A COMPROMISING POSITION

Dragging herself up instantly from where she had fallen and ducking under his elbow, Elizabeth righted herself on the carriage seat. She was tongue-tied from an excruciating awareness of his muscled thighs moving against her moments before.

A carriage appeared from around a curve, and she ducked her head, shielding her features with the bonnet brim as it rolled past.

"Afraid of being seen with me?" Chan asked in annoyance. "Other women beg me to take them up for a ride."

Clinging to the curved seat rail, Elizabeth leaned away to avoid the touch of his spread legs. "Maybe you take *them* up without grabbing them off the ground," she said tartly. "Ladies prefer not to be seen rumpled and dirty, looking as if the rake who's driving has ravished them in the road."

His burst of laughter was hardly the reaction she expected or wanted. "When I ravish you, I promise it won't be on a public highway." His sidelong look prickled along her skin, covered and uncovered, like a dangerous promise. "You'll be far more responsive on cool sheets scented with lavender."

Other *Love Spell* books by Pat Cody:
KEPT BY A COUNTESS

His Wicked Will

Pat Cody

LEISURE BOOKS   NEW YORK CITY

A LEISURE BOOK®

November 2000

Published by

Dorchester Publishing Co., Inc.
276 Fifth Avenue
New York, NY 10001

ISBN 0-8439-4791-8

For my personal research librarian, Karen Stevens, who knows how to communicate with librarians in England to make materials appear. For my patient critique partners Geralyn Dawson and Sharon Rowe. For my other Nurses of the Spirit in the difficult deadline time for this book, Sally Mollenkopf, Jan Pinkston, and Sue-Ellen Welfonder. Saying thanks isn't enough and repayment isn't possible.

Chapter One

Bath, 1810

"Damned if that isn't her!" The new Duke of Ashcott twisted on the seat of his curricle to glare over his shoulder, letting the reins drop.

Startled by his friend's angry outburst, Lord Chandler glanced back over the folded carriage bonnet at the swarms of shoppers on Milsom Street. "Who?"

"The tart who tricked a fortune out of my father." Ash scowled. "Lucinda's here in Bath, not Bristol at all. Stop her, Chan."

Charles Norton, Viscount Chandler, stifled the urge to snatch the leathers as the team veered toward the shops. "The street's full of females. How the deuce do you expect me to know which ones are tarts?"

Turning back in time to keep his pair of matched bays from trampling anyone, Ash said with urgency, "Blue spencer, cottage bonnet with bronze ribbons." Drivers behind them shouted complaints as he reined in his team, blocking half the street. "Hurry, before the blasted doxy gets away."

Chan didn't relish accosting a strange woman in a public place, soiled dove or not. "How do you know it's Lucinda and not a look-alike?"

"I should know the harlot when I see her. She passed me in London, nearly as close as I sit to you now, cozied up to Father in an open landau." Impatient as usual, Ash struggled to get his game leg under him. "Here, you take the reins. I'll go after the jezebel myself."

"And murder her on the street in front of witnesses?" Chan avoided mention of Ash's impairment, with its guilty reminders. "I'll see if she's the right woman before you get hold of her. We'll meet at the Bear Inn after I learn where she's living," he added in resignation, feeling for the slick metal step under his boot to swing himself down from the carriage.

"No, bring her straight to me at the inn. Tell her she won't keep a shilling she stole from my father's estate." Ash sounded as angry as the drivers he blocked, shouting and cursing above the clamor of street criers, wheels, and harness.

Chan set off up the street. He wouldn't deliver the woman or the message, though he wouldn't stand arguing about it. If Ash expected him to drag an unwilling female to the Bear Inn for a public brawl, he was moon-mad. Threats were hardly a good way of dealing with women. He'd learn if this was Ash's Lucinda and discover her address. That was enough.

Legs stiff after a long spell of sitting in his friend's carriage, he scanned the foot traffic ahead. Only three blue spencers in sight.

Lengthening his stride, Chan caught up with the first woman wearing a fitted blue jacket, which ended just under a full bust the old duke would have appreciated. Bending to glance under her bonnet brim as he passed, he eliminated her as Lucinda. The bonnet encased a face like a pig's, complete with a mole sprouting stiff hairs. The woman wouldn't have inspired Ash's father to take her into his bed, much less leave her a fortune.

Ducking under the lintel into a glover's after the second female wearing blue, Chan stopped just inside while his eyes adjusted to the dim light. Three female customers and a frock-coated clerk glanced his way.

This woman in blue was more like it, just plump enough to make a good armful. She caught his eye and smiled, looking him over with evident interest. She was forward enough to be a woman of pleasure.

"Lucinda!" he said, sweeping off his beaver hat as he approached her. "I thought I saw you step in here."

Her mouth curved from a smile to a pout. "I'm sorry; you've mistaken me for someone you"—her gaze swept him head to foot with approval—"*already* know."

Grinning, he left the shop faster than he had entered. The woman wearing the third blue spencer might already have disappeared. Like as not, she wasn't Ash's mercenary jade either, but he'd agreed to follow her. He never failed Ash.

That was luck; the woman stood a few doors farther on, looking into a shop window. Her poke bonnet was tied with bronze ribbons, as Ash had described the ladybird in blue.

Searching his breast pocket as he approached her, Chan drew out a dainty handkerchief handed to him in Hyde Park yesterday. Good thing he'd worn the same coat again on the road. As he reached the shop window, he held out the trifle of lace, smiling. "You must have dropped this."

Staring in at the books on display, the woman didn't seem to realize he had spoken to her. A doxy who sighed over tomes instead of gowns and jewels was a novelty. He nudged her elbow, holding out the dainty square.

Starting, she looked first at the folded handkerchief,

her face hidden by the dipped bonnet brim. Then she stared up at him.

At first glimpse of the lovely face tilting up to his, Chan clenched the lace handkerchief. Ash's father hadn't deserved a glorious beauty like this, even if he was a duke. Languid lids curved over large eyes that had to be hazel, though he could have sworn they glinted more golden than the sun-warmed Bath stone surrounding them. The most sensual lips he'd ever longed to kiss formed a prim line. The golden cat-shaped eyes swept him with a look women rarely turned on him—disdain.

"It isn't mine," she said in a musical voice that caressed his ears like the rich, clear notes of a French horn playing low. Despite its dulcet tone, it sounded accusing. "You're chasing a female with red hair, from the color of the curl showing through the linen."

Glancing down, he saw what she meant. Serena must have folded a lock of her hair into the handkerchief she pressed into his hand in Hyde Park, meaning for it to remind him of her while he was out of London. He hadn't even looked at the talisman, just slid it into a pocket and leaned over to claim a quick kiss as they passed behind a shrub.

Red hair seemed tawdry in comparison to the rich golden color of the curls nestled under Lucinda's straw bonnet. Even in shadow, her hair gleamed with the varied hues of yellow Baltic amber. Hastily he stashed the handkerchief again.

"It was just a pretext to speak with you anyway," he admitted, smiling. "Let me carry your parcels as you shop, Lucinda."

The pretty lips parted for a quick snatch of air as her eyes widened in the blanching face. "You . . . you're mistaken. I'm not—" Backing away, she held a paper-wrapped package before her breast like a shield. "Stay away from me!"

Before he could grasp her arm, she turned and rushed

away, nearly running on a street where shoppers sauntered. Her obvious fear and flight were all the admission of identity he needed.

Setting off in pursuit, Chan wondered why she had panicked. Surely Lucinda expected the old duke's heirs to search for her, with sixty thousand pounds at stake. The appearance of a hound hot on the scent shouldn't even startle her.

As he caught sight of her weaving through the throng ahead, he admired her grace. The woman couldn't make an awkward move if she tried. In the brief moments since he first saw her, he'd noticed she was supple as a dancer, every motion of her head and hands as graceful as a gliding gull.

Now she flowed away from him like an outgoing tide, and he felt an urgent need to catch her before she retreated beyond his horizon. Little wonder she had bewitched the old duke into signing a will in her favor, with more beauty and grace than any actress on London's stages.

Chan held his breath as she stopped half a block ahead, then dashed halfway across the swarming street. The wheels of a post coach must have smudged her white skirts as it rumbled in front of her. He broke into a run.

Catching her arm just as the coach clattered past, he said through clenched teeth, "You little fool! You'll never live to fight for a fortune, taking risks like that."

She pulled against his grasp. "What I do is no concern of yours. Let go of me, you devil! I don't know you, and despite what you think, you don't know me."

"Perhaps not, but you'll prefer dealing with the devil over my friend Ash." He locked her against his side with one arm to keep her from escaping again.

She breathed like a scared, wounded creature fighting off help it couldn't understand. "We have nothing to talk about; I'm not this person you named."

"Then we'll talk about nothing. I'm always ready for a conversation with a beautiful woman." Perhaps he should have expected this denial from a woman who surely lived by her beauty and wits. Chan felt a twinge of pity for the lovely light-skirt. She'd chosen a rough road, unless she renounced all claim to the fortune she'd lured an old man into leaving her. Grief and betrayal made a poisonous mixture, and Chan's friend Ash would never swallow it without a fight. His father's legacy would certainly be contested.

Hurrying the woman between a dray and the turnip cart following it, Chan gave her a little distance but kept a firm hold on her arm.

"Let go; you're hurting me," she said, pulling against his grip. The golden eyes shot sparks of contempt, not pain.

"If you stop fighting me, you won't feel a twinge of pain," he assured her. "I'm holding you by the elbow, so no one will notice anything unusual if you don't struggle. Cooperation is to your advantage. I'll see you home, where we can talk privately."

"I don't allow Satan's spawn like you in my home." Loathing suffused her features as she stared at him, but her elbow went still. "Do you always have to use muscle to force a female to listen to you?"

Amused, Chan also felt slightly offended. Other women who had called him a devil meant it as a compliment. Keeping her close as they moved through the crowd, he put menace into his tone. "Call me what you like. We can walk quietly to your house or I can drag you there like a balky mule."

Chin thrust forward, she said, "I don't take strange men home, and you're the strangest I've encountered. You won't pass through my door."

"I go where I choose," he informed her, surprised to be trading insults with a loose woman on a public street.

The shop-lined bridge over the Avon River lay to the

left as he hustled her to the corner of Northgate Street. Chan stopped, looking down into her defiant face. "I don't use females roughly, but you can become the exception. You've injured my closest friend, and I won't see him suffer. Lead me to your house, or I shall drag you down to the stinking Avon and douse you in it until you're ready for a change of mind and clothing."

The huge golden eyes grew larger. "You wouldn't dare do such a thing to a lady in broad daylight with people about."

"Won't I?" Gripping her elbow more firmly, he headed for the bank at the near end of the bridge. "You'd have cried out already if you expected anyone to believe your story over mine."

"Wait!" she cried, planting her half boots in the dirt. "You really would duck me like a suspected witch, you archfiend!"

"Call me Lord Lucifer if you like." Chan had no intention of soaking the little beauty in filth when the threat would suffice. "I'm not a man to trifle with when his friends have been wronged. Do we go uphill or cross the bridge to reach your house?"

Glancing up Bridge Street and then across the Avon, she gave him a measuring look. The little hussy still hoped to mislead him.

He could admire her spirit, even if it was wasted against his determination. Too bad he couldn't flirt instead of menacing her, but she had made this as much a personal challenge as a favor for his friend.

"Bath isn't nearly big enough to hide you from me, if you think you can get away now." He smiled to avoid drawing the attention of passersby but put a threat into his tone. "I don't quit when I've set myself a task, and I will know where you're staying before we part company."

The bonnet brim hid her face while she hesitated, and then she headed for the bridge. "Across here," she said, her voice sounding small and breathless. "I'm staying at the Sydney Hotel."

She walked quickly, slightly in front, though he didn't let go of her elbow. He didn't trust her that much. Threading through the crowd surging across the bridge, she hurried on, pausing at the broad diamond intersection of Laura Place for a break in the traffic flow.

Halfway down Great Pulteney Street, she broke the strained silence, shooting him a brimstone look before she spoke. "How do I convince you I'm not who you think and that I've never met, let alone injured, your friend?"

"Actions speak louder than words," he replied, steeling himself against the contempt in her molten gaze and voice. "You ran when I called you by name. That confirms who you are and what you've done."

Anger mixed with grief and fear as the lovely face turned toward him briefly. "Damned by association," he thought she muttered, though it made no sense.

He'd best be on his guard with this conniving, exquisite creature. What a pity that treachery and loveliness could be wrapped together in one supremely tempting package.

At the end of Great Pulteney Street with its tall town houses, they paused as carriages turned onto Sydney Place. Down a short left arm, the street ended in open ground, with Sydney Gardens to the right. That popular destination drew more vehicles and pedestrians to this area than the residents alone accounted for.

Shoulders well back, Lucinda preceded him across the street and to the entrance of the massive hotel building, barely a decade old. Stopping, she said with animosity, "We'll part here. You know where I'm staying. If your friend has a complaint against me, bring him to this hotel."

Despite the scornful glance at him, she darted nervous looks about. He'd best make certain she had rooms here.

Removing his tall beaver hat, Chan drawled, "Leaving you to face the strangers in a hotel's public rooms alone would be rag-mannered. I'll see you safely inside."

Lips tight, she said, "Very well," and entered the hotel. Her nod at the porter just inside the door, and his answering grin, quieted Chan's suspicions that she was a stranger here.

Stopping at the stairs to the upper floors, she said with controlled passion, "Even Lord Lucifer wouldn't follow an unrelated female openly to her rooms. Carry your report back to your crony and leave me in peace."

He deserved the whiplash in her tone, for he wasn't proud of bullying this beautiful, intrepid woman. If only he could have met her under different circumstances, how pleasant could be this parting, with a promise to meet again. Sliding his hand from her elbow to her fingers, he bent over them as he would a lady's.

"I'll be back," he warned her. "You won't have time to pack your belongings and pay your shot before Ash and I return. Don't think you can run away from me, Lucinda."

"I hope you're run over by a speeding coach laden with baggage before you can report to him, Lord Beelzebub." Snatching her hand out of his clasp, Lucinda whirled away and up the staircase.

Watching her scurry up to the landing, Chan leaned on the polished banister. Flashes of her trim ankles in white stockings made the wait worthwhile. She didn't look back.

Deep in thought, he strolled across the hotel's elegant reception room and stepped outside. He felt in a waistcoat pocket for his watch and looked upward to the slanting sun. Ash was no doubt waiting impatiently, but Chan was in no hurry to report on his encounter with his friend's enemy.

Leaning against a tall pillar, he pocketed the watch again. Lovely Lucinda was a puzzle with pieces that didn't fit well together. He wanted time to figure out which parts didn't match Ash's tirades against her.

Before the old duke died, Ash had talked about his father's doings no more than most men. He might have mentioned that the old duke had set up a new mistress, but that was hardly remarkable. No reason for either of them to discuss Lucinda before the will was read.

Ash hadn't called her an old harpy, but Chan had expected the duke's mistress to be older than Lucinda appeared. She might be a year or two beyond twenty. Not that plenty of elderly men didn't prefer a downy chick to a full-feathered hen.

Yet the old duke had been a man of culture and taste, quiet in his pursuits. Not a man he'd expect to sow wild oats in his last years with a young filly. But youthful as she appeared, Lucinda had been studying a display of books when he caught up to her on Milsom Street. She might have a mind informed enough to entertain a mature man, and her beauty alone would entice any male to set her up for his exclusive pleasure. Chan could fancy her himself.

Shifting his shoulder against the pillar, Chan noticed a flutter of white off to his right. A graceful young woman in a white walking gown appeared from the side loggia of the hotel and headed down Sydney Place toward the gardens.

It was odd for a woman to go walking without a wrap in the cool spring air. Females usually shivered in thin muslins while men roasted in heavy wool coats. He straightened and stared past the column's concealment.

On Sydney Place, the short row houses squatted in less splendor than their soaring neighbors in Great Pulteney Street. He'd see if this shapely woman entered a door or the garden entrance.

A moment later the white-clad figure turned to cross the street, and he spotted the bundle she clasped before her. Besides a wrapped parcel like Lucinda's, an edge of blue showed between her white gown and the package.

The little schemer must have removed the blue spencer before leaving the hotel from a side entrance. Good thing he'd been in no rush, or he would have taken back the wrong information about her whereabouts. Lucinda was every bit as cunning as Ash said, but she wouldn't make a fool of him.

While he watched, she ran up two steps of a small town house and worked the knocker as briskly as a pump handle. The instant the door opened, she pushed inside.

Leaning around the pillar, Chan caught a quick glimpse of three laughing faces at the door before it shut—pretty faces of girls younger than Lucinda. Girls just old enough to attract men's notice.

Tension knotted his shoulders as he noted the town house's number. The strumpet wasn't staying at the Sydney Hotel at all. She had rented a residence in a decent area where men hired holiday lodgings for their families.

Chan burned with indignation. From the gaggle of girls answering the door instead of a properly uniformed maid or footman, it appeared she had returned to her old business.

Ash's inheritance was paying for a house where her girls could service men just as Lucinda had his father.

Chapter Two

Half an hour after arriving home, Elizabeth Merriman poured tea for her aunt Delia Lindsey with unsteady hands. They'd both suffered a shock in the last hour.

Who was he, the ominous stranger who had called her by the name she had erased from their lives?

Call me Lord Lucifer, he had said with easy sarcasm. Whatever his real name, the dark title fit the menace of his probing gaze. He looked the part of a fallen angel, with a face that could lead unwary females into temptation and ruin. His features were saved from sculpted splendor only by a jaw too square and pronounced, as unyielding as his will.

Adding hot water to the cup, she achieved the dilution for black bohea that Aunt Delia preferred.

The devil's threats, if carried out, would end her plans for a useful life here in Bath. Only by appearing entirely respectable could she prepare local girls to support themselves, without need to rely on any man.

Aunt Delia leaned back on the small sofa in the drawing room, her feet up along its length, smelling salts clutched unopened in one thin hand. "Two lumps, dear," she murmured, laying a hand over her heart. "I vow, I can't make a fist after all the commotion."

Stirring the fragrant brew for her aunt, Elizabeth felt as if she whirled in a vortex hotter than that in the delicate cup. She wanted time alone to recover from the unnerving encounter with the most handsome rascal she'd been unfortunate enough to meet, but Aunt Delia needed her, and her aunt came first.

What her aunt didn't need was any mention of Lucinda within her hearing. After several years of vague spells, Aunt Delia's failing mind still retreated into the past when reminded of that name. One day she might not return to the present, and this aunt was the only family Elizabeth could still claim.

"You look hot, dear, though the day seems blustery to me," said Aunt Delia, wrapping her paisley shawl closer. "I'm afraid you're as overset as I am by the morning's events."

Elizabeth started, missing the cup as she poured her own tea. "How could you know—" She bit off the question. Aunt Delia referred to the upsets here at the house, not her recent diabolical acquaintance.

Forcing a smile, Elizabeth tried to look serene. "Perhaps I am a bit warm. It's humid for March, and I rushed home faster than I should have."

"I'm glad you arrived when you did. Those silly girls of yours only squealed and jumped up and down." Aunt Delia put an unsteady hand to her forehead. "Heaven knows I'm no midwife. You'd expect workhouse girls to have more experience than I of birthing."

The girls might have managed better without Delia's conniptions, as they'd described Elizabeth's aunt's state before Elizabeth had even gotten inside.

"It isn't every day a stray cat has kittens in a lady's dolly tub," Aunt Delia said, sipping tea. "If the girls

21

hadn't put the sheets in it after changing the beds on Saturday—though they know laundry is done on Mondays—an expectant mother couldn't have chosen it for her accouchement."

"I'll tell them to pile soiled sheets on a bench in the scullery in future." Linen wasn't Elizabeth's present concern, unless it was the crisp neckcloth tied with precision under a chin firm enough to threaten persistence.

Elizabeth glanced up to see Aunt Delia's forehead creased in the puzzled look she wore too often these days. "I would have spared you the unsettling view of a cat giving birth on Merriman marked linen, but moggies will drop kits in their own time, no matter how firmly you order them to stop."

Lord Lucifer seemed no more likely to halt a hunt than a cat to stop birthing a litter. Could she hide until he left Bath?

"Don't you agree?"

Recognizing a query without knowing what it was, Elizabeth held out a plate of sliced seedcake to cover her inattention. The silver server rattled against the sprigged Merriman china, the best legacy from her kinfolk. Family was too often like deadly quicksand, ready to suck you under if you let them close.

"You're as unsettled as I am, and no wonder." Aunt Delia peered at her with clouded, vague blue eyes. "We don't need a house full of cats when you've already filled it with stray girls. You won't let them up into this part of the house, will you, dear? The cats, I mean, not your girls. I don't expect you to run them off, though you should, you know. The cats, that is, not the lasses." She looked aggrieved. "Though they aren't really your girls—you aren't likely to have children when you won't even consider marriage."

"I'll tell the girls to keep the kittens in the scullery." Avoiding the matrimony debate, Elizabeth passed a plate of individual jam tarts with both hands to steady it.

"Why don't you try a tart, dear? Cook didn't brown the pastry as much, far more to my taste." Aunt Delia stretched across the tea table to help herself to another.

What Elizabeth wanted more than sweets was a chance to catch her breath and think. The morning's encounter could be ruinous if the rogue found her.

Once again a man would decide her fate—unless she could outwit him. Yet this time she was older. This time Elizabeth would protect herself and safeguard Aunt Delia as well.

The tall rogue with searing eyes was the sort of man she despised, treating women carelessly, using a love token from one to approach another. She pitied the deluded redhead who must have offered him her heart along with the curl. The poor thing would need her handkerchief back and a dozen more, if she loved him.

Discovering pastry crumbs on her muslin skirt, Elizabeth realized she'd eaten the rest of the jam tarts without tasting them. *Drat the man!* She'd vowed to cut back on sweets; her lapse was all his fault.

"Did you hear me, dear?" Aunt Delia interrupted her useless self-harangue. "Would you set the seedcake nearer, where I can reach it without straining my shoulder?"

As she slid the plate across the round tripod table, a loud pounding rose from the ground floor below, as if someone meant to batter in the door. Elizabeth jumped, sloshing tea onto her white muslin skirt.

Holding her breath, she listened.

Shortly an angry male voice rumbled up the stairs like thunder threatening an approaching storm. Another man spoke in a quieter tone. Elizabeth crashed her cup onto the saucer.

Not him, not here!

"Who can that be?" Aunt Delia cocked her head like a terrier. "Did I forget we're expecting callers?"

Elizabeth cringed. How had he found her? Leaping

up, she headed for the door. "It's nothing," she said, searching for a sensible explanation that would keep her aunt here in the drawing room.

Aunt Delia leaned forward, listening, as Elizabeth opened the door into the passage. "It sounds like men's voices to me. I don't call gentlemen visitors nothing." A growing interest in romantic nonsense sometimes marked Aunt Delia's mental oddities.

"Most likely it's just a tradesman. Drink your tea and have another slice of seedcake." Latching the door securely behind her, she hurried to the stairs. Little as she relished facing Lord Mephistopheles and his friend, even less did she want to expose Aunt Delia to befuddling reminders of Lucinda.

The sound of the door closing must have alerted the callers to her presence. By the time she crossed the passage to the top of the stairs, the two men were staring upward at her. Below, Sally looked their guests over with far too much interest.

The slighter man looked furious; he had a red face and clenched fists. Yet Lord Lucifer's sharp-eyed restraint was more menacing. Little got past him, and Elizabeth had much to hide.

Legs limp as boiled asparagus spears, she descended the stairs. Chin high, she spoke to Sally on the way down, hardly finding the breath to speak. "I'll see to the gentlemen; you may return to the kittens."

Reluctantly Sally edged away, looking back over her shoulder at the two men.

"Kittens?" said the dark one, his gaze scornful. "I've heard girls called *cats* in these houses, but I didn't expect you to be that frank about your business."

"I beg your pardon?" Elizabeth said, bewilderment overshadowing her anxiety.

Scowling, he stepped forward to confront her as she reached the small entry hall. His closeness surrounded and smothered her, as it had when he had gripped her arm on the street. Elizabeth felt as if the space had shrunk, as if his unwelcome male presence used up all the air in the house.

Lord Lucifer frowned. "Your kittens are too pretty to overlook. Don't deny choosing them to lure men here, Lucinda."

Liquid fire blazed through her veins at mention of the disowned name. She traded stares with him. "I don't know how you discovered where I live, but I don't want you calling here."

"This isn't a social visit," said the smaller man with a snarl, pushing forward with a pronounced limp. He radiated hatred. "I don't make daylight calls on women who earn their livings on their backs."

If he had struck her, she wouldn't feel any more shocked. Momentary regret for his physical impairment dissolved into rage. Gripping her hands together, she faced him with effort. "Your senseless insults make you no more welcome here than your bullying friend."

The limping man sneered. "I don't want a welcome. I want the legacy you stole from me."

"I've stolen nothing." For the first time she regretted her choice to employ no males. A burly footman would have backed her against these two intruders. "If you don't leave at once, I'll send for the watch to remove you."

"Let's send for the charlie, as Madame Lucinda suggests." The limping man's voice rose and roughened. "He can take up the thief who insinuated herself into an old man's bed and will."

Lord Lucifer laid a hand on his fiery friend's shoulder. "You don't want that notoriety. Let's sit down and try a rational discussion instead of verbal fireworks. This can be resolved quietly between you."

"No! I don't discuss theft with a criminal," the limping man bellowed, red-faced. He slapped the wall beside her with his hand and she flinched. A candle fell from its wall sconce and he kicked it, jerking away from Lord Lucifer's restraining touch.

It was too much to hope that Aunt Delia hadn't heard the entire violent outburst. The click of a door latch from above confirmed her fear. Elizabeth reached behind her for the support of the newel post.

Swallowing her pride, she begged: "Please, you must leave at once. My elderly aunt isn't well and you'll disturb her. I'm not the lady you want, I don't have your money, and I can't help you get it."

"I'm not looking for a lady," said the limping man through gritted teeth. "I've found the right fancy piece."

A touch on her shoulder from behind signaled Aunt Delia's arrival. Glaring at Lord Lucifer, Elizabeth turned to urge her aunt back up the steps. "I'm sorry these men disturbed you," she said more calmly than she felt. "They've come to the wrong house. Please go finish your tea while I see them out."

"I can drink tea anytime," said Aunt Delia with a smile for Lord Lucifer, evading Elizabeth's hands. "When we have handsome callers to entertain, we must send for the decanters. Call your girls to do the honors, dear. They can use practice at serving gentlemen. I'll take our visitors up to the drawing room."

The men exchanged knowing looks. Elizabeth cringed. Aunt Delia had innocently confirmed their impression that this was a house of ill repute. In desperation Elizabeth said, "These men aren't acquaintances, and we mustn't delay them."

"They look familiar, dear. Perhaps I know your fathers." Aunt Delia waited expectantly, looking between the taller males like a harmless sparrow standing between predatory hawks.

Either man might say that dreadful name again any moment. Elizabeth dodged between Lord Lucifer and the limping man and snatched their hats off a side table.

"They must go," she said firmly. "Good day, sirs. I hope you discover the person you want."

Pinning her hopes on the devil, she thrust a curly-brimmed beaver at him.

Ignoring the hat, Lord Lucifer made a graceful leg as he bent above her aunt's hand. "My father's been dead many years, ma'am, but he was fortunate if he knew you. I'm Charles Norton, Viscount Chandler, and this is the Duke of Ashcott."

Horrified, Elizabeth dropped both hats. She stared at the limping man, who was actually the old Duke of Ashcott's son. He glared back with loathing. She had fervently hoped never to set eyes on him. Bending to retrieve the headgear gave her a moment to recover a civil expression, though her stomach still imitated a landed fish.

"Yes, indeed. I should say I did know the former viscount and duke." Aunt Delia gave a girlish laugh as she took the viscount's arm. "Come along upstairs, and I'll tell you stories of your fathers they'd rather you never heard."

Stopping Aunt Delia simply by standing still, the devilish viscount smiled at her as she turned back from the stairs. "I'm sorry; we can't stay this time. Yet will you tell us who you are, since you know our families?"

Polite introductions and unfamiliar names might defuse the young duke's anger and get rid of both men. Elizabeth gestured to her companion with one of the hats she had rescued from the floor and said in a formal tone, "This lady is my aunt and companion, Miss Delia Lindsey. I'm—"

Aunt Delia interrupted, shaking her head. "Young ladies don't introduce themselves to gentlemen, dear. This is my delightful niece, Miss Lucinda Elizabeth Anne Merriman."

Elizabeth closed her eyes against the pair of accusing male stares drilling into her. Why did Aunt Delia have to recall all her given names when she rarely remembered the right day of the week?

"I knew it!" said the duke with vicious satisfaction. "I couldn't mistake those bedchamber eyes. You're Lucinda, all right."

"You already know my Lucinda?" asked Aunt Delia, sounding bewildered. She looked down, frowning, then studied the young duke. "Yes, of course you do, Ashcott. What am I thinking?"

"Not as well as I'm about to know her," said the duke to Elizabeth. "But I know all about her kind."

"You're quite right," Aunt Delia hurried to assure him, her voice quavering as she looked about in bewilderment. "She's noted for her kindness throughout the county. No one's ever treated me as well as Lucinda does."

Elizabeth heard the exchanges as if they were runaway horses, pounding toward her aunt with deadly speed. She couldn't guess which way to jump to save Aunt Delia from the growing confusion that could fog her mind for days.

Ignoring her aunt, Ashcott stepped toe-to-toe with Elizabeth. "You're about to learn what it means to cross me. Either you renounce all claims against my father's estate in writing, or I'll see you in chancery court."

"Court?" murmured Aunt Delia, twisting her handkerchief. "It's far too late for courting. If you're ready to talk marriage at last, best tie the knot at once."

"Marriage?" bellowed the duke, glaring toward Aunt Delia and back at Elizabeth. "Let's get one thing straight: you'll get nothing from me but trouble. I'm not a weak old man you can bend to your devious will."

"Your will," muttered Aunt Delia, putting a hand to her temple and slowly shaking her head. "I told Lucinda not to count on that if you couldn't marry her."

The duke turned to stare at her, openmouthed.

Elizabeth went to Aunt Delia, choking back tears.

These horrible men had utterly confused her. Now the waking nightmares would start, and who knew when she would return to a semblance of herself again.

"Don't fret, please," she said, trying to make her tight throat produce a tone of reassurance. She felt ripped in half, trying to comfort Aunt Delia and at the same time chafing to pitch the duke and his friend into the street. "These men are just leaving, and we can finish our tea in peace."

Lord Lucifer loomed above her, though she should think of him now as Lord Chandler, if she had to think of him at all. He gazed at Aunt Delia and then stared down into Elizabeth's face with searching intensity.

As he reached for his headgear, she glared back in fury and dropped both beaver hats, on purpose this time.

In a swift swoop like a bird of prey, he picked them up. As he straightened, he murmured, "Your companion doesn't seem to know your business with the duke. I'll get Ash out of here before you dent these brims past steaming back into shape. But don't try to bolt; I've proved I can find you despite your tricks."

Holding out his hat to the duke, he said louder, "It isn't polite to interrupt these ladies at tea, Ash. Now that we've introduced ourselves, we can call again later."

When the young duke scowled, the viscount said to him in a warning tone, "Business and tea parties don't mix. You don't want to bore Miss Lindsey with affairs that don't concern her."

Snatching his headgear from the viscount, the duke said to Elizabeth with a snarl, "You'll see me again. Soon. You'd best think over what I said and be ready to sign an agreement when I return."

"How kind to reassure us you'll call again." Beginning to tremble, Aunt Delia gave a tentative wave.

The duke looked her way and shook his head. Jamming on his hat, he lurched out of the house in his torturous gait.

Lord Chandler bowed over Aunt Delia's hand, then gave Elizabeth another measuring look before following the duke.

"Poor fellow; what a nasty limp." Aunt Delia looked distraught and puzzled. "I didn't recall the duke had injured himself. The viscount is a fine figure of a man, though, as you must have seen for yourself. Well-spoken, too, and without a wife since his son's birth. He's a far better choice than the duke with his sickly duchess. Ashcott can't marry you." Her eyes glistened with tears.

The young duke and the viscount had become their fathers to Aunt Delia, with that despicable name scrambling her perception of time. Elizabeth groaned, heartsore with this evidence of her aunt's retreat to earlier years. She felt abandoned all over again when her aunt no longer knew her.

"You like the viscount, don't you, Lucinda, dearest?" Aunt Delia asked anxiously as Elizabeth urged her up the stairs. "I noticed the two of you talking together over the hats."

Being called by that hated name in her aunt's confusion was doubly painful. The anguish Lucinda brought on Aunt Delia was reason enough to avoid any link with her, even if her very existence didn't threaten Elizabeth's work and reputation.

Lucinda had abandoned them without regret.

If betraying Lucinda wouldn't betray herself, she would hand the selfish woman over in an instant. Elizabeth's charitable efforts would count for nothing, besmirched by the offal of the other woman's licentious lifestyle. Worse, hearing the old scandal served up all over town might turn Aunt Delia's mind permanently to the past, lost to Elizabeth forever.

For now, Aunt Delia must be calmed and encouraged back to reality. Elizabeth would send down for hot water to make her fresh tea, and maybe a few of the tarts were still left.

On second thought, considering the names she'd been called today, she never wanted to see tarts again.

"Calm down, before you ruin a fine pair's mouths," Chan advised his friend. "You're driving them like a pair of donkeys."

Still scowling, Ash glanced over, but tension eased from the fingers threading the reins. "No wonder I'm heavy-handed after dealing with that doxy. Why did you drag me out before I was through with her?"

"Because you were ranting like a fishwife and upsetting the old lady." It had seemed to him that Lucinda's concern was more for her companion than herself when Ash's temper exploded in her entrance hall.

"Upset the old crone? I didn't know what she was talking about most of the time. As for the young strumpet," Ash said, skirting a cart delivering a barrel to the Sydney Hotel, "I'd like to get Lucinda's conniving neck in my hands long enough to squeeze a confession from it."

An image overran Chan's mind, of his own fingers stroking the slim white throat rising from the woman's prim neckline. Of his lips finding the pulse that had throbbed visibly in a delicate vein while she faced them down with dignity.

No, he mustn't follow that inviting road further. Not with his best friend ready to throttle the woman. "You were too violent with her if you hope to achieve a reasonable settlement."

The duke yelled at a dog chasing the carriage before glaring at Chan. "I never expected you to jump to a tart's defense instead of your best friend's."

"Don't call her a tart." The word grated against Chan's mental image of the young beauty. "Whatever she's done, Lucinda's too elegant for that vulgar term."

31

Ash flashed him a knowing look. "See? You're doing it again. You don't like the truth about her, just because of a pretty face. This particular piece of delectable fruit has a rotten core, old man."

Uneasy, Chan stared down Henrietta Street as they drove into Laura Place. "That's too harsh. It isn't as if she set out to do you personal damage."

"Might as well be hatred as greed that motivates her. Either way, the kick in the crotch feels the same to me." Ash's set face looked as hard as the stone under the iron-rimmed curricle wheels. "I'm out sixty thousand pounds whatever her reason for gulling Father. Not that I mean to lose a groat of my rightful inheritance to the old man's bed warmer."

They were slowed by the crowd of conveyances crossing the Avon River bridge.

"The law's decisions are costly and slow," Chan reminded him. "The longer the courts muddle in the estate, the more time she has to spend funds your father already put in her hands."

Ash swore, turning away from the inn at the city side of the bridge before Chan realized his intention. "Don't expect me to settle with her. I don't make deals with round-heeled women, and I won't go begging, hat in hand, for what is by rights mine." He glared at Chan. "I thought you came along to help me, not champion the woman who has stolen from me."

Ash was in one of his foul moods. He'd grown quick to anger, more likely to see the black view, after the youthful incident that lamed him. Chan supposed that constant pain didn't sweeten a man's disposition. Still, putting up with ill humors was small beer to Chan, when he was the reason behind the injury.

"I am trying to help you," Chan said. "Women get stubborn as mules when men push them. The more you rant at her, the less she'll hear a word you say. Approach her diplomatically if you want to settle this quickly."

"Don't expect me to mince around a whore like a lady in her drawing room. Call a sow a silk purse if you want, but I call a harlot what she is."

Chan clenched his fists, surprised that he cared what Ash called the young Lucinda. He usually allowed his friend's ire to wash over him like rainwater, waiting for the storms to blow themselves out.

Ash looked around him as they slowed among the press of vehicles behind Bath Abbey. "Where are we, confound it?"

"You took the opposite direction from the Bear Inn back at the bridge. And if you insist on racing along in a blind rage when you deal with Lucinda, you'll find yourself on the wrong road to salvage a fortune, too." Chan flung an arm along the carriage's folded hood, satisfied he'd offered his best advice.

"I know where I am, and I know what I'm doing." Ash grinned, his mood changing as quickly as his route. He guided the pair onto less crowded South Parade, hardly slowing as he rounded the corner without warning. "This leads to the Bristol tollgate. I meant to take a little spin all along." The curricle lurched into a hole and out again.

Chan shook his head. "You don't want to admit that my advice about Lucinda makes sense any more than you'll confess you took the wrong turn."

"You always make sense, curse you. But I won't offer the greedy trollop a deal." Ash eyed Chan in challenge. "Tell you what: if you think you can convince her to set aside all claim to my inheritance, I'll stay away from the little madame while *you* try it."

Hands palm-out, Chan said, "No, you don't; I'm not carrying those hot coals for you. It's your inheritance, and you can leave it to the bagwigs to sort it out by legal means."

Ash's glance was reproachful. "You said you'd support me through this the night I told you about the will."

A miasma of damp cellars and too many people in too small a space rose from the crowded western quarter of Bath they drove through. Ash's reminder was no more welcome than the stink in the street.

Chan had no heart for bullying Lucinda, even for this friend to whom he owed his life. But he remembered Ash's set, tragic face after hearing his father's will read. Ash had grabbed Chan's arm as he left the library, dragging him along to the stables, where he demanded mounts for them both. During their wild, pounding ride over the estate, he'd cursed into the wind, demanding to know what he'd done to deserve his father's insult.

Never before had Chan seen his friend in such a state. They had spent that night in a hedge tavern, drinking Blue Ruin without drowning Ash's grief at losing more than his father. It was impossible to comprehend how or why his friend's father had chosen his mistress over his son.

Therefore refusing Ash now wasn't easy, but Lucinda's air of pride and protectiveness made Chan reluctant to besiege her. Shaking his head, he said, "Support isn't the same thing as acting for you. I'm just along for the ride. You'll have to do your own talking to that temptress."

"Afraid you'll succumb to her charms?" Ash jeered.

"I can handle lovely women," Chan said, annoyed by his friend's taunt. "This one is your problem. You'll have to make do with my company and advice."

"I can find better company than you with the Bear's chambermaids, and your advice flows too freely already." A grin softened Ash's insults. "You've always preferred a better class of light-skirt than I. Give me a simple taproom wench anytime, satisfied by a coin instead of jewels and carriages. You're the one to convince this elegant canary bird to give up."

When Chan didn't respond, Ash nudged him with an elbow. "We never let each other down."

Chan grimaced. That blow hit too near the heart.

Ash added, "You said yourself I'm bungling the job."

"Much you care what I say." Striking his knee with a closed fist, Chan grimaced. Ash hadn't reminded him straight out of the old obligation, but Chan never forgot it. A friend didn't almost lose a leg because of you and then ask for your help, only to be turned away.

Groaning, he said, "I can't guarantee the outcome. You may be sorry you involved me. But I'll speak to her about settling the matter out of court. Now that we know she's Lucinda, she can't pretend ignorance about the legacy any longer. Surely she'll realize other wealthy men can't be bled if the courts decide she defrauded a duke."

"That's the winning ticket," Ash said with satisfaction. He glanced down at a pair of street urchins who ran alongside them, racing the carriage. "Give her the night to think over my threats. Challenge her first thing in the morning." His quick look at Chan was sincere and grateful. "I knew I could count on you in the crunch."

Wincing, Chan wished Ash had chosen a different word, one that didn't recall the sounds of sliding rock in that cave. He had been behind Ash when the first stones rattled over them, knocking him half-senseless. If Ash hadn't stopped to shove Chan into the main chamber first, he wouldn't have been pinned down. He wouldn't limp in agony now.

It wasn't as if Ash had asked him to cut his heart out for him. Negotiating with a beautiful woman of accommodating morals on his friend's behalf couldn't begin to repay his debt.

Chapter Three

Using his ebony cane, Chan knocked on Lucinda's door the next morning. Sunlight glinted off the golden stone of the Sydney Place town house with the promise of a fair day. He waited.

Where was the girl who answered the door yesterday? Backing up a couple of steps, Chan looked up at the windows above. No movement of curtains there or to the side of the door. Perhaps Lucinda had decided the only safe way to deal with discovery was not to answer the door at all.

Determined, he applied the cane to the door panels again. And waited.

If he must, he'd find his way behind the long row of connected houses. Kitchen doors were never locked before bedtime, and he'd talked his way through back entrances before. He'd give Lucinda another minute to admit him before making a less conventional approach.

Four minutes later, he reached the rear of the sixth house in Sydney Place. A door stood open, and he stepped into the shadowed space, his heel scraping on the flagged floor.

"Mercy!" squealed a plump woman, looking up from the deal table centering the long kitchen. "You didn't half frighten me, popping up like Old Nick." She raised floured hands from a doughy mass and stared at him. "Bless me if you don't have the look of him, too, with those slanted black eyes, even if I never knew the devil dressed like a proper gentleman."

Sweeping off his hat, Chan sniffed the air and grinned. "And I never realized angels bake bread. I could savor a slice or two of a loaf, even if I just ate at the Bear."

"Not one of my loaves, you won't." Though she frowned, the cook's gaze was more familiar than unfriendly as she looked him over as if he were a rooster that might do for the stew pot. "The first rising's still in the oven. What are you up to, coming to the back of the house like a tradesman? You must want the ladies."

"I knocked at the front," Chan said, sniffing his way to the brick wall oven. "It seems no one heard me. Then I followed my nose to the best bread I've smelled baking in Bath."

"Must have been a new experience, a lady's door not flying open to you." Reaching for a cloth, the cook scrubbed her hands and lower arms with it. "Miss Merriman might be giving her girls lessons and didn't hear you," she continued. "If you'll come this way, I'll take you up and see if she's free."

Bustling across the room to a dark, narrow staircase, she glanced back. Chan followed at once. No need to tell the woman he wouldn't allow Lucinda to refuse to see him.

"Who shall I tell her has called?" she asked a bit breathlessly as she labored up the steps ahead of him.

"She's expecting a visit this morning," Chan said. "You won't need to announce me."

Nodding, the woman said, "About her girls, no doubt. She'll be glad to know of a place for one even before they're trained. But you'll have to wait for her services. Miss Merriman doesn't let the girls go until she's certain they'll give satisfaction."

The woman whooshed a couple of deep breaths at the top of the stairs before starting down the long passage. Ahead of them stood the front door that hadn't kept him out, where lazy dust motes drifted in shafts of morning sun.

Cook glanced into the first doorway on the left.

What might the day's lesson be? Chan wondered. If girls received training as mistresses, he wasn't aware of it. Surely the basics came naturally, and a man preferred to teach a partner his particular ways. Though he had heard of Oriental practices few English ladybirds would know. Perhaps the old duke had taught Lucinda skills she passed along to her chicks. Intriguing, if so. Even titillating. He'd best squelch such thoughts for now, considering he wore knit pantaloons.

His plump guide stopped at a door to the right, saying, "The gentleman's here, miss."

"How did he— Never mind. I'll come at once." Lucinda's voice sounded startled at first, with a sharp intake of breath before she finished the speech.

Chan guessed she hadn't expected a visitor to be announced after the knocking stopped at the front door.

Her grim voice came nearer, as if she crossed the room. "I'll see to him, Cook. You may go."

The woman curtsied and headed for the servants' stairs.

Chan walked through the open door. He didn't mean to be kept standing in the passage like yesterday. Just inside the room, he stopped, surprised but amused.

"You again!" she said as if he were a mangy dog tracking in filth. "I expected the duke."

Lucinda hefted a long iron utensil in both hands, hold-

38

ing it like a singlestick weapon. It looked to be an oven rake. Her expression was determined, but her hands trembled. He hadn't expected a welcome, but being bludgeoned by a nervy woman was no part of his plans.

Maybe he should try to calm her first, in self-defense. "Surely your cook needs that implement, as today seems to be baking day." Casually he grinned and strolled across the small room. A quick glance around showed him it was furnished as a household office. A cluttered table held papers and books, and a shabby upholstered sofa squatted with its back to the window.

Sauntering over to the sofa, he dropped onto it, stretching his legs full-length on the Berber carpet before settling one boot over the other at the ankle. Maybe she wouldn't be tempted to strike a man who was already down.

"Don't make yourself comfortable," she warned him, waggling the oven rake. "I didn't invite you to stay, let alone sit."

"Dogs are told to sit and stay, not men," he drawled, folding his hands across his waistcoat. She was edgy as a cat, worse than when Ash had barked threats at her. Signs of exhaustion shadowed the beautiful face, as if she hadn't slept. "Why don't you have a seat, too, and we'll talk."

The glinting eyes narrowed and the pert little chin jutted. Spirited women attracted him, and despite signs of fatigue and alarm, she stood firm. She might just swing that oven rake, if she lost control. His muscles tensed to throw himself off the sofa if she started a backswing with the hooked iron rod.

"We have nothing to discuss." She spoke fast, her tone tight. "You can't think you're welcome here after pushing your way in yesterday and unsettling my aunt."

That was a pity, the old lady's confusion. He'd noticed how little sense she made the longer they talked. Nipped by regret, he straightened, propping an ankle on his knee. "How is Miss Lindsey? I'm truly sorry if our call disturbed her. She struck me as a very game old girl."

The oven rake lowered a notch. "After a late night that did her no good, she's still sleeping this morning. I hope she won't remember your visit yesterday when she wakes. If you leave now, she won't be upset further."

The crease between her graceful eyebrows betrayed her concern for her companion, and faint smudges beneath her eyes meant she'd sat up late with Miss Lindsey. No doubt she cared deeply about the older woman. Still, Chan had to put Ash's needs first. Besides, he reminded himself, his plan benefited her, too.

"I don't understand why seeing me should upset her." Settling into the chair, he watched her growing discomfort.

Moistening her lips, she looked away from him for the first time, no longer meeting his eyes. "Having you burst in here would upset anyone."

The old lady had welcomed them. Maybe Lucinda had more to hide than a fortune she didn't want to return. He'd know all her secrets in time, but first he'd deal with Ash's legacy.

"You don't have to worry about defending Miss Lindsey or yourself from me," he said quietly. "I'm here to make things easier for you, not cause trouble." He patted the sofa cushion. "Why don't you sit down instead of shaking that thing at me?"

"This is my house, not yours. It isn't your place to offer seats. This"—she jerked the heavy oven rake up like a musket—"was meant as a welcome for the duke after his threats yesterday. He's the one I expected to see."

"You don't want Ash to call on you again," he assured her in a mild tone, admiring the way her full breasts pushed against the tight bodice of her printed muslin gown as she flourished the rake. "Ash couldn't hold his

40

temper in front of an archbishop. Now I'm a reasonable man, always willing to talk things over and find a solution that lets everybody win. Not Ash." He shook his head. "It's his way or no way. You're much better off dealing with me."

"I refuse to deal with either of you," she said, shifting her curvaceous weight from dainty slipper to slipper. Holding up an iron oven rake must be tiring to those rounded, elegant arms, or she was growing edgier by the moment.

"Your business doesn't involve me," she continued, her voice rising toward panic. "I won't be tainted by it."

Before she finished speaking, Chan sprang out of the chair and wrested the iron utensil out of her grasp. After one lunging effort to retrieve it, she backed away from him along the table, looking as if she expected to be murdered.

As if he'd injure a woman. Annoyed she thought so, he marched to the door and tossed the oven rake into the passage. It landed on the patterned runner with a dull thud. Closing the door, he set his shoulders against it and stared at her.

From behind the table, she glared back, hugging herself. Getting past her barriers was no easy task.

"We aren't making any progress like this," he said with a wide gesture. Coming here to intervene for Ash had seemed simple while he chewed on beef and bread at the inn this morning. He'd awakened with a plan that made sense for all three of them, a plan that benefited Ash without leaving the lovely Lucinda unprotected. He hadn't expected to feel like a browbeater, and he didn't like it.

Chan had to make Lucinda understand where her best interests lay, with him as her ally, not her enemy. At least he wanted to replace that look of loathing and dread.

"I don't want Miss Lindsey upset any more than you

do," he said, not moving away from the door. He'd keep his distance for the moment. "Ash can be hasty, saying and doing the first thing that enters his head. That's why I agreed to come here for him. You and I can talk like two reasonable people, find a solution that leaves you both better off."

Lucinda grasped the back of the chair at the worktable, not taking her gaze off him. Watching the rapid rise and fall of her breast was too distracting, so he watched her hands instead. They could tell him when he'd begun to win her confidence. For now she gripped the chair's top rail so her knuckles showed white, and he regretted her anxiety and fatigue. She'd feel like a frightened bird in his arms right now, and soothing her would feel better than this badgering.

Instead he continued in a quiet tone, "I promise I won't make a fuss or talk in front of Miss Lindsey if that's what you want. But I have to warn you, Ash isn't going anywhere. And as long as he's in Bath, I won't leave him. Can't we try to resolve this without making him return? I guarantee there's less chance of me disturbing your aunt."

Her knuckles showed less tension. Looking indecisive, she said, "I can't give you what you want."

"All I ask is a chance to talk with you." He spread his arms, hands open in a gesture of goodwill. "You don't have to admit anything; just hear me out."

Looking anywhere but at him, she caught her full lower lip between her teeth. For an instant he could almost taste her. If things went according to his plan, he would—every tantalizing, beautiful inch of her.

Leaning over the chair, she asked, "Will you go away after you have your say? You won't make a scene and wake Aunt Delia?" Her hands cupped the side rails of the chair, moving up and down with a slight twisting motion.

Chan couldn't look away from the movement. A

woman's hands had never fascinated him this much—at least when they weren't touching him. "I have no intention of disturbing either of you."

Yet Lucinda disturbed him. Every time he saw the woman, she stirred him as if he were again a randy schoolboy.

"Very well." With a resigned sigh, she crossed her arms under her full bosom. "Talk."

He moved away from the door, toward the window. If he was to speak sense, he had to look at something besides Lucinda's lush body.

"Ash is determined to have the legacy that was left to you—very well, to Lucinda—returned to the estate." He amended his words as she began to interrupt. "He isn't willing to compromise on that purpose."

"Did his father leave him nothing?" she asked, sounding curious for the first time. Maybe she was relaxing enough to hear reason.

"Of course not. As his father's heir, he receives all the entailed property and some of the unentailed."

"Which includes rents on several estates, I would guess."

Lucinda surely knew the terms of the will; the old duke must have talked about it as she'd wheedled herself a legacy. "Indeed. Ash might have to practice economy for a change, but he can live comfortably on the income from the estates." He smiled. "To him it's the principle of the thing more than the money, significant as sixty thousand pounds are."

"Do you think I don't understand honor?" She looked offended. "My principles are higher than yours and the duke's appear to be."

No sense in getting drawn into that argument. Chan continued, "Ash isn't making an idle threat about taking this matter before chancery court. He would spend the entire sum in question on solicitors rather than let you— the wrong person—have it."

Not only did she look unmoved, she hardly seemed interested. Could she be totally naive about litigation involving an aristocrat and a kept woman?

"Any court case involving a duke will rate full coverage in the papers, and society will feed on every detail." If he had to spell it out for her, he would. "Those most likely to read the news on a regular basis are men of means, men a woman with girls to place wouldn't want to offend. Are you ready to be named in a chancery court case for undue influence?"

Chin up, she spoke with trembling lips. "But my girls need the work I find for them. I won't let the duke ruin their chances."

"If you persist in claiming a fortune that should go to Ash, he'll ruin you," Chan warned her. "He won't stop with getting that legacy set aside. He'll see that no man of rank is ignorant of your unfortunate influence on his father. He'll have you watched by the law to the point that your neighbors will clamor to have you removed from this street."

For a moment he thought she would speak, but instead she covered her mouth with a hand and turned her back, looking distraught.

Perhaps it was time to suggest his plan for her reprieve. Joining her behind the table, he lowered his voice. "Whatever the reason the old duke left you a fortune, you don't have to suffer because of the legacy. I know how to fix this so neither you nor Ash comes out the worse."

She stood before a dark framed landscape, head down. "Go on."

"Just sign a statement renouncing the legacy. That will send Ash away satisfied." He hurried to the next part of his plan, eager to relieve her worries. "You won't lose by doing the right thing. I can provide for you for the rest of your life."

Her quick intake of breath didn't surprise him. His

offer was unusual and generous, but she wasn't aware that he owed Ash his life.

Placing his hands on her shoulders, he said, "You can choose a house in a good neighborhood in London, and I'll put the deed in your name. I'll set up an annuity giving you an ample income for the rest of your life, totally under your control. You can send your girls away and never have to worry about finding another man to keep you."

Though she had stiffened at his first touch, Lucinda twisted free as he finished his offer. Scooting away, she put the table between them again.

"How like a man," she said in a quavering voice. Her golden eyes dominated the tired, pale face. "You'll arrange a mere female's life to suit yourself! You and your friend have insulted me since the first moment you accosted me in Milsom Street."

Stumbling away as if blind, she sank her face in her hands. "Haven't I endured enough from Ashcott men? Can I never be free?"

Pushing back loose hair, she said, "You invaded my house and upset poor Aunt Delia. And now—this!" She sputtered over words for a moment. "Now you make this disgusting proposal as if I were a common whore!"

"Hardly, my dear." He rounded the table, wondering how to rephrase what seemed like a generous offer. Histrionics from a courtesan weren't unusual in negotiations, but could she be greedy enough to expect more? "Common trollops don't rate property ownership and an annuity. Even the highest fliers aren't set up for life by protectors."

"Protectors, indeed; you mean *jailers!* Don't expect gratitude for your—your insulting *proposition*," she said, hands clenched as she kicked at the curtains. A delicious flush suffused her throat and face.

Chan reached for her and she jerked away, almost hissing at him between her teeth. Puzzled, he asked,

"What more do you want, wooing? You're hardly an innocent. Though this is basically a business arrangement between us, I promise to treat you with consideration as long as we're together."

Flinching away as he approached her again, Lucinda threw up crossed arms. "Don't touch me! The only reason I'm not screaming at you is to protect Aunt Delia from waking and hearing you defame my character. You've had your say as promised, and I don't have to endure more of this."

Stopping, Chan wondered if she really feared him. Surely the old duke hadn't mistreated her.

"Now you can listen to me," she said in a low-voiced command. "Your friend's father left me no legacy. And even if you attracted me in the least, which you don't, I wouldn't be your scullery maid, let alone anything that required closer contact."

Watching this puzzling display, Chan marveled at the fire in her eyes, like an inferno snapping sparks in all directions. What a magnificent woman she was, more vibrant and alive than even the opera diva who had shattered every dish in his house in her passions. He wanted to revitalize himself with Lucinda's energy, lead her to express this ardent side of her nature again and again.

"You could come to appreciate my touch far more than an old man's," he assured her, advancing as she retreated. One more step backward and the sofa stopped her. He watched her eyes dilate as she realized she could flee no farther. Characteristically, her chin rose. That defiant move made her shapely mouth too accessible to ignore. He wasn't a man to resist temptation.

Chan caught her into his arms and pressed his lips to hers in the same move. She went still, and he took the moment to taste her sweetness, to show her the passion they could build between them.

Even as he longed for more of her than he could know in a lifetime, she exploded out of his hold. He felt bereft, cheated on the brink of discovering something truly profound.

Otherwise he might have sidestepped the kicks she aimed at his shins. She emitted pent-up squeaks of rage, considerate of waking her companion even in wrath.

"You horrid man! Do you think every woman wants you grabbing at her? I'll teach you to force your wickedness on me!" Catching up a cushion from the sofa, she attacked him with repeated blows, dancing around him as he dodged.

If she didn't look so angry, he'd have laughed. She hopped off the floor with each swing, wielding the cushion with all her might. As many feminine tantrums as he'd survived, this was the nearest to silent one he'd seen.

More than ever, he wanted to push this woman down on the sofa and hold her against him, persuading her to match passions with him. Ducking a blow, he said, "You're even more enticing in a temper, my girl."

"Will you never hear me?" she cried aloud, sounding desperate and anguished. The tone rebuked him. Flinging away the cushion, she snatched a heavy book from the worktable and turned on him.

Throwing up his hands, Chan said, "Wait! You could do real damage with that."

"You're right," she said, dropping it again. "My books are too precious to risk the bindings on your hard head."

Stalking her around the table, he watched her scrabble at the standish for another weapon, knocking a ledger to the floor. When she found the ink pot, he pinned her wrist to the table, holding her there with enough force to contain movement without bruising her.

"Let go of me," she said between clenched teeth.

"Not flaming likely," he replied. "This is one of my favorite coats, and ink won't improve it or my disposition. Settle down, you little hellcat. If you don't like my offer, just say so. But you *will* get your claws out of Ashcott's legacy."

Panting, she twisted her arm in an effort to get free. He needed only one hand over her wrist to control her struggles. She said with a gasp, "I have no claim on any estate."

"Then you won't object to signing a statement saying that," he said, wishing he weren't aroused by the angry looks she fired at him between tugs at her captured wrist. He shouldn't want a woman who wasn't attracted to him, but it was difficult to ignore the lavender scent of her hair as it brushed his face in her efforts to pull free.

Abandoning the fight for a moment, she stared at him with disgust. "I should sign and be rid of you," she said. "Much good the wrong signature will do your precious duke, but if that's what it takes to get you out of this house forever, then I'll do it! What name do you want signed? Lucinda? Very well; I'll sign any document you want as Lucinda—whoever. What last name do you want me to write?"

That was a good question. Ash had never put any name but Lucinda and vulgarities to his father's mistress.

Chan stared at her flushed face and mussed hair. It hung halfway down to her shoulder on one side, with curls loosened around her face and neck, and damned if she wasn't the most seductive female he'd ever seen.

Also the most incensed. No woman this far gone in emotion could think straight enough to practice wiles. Might she really not be Ash's Lucinda despite his friend's conviction?

"If you aren't Lucinda, you have to be her twin sister," he said, and watched her complexion fade from flushed red to paper white. For a moment he thought she would faint.

Just as he was about to let go of her wrist to catch her as she fell, she jerked against his hand again. Leaning forward, he increased the pressure of his hold. "Is that it?" he demanded. "Are you protecting a sister?"

Fierce relief filled him. Perhaps she hadn't been the duke's darling. Maybe she hadn't yet belonged to any other man. That would make taking her for himself even sweeter. Like Harriette Wilson's siblings; if one sister became a ladybird, the other rarely shunned the same plumage.

"Tell me the truth and I'll let you go," he said. "Is it your sister who earned the legacy from the old duke? I can appreciate loyalty to family, but you can't protect her forever. Tell me where to find the old duke's Lucinda."

"I can't," she whispered, sounding choked. "You ask too much of me."

"I understand the indebtedness you feel to a sister," he assured her. "Ash is my brother in all but blood. As much you want to protect your family, I want to help him." He hardened his mind against her anguish. "You'll lead me to the right Lucinda or I'll ask your aunt's help."

"You mustn't disorient her still worse." She sagged onto her elbows atop the table. Concerned, Chan put his free arm around her for support and felt her whole body quiver.

"No," she said, her voice trembling but fierce. "This time you could make her disappear into the fogs of the past forever. Aunt Delia's all I have left."

Her voice broke on the last word, shaming him for tormenting her. Had the sixty thousand pounds been his, he would have released her and left without another word. Had the legacy represented only money to Ash, he wouldn't even be here. But much as he sympathized with this lovely woman, he had a duty to his friend.

Gently he released her wrist and leaned over her, a hand flat on the table at each of her elbows. She didn't seem to notice he'd let her go, bent in her private grief.

Hardening his resolve, he said, "I don't want to hurt you or Miss Lindsey. But I can't leave Ash to grieve his

49

heart out over the injustice of his father's will. He has to recover his legacy or he'll always feel he's lost the father he knew."

Her shoulders convulsed without sound.

"I don't care what Lucinda did or didn't do; I'm not set on causing her trouble, either," he assured her. "If you lead me to the right Lucinda, she won't suffer any harm from me. Give me the culprit, and I'll get Ash out of Bath and out of your life."

A shudder and sniffle answered him, and she reached into her sleeve for a handkerchief. After a couple of quick swipes, she said in a muffled voice, "If you'll stop crouching over me like a hen with chicks, I'll find the address you want."

Success at last. Feeling no satisfaction, Chan stood up and stepped back. He watched as she scrabbled through the litter of papers, folded and flat, on the table. He'd be amazed if anyone could find anything in the confused piles.

Lifting papers at the back of the table, she uncovered a letter. She let the other papers fall, ignoring those that slid onto the floor to seize the folded sheet. Fumbling the pressed stationery from its cover, she crushed the correspondence in a fist and held out the addressed sheet.

"Here's a letter from the Lucinda you want," she said, sounding worn beyond caring. "The direction on it is the only information I have or want about her. Take it and leave me alone."

Looking down at the superscription written in a looping, feminine hand, he read out, " 'Lady Enfield, Greystone Cottage, Farmborough.' " The hamlet was about ten miles distant on the road to Wells from Bath, hardly a fashionable address. Suspicion crawled through his mind. Did she mean to trick him again, as she had by running upstairs at the Sydney Hotel?

"Lady Enfield, indeed. A titled lady will know where to find the old duke's mistress?" he asked harshly. Decent females didn't associate with kept women.

Despite wet eyelashes and a pink nose, she said with dignity and defiance, "Why wouldn't a lady with a title know as much about your Lucinda as I?"

Chan stared at her, feeling ashamed and annoyed by turns. The longer he was with her, the less he knew this female. He made a decision. "We'll call on Lady Enfield together."

"Not me; you don't need me." Backing away, she shook her head, sending pins flying. "I won't see that woman."

"I'll need an introduction," he said, puzzled at her vehemence, especially about a sister. "You know Lady Enfield; I don't. You're coming along to ensure she'll receive me."

"But I don't know her; I can't matter to her now." Her speech was fast and shrill, her eyes wide and imploring.

"If she doesn't know you, you never mattered. Which is it?" Contradictions usually meant lies.

She appeared more afraid now than when he'd first arrived. "I haven't seen her in ten years. She can't care to see me after all this time."

Curious. Whatever her dread of Lady Enfield, he needed her if he were to fix things for Ash. He couldn't be distracted by any other consideration. "More likely she'll be happy to see you again after so long."

Heading for the door, he opened it wide. Turning, he spoke softly but with total conviction. "I'm calling on Lady Enfield, and you're coming with me. I can wrestle you out the door as you are, with your hair falling down for the neighbors to see and gossip about. Or you can go up to your room like a sensible woman and tidy yourself, put on a wrap and bonnet, and send one of your girls to the Sydney Hotel with a message that I want a curricle."

"Please don't do this to me," she whispered, her face contorted and pleading.

If he let her see how difficult this was for him, he'd never find Lucinda for Ash. "The alternative is to wake up your aunt and see if she will come. I mean to find the duke's Lucinda, and if you aren't the right one, someone here will lead me to information about her. Who is it to be?"

For a moment she twisted her handkerchief, obviously holding back tears. Then, blowing her nose into the ridiculous scrap of lace, she straightened her spine. Pushing back her loosened hair, she marched past him, tragic and proud as if facing the guillotine.

Damned if he didn't have to admire her.

An hour later, Chan admired her still, as he pulled his team off the road to Wells before reaching Farmborough. After leaving him to prepare for this journey, she had cooperated quietly and with dignity.

From directions he'd asked of a farmer in a nearby field, this graveled drive led to a stone cottage behind tall hedges, the home of Lady Enfield. The lady kept to herself, the farmer had confided.

Beside him, his companion sat still as a marble column on a plinth, silent as she had been on the entire drive from Bath. If she'd raised her head on the journey, he hadn't noticed.

Easing his hired pair to an uneven halt on the graveled circle before the three-storied house, he waited to see if their arrival was noticed. Within seconds, a boy dashed from the doors to his horses' heads. Nodding to the lad, Chan swung down from the curricle and crossed behind it to his unwilling passenger.

"I don't know what to call you," he murmured, looking up at her on the bench seat. "If you prove not to be Lucinda, are you called Elizabeth?"

Her bleak gaze met his, the golden color drowned in

52

the shadows beneath her bonnet to flat hazel. Her lips trembled, and she whispered, "If you have any mercy in you, let me wait here."

Looking away, he stared at the plain stone facade of the house. He had to be cold as stone, hard as rock if he were to be successful in this quest. Putting out a hand, he said, "Come along."

To compensate, he helped her down and into the house as if she were an invalid. When she held herself as distant as his grasp on her elbow would allow, it stung.

By the time an elderly manservant met them with a salver for cards, Chan's mood was as dark as the interior of the old house. Small windows let in little light, even in the drawing room overlooking the garden where they were shown to wait for Lady Enfield.

Lucinda-Elizabeth pulled away at once to stand at a far window, and with no way out of the room except past him, he let her go. Her arm within his hand had communicated the stark tension he'd felt from her throughout the miles between Bath and Farmborough. Her body seemed brittle enough to break under the odd stress this visit imposed.

Watching her, he almost missed Lady Enfield's entrance. A whisper of silk skirts and a quick intake of breath told him they were no longer alone.

Turning to bow, he stopped when he realized Lady Enfield's attention was fixed on his companion, as if he weren't even in the room. Then his gaze was riveted on the lady, and social conventions were lost.

Chan looked from Lady Enfield to the tense figure at the window, her back to the room. If the lady were the true Lucinda, little wonder Ash had thought Elizabeth to be her. Lady Enfield mirrored the younger woman, face and form, as she would look within several years' time.

Lady Enfield's features didn't look older so much as muted, as if a charcoal drawing had smudged to less sharp lines. The same golden eyes glowed with warmth, but their light was dimmed. The sense of energy about the curvaceous body was more subdued. The aura of sensuality they both wore like a misting of delicate scent offered a deeper, more mature appeal. Lady Enfield was the old duke's beloved Lucinda—of that Chan was now sure—her worth easily sixty thousand pounds.

Not a twin, then. Was she Elizabeth's older, sadder but wiser sister?

Chan looked back at the younger woman to find that her body appeared stiffer, as if she had stopped breathing to listen.

"Oh, my dear. I'm so grateful you've come at last." Lady Enfield's rich, low voice throbbed in the silence like a prelude offered in a cathedral.

Elizabeth finally moved, turning about as slowly as was possible. As her face came into view under the bonnet's brim, Chan felt stunned. If she had been silent and stolid before, she now looked pale and waxen, as if laid out for burial rites. The lovely features were wiped of emotion. Only her eyes were alive, molten and accusing.

"Elizabeth—please!" Lady Enfield's plea choked off as she held out her arms, inviting an embrace.

The younger woman moved toward them, slowly at first, then gaining speed. By the time she reached Lady Enfield, just inside the door, Elizabeth was running.

She fled past the lady, her soft, slippered steps silent on the carpet, then shushing over the polished boards in the entrance hall. The sound receded, merged into that of shifting gravel outside.

Lady Enfield stood with her handkerchief over her mouth, her great golden eyes pooling with unshed tears.

"I'm sorry," Chan said, shaken by disturbing undercurrents eddying about him. "I don't understand."

In a valiant effort to smile, her generous lips twisted. Her voice low and musical despite tears, Lady Enfield said, "Neither does my daughter."

Chapter Four

"You don't look old enough to be Elizabeth's mother," Chan blurted without thought, glancing toward the door. Where had Elizabeth gone in her disturbed state?

Lady Enfield didn't seem to notice his lapse, wandering down the long drawing room as if lost. "I should never have begged her to come here," she murmured in a choked voice. Turning back, she said with effort, "You must go see to Elizabeth. She won't welcome my concern, I fear."

Before he could agree, she hurried into distracted speech. "Forgive me for sending you off abruptly without the usual courtesies. You must be her friend, but I don't know you."

The assumption of friendship nipping at his conscience, he bowed. "A mother's anxiety for a daughter is only natural. I'm Charles Norton, Lord Chandler, happy to be of service to you or Elizabeth."

"Lord Chandler," she repeated, her fingers worrying a jet necklace like a rosary. "I know you only by reputation, but that makes me hope you don't judge me too harshly. How did you come to bring my daughter here— did Delia make her visit? Why did she come if she didn't want to see me?"

Chan didn't want to discuss this sore subject. He wanted to find Elizabeth, to learn what damage he'd done by forcing her here. Despite that urgency, his business with Lady Enfield had to come first. He had to keep his foot in Lucinda's door if he was to help Ash. "I can explain it to you more fully another time, when we aren't both distracted by concern for your daughter." Trying to lighten the atmosphere in this house of shadows, he smiled. "She's capable of taking my curricle back to Bath without me. I'd best go find her, if you'll say I may call again."

"Thank you for your courtesy. It's welcome, if unexpected." Walking to the window where Elizabeth had stood, she laid a hand on the glass where her daughter had touched it. "Society has ignored me since I broke its cardinal rule of discretion ten years ago."

"No one who looks like you or Elizabeth could ever truly be ignored."

The trite flattery came easier than the discussion he should pursue. Though Ash's interests should take precedence, the need to find Elizabeth and learn her state of mind distracted him. "Perhaps later I can help you in this difficult situation."

"Perhaps you can." Golden eyes measured him with a glimmer of hope from across the long room. "You must have earned Elizabeth's trust since she asked for your company at this meeting. Perhaps you would agree to speak with her for me, persuade her I never meant her to suffer."

His offer of help had been meant only to ease her social isolation, not to act as go-between with her daughter. The old duke's legacy would further alienate Lady Enfield from society if she went to court over it, a situation that might give him a bargaining point with this woman. Honesty forced him to admit, "I'm not certain your daughter will speak to me again after today. You can find a better emissary."

The full lips so like her daughter's trembled, reminding him how much he'd upset Elizabeth. "You underestimate yourself, Lord Chandler," she said. "Your reputation makes me believe you're very persuasive with my sex."

"Your daughter is no ordinary woman." That was a gross understatement of his opinion of Elizabeth.

"She's lovely, isn't she?" Shadows fled from her large, luminous eyes as they lit with joy. "Even as a girl of twelve she didn't show the usual awkwardness in the change toward womanhood." A haunted look crossed her face. "Will saw her beauty then, too. He said a girl on the verge of womanhood must be protected from the kind of household we could share."

Will. It took a moment for Chan to realize she spoke in this heart-wrenching tone about the sixth Duke of Ashcott, his best friend's father. Her lover.

Head bowed, she said, "He was right. Sending her away was for the best. But I didn't realize fully what separation from my child would cost me. You make the choice that seems best for those you love, but living with it . . . can become a daily death."

Though they'd just met, Chan wanted to comfort her, this woman he must persuade to give up the legacy from her beloved. But first he had to find Elizabeth. He had brought her here against her wishes, and she had left this room distraught as a result. The least he could do was get her safely home again. "If Elizabeth will discuss it with me, I'll do as you ask. But now I really must find her. It isn't good for her to be alone, as upset as she seemed."

Nodding, Lady Enfield headed for the entrance hall, graceful as her daughter. "I'll see you as far as the door;

she won't want me to come out. Promise you'll return soon, though, to tell me if she recovers fully from this meeting. She's refused to see me these last ten years, and even began to return my letters after a while. I never meant to hurt her, and I pray she will someday believe that. Even if she can't be persuaded to listen to my side of things at once, please come back and tell me how she is." Tears seeped from the corners of the woman's rounded eyes without her notice, as if they were frequent companions. "I long to know what her present life is like, even if she has no place for me in it. Will you come again?"

The promise came easily. "Of course I will." Taking her cold fingers, he bent above them in a proper salute. Whatever mistakes Lady Enfield had made, she still paid a high price for them.

The lane's dust swirled up from each slipper as Elizabeth set one foot in front of the other with careful deliberation. She wouldn't think about the woman behind her. She would concentrate upon getting back to Bath, upon getting on with life without letting the past besmirch it.

Half boots would have made the ten-mile walk far easier, but she'd been pitchforked into this loathsome journey without adequate time to prepare. Not that any amount of preparation could have eased the ordeal of that unwelcome meeting. The voice, so long unheard, had jangled every nerve inside her, tangling her feelings into a snarl of threads that could never be untied.

No, she wouldn't think of that woman. All that mattered now was getting herself back to Bath and Aunt Delia, one step at a time. What couldn't be cured must be endured. Trust was fragile as an egg, unfixable once broken. And her trust in her mother had been broken long ago.

To Elizabeth, her mother had died when she was a

child of twelve—when her mother had chosen to abandon her child.

Head down, Elizabeth saw no more of a passing dray than the giant hooves of the shire horses and the heavy wheels rimmed in metal. She held her breath against clouds of dirt rising to sift over and stifle her.

Along the outer edges of her consciousness, she heard a carriage pass and pull up ahead. Whether friendly or threatening, she would refuse all offers of a ride. She couldn't carry on a civil conversation as if nothing had occurred, and as for dangers of the open road, nothing worse could befall her today.

"Climb up."

It was the dictatorial Lord Chandler again. That would teach her to think the worst was over. His curt order only moved her feet faster as the jumbled feelings of the past quarter-hour boiled over. He had turned her comfortable world on end, but he would never again impose his will on her. A fresh blaze of anger replaced her disgust at being forced to accompany him into that tainted house.

"You can't walk ten miles in thin slippers. Come up into the curricle like a sensible woman." The awful man eased the horses forward, wheels creaking a protest at the slow pace, to keep beside her. "You don't want to go this way."

She looked into the diabolical darkness of his eyes, but she couldn't think. Speeding her steps again, she almost ran along the rutted surface of the well-traveled lane. Stumbling, she caught at the carriage's swan axle to steady herself, then flung away from it. Taking even instinctive help from this man demeaned her. Her hands clenched in growing wrath against his interference, she marched on.

"Walking back is hardly appropriate for a gentlewoman. You rode this far with me; you might as well ride back."

Elizabeth despised his logic and his reasonable tone.

Throughout his wrongheaded torments, he had kept control of himself and controlled her while she beat against him in useless reaction. Never again would she allow him to dictate to her.

Despite her silence, he persisted. "You're so covered with dust your own mother wouldn't know you. It's silly to—"

Her fuse burned up, Elizabeth exploded. "I have no mother! I was abandoned by the woman who gave birth to me—for her lover! She has lost the right to call herself a parent."

Holding in the pair as they shied ahead at her outburst, Lord Chandler urged them back beside her as she marched forward. "Lady Enfield impressed me as someone who cares deeply about you."

It was a mistake to discuss anything with a know-all male. Elizabeth felt fine sand grate between her teeth as she clenched her jaw. Lord Chandler was just as intrusive and irritating.

"She urged me to follow and look after you." He leaned over her from the curricle as he spoke. "That doesn't sound like an uncaring mother."

His defense of a woman who could send her child away for a mere man made her tremble with rage. "If you admire her so much, go back and stay the entire day with her. You're two of a kind, a seducer and the seduced; no wonder you defend her."

He didn't react at once and she hurried on, wanting to be rid of his looming shadow. Then he said calmly, "It's easier to judge others than to try understanding them."

How could anyone support that woman's behavior? "I don't claim to be perfect, but I'd never abandon my child—never! That may seem like a minor fault to you, considering you've probably left litters of bastards behind you."

That drew a stifled curse. "You're no closer to the

truth than you are to Bath, and if you stomp along in this direction, you'll never get a step closer to either one." His sharp tone cut across her hot sense of injustice like a cold wind. "Stop acting like an emotional female and get in the carriage."

How dared he sound amused and superior after this day of distress he'd inflicted. As she whirled toward him, her skirts whipped her sore ankles. "Stop telling me how to think and act. You assume you know exactly what everyone should do about everything, and you don't know the first thing about who I am, what I've endured, or how I feel. Drive on, sir—to Hades! You won't take me with you."

His gaze was fixed and narrowed on her, eyes brilliant and hard as coal. Feeling hot and cold by turns as a blaze built within their dark depths, she refused to look away.

Danger flared in his eyes like the sun's flash in a mirror, and she wavered. Unable to maintain her righteous glare under his furious intensity, Elizabeth picked up her skirts and fled down the road.

The man was a menace. He'd hounded her through the streets of Bath, run her to her ground at home and ruthlessly kissed her, then forced her to accompany him to the last place she meant to go. Running might be undignified, but facing his fury was foolhardy.

Her gasping breaths filled her ears along with the pounding labor of her heart and feet. Through this haze of sound the relentless clatter of harness and hooves beat along her spine. The curricle drew even with her. Almost sobbing, Elizabeth laid a hand against the stitch in her side and turned to jump a ditch and dash into a field. He caught at her shoulder, though, and, as she slowed to twist away, slipped an arm around her waist.

Elizabeth felt herself scooped off the road and slapped against the curricle's side. The horses whinnied and reared as she dangled from Lord Chandler's arm in a dust storm, shrieking and blinded.

"Stop fighting me, you little fool, or I'll drop you on your pretty rear in the road," her abductor threatened somewhere above her head.

"Please do," she cried, clinging to his arm and shoulder out of reflexive self-preservation. She'd never felt so helpless and imperiled, flopping like a child's doll hung out of this carriage. Flashes of lurching ground met her tearful eyes. She'd fight loose from the muscular arm crunching her ribs if she could shake off the vision of herself crushed under uncurbed hooves.

Shifting along the seat, Lord Chandler pulled her inside. Her bottom bumped over the side rail and thumped onto the leather cushion of the seat. Clamping her against his side under his elbow, Lord Chandler leaned away for balance, taking the reins back into both hands. She couldn't break free from his powerful hold and didn't dare do battle with rearing horses ready to overturn the curricle in the ditch.

"Let me go," she said in a gasp, bent backward at an awkward angle between his body and arm. "Someone will see us."

"You might have thought of that earlier." Scowling, he didn't loosen the vise of his muscular arm. "Walking alone down a public highway toward Wells looks far more foolish than riding to Bath under my"—he looked down at her, bent across his lap, and grinned—"protection."

Realizing she'd set off in the wrong direction didn't improve her temper. "You can just remove your *protection* from my body this instant."

"Do I have your word you won't leap out of the curricle at the first opportunity? I don't care to put the horses through this ordeal again."

Squirming brought his arm into searing contact with her breasts. Flinching, she said, "It didn't do me any good, either, being snatched up like a mail pouch by a coachman. Let me go, you bully. I can't breathe!"

"If she can bitch, she can breathe," he muttered. As he brought the pair under control at last, he insisted, "Do I have your word?"

"Yes," she promised with regret. As he raised his arm and freed her, she fell across his thighs.

Dragging herself up instantly and ducking under his elbow, Elizabeth righted herself on the seat. Close contact with a man's pantaloons wasn't part of her experience in a female household. She tugged her bonnet off its sideways position over one ear, careful not to look at the lower part of his body. She was tongue-tied from an excruciating awareness of his muscled thighs moving against her moments before.

A carriage appeared from around a curve, and she ducked her head, shielding her features with the bonnet brim as it rolled past.

"Afraid of being seen with me?" He spat the question as he maneuvered the pair in a tight three-point turn on the now empty road. "Other women beg me to take them up for a ride."

Clinging to the curved seat rail as the curricle lurched in the final turn toward Bath, she leaned away to avoid the touch of his spread legs. "Maybe you *take them up* without grabbing them off the ground," she said tartly. "Ladies prefer not to be seen rumpled and dirty, looking as if the rake who's driving has ravished them in the road."

His burst of laughter was hardly the reaction she expected or wanted. "When I ravish you, I promise it won't be on a public highway." His sidelong look prickled along her skin like a dire premonition. "You'll be far more responsive on cool sheets scented with lavender like your hair. A woman who feels safe and secure is more inclined to lose herself wholly to a man's embraces."

The wicked image unnerved her more than landing on his lap had. She wanted to hit him. "Don't confuse me

63

with my mother. We might look alike superficially, but we don't deal with men the same way. This is why I avoid her, knowing men will assume the worst about me if they know we're related."

"Your mother has put her passions to better use than you have." This time his glance seemed to find her lacking. "Wait until you understand men as well as she, before you decide what they assume."

"Understand men!" Gripping her upper arms, she pushed against the footboard with her toes. "I've understood far more than I care to know about men since I was a girl. I don't have to *know* them in every possible sense of that word to choose to stay out of their overbearing clutches."

His smug grin taunted her and frayed her temper further.

"Some clutches give more pleasure than others. If you got to know a man in the right way, it might take some of the starch out of your petticoats."

Furious, she rounded on him. "Your drawers could benefit from a great deal less starch in— Oh!"

Feeling her face flood with heat, she stared off toward the horizon. She had never thought, let alone said, such an improper thing in her life. This just illustrated the evils of associating with men. Nearly crying with frustration, she said, "See what vulgarity you made me speak."

Laughing, he leaned toward her. "At least you know what men cover with drawers. That's a beginning."

Lips compressed, Elizabeth kept her head turned away. She was more interested in an ending, but no good would come of saying that to this wicked man. She'd ride the rest of the way home in disapproving silence.

Besides, bandying words with Lord Lucifer had burned her quite enough already.

*　　*　　*

None too soon to suit Elizabeth, Lord Chandler guided the pair down Bath's Great Pulteney Street toward home. As he turned behind the Sydney Hotel to its stables, she said sharply, "No need to leave the horses here. Just stop in front of my house and I'll jump down."

"I took you away from your home and I'll deliver you safely inside," he said in his inflexible manner.

"That's hardly necessary." She would tolerate his high-handed manner one last time, since she never had to see him again after today.

As they reached the steps before her door, she hurried ahead, ready to leave him standing on the stoop without a word. The door burst open and she stopped short.

It was Sally, who led the other two maids as they pushed through the portal. Cook hovered behind them, wringing her hands in the towel tucked in at her ample waist.

Please, God, let it simply be a problem with the kittens. The level of distress in the four faces made the newborn creatures unlikely to be the source of trouble.

"She wasn't in her bed, miss, when I took up her chocolate," Sally cried, seizing Elizabeth's arm. "Miss Delia's wandered off!"

Chapter Five

Elizabeth couldn't draw a breath into her lungs. The worst had happened, the thing she had dreaded since Aunt Delia began stepping outside reality and losing herself in the past.

Somewhere in Bath her elderly aunt wandered alone, frightened and disoriented.

The other two maids crowded close behind Sally, sniffling and red-eyed. "We should call the constable," wailed Nell, wiping her nose on her sleeve. "Miss Delia is as helpless as our newborn kittens."

Suze spoke well above her usual shy whisper. "I'll knock on every door in the street if you say the word, mum."

Cook met Elizabeth's questioning look across the milling maids, concern puckering her plump features. "It's true, Miss Lizbeth. I sent up the morning tray about noon as you said, and Sally ran back down the stairs without it, allowing as how Miss Delia wasn't in her room. We've looked around the streets close by, but I was loath to go farther afield, not knowing when you might return and find the house empty."

"Yes, go for the constable, Nell," said Elizabeth, apprehension making her stomach lurch. "We must find her at once." In her anxiety, she hardly knew what to do herself, let alone how to direct the others. "We'll each take a street on this side of the bridge and call at every house in case she's been seen."

Hands to her head, she felt almost dizzy with anxiety. The bridge and the Avon brought frightening images to mind.

"Wait." Lord Chandler's deep, quiet voice at her shoulder stopped her servants. "Let's think a minute before starting the search."

Elizabeth wanted to scream at his delay. Her beloved aunt wandered lost, endangered, and this man insisted on taking command.

"I won't keep you any longer with my personal concerns, Lord Chandler." She glared at him. "You'll want to hurry back to your friend."

Big hands clasping her shoulders, he said with grave sincerity, "Let me help, Elizabeth. The more of us looking, the better, and with me along, you can go places a lady might not be safe alone."

His firm grasp brought an unexpected feeling of support in this crisis, an unaccustomed sensation. Major or minor, she dealt with her household's incidents alone. She didn't want to take his help, but he was right in what he said. This was no time to allow personal antipathy to get in the way of her aunt's safety.

"Very well," she agreed. "You search all the places men gather on this side of the bridge."

"Let's not scatter in different directions like sheep," he said. "Miss Delia may need to be carried back if she's wandered far, and two of your girls could bring her home more comfortably than one. Also, your aunt might find her way here while we're out looking. Someone should stay in the house."

Everything he said made sense. Nodding once, she said in a rush, "Cook, will you watch for her here? Sally, ask at neighboring houses whether anyone saw Miss Delia pass by. Nell and Suze, search Great Pulteney Street and the recreation ground east of it."

Poised to hurry down the steps, she stifled her anxiety-fed anger as he stopped her again with a hand on her arm.

"Does your aunt especially enjoy visiting a particular spot near here?"

"She usually chooses to walk one of two places," she said, near tears of impatience to be searching. "Sydney Gardens or Bathwick Park."

"Even confused, she might follow familiar routes," he said. "As much ground as Sydney Gardens covers, your maids might look there first, while we search toward Bathwick Park."

Accepting his logic, she nodded quickly at the maids. As they scurried across the street, Elizabeth led the way toward the far end of the town house row, nearly running. "I'm going this way, to look across the fields before turning back toward the park."

"We'll find your aunt," he assured her, keeping pace without a sign of exertion.

"But will we find her in time?" Fretful tears clogged her throat, preventing her from saying more. As they reached the end of Sydney Place, she shaded her eyes to stare toward distant Cleveland Bridge and back along the riverbank toward Bathwick Park.

Befuddled after yesterday's disastrous visit, Aunt Delia had likely gone searching for Lucinda. When disoriented like this, she asked for Lucinda constantly whenever Elizabeth left her sight.

Had she been at home when Aunt Delia awoke, her aunt wouldn't have left the house. If Lord Chandler hadn't forced Elizabeth to accompany him this morning, she would have been home. She would never forgive Lord Chandler or *that woman* if her aunt was harmed.

Clasping her elbow, Lord Know-it-all looked over the fields along the Avon, too. She stepped away from his unwelcome touch. The last thing she wanted was the distraction of his hands, when the need to find Aunt Delia built in her head with the pressure of an oncoming storm. Frowning, she focused on the riverbank, watching for any sign of movement.

"Don't torment yourself by thinking the worst," he said with reassurance she couldn't accept. "I doubt your aunt would climb down a high bank to the river. The natural instinct for self-protection stays active even when minds lose ordinary memories."

"But she might fall if she got that far." His insight into her fears surprised her. Swallowing her threatening tears, she asked on a note of challenge, "How do you know so much about older people's minds?"

"I learned what little I know the way most of us do, within my family." He scanned the broad expanse of undeveloped land stretching all the way to the London road across the river.

"You're right about the park. My aunt is more likely to wander toward an area with people, looking for me—or Lucinda, as she thinks me to be in these mental states."

How she hated to be mistaken for that woman. Elizabeth headed across the fields toward Bathwick Park at a fast pace.

At least Lord Chandler didn't doubt the serious nature of this search, judging from his sharp gaze in all directions as they walked. For the first time she considered him as a typical person with a family, not just a devilish fiend set on hounding her. "You have an older relative who's easily confused?"

"I did have. A few years back *Grandmère* became

vague and easily lost herself even on our familiar grounds. I asked her elderly abigail to sleep on a truckle bed in her room, but Gran still got outside a night or two—probably confused when she awoke. She wandered as far as a nearby lane once, uncertain where she was."

His tone didn't change, but his expression betrayed the anxiety he'd felt. "A late traveler mistook her for a ghost in her bed gown and shot at her as she stood in the road." He was quiet for a moment. "I had her moved from the dower house to rooms near me at Chandler Hall."

His simple statement spoke eloquently about a horrible time when he had feared for the safety of a relative he loved. Elizabeth easily imagined the guilty fear of searching for an elderly lady in darkness, hearing a shot shatter the silence, and rushing toward the sound expecting the worst. "At least no one's likely to fire at Aunt Delia in broad daylight in Bath, even if she left home in her night rail."

"I should have thought to ask what she wore," said Chan, smacking his forehead.

"Aunt Delia is my responsibility," she reminded him at once. "If anyone should think of everything that might help locate her, I should." In fairness, she admitted, "You were far more rational about the search than I was able to be."

Looking no less concerned or worried, he said, "Being logical isn't the usual reaction when a family member is endangered. I feel terrible that she's missing." His tone conveyed anguish. "I also feel responsible."

As he looked around them, grimacing, she realized he couldn't meet her eyes.

"If I hadn't made you leave early this morning, your aunt would have found you nearby when she awoke. She probably wouldn't have left the house."

His echo of her earlier thoughts surprised her.

Hunching his shoulders, he sighed. "I'm sorry, Elizabeth. My mistrust of you led to this danger for your aunt. If she has suffered the smallest scratch, you may use your cook's oven rake on my thick skull, and I won't lift an arm to stop you."

Perhaps she thought a bit better of him for accepting his share of blame. Still, she had no energy to waste on his guilt now with Aunt Delia alone and at risk. "Maybe no one is at fault, any more than when your grandmother wandered away from the house. We do our best to protect our elderly relatives, but hedging them with guards and locks would deny them the good days they can still enjoy."

His warm, dark-eyed glance was grateful.

Hurrying along the middle path into the park, Elizabeth shoved aside thoughts of feelings. "Finding Aunt Delia safe is all that matters now."

"I don't see anyone alone among the strollers and nurses with children." He gestured toward Henrietta Street, which fronted Bathwick Park, then toward open fields. "Let's search among the trees beyond the oval drive."

Elizabeth veered in that direction, cutting across the scythed grass to save time. Trees and shrubs stood in clusters, rustling leaves as if exchanging gossip, wearing the light yellow-green of new growth.

Though Elizabeth wasn't cold in her spencer despite the sharp spring breeze, Aunt Delia might have left the house without a wrap. Catching a chill was dangerous at her age.

Her heart pumping, she walked faster, and Chan easily kept up, lengthening the stride of his long, lean legs. As they passed each leafy retreat, she searched the site quickly with eyes that teared in the light wind. Chan left the path from time to time to check rises and depressions of the ground, his speedy pace returning him to her side before she could have reached those spots. This terrain

71

provided areas where Aunt Delia could be hidden from a searching glance if she had fallen. Checking it would take twice as long without him.

About to pass a stand of oak, she paused, watching intently.

"What do you see?" He stopped behind her, a steadying hand on her shoulder.

"It may have been nothing more than a hare or a skylark." She waited, intent. "I thought I saw movement—yes!" Hope propelling her feet, she left the path at a run and dodged through the trees.

Relief lightened the boulder she'd carried in her chest for the last quarter-hour. Beyond the copse, Aunt Delia sat facing the remains of the former Bathwick estate, looking small and fragile as she hugged her elbows and rocked.

"Oh, no!" Elizabeth's heart clenched. "She's come out in her nightclothes. She must be freezing."

"You approach her first," murmured Chan. "Seeing someone she doesn't know well might alarm her."

Nodding, she slowed to a walk and regulated her breathing. He was right; best to arrive quietly and make little of the situation. The important thing was to get Aunt Delia home and warm as quickly as possible.

Circling to come upon her more from the front, Elizabeth crouched beside her aunt. As the older woman looked up, Elizabeth took her thin, cold hand between hers. "Hello, Aunt Delia. Have you enjoyed your morning walk? I'm sorry I wasn't home to come out with you. Let's turn back now; it's past time for a luncheon and I believe Cook's making Bath cakes today."

Her aunt's bleak features lit as the pale eyes searched her face. "There you are, Lucinda, dear. I thought I'd find you in the garden with Will, but you weren't there. Then . . . well, I don't know where I walked."

The ache of finding her aunt's mind still far in the past bored deep into Elizabeth's chest. Taking off her spencer, she laid it around Aunt Delia's shoulders and hugged her. "I'm not walking with Will today," she said gently, feeling her aunt tremble. She had to get the woman off these damp weeds as soon as possible. "Lord Chandler accompanied me. Do you recall Lord Chandler, who called on us yesterday?"

As Elizabeth looked around for him, he approached on the other side, sinking down on one knee to smile at her aunt. "You seem to be enjoying the sunshine," he said quietly. "It's good to see you again today. Are you very tired from your long walk? May I help you up?"

His manner and tone showed Elizabeth he spoke as naturally to confused old ladies as to young ones.

"Lord Chandler." Aunt Delia's thin voice strengthened with satisfaction after peering at him for a moment. "I'm relieved to find Lucinda in your company. A widower's far better for her than a married man, but don't tell your friend Ashcott I said so, as he's a very good man in his own way. Just unequally yoked, as the good book says."

Elizabeth ached at this evidence of Aunt Delia's confusion. She appeared to think Lord Chandler was his father.

Trying to shift position, Aunt Delia caught her breath and said, "Yes, I believe I'll need a strong arm to help me rise. I've grown a bit stiff sitting here."

Turning to Elizabeth, she blinked faded eyes and frowned. "I can't recall how I came to sit down on the ground. It's far too cold to sit here as if attending one of those horrible picnics people insist on holding when they have perfectly good dining rooms." She sounded plaintive and a little afraid. "My gown feels quite damp, and you know I can't bear dampness for any length of time without coming down with an ague."

Rearranging the fabric over her lap as she prepared to rise, Aunt Delia looked at Elizabeth, confused and horrified. "Merciful heavens, I'm wearing my bed gown outdoors!" Tears collected in her eyes, and her lips trembled as she glanced about. "You'll have to forgive me, Lord Chandler, for coming out without dressing properly. I can't think what made me do so."

About to cry herself, Elizabeth hugged her again.

"You look charming." Lord Chandler spoke as if ladies sat on the ground in nightclothes every day. "If you'll slip your arms into that pretty blue spencer and button it, no one will notice any difference from the white muslins ladies usually wear these days."

For once grateful for his easy manner with ladies, Elizabeth helped her aunt find the spencer's armholes. Chan continued to chat and flirt with her as normally as if they sat together at the Pump Room on a rout bench. Color returned to Aunt Delia's face as she smiled and responded to him.

When Elizabeth had fastened the last button, he rose and asked her aunt, "Are you ready to see if you're comfortable standing? Will you give me the pleasure of helping you up?"

Elizabeth's heart filled at his gentle consideration for Aunt Delia's pride.

At her aunt's nod, he lifted her smoothly onto her feet, keeping steady hands under her arms while she swayed a bit. Without making a fuss, he allowed her to stand on her own as much as she could, getting her bearings.

Elizabeth noted with concern her aunt's thin embroidered house slippers, damp and dirty from the long walk. Surely she couldn't make it back to Sydney Place under her own power.

"I think I'm ready to go home now," said Aunt Delia, taking a tentative step. She crumpled, caught at once in Chan's ready clasp. "My knees don't seem to support me," she said in a gasp, clinging to his strong arms.

"Probably you've only overdone a bit by walking so far," he reassured her. "If you'll allow it, I can carry you home faster than I could go for my carriage." Grinning, he added, "I promise not to take ungentlemanly advantage while I have you in my arms."

Smiling in return, she raised her arms like a trusting child to be picked up. "How disappointing. However, with Lucinda looking on, I suppose we'll have to mind our manners."

As he lifted and cradled Aunt Delia with tender care, he looked briefly at Elizabeth. How could she have called his face darkly dangerous and threatening, when it showed only compassion as he looked down at her aunt?

When his gaze shifted fully to her, Elizabeth felt a jolt from its intensity.

"The pavement on Great Fulteney might make the trip a smoother ride for your aunt in that direction, but we can get Miss Lindsey home sooner through the park," he said, consulting Elizabeth. "I think I can avoid jostling her too much, especially if you go ahead and pick the smoothest ground."

"Let's take the shorter route," she said, setting off at once. How kind of Chan to realize she would prefer not to expose Aunt Delia to curious eyes. His long shadow fell within her peripheral vision as they walked, so she knew he followed close behind her with his precious burden.

Relieved as she was to find Aunt Delia, another thing gnawed at her peace of mind. A crack had appeared in her black view of Lord Chandler, and the chink of light disturbed her opinion of him. She didn't trust him any more than she did other men. They couldn't be depended on. Like her handsome father, they all had more important things to do than bother with the ladies at home. If they appeared to offer help, it benefited them more than their families. Or so it had always seemed.

Yet Chandler had gone out of his way to help find Aunt Delia, and he had shown the greatest consideration for them both in this terrifying situation. To continue showing contempt for him after his kindness would be mean-spirited.

Despite the hard angles of his darkly handsome face and his overly rational nature, Chan appeared to have a genuine, concerned side to his nature. Joining in her effort to find her aunt, he had been responsible and dependable. How irritating to be forced to think better of him.

As she hurried toward home, she heard Aunt Delia murmur, "It's a sin for a man to have hair that curls while ladies have to tie theirs up in rags. You're even better-looking this close up, Chandler. No wonder ladies can't say no to you. I don't know why Lucinda prefers that long-faced Ashcott to a devilish flirt like you. He never seems to smile, while it always lifts my spirits to have you around."

"Then I'll have to call on you daily."

Elizabeth heard his amusement as he answered, imagined the twinkle in his dark eyes, pictured the curve to his tilting lips.

"I certainly want you to stay in good spirits," he continued. "Maybe in time you can help me persuade your niece to prefer my looks to any duke's."

Less than an hour ago Elizabeth would have squelched the idea of Chan darkening her door again. Aunt Delia thoroughly enjoyed having callers as often as possible, though, and the extra mental stimulation might speed her return to her normal state of mind.

To be reasonable, Elizabeth had to admit that Chan was nothing if not stimulating.

Half an hour later, Chan entered the cluttered premises of Number 5 Bridge Street. A jumble of male voices in avid discussion of sport met him at the door.

Fly fishing and live bait poles hung on each wall; nets of every shape and handle length lolled in umbrella stands. He might have guessed he'd find Ash at his favorite fishing-gear shop even if he hadn't left word at the inn.

Among sprawled tackle and spellbound patrons, Chan spotted his friend leaning against a counter. Ash rested his game leg by propping that booted foot behind him, his weight on the other side. Joining him, Chan nodded to the merchant and said, "Let's go lift a tankard and talk."

"Look at this one!" Ash held out a tied fly on his palm, a trifle of colored feathers and silk threads hiding a hook.

Chan wanted to relate the day's earlier activities to his friend, not size up angling equipment at J. Grant's. "Looks good unless you're a fish. Come on; we need to discuss what we're doing here."

"Nothing to discuss." Ash laid down the yellow fly to pick up a double-hooked one. "You're looking out for my interests, and I'm going fishing. Haven't tickled a trout's fancy in far too long."

"You've made a mistake," Chan muttered, not wanting to spread Ash's business around town, but wanting to impress him with the need to talk. They could easily be overheard in this popular gathering spot for sportsmen.

"No mistake, I'm going fishing. Grant holds the rights to a lively stream in Bathampton, and I just had a license written up." Ash hefted a long-handled angler's net that had leaned against the counter beside him. "See the reach of this thing? I can net a catch without stepping much closer than my casting spot."

This reminder of Ash's limited range of mobility made Chan wince. Fishing was a sport Ash could enjoy and excel at, like other men. It was a shame to drag him away from an afternoon of trading tales and fingering flies as he planned future catches.

The task he'd taken on for Ash had changed in several telling ways during the morning, however, and he needed to make Ash aware of the true situation. "You can fish tomorrow morning before the sun's too bright. Come have a drink with me now and I'll tell you about my call on the ladies."

Ash looked around with interest. "That's different." Winking at the clerk, he said, "The only excuse not to fish is a female, especially one who's going to pay you instead of the other way around."

Relieved, Chan said, "I'll go get the carriage."

"No need, the Saracen's Head is just up Broad Street." Ash headed for the door with his newest net. "We won't wait around for horses to be put to for a distance of three blocks."

Chan wouldn't have considered getting the curricle for himself if the pub had been across town, but even short walks pained Ash. His friend's poorly set leg couldn't be counted on to hold him steady, particularly on inclines. Built in a bowl, Bath's sloped streets kept chair bearers in business. A pity Ash would never let himself be carried in a sedan chair, but he said they made him feel like a woman or an invalid.

Away from his beloved fishing gear in the pale afternoon sunlight, Ash showed the expected interest in Chan's activities of the morning. "Did she admit to fleecing Father? Did you lay down the law to her?"

"This whole situation turns out to be more involved than we thought. I'll explain at the Saracen's Head in a quiet corner." Chan didn't really want to get into a full discussion on the street. He never relaxed his guard when they walked anywhere, ready to support Ash if he stumbled.

"Involved?" Ash sneered. "Don't tell me you're still salivating over that little piece of goods."

Chan had to right this opinion of Elizabeth. "You were wrong about her, Ash. She wasn't the old duke's *amour* after all."

"The devil you say!" Already Ash breathed hard from

the pain of walking on the crooked leg. "I'd know those bedchamber eyes anywhere."

"The lady we called on isn't the only one in her family with those lovely eyes," Chan said carefully, not wanting to be specific on the crowded street. He glanced around at the people inconvenienced by Ash's slow gait.

"Lady, my bare arse." Ash grimaced as he slipped on a cobble as they started across Northgate Street. "You mean there's two of them? Twins?"

Hearing snickers from behind, Chan glanced back to find two street urchins lurching along behind them, mimicking the awkward movements Ash made to swing his gimpy leg forward. His hand itched to swat their bottoms.

Noticing his distraction, Ash looked back to see what had attracted Chan's attention.

As the two noblemen stopped and turned, the boys ran, dodging around Ash toward the far side of the street. The smallest one made a good effort at getting away, but Ash lunged forward with his new fishing net, slipping it over the boy's head and down the skinny shoulders.

The taller lad twisted into the crowd on the other side of the street and disappeared.

"Caught myself a sprat!" Ash exclaimed. "Hang on to him, Chan, while I decide if I'll throw him back or fry him."

Elbowing at the coarse netting, the small boy fought for his freedom. Chan grasped him by one bony wrist, getting the net off without letting him go. He hauled the lad across the street, stopping in front of Saint Michael's.

People passing through the three-way intersection stopped to laugh and jeer. A few scolded the dirt-crusted child but several ordered Chan to let the boy go. He'd seen crowds turn ugly over less, but letting the urchin get away without a lesson about mocking others' afflictions didn't seem right. The boy yanked against him, yowling like a trapped cat.

"You and your fleet-footed friend should be in a traveling fair," Ash said to the boy, grinning and ignoring the growing rumble from the onlookers. "Bet you'd be particularly good at mummery."

He waved the onlookers closer. "Stay and watch the show with me if you like, folks. This lad should know a few tumbling moves or a song to entertain us. What about it, boy? I have a shilling in my pocket that says you can give a better performance than limping."

Ash's humor surprised Chan, though he knew that his friend had worked hard to overcome his embarrassment at his condition. Chan doubted he himself could have endured the taunts from fellow students and village children when they'd been younger. But Ash had learned; he had once explained that if he couldn't fight and win with his fists, he'd best tormentors with his wits.

The ragamuffin looked abashed at talk of talents. Seeing Ash pull a coin from the slanted inner breast pocket of his blue coat, the boy's expression changed to eagerness.

"I can whistle," he confided, hungry eyes on the coin. "Want to hear me whistle?"

Ash leaned a shoulder against the stone front of Saint Michael's, probably to ease the pressure on his sore leg and hip. Holding up one shilling, he said, "Whistling will do, if you know a cheerful sailor's ditty. No dirges for me."

"Aye, Captain," said the cheeky boy. Striking a pose, he spread his thin lips and produced sound from between his teeth that set Chan's teeth on edge. No one could accuse the boy of musical talent. Onlookers turned away, going on about their business, as Ash flipped the child the shilling.

"Show me how you do that," Ash said in admiration, waving the boy closer. "I never got the hang of whistling through my teeth, though I do a fair tune the usual way."

Chan stood by, restless, as the two exchanged rude comments on Ash's efforts to whistle. Anyone who knew him less well would figure Ash didn't care much about efforts to reclaim his inheritance, taking time to whistle with a street child instead of learning about the morning's events. But Chan knew his friend's true need to make this child forget his limp. Ash wouldn't even lose face to a nameless child if he could prevent it, let alone lose a fortune that represented his father's feelings for him.

Searching his pocket, Ash found another coin. "That lesson was worth more than your performance," he said to the boy, handing over the money. "Keep this out of sight of your cowardly mate who ran. Find yourself a friend who'll stay with you in trouble as well as play."

The urchin's face radiated wonder and joy through its topsoil as he bobbed his head at Ash and ran.

Heading up Broad Street, Ash attempted to whistle through his teeth again, breaking off to say, "My advice to the tadpole was worth far more than the money, if he'll take it. The friends who stand by you at his age are the ones you can count on at ours."

His grin as he punched Chan's shoulder took the mawkishness from the compliment. Chan's pleasure was stained with guilt. Knowing his friend valued his loyalty felt good, but this morning he had failed to arrange the settlement his friend had desired he effect—and his view on the entire situation had changed.

As they passed the Saracen's multipaned windows, Chan glanced inside. The place was as dim and close as he recalled, with low ceilings and dark paneling. As he pushed through the pub's door, the sharp smell of hops surged out to greet them. In the afternoon, only a thin company occupied heavy tables standing too close together. "Find us a corner where we can talk privately and I'll fetch the pints," he told Ash.

Minutes later he set a tankard of dark ale in front of his friend and settled on the same side of the scarred table with him. That seemed easier than facing Ash. Words could wait while they drained off a fourth of the mellow local brew.

How would he account for his renewed distaste for the job he'd agreed to do?

Setting down his drink, Ash leaned forward, easing his leg by propping his heel on the bench opposite. "What did she say about giving back my inheritance?"

"Which she?" Chan asked. "Lucinda or her daughter?"

Swearing, Ash thumped his thigh. "Then you meant it about two of them, and they aren't twins. The mother must have begun breeding young, for I would have sworn it was the same woman."

"You were fooled by the eyes," Chan confirmed, "though mother and daughter are as alike as peas in a pod. The little beauty you harangued is definitely not your father's Lucinda."

Ash rubbed his chin, looking suspicious. "How do you know? Did you see the old man's bed warmer or take the chit's word for it?"

"I spoke with them both," Chan said, remembering what their visit and his suspicion had cost Miss Delia Lindsey and Elizabeth.

Briefly he recounted the events of the morning to Ash, or rather a summery of getting an address for Lady Enfield and confronting that lady. Ash wouldn't be interested in how Elizabeth felt in his arms or the odd sense that she belonged there. Stripped of his unaccountable reactions to the provoking, desirable daughter, the tale didn't take long to tell.

"They're not women of casual virtue; they're ladies," he concluded. "We have to approach them with respect if we want to resolve this matter of the legacy."

"Lawsuits can be brought against people of high estate

as soon as low." Ash frowned into his tankard. "If they steal, people are thieves, whatever else they're called. Besides, even if she really can claim a title, this Lady Enfield proved her real quality when she chose to live openly with my father, knowing my mother was alive."

"You have to admit your parents weren't a close couple," Chan temporized. "It isn't as if Lady Enfield tempted him away from a loving wife."

Ash rounded on him, his face flushed. "Mother couldn't help her weak constitution. It isn't like she chose to be practically bedridden. Father didn't have to flaunt his trollop in the face of the world."

Instead of answering, Chan took a swig of ale. In his opinion, the duchess enjoyed her poor health. Far from being bedridden, she suffered in public at every opportunity. Where some ladies housed a priest or vicar to nurture their souls, the Duchess of Ashcott kept a pair of pet physicians to tend to her numerous health complaints.

"My mother was a dignified duchess for my father," Ash insisted, "and I never thought you would say differently."

Chan stared up at the soot-blackened ceiling, feeling defensive toward Elizabeth's mother instead of Ash's. "The story going around was that if the duke wanted to see his wife in her rooms, he had to listen to cautions from her medical attendants first. Surely that is enough to cool any husband's ardor."

"Ardor be damned," Ash said, kicking the table's underside as he shifted on the bench. Men glanced around at them from other tables and turned back to their pints. "A man can find a bit of muslin anywhere. He doesn't have to set up house with a woman and give her all his time and attention."

No wonder Ash preferred a variety of wenches in taverns to a cozy house with a congenial mistress. He sounded almost jealous of his father's long devotion to a lady. Odd that his nose was put out of joint by a common enough situation in the ton. Both partners in arranged marriages often found love as well as passion with someone outside the usual businesslike unions.

Not that Chan would want to marry a pedigree or fortune himself. Someday, when he had to do his duty by his family name, he hoped to find a lady he enjoyed in and out of bed, like his mistresses. Someone as lovely and personable as Lady Enfield.

Chan recalled the woman's shadowed house and face. She seemed far above Ash's perception of a wicked woman. In fairness to her he felt compelled to reason with his friend. "I heard as the port went around my father's table that the duchess wouldn't even give your father the usual 'heir and a spare' to ensure that the title continued."

Ash loosened a string of curses hot enough to curdle milk. "You're as big a gossip as any old biddy if you've listened to such stories about my parents."

This time when other patrons looked around, they stared longer. Quietly Chan protested, "It was common knowledge they lived as separately as the Duke and Duchess of York. I don't go around encouraging tattle. Half of what I know, you let fall yourself. I'm no more a gossip than you are."

Mercurial as ever, Ash raised his tankard in a salute and laughed. "Then your tongue hardly wags at all." He sobered again. "What you heard about my parents' living arrangements doesn't matter. Point is, everyone talked about it after the old man set up house with Lucinda. My mother was a faithful wife and deserved better of my father than public embarrassment."

Chan tried to hold back a response and couldn't. "Some older ladies don't seem to enjoy the temptations of the flesh, though." He spoke in a light tone, not wanting to set Ash off again. He also wanted to encourage Ash to rethink old reactions instead of clinging stubbornly to the views he'd always held. "Your mother might even have been relieved to pass along what she saw as the duty of marriage, considering her health problems."

"My mother is delicate, sensitive," Ash protested, glaring at him. "You couldn't expect her to have the base urges of ordinary women. She would never have taken notice of my father's normal male needs if he'd satisfied them with the ordinary discretion of a gentleman."

Maybe Ash didn't like to think of his mother in that way, but Chan believed most women felt the same passions as men, given the opportunity. He wouldn't insist Ash look at a scene he obviously didn't want to view, but he could understand how his friend's father had needed more than an occasional quick tumble with a stranger.

Chan had discovered that sharing a woman's thoughts and tastes, enjoying her company outside bedchambers, added a deeper level of gratification to satisfying one's physical appetites.

"Maybe your father needed a friend," he suggested. "Most females listen differently from men, and you can tell them things you can't tell another man. They offer other comforts as welcome as those found between the sheets."

"He could have damned well talked to my mother or his sisters," Ash said loudly enough to make the publican look their way, his brows drawing together.

"Different men, different needs." Chan smiled to reassure the pub's keeper. Best turn their talk to more general paths before they were told to take an argument outside. "I see a woman as a fascinating gift package, an entire personality to be unwrapped and discovered layer by tantalizing layer. The anticipation of what you'll discover next about a woman when you've been together awhile is a delight."

Ash snorted, moving his tankard in circles on the dark wood of the table's surface. "All cats are gray in the dark. This particular yellow-eyed pussy already stole enough from my family without depriving me of my full inheritance. What arrangements did you make for her to sign papers refusing the legacy?"

Shifting on the hard bench, Chan lifted his pint and looked for the publican. "Want another?"

"Not before you give me something to toast."

Chan set down the tankard and leaned back. "We didn't get an opportunity to discuss the will's terms. Lady Enfield and her daughter hadn't seen each other in a decade, and they were, well, disconcerted. Much good it would have done to talk business to a lady up to her eyelids in a high drama of emotions."

Hitting the table with his fist, Ash said, "Damnation! Sounds like the doxy managed to get around you with the usual feminine tricks." He shook his head. "You'll have to harden your heart to deal with this woman as she deserves."

"You couldn't have done differently yourself," Chan protested. He searched for the right words to explain his actions. "Lady Enfield is a lady in mourning, Ash. Her house emanates sorrow—aside from her grief at separation from her daughter. I believe she cared deeply for your father."

Scowling, Ash said, "Naturally she'd want you to think that. I would have seen through her act at once. All a woman has to do is pour like a water pitcher in front of you, and you can't see dung in horse droppings."

Chan clenched his jaw and straightened on the bench. "I understand ladies better than you, for you prefer women who wear aprons. Believe me, Lady Enfield deserves a little compassion, if you have to go ahead with this business. It wouldn't hurt for us both to offer apologies to Miss Merriman and Miss Lindsey for our insulting visit to their house, either."

"The damned daughter again!" Awkwardly, Ash rose from his seat. "I might have known you'd be distracted by the harlot's performance because you're drawn to a younger pair of the same eyes. Lucinda was no lady, and she stained her spawn with the same blacking when she chose to live openly in sin. The apple doesn't fall far from the tree, and you're as gullible as Adam in the Garden of Eden where a pretty face is concerned."

Taking Ash's arm, Chan urged him back down on the bare bench. "Every apple on a tree isn't rotten, and they don't all become tarts, either. Elizabeth is a beauty, as much like her mother as a daughter can be in looks, and she'll be fortunate to have her mother's ability to love with her whole heart, too."

"At this rate you'll be setting the chit up as your next mistress," Ash snipped as he moved away on the bench. "Just don't bring her along on our romps. I can't overlook a small matter of larceny, even if you can. I expected your friends to mean more to you than a thief and her offspring."

Perhaps his earlier plan to make Elizabeth his mistress in lieu of the duke's fortune wouldn't have worked out after all. He could hardly have kept a woman his best friend refused to go near.

Patiently Chan said, "I'm not setting up Elizabeth as my mistress. She's the daughter of a baron, I suspect, as her aunt's name is Miss Lindsey. I suspect Miss Merriman's surname is also Lindsey. That's a decent family. Seems like the present holder of the Enfield title is only a distant connection of the father, though, as the family is dying out."

"A little gossip with some of the local biddies should clear up all the details for you," Ash said with a sneering look.

Chan's hold on his temper slipped. "You're as nasty

as Cripplegate at his most foul, and I don't have to take your insults when I'm doing you a favor." Wishing the words unsaid, he closed his eyes. What was this imbroglio leading them into, for him to throw Ash's infirmity in his face? Sincerely, he apologized. "Sorry, Ash. You're nothing like Lord Barrymore, and I shouldn't have said it."

His jaw working, Ash fiddled with his tankard. Finally he grimaced and said, "You may not be all wrong. Old Cripplegate and I both limp, if not from the same cause, and I like to think I can fiddle the reins as well as the old reprobate."

No, Cripplegate's clubfoot was an act of nature, while Ash's limp was the result of self-sacrifice for a friend. Chan felt still worse. "You drive to an inch except when you land me in ditches."

Ash gave him a quick sidelong look. "I've overturned us only once, not that you'll let me forget it." He lifted his tankard and held up two fingers to the publican. "My turn to buy. I'll keep your throat wet enough to speak with the eloquence of a diplomat, so you can bring me a signed release from Lucinda after the next call on her."

"I'm as eloquent with ladies as you are with reins," said Chan, pushing his empty pint aside. He'd hoped to get out of his agreement to negotiate a settlement for Ash. Instead, he now felt locked into it, to show Ash his loyalty.

Chan's plate was too full of promises to people with opposing needs. Ash had to come first, of course, even if Chan had less stomach now for persuading Lady Enfield out of Lord Ashcott's legacy.

He'd also promised to bring Lady Enfield accounts of her estranged daughter's life. Considering Ash's unreasonable antipathy to the daughter as well as the mother, he wondered at the wisdom of his seeing too much of the fascinating, infuriating Elizabeth. Now that the necessity of seeing her was removed, maybe he needed to break off contact—before her undeniable attraction created more difficulties between him and Ash.

Still, he'd promised Miss Delia visits, and the old dear didn't deserve to be snubbed. Her efforts to hold on to her dignity as her mind deserted her reminded him vividly of his grandmother's pride, right to the end.

Visiting the older lady didn't require him to lose his head over the young one. He was hardly a boy in his calf years, and he prided himself on his self-control.

After all, he'd taken a couple of the highest fliers in London into keeping since his youth. He was in no danger of losing his heart to the prudish Miss Elizabeth Merriman of Bath.

Chapter Six

"I always liked this china, dear, and I'm glad you chose to keep it after Enfield's passing." Aunt Delia pushed a slice of turnip across the flowers scattered over a Meissen plate. "I wouldn't have blamed you for packing the entire set off to the auction house."

Though she seemed well enough physically to come down to dinner three days after wandering away from home, this remark suggested that her aunt's awareness remained in the past. Elizabeth pushed at her turnips, too, fretting over Aunt Delia's slow return to lucidity. "Of course I'll always keep the family china. Why wouldn't I?"

"Reminders of Enfield can't be that welcome to you." Aunt Delia's reproachful look hinted at shared secrets. "And now that you and the duke have . . . well, renewed your former acquaintance, you have even more reason than before to put away reminders of the distressing time with my brother."

Elizabeth put down her heavy silver fork, though they

had hardly begun dinner. "What do you mean, Aunt Delia?" Normally she didn't encourage her aunt's delusions or talk about the past, with its reminders of her mother, but this was new. "Everyone loved my father. Why would you feel our time with him was distressing in any way?"

Aunt Delia cut the turnip slice into increasingly smaller bits. "Oh, my dear. How brave you are, still pretending an arranged marriage couldn't have suited you more."

These convoluted conversations with her aunt could easily scramble Elizabeth's wits, too. She leaned forward, willing her aunt to recognize her. "It's easy to confuse events from years ago, to add impressions from other sources. I recall only good feelings and individual scenes from those days, myself, like precious pictures hanging in my mind. We were always together, the three of us, day after day, and everything was perfect then."

"Nothing is ever perfect, dear, and John was far from that. The three of us were indeed always together, you and me and the child. Rarely John." She made a face of distaste. "You know very well John hated the country, too busy with the prince and his *affairs* in London for us."

Like the compulsion when passing a carriage accident, Elizabeth couldn't look away as Aunt Delia began mashing turnip pieces with the tines of her fork. She mustn't allow her aunt's wandering talk to mangle cherished memories. "Father had duties in the House of Lords. He always brought me presents when he came home, and said how much he had missed me."

"Presents don't replace companionship and real sharing of life's little daily doings." Picking up her knife again, Aunt Delia began mincing the slice of boiled beef. "I won't force you to discuss your feelings; you always prefer not to criticize John, even when I do. I admire your loyalty, little as he deserves it."

"Father deserved the best of everything." Elizabeth softened the sharp tone that had spurted out in protective anger. "I only wish he'd lived long enough for me to know him longer and better."

Aunt Delia sighed and shook her head, stirring minced beef and turnip together. "He had room in his heart only for himself, even as a boy."

Her aunt was muddled, perhaps reliving Delia's own parents' marriage. Father hadn't neglected Elizabeth in the least. If he had, she wouldn't hold his memory in her heart, knowing she could never measure up to its heritage.

Father had been a whirlwind of energy and gaiety, his visits to Enfield Hall a celebration. For the days he was home, she could hardly bear the endless stretches of time in the nursery, eager to be summoned to the lawn or gallery to romp with him for an hour. He was the most exciting, amusing man in the world.

Hadn't he assured her that he left her only to wait on the Prince of Wales? Only the prince and his own death had forced her father to leave her. He hadn't chosen to abandon her, as had her mother. He couldn't argue if the future king of England wanted his company.

Poor Aunt Delia must be even more confused than usual, to malign her younger brother. Concerned, Elizabeth tried to guess from the mashed food on her aunt's plate if she'd eaten anything at all. "Aren't you hungry tonight? The beef is really very tender."

Aunt Delia sighed again and laid down her fork. "I'm sure it's quite good. I just don't fancy it."

"Could you eat stewed apples, perhaps? Cook meant them for breakfast, but I'm sure there's plenty for you to have a taste with the beef. They smelled wonderful simmering with cinnamon. Let me ring for Sally."

Pushing back from the table, she went to the bellpull and yanked it. Where had Suze gotten to, and why had she been the one to bring in the hot dishes tonight?

Surely it was Sally's turn to serve at table. Even if Suze had traded duties with Sally for some reason, they both should know by now to stay in the room throughout the meal just in case of needs like this.

A little annoyed that her lessons hadn't sunk in better, Elizabeth waited impatiently for the dining room door to swing open. When it did, Nell burst through, dabbing her eyes with the edge of her long apron.

"Has something happened?" Elizabeth couldn't guess why Nell would now appear in place of Suze. Nothing seemed to go right during the times Aunt Delia wasn't herself.

"No, miss. What can I bring you?" The girl twisted her hands in the apron, snuffling, her head down.

With growing concern, Elizabeth crossed the room and laid a hand on Nell's shoulder. "You don't come to the dining room in tears when Suze was the one serving dinner, without me guessing that something isn't right. Is someone injured? Does Cook need me in the kitchen?"

The maid edged away, clasping her hands dramatically. "Oh, no; you mustn't go down to the kitchen. Cook will murder me!"

"No one will be murdered in my house." Worried now, Elizabeth hurried to the door, speaking over her shoulder. "Stay here with Aunt Delia while I go down to see for myself what's happened." She added to her aunt, "I'll ask Cook to warm a serving of the apples for you while I'm down there."

It never rained that it didn't pour. As she hastened through the dim evening light in the passage, she wished that life could be a bit more settled than it had seemed lately. Opening the door onto the servant's stairs, she heard Cook speak from the kitchen below.

"What do you mean, her brush is gone?"

Suze's timid voice was hardly audible, but the distress in it made Elizabeth take the rest of the steps faster than the lack of light warranted. Rushing into the kitchen, she asked, "What's this about something missing?"

Cook turned quickly, a plump hand over her mouth. "She never told you, miss! I warned Nell not to worry you at your dinner, as much as you have on your mind already with Miss Delia like she is."

Holding back a sharp retort about who was responsible for events in this house, Elizabeth said, "Nell didn't explain what was wrong, though I could see from her face it wasn't a cut finger that kept Suze from coming back to the dining room. What's the trouble?"

Cook shook her head, glancing at Suze. "It's Sally again. This is her night to serve, but she hasn't been seen for two hours and more. She came through my kitchen, saying she'd gathered a basket of odds and ends from the larder to take to old Mrs. Winston at number nine like you want, rather than let them go to waste. What with seeing dinner readied, I didn't realize she hadn't returned until right on the dinner hour." She frowned at Suze, who threw up her apron and sobbed into it. "Silly girl didn't say anything earlier, didn't want to get Sally into trouble over not showing up to serve dinner."

Elizabeth crossed her arms over the empty space where her stomach lurched. Little wonder Suze had assumed Sally was lingering down the street too long. Sally liked to gossip with other servants in the area behind the town houses far too much. Especially when footmen lounged out back. The girl was far too friendly with males for her own good, despite lectures and warnings.

"Sally's brush isn't on the dresser?" That raised disturbing possibilities for a girl too susceptible to the lads.

"Yes, I just sent Suze up to the girls' chamber to see if Sally might have gone up to have a lie-down and fallen asleep. Suze says her things are gone, and she found this where her brush should have lain."

Cook handed over a crumpled piece of paper that Elizabeth recognized. She'd given the girls a list of tasks to be learned by taking turns doing them, and the sheet scheduled which days each of them worked at various jobs.

On the back of the schedule, a message was printed, actually more scrawled, in pencil.

Dont wury about me Im going to Lundon for a ril job thank Mis Lizbeth for me anyway.

Even after translating Sally's creative spelling, Elizabeth stared at the paper without taking in the note's full meaning. Sally headed for London? Surely this was just a game, Sally's high spirits coming out in a foolish prank. Sally wouldn't just run away from the comforts here, head for London without a shilling to her name.

"Ungrateful girl." Cook's mouth tightened as she shook her head. "You take her out of the poorhouse, and this is the thanks she returns. Running off with the first footman who promises her the moon. Muck is more likely what she'll get."

Suze emerged from her apron, red-nosed and pink-eyed. Timidly she protested, "It wasn't a footman."

Elizabeth went to the girl, speaking gently to keep her from retreating into tearful silence. "Suze, if Sally's said anything to you about wanting to leave here, it would help me protect her if you'll tell me about it."

Twisting the corner of her apron in both hands, the girl swallowed hard. "I don't exactly know anything, miss. She didn't really tell me for certain."

"You want to keep your friend from making a horrid mistake that could ruin her chances for a decent life, don't you?" Despite her need to rush out after her missing charge, Elizabeth remembered that Lord Chandler had stopped to determine the most likely place Aunt Delia might go when she left the house. "Have you heard

Sally talk about any particular young man? Perhaps someone at the market?"

"She flirts at market. She carries on, teasing-like, with anyone, but she doesn't mean any harm by it." Suze barely whispered the admission. "I thought it was just fancy, her tale of meeting a duke; I never thought she had for real."

Chills gnarled her stomach as a single word from Suze's story clanged in her head. *A duke!*

Ashcott, of course.

What other duke would come to Bath these days, let alone linger here? Who else but Lord Chandler's hateful, bullying friend had turned her comfortable life topsy-turvy since he set foot in town? She could easily believe he would entice a green girl away from the protection and opportunity in this house, if only to strike out at Lucinda through her daughter.

Lucinda and the duke were two of a kind, leaving innocent people littered behind them as they rode rough-shod down their own selfish roads. She wouldn't allow Ashcott to ruin Sally's life in some misdirected effort to wound her. Sally was Elizabeth's responsibility, and no man would harm her, even a duke.

Elizabeth was halfway across the room to the stairs when Cook cried out, "What are you planing to do, Miss Lizbeth?"

Surely that didn't need saying. "I'm going to get Sally and bring her home."

"But a duke!" Cook's usually placid face crumpled. "If the silly girl's had her head turned by promises no man keeps to her kind, you won't face down a duke by yourself."

Feeling hot and weak with anger, Elizabeth snapped a reply. "Who else is there to deal with this man? Aunt Delia? Our dear friend Lord Chandler? I'll return presently—with Sally."

Whirling away, she dashed up the stairs, pausing to

put her head into the dining room. "Serve Aunt Delia the sweet and stay with her until I return."

Leaving the two gazing openmouthed, she slammed the door and rushed up to her bedchamber to seize a cloak and reticule. Flinging the cloak over her shoulders as she took the stairs again, she yanked open the front door and ran into the early darkness.

As many people as came to events at Sydney Gardens and the hotel, surely she could find a hackney at once. There. One had stopped outside the hotel.

Racing across the street, she elbowed a gentleman aside as he descended from the coach. Before the driver had pocketed his fare, she said to him in a snarl, "The Bear Inn, and don't dawdle."

Inside the coach she flung herself against the seat, breathing in deep gulps that had more to do with her rage than running. The straw on the floor of the carriage hadn't been changed lately enough; its fetid damp suggested the dark squalor feeding her fears.

If Ashcott ruined Sally, she would make him pay for it. No one had the right to take another person's dignity and choices away when they were too young to look out for themselves. Ashcott could kick the wall all he wanted; he wouldn't scare her.

Leaning forward, she beat on the wall behind the driver, peering through the sliding panel behind him. "Hurry!" she shouted.

Ignoring his grumbling answer, she threw herself against the seat back again, staring out at flickering torches burning outside the bridge's shops. She'd like to set fire to the seat of his pantaloons, the high-and-mighty duke who thought he could ruin girls' lives at a whim.

Like father, like son. The Ashcott men indulged themselves at any cost to anyone but themselves. Not this one, though, not this time.

As the carriage left Bridge Street, she fumbled in her reticule for a coin, ready to hand it through the panel to the driver the instant he reined in his horses at the inn. She was ready for this confrontation—more than ready. She would endure no more meddling in her life by Ash-cotts, and the duke was about to learn it.

Too focused to feel the full impact of staring bystanders, she jumped down from the hackney. Stumbling, she almost lost her balance. When a man lounging nearby caught her arm, she fought out of his hold. Turning on him, she said between gritted teeth, "Get away from me. Now."

The big man stood back, holding up both hands. "Fall on your ass next time, then, missy. It's no skin off my rump."

Facing down the hulking stranger gave her courage and fed the twin flames of rage and determination. Into the Bear Inn she marched and found the innkeeper's wife at once. "Which room is the duke's? It's urgent I find him."

The woman sized up her good cloak and dress in the wavering candlelight with a quick glance. "But miss, you can't go above stairs to a gentleman's room. It's not seemly."

"It'll be too late for *seemly* if we stand here arguing about it. Is he in the double chamber with its own sitting room at the back?"

"But he said he wasn't to be disturbed this evening."

"I'm more disturbed than the duke will ever be."

The woman hadn't denied that the Bear's best rooms housed the duke, and that was enough. Elizabeth headed for the dark stairs to the floors above, assaulted by raucous voices from both outside and inside the public room. Her nerves strummed with fury, and her muscles trembled as she mounted the stairs. If she had to vanquish every male in this place, she'd get Sally out and home again.

In the upper hall, she strode to the end of the carpeted corridor. She'd seen these rooms before when the Bath &

West Improvement Society hung an exhibition of paintings where it could be locked safely away at night. Naturally they would be offered to an aristocrat with Ashcott's power and influence. No doubt he had planned on a private exhibition tonight, but she was about to steal his main attraction.

Raising a fist, she beat at the door of the chamber. When no one answered, she rattled the knob.

"You can hold your horses out there." The duke's snarling tone reached her through the door panels. She raised her chin, doubled her fists, and sucked in a deep breath.

As the sound came of the key turning in the lock, he added, "I told you not to bring supper before midnight."

The door swung open, and before he had stepped into its opening, she threw her weight against it and pushed through. "You'll be taking supper by yourself tonight, Ashcott, and sleeping alone, too. Where's Sally?"

Clad in pantaloons and the finest linen shirt, rumpled and open at the placket, the young duke stood staring at her as she swung around toward him. A quick glance around the sitting room with its sofa, chairs, and writing desk revealed a tray with bottles on a side table. No sign of Sally, but the door into the next room was closed.

"The girl isn't your concern now, wherever she is." He sneered as he stared back with negligent contempt. "You can forget about her, for she's found a better protector than you could have hoped to provide."

Going straight to the fireplace, Elizabeth chose the poker from the tools lying in order against the clean grate. "I'm all the protection my girls need, as you will learn to your sorrow if you don't let her go at once."

Ashcott leaned against the wall near the door, crossing his lame ankle over the sound one as if she hadn't threatened him. "I can't let someone go who isn't imprisoned. You'll just have to accept that your little nestling has flown before you could make her a bird of paradise and line your own pockets."

Flexing the poker, she felt violent madness thrust its way through her on her charge's behalf. "Sally's naive, too gullible to see through lechers like you Ashcotts. She's not what you mean to make of her, and she never will be. If you've violated her already, I'll kill you where you stand."

"What?" He drank from the cut-crystal glass he held and laughed, his indifference and derision scorching her. "Don't want your girls taking up where your mother left off? Most madams are delighted to supply a duke."

The space between them burned from candlelight yellow to flickering red as her blood roared in her ears. His superior, dismissive stare and the hand raising a crystal glass to drink recalled a scene she had endured before. Twelve long years ago, another Ashcott had shown no regard for a mere girl. This duke wouldn't have it all his way.

Fury possessed her body and soul. The poker raised without conscious direction from her, and she advanced on the duke, swinging it in a curving arc.

The sound of glass shattering into smithereens stopped her. For a moment she stood staring down at shards of bright glass in a spreading puddle, glinting in the light from the wall sconce above it. The duke must have leaped aside as she swung. Her weapon had connected only with his glass.

Her enemy scrambled to get up from an elbow chair he'd fallen over. He scuttled crab-fashion, cursing as his bad leg twisted under his weight.

In dazed wonder, she raised the poker, considering its blunt black iron tip. This would have killed him if she'd hit his head instead of the glass. She had almost committed murder. For an instant she had wanted to kill the duke.

Feeling a tug on the poker, she let go, glad to relinquish the weapon if not the horror.

"Chan! Thank God you heard the commotion and came over." The duke leaned against the wall and winced, reaching for his lower leg. "This crazy bitch just tried to kill me."

The room and events in it had taken on the quality of a nightmare, the worst of her life. This couldn't be happening. One moment she had been determined to take Sally out of here, and the next was a mad kaleidoscope she hadn't willed to happen.

Lord Chandler asked his friend, "Were you hurt?"

Ashcott straightened slowly. "No, she broke my glass rather than my head, but not because she didn't try."

"What did you do to set her off?"

The duke cursed. "Do to her? I'm nearly murdered, and you defend the slut's spawn?"

The poker hit the floor and Elizabeth started at the sound. Big hands closed urgently on her shoulders and turned her away from Ashcott, then put back her hood. She looked up slowly, from long leather boots, up knit pantaloons, across a thin linen shirt's broad expanse, to the black shock in Lord Chandler's eyes. His fingers dug into her shoulders, but she deserved the pain.

"Elizabeth?" Disbelief molded his dark features. "What are you doing here?"

"I could have killed him." Toneless, her voice didn't sound like her own. Was she possessed by the same devil she had accused Lord Chandler of being?

"Damn right you could have." Ashcott sounded outraged.

Chan stared at his friend, accusation hot in his eyes. "What did you do to her, Ash, to make her come after you with a poker? What's she doing in your rooms?"

Ashcott closed his eyes as he leaned his head against the wall. "I certainly didn't try to ravish her, if that's what you think. She's not my style and you know it."

"Is that true, Elizabeth?" The pressure of his fingers began to dig into her shoulders, despite her cloak. "Did he threaten you?"

"You need my word backed up by the doxy's daughter?"

Twisting out of Lord Chandler's grip, Elizabeth felt herself slip back into her own skin. Sally was the reason she was here, the reason she had forgotten herself so far as to threaten the life of another human being. That horrifying truth about herself would have to be faced, but for now other business demanded her attention.

Elizabeth headed for the closed door into the next room.

"Wait." Lord Chandler caught her, trying to see her face. "Are you all right? Why are you here?"

"Save your concern for your friend," she answered, still feeling at odds with her usual nature. "I followed Sally here when this note was found in my girls' room."

Pulling the crumpled sheet out of a pocket under her skirts, she thrust it at Lord Chandler and wrenched open the door to the other chamber.

The few words didn't take long for the viscount to scan. "Ash, if you know about this, it's the stupidest stunt you've pulled yet."

The duke groaned. "Who knew the chit could write? Most servants can't."

Entering the dim bedchamber, Elizabeth looked around quickly for her maid. The bedcovers were rumpled, but neither the bed nor the bench at its foot was occupied. Could she have been wrong, believing Sally had come here to be seduced by the duke? Merciful heavens, she might have murdered him over a mistake.

"Sally?" She moved blindly into the room, feeling through the dark within her soul as much as within these strange surroundings.

A whimper came out of the shadows, like a puppy

closed away from its mother in the night. "Sally, is that you? Are you hurt?"

If he'd injured Sally, she'd have Ashcott before the magistrate, duke or not.

A soft scuffling sound came from the general area of the bed's far side, and she moved toward it.

From the next room, she heard Lord Chandler speak in exasperation. "What the bloody hell did you mean, Ash? You lured one of Elizabeth's girls here with a promise of a job in London?"

A shadow rose up beside the bed, and Sally's choked voice came out of the gloom. "He said he knew Sheridan, called him 'Sherry,' said he could get me in as a dresser at the theater, with a chance to be on the stage myself one day. Doesn't he know Sheridan after all?"

The last sentence ended in a wail as Elizabeth reached for the girl in the near darkness and pulled her into the safety of her arms. Patting her back as she sobbed, Elizabeth realized that the scent of brandy wasn't all coming from the broken glass in the other room. "Oh, Sally, how could you listen to a man I had barred from the house? I warned you never to trust men who offered you gifts."

"But it wasn't a gift, Miss Lizbeth, it wasn't." The girl hiccuped between words, swaying as she leaned against her. "I was to have a proper job, in London, in the theater. Will he not take me to London now?"

"Hush, dear. Don't cry any more." That heartless corrupter had made Sally drunk, and it probably hadn't required much costly brandy to do the job. "London is a great, smoking, nasty place, and women at the theaters have to do most of their work on their backs. You'll have a far better place than that, I promise, no matter what he's done to you."

Easing Sally toward the doorway so she could look her over in the faint light from the sitting room, she tried to make out the state of her clothing. "Has he interfered with you? It doesn't matter, either way. It isn't your fault

103

if he has. I'll take care of you no matter what's happened."

"Inner feared?" Sally's head lolled back loosely before she straightened it and squinted past Elizabeth into the next room. "I wasn't afraid of him, not one bit. The drink burnt my gullet and I didn't really want much of it, but the duke said everyone in London drank it and it would grow on me."

She giggled into her hands. "It didn't. But my head grew on me." She swung out one hand, leaning in the same direction. "I got so dizzy I asked if I could just have a moment's lie-down, and the silly duke said certainly and that he would lie down with me."

Shaking her finger, she assumed a vicar's voice from the lectern. "But the good book warns against lying down in sin, and I figured that meant the kind of lying the duke wanted to do."

Sally nodded wisely. "I know that look in a man's eye even if he is a duke. So when we came in here, I just fell on the floor and rolled under the bed, and he's been trying to coax me out ever since."

Fiercely glad and relieved, Elizabeth hugged the girl again. Thank heaven the poorhouse made the orphans march to church every Sunday and start every day with Bible lessons. Sally's quick wits, even befuddled, had done the rest.

"Is she unharmed?" Lord Chandler spoke from the doorway, concern and chagrin mingling in his tone.

"No thanks to your crony." Elizabeth's anger hadn't completely dissipated with the shock of discovering how far astray her unchecked emotions could carry her. This near seduction wasn't Lord Chandler's doing, but he couldn't be that different from his friend. "Sir, this child is tipsy."

Sally giggled and sank down on the side of the bed, then fell back, laughing aloud.

"Back teeth awash, it sounds like to me." He leaned

over for a closer look at the girl. "But is she in the same state as she came, otherwise? Ash swears he didn't harm her, as he couldn't get her to come out from under the bed. He doesn't lie to me."

"He didn't do his worst, if that's what you mean." Elizabeth needed to make someone pay for Sally's shameful state. "She can hardly be the same after an experience like this, though. Don't think I can overlook his lies and lures to a girl in my care, even if you can."

Lord Chandler drew himself up, shoulders square, looming above her in the faint light from the other room. "I don't approve of the duke's actions, but he's my friend. You might try to be a little more charitable, considering you could have killed him."

From the other room, Ashcott said, "Indeed!"

Despite her guilt, Elizabeth resented Chan's defense of the other man. "I suppose you think seducing a young orphan is a gentleman's prerogative. I shouldn't have expected any better of you, when you're thick as thieves with the man."

His full lips thinned and his dark brows sloped toward each other. The surge of anger emanating from him struck her like a palpable force.

Control tightened his voice. "If I'd known he meant to try this, I'd have stopped him. I'm sorry he chose your maid to go after. Before he sleeps tonight I'll have his word it won't happen again."

Folding her arms, she shrugged. "How can you trust the word of a man who could ruin a young girl's life?"

His jaw jutted in the darkness. "He's my friend and his word is good. He's never lied to me."

How could a man of honor defend the duke's behavior? "But he lied to Sally, and very likely to dozens of other girls who had no one to protect them."

"His actions are his, not mine. I don't have control or responsibility over him." He shook his head. "Ash isn't perfect, but neither am I. I'm his friend, not his judge."

Though she still wanted to lash out at both men, Elizabeth was reminded of her responsibilities. Sally had to be taken home and sobered up.

Leaning over the girl, Elizabeth encouraged her to sit up. "He deserves a judge more than a friend right now, and I mean to arrange for one."

Raising Sally off the bed easily by her elbows, Lord Chandler steadied her. Elizabeth stepped away from close contact with him.

"I understand your urge to haul him into court, but don't forget he's a duke," he said. "You'll have to take Sally to London after all, if you can get him indicted, for a duke can be tried only in the House of Lords."

The injustice of it stirred rage in her midsection all over again. "No wonder dukes act like they can take whatever they want." Once more an Ashcott had won—but not the whole game this time. She had arrived in time to thwart his plans for her maid. "I'm taking Sally home. I need a carriage, but I'm not leaving Sally here with that predator to call for one. Can you at least act against your friend far enough to hail a hackney for me?"

"I don't support what Ash did. He knows that, though I haven't finished explaining my views about this to him." He moved toward the door. "Bring Sally through here. You can wait in my rooms while I have a closed carriage brought to the rear of the inn. You don't want to make a parade of her through the crowd at the front."

"That will do." She knew she sounded stiff and shrewish, though his consideration for her feelings and Sally's made her feel cruel for lashing out at him. He had showed kindness to Aunt Delia by visiting each day since helping to find her, and he had offered Sally consideration tonight. Still, when he could be misjudged by the company he kept, that was his problem.

Averting her eyes from the man she'd come close to killing as they passed through the sitting room, Elizabeth guided Sally's wayward steps out into the passage toward the door across the hall.

Candles lit Lord Chandler's neat chambers, and nothing more than a newspaper closed into a book seemed an inch out of place. Trying not to look at the poster bed in the next room, Elizabeth eased Sally onto a chair and stood protectively over her. She hadn't expected to find herself in two men's private chambers tonight.

Chandler hesitated at the door, gazing at her for a long, serious moment before unclenching his square jaw. "I'll call for a carriage and come back to carry your Sally down to it."

"I appreciate your help. Even if it was your friend who made it necessary." She forced a civil tone, even if she didn't feel mannerly at the moment toward any man. "I can take care of Sally now. If you'll simply call the carriage to meet us and give us ten minutes, you can have your room to yourself again."

"You're welcome to my help in any circumstances." The viscount's dark features looked careworn, as if her concerns worried him as much as his friend's. "I couldn't rest tonight if I sent you off with this poor girl in this state. I suspect you've never heaved a jug-bitten friend down stairs, let alone in and out of a carriage and into a house. It's an easier job if we manage together."

Little as she wanted to be obligated to him, he made sense as usual. "I'll expect you in a few minutes, then."

When he closed the door quietly, Elizabeth sank onto another chair and gazed at Sally, who was lolling awkwardly with her eyes closed and her mouth hanging open.

This was what happened when a female listened to a man. Here she sat, waiting for a man to see her and her drunken maid-in-training home. Lord Chandler made his offer sound logical and reasonable, yet she felt the danger of listening to him. Accepting help from him made her uneasy.

Had poor Sally felt the same way about the duke's blandishments, wanting what was offered while fearing its cost? Maybe her lecture in the morning wouldn't be quite as harsh to Sally's sore head as Elizabeth had first planned.

Chapter Seven

Flinging the pencil onto the account ledger, Elizabeth shoved away from the table that served as a desk in her household office. Sally stood in front of it, twisting one end of her apron, pale and squinting against the morning light.

"Close the door, please."

Little as she liked to deliver lectures, Elizabeth couldn't allow last evening's events to fade without making certain the lessons were clear. Sally had skirted absolute ruin.

She waited until the girl had staggered to the door and returned. "Your head aches this morning, doesn't it?"

"Yes, miss, and I was ever so ill when Cook poked me out of bed at dawn to help start breakfast." The girl's complexion still looked slightly green. "I never would have believed rashers of bacon cooking could smell worse than pig shit."

Elizabeth must remember to thank Cook for that object lesson. "Pig . . . ordure . . . isn't a suitable subject for discussion with future employers, Sally, particularly ladies. But we have far more serious matters to talk about this morning, don't we?"

Sally's nose reddened as her face crumpled. Tears oozed from her big eyes, and her shoulders heaved. Elizabeth felt like a bully as the girl's silent misery spilled down her cheeks, but she had to be certain the silly maid understood how close to the dung heap of total degradation she had been led.

The damnable duke deserved far worse than a lecture. Instead, he could brag to anyone who would listen about the one who just barely got away. As if a servant girl's virtue were nothing more than a fish to be landed.

Little as she could excuse her slip over the edge into violence last night with the poker, the provocation had been great. By taking her virtue, the duke would have taken the girl's life in a sense. The only work open to her then would have been further abuse at the hands of men.

"This isn't the first time you've allowed too much interest in males to earn you a scolding, is it?"

"No," Sally choked out one word before managing another. "Miss."

Hardening her heart, Elizabeth continued. "You've been late for your evening duties twice because you loitered out back to flirt with footmen from nearby houses."

"Yes." Sally wiped her streaming eyes with her hands. "Miss."

"A girl in service can't afford to encourage followers. You don't yet have a place to provide yourself with a secure future, and you've put the chance of doing so at risk. Do you realize that no employer would have come after you last night? The duke would have set you out in the streets either here or in London, and that would have been the end of respectability for you."

"But he promised me a job." Sally wailed and winced

at the same time, clasping her temples in both hands.

Biting back a curse against men who made promises they wouldn't keep, Elizabeth left her worktable to stand at the window beyond Sally. The next part was difficult to say.

"It's vital that you listen and remember what I tell you now. No matter how attractive and kind men may seem, they always put themselves and their own interests first. Any woman who believes what a man promises will end in tears and tatters."

Facing the maid again, Elizabeth repeated the caution for emphasis. "A man who shows interest in you is really acting for his own good. He doesn't care about the effect on you of what he wants, even if it destroys your only source of food and shelter as well as your reputation."

Her hands clasped, Sally's pinched face begged. "But we all know you don't like gentlemen, miss, and this one seemed so kind. I'd let him into the house myself when he and his friend called here."

Turning back to the window abruptly, Elizabeth clasped her hands, too. "It is never proper for servants to speculate about or discuss their employers' private lives. Not with each other and never outside the house if they want to keep their places. I see I've failed to cover a number of important lessons with you girls."

Merciful heavens, what must Bath residents think of her, if these orphans from the workhouse believed her to be a man-hater? Gossips would label her as being like the ladies of Llangollen, who had set up housekeeping together in an unnatural affection.

Crossing her arms, she towed her drifting mind back to saving Sally. "As for admitting the duke, you've opened the door of this house to the coal deliveryman, too, but that doesn't mean you won't get blackened if you throw yourself into his arms."

"Yes." Sally gulped down a new sea of tears. "Miss."

"Ladies of independent means may choose to include gentlemen in their social lives or not. Miss Delia enjoys their conversation, so I don't keep gentlemen from calling here." That explained Lord Chandler's calls satisfactorily. "However, servant girls have to protect the only means open to them to earn their keep. If they want regular meals and a roof over their heads for a lifetime, girls without families in particular must reject all male attention."

Sally sniffled, showing doubt in one quick glance. "But what about marriage, miss? Don't orphans and servants deserve a chance to be loved and wed, too?"

Now Elizabeth's head was beginning to ache, and *she* hadn't overindulged in wine last evening. "Of course you deserve to be loved, and if I didn't care about you, I would never have come looking for you and brought you back here." She felt impatient with this foolish girl for believing any man would offer more solutions than dilemmas for females. "I want you to use your head for a moment, even if it is fogged with fumes because a man plied you with wine. Think back to the workhouse where I found you. How many of the women in that horrible place came to it because they had trusted men?"

Sally frowned behind wet cheeks and twisted her apron's corner. "You mean like them that had babies without fathers, or got turned off their jobs without a character letter, or their husbands disappeared on them and a litter of young'uns, or them that got too old to be on the game anymore?" Sobs shook her shoulders. "But it will be different for me, miss. I just know it. Men have always wanted to be good to me, and just because the duke was a trickster doesn't mean they all are. You must know it at heart, for you let his friend bring us back here last night."

Accepting help from Lord Chandler was different. Elizabeth knew it was safe to accept his help, even if she hadn't thought about the reasons.

Feeling defensive, she tried to explain the distinction both to Sally and herself. "I simply used the viscount's superior strength and experience with a drunken person to get you back here with as little notice of your state as possible."

Sally looked down, reddening at her severe tone.

"Pretty girls like you are especially vulnerable." Elizabeth couldn't help softening her scolding. "As a servant in a decent household, you'll find yourself working alongside males, and you'll need their cooperation in some tasks. That doesn't mean you'll smile and flutter your eyelashes to get it. Respect yourself enough to offer and accept help without demeaning familiarity between you."

"But I like to smile at men and see them smile back." Sally's wet face looked earnest. "I never feel mean about that, miss."

"*De*meaning, not mean. Demeaning is about the same as belittling." Unfortunately, she had begun to discover what Sally meant about the pleasure of trading smiles with males. Or at least with Lord Chandler. "When a man's intentions are honorable, he doesn't go beyond the line of proper behavior with you. Anything that's said or done between you could take place in front of your mistress or the vicar."

The feeling of being kissed by Lord Chandler, of lying across his lap in the carriage, reeled through her senses. Sternly, she banished it. "Do you understand what I'm saying?"

The flow of tears had stopped while Sally put her head to one side. "Can't say that I do, begging your pardon, miss. If a man never does or says anything he couldn't in public, how will a girl ever get a chance to raise babies?"

Something deep within Elizabeth stirred: the regret that she felt when she watched children with their nurses in the parks. Even looking in on the newborn kittens brought on a strange, sad yearning, though touching the tiny, squirming bodies sent their silky warmth up her fingers and arms all the way to her heart.

Her own succumbing to silly emotion had to be curbed if she was to set Sally safely on the path to independence. "It's sad but true that most girls who go into service have to set aside rearing children of their own. Women in service who marry often end up in the workhouse, too, raising children in conditions of near starvation. Look around Bath when you go to market at the number of thin, dirty waifs running the streets in rags. Would you want to bring children into the world to exist like that?"

"I wouldn't let my children starve," Sally said stoutly. "My man wouldn't be that sort, either."

"Perhaps you need a couple of hours off to go back to the workhouse." Elizabeth was losing patience with Sally's stubborn fantasies. "Talk to the women there and see how many of them believed the man they listened to would be different. Maybe then you'll be convinced of the truth of what I say. That's a very good idea, in fact. Wait until tomorrow when your head isn't swimming and aching with the effects of a man's attentions, and go visit the place where I found you. Maybe you need a reminder of where women go who believe men's blandishments."

"No, please, miss, don't send me back." Sally fell to her knees, bawling. "I won't ever speak nice to a man again; cut my tongue out if I do. I can learn to look at them like cockroaches, miss, just like you. Please don't send me back there."

Feeling worse than if she'd kicked the mother cat, Elizabeth hurried to the sobbing girl and hauled her to her feet. Thrusting a lace-edged handkerchief into her hands, she patted Sally's shoulder. "I said *visit*, not go back to stay. You really must pay more attention to what I tell you."

Shaking her head at the proffered handkerchief after Sally blew her nose loudly into it, she said, "Put it in the laundry. I'm not threatening you with dismissal; I just want you to see clearly what your choices are. Your best chance to have the comforts of a full belly are in service."

That didn't sound right. "A regularly fed stomach, I mean. Otherwise, you'll have a full belly from being with child, without any means to provide for the child or yourself."

The expression of despair Sally showed for an instant, before hiding it in her apron, made Elizabeth's chest hurt. "It isn't fair, I know," she continued. "It is reality for most women. They trust a man's cajoling promises and they pay for the weakness with a lifetime of loneliness and misery. I want better than that for you and for all my girls. I want you armed to earn your living so you need never listen to any man's lies."

"How do you know if a man's"—Sally gulped down a noisy sob—"lying, though, miss?"

"If he's smiling and talking, he's probably lying." Much as she believed this, Elizabeth felt stultifying sadness as she said it. She sighed. "Assume he is, and you'll be safer than if you give a male the benefit of the doubt."

"Oh, miss, what a horrible way to live, though." Sally's tears flowed over an indignant expression. "Life won't be worth living if I can't have a bit of fun now and then."

"A moment's pleasure is hardly worth a lifetime of regret." If she had to be more graphic, she would. "Do you regret what you did last night?"

Sally nodded, sniffling.

"Think how much worse you'd feel sitting outside the Bear Inn right now with a throbbing head and no prospect of dinner or a bed tonight—unless you paid for it by allowing yourself to be abused again. You couldn't expect any decent woman to hire you or any decent man to marry you. Is pleasure worth that?"

Sally's forehead wrinkled. "I know I'm supposed to think it isn't, miss. But did you ever just want to be held in a man's arms for a while? Just held all nice and cozy in a place that feels safe and good?"

Startled, Elizabeth realized that she knew the feeling Sally described. It was one she fought off when it attacked her, but it was as much her own enemy as any servant girl's.

"That's a weakness that intelligent women learn to control," she said, putting stern conviction into her tone. "Men don't curb that weakness, and that's why we must protect ourselves from them."

Suspecting she had done a poor job of convincing Sally, she decided to let the effort go for now. Better to repeat the lesson to all the girls and hope Sally accepted it better for hearing it more than once.

"You may go back to your duties now. It isn't fair for your mistake to heap extra work on Suze and Nell. I expect you to carry on as usual, no matter how poorly you feel from last night's excesses. I want you to think about what I've said, for the danger from men won't go away like your sore head. Go on with you now."

Heading back to the worktable, Elizabeth determined to focus on the household accounts despite the uneasiness the lecture to Sally had stirred. Along with the sound of her office door opening, she heard a knock on the entrance door to the house.

"You're closest, so you might as well answer that. If it's a friend to visit Miss Delia, show them up to the drawing room. She might have nodded off, but she won't want to miss company."

Settling behind her table, Elizabeth sat down and picked up the first tradesman's bill. Resolute, she ignored the office door closing and Sally's footsteps receding along the passageway.

The deep tones of Lord Chandler's voice reached her ears. Elizabeth dropped the bill and listened without hearing what he said. She heard the sound of his footfalls fading up the stairs, knowing when he reached the third riser from the top by its characteristic squeak. From above, she heard the drawing room door open and then close.

Perhaps she should go make certain Sally left the room at once instead of dawdling about to gawk at Lord Chandler's dark good looks and formfitting attire. Her aunt might forget to order tea or offer wine to their guest. The fire might need making up in the drawing room or even have gone out.

Hearing Sally's footsteps return down the stairs, skipping as if she had not a worry in the world, Elizabeth reined in her wayward impulses. She would remain here like a sensible woman instead of a silly servant girl with an easily turned head. She had duties to tend to, and Aunt Delia could entertain her caller very well on her own.

Lord Chandler knew about her aunt's confusions of time and identities. He had shown understanding and sympathy for her problem. He would be kind even if Aunt Delia rambled a bit. How comfortable to have someone else who could entertain her aunt with as much care for the older lady's feelings as she would take herself.

Half an hour later, Elizabeth set aside the bills she'd stared at without recording one in the ledger. As often as Lord Chandler called, she should be able to ignore his presence in her house, especially when he was a floor above with two doors closed between them. Yet it was almost as if he sent out waves from himself that washed all effort at concentration out of her head.

Why bother to stare at accounts when she couldn't recall a single bill she'd read? Checking last week's figures was equally impossible. She'd forgotten the subtotal halfway through the column of figures three times. Math was difficult enough without the distraction of Lord Chandler in the house.

The image of the tall man lounging on a chair in her withdrawing room, legs outstretched before him, filled her inner eye again. How could a man with such long, muscular legs look completely at ease on an elbow chair he dwarfed?

The drawing room hardly felt like her own anymore, as much as he occupied it these days.

Elizabeth threw down her pencil.

Even the furniture arrangement was no longer hers. He'd come up with the notion of moving the sofa on his first call. Finding Aunt Delia reclining in the center of the room with a book of flower engravings, he'd protested that the light was poor.

"You need sunlight and an interesting view of the neighbors' comings and goings," he'd told Aunt Delia, lifting her from the sofa onto a chair as if she weighed no more than a cushion.

Of course Aunt Delia had been delighted with his attention. What woman wouldn't be pleased to have a handsome rascal fuss over her as if she were the most important female in his world?

He had shifted the heavy upholstered mahogany sofa with its one raised end as easily as he had her aunt. Then he'd laid Aunt Delia on it again, piling cushions behind her and asking if she could see the street without strain from that angle.

Not that her aunt had looked at the street much after his effort. Who could take their eyes off a man who'd removed his coat to move furniture?

Elizabeth leaned back in her chair.

As he lifted furniture, his thighs had bulged against the seams of his pantaloons as if they might burst. The thin linen used for shirts these days was disgraceful; she could nearly see straight through it. Every muscle in his shoulders and arms had strained visibly against the fine fabric as he carried the sofa from the middle of the room to the wall fronting the street.

Straightening the pen tray, she frowned. He hadn't bothered to ask her permission to rearrange her room.

Of course Aunt Delia had enjoyed looking out at people passing along Sydney Place in vehicles and on foot with the sofa in its new spot. She hardly rang the little handbell more than once in half an hour when she was alone up there these days.

Aunt Delia wasn't alone right now. Lord Chandler was probably telling her stories about people she had known in the past, making her laugh. One of the girls had passed by, probably taking up a tea tray, and she could just imagine him insisting on pouring out tea and handing Aunt Delia cakes, teasing her into eating.

Few men knew how to brew, let alone serve, a decent cup of tea, but the viscount did. Perhaps he had learned when his grandmother needed close attention. Why would he visit an elderly lady every day, a man who must surely have the ladies of Bath in an uproar of efforts to attract his notice?

Silly women, with nothing better to occupy their time than thinking about men.

Springing up from the worktable, Elizabeth clenched her teeth. What had she been doing for the last half hour that wasn't just as foolish as the actions of any lady of more leisure than sense?

Heading for the door of her office, she crossed the hall toward the servants' stairs. What she needed wasn't solitary duties, but people to distract her. She'd look in on Cook and the girls during the pastry lesson scheduled for this morning.

Elizabeth yanked open the door onto the enclosed stairwell, hurrying down the steep risers faster than was safe in the dim light. Making certain the girls paid attention to Cook's lesson was a more useful occupation for her mind than thinking about a man who seemed to know too much about pleasing women of all ages.

Cook's voice reached her before she entered the long room with its stone-flagged floor. "That's good, you have a right light hand. No more strokes than you can help as you stir in the liquid."

Reaching past Suze to flick a few more drops of water into her bowl, Cook looked up from the deal table centering the room. "What can I get for you, Miss Lizbeth? Do you need more hot water or cakes? You should have rung instead of walking all the way down here."

Feeling like an outsider to the little group gathered around the table now that she was here, Elizabeth shook her head. "Miss Delia will have Lord Chandler ring if they need anything. I was just catching up on some work in my office and wondered how the pastry lesson is coming."

"What? Miss Lizbeth, you didn't walk out on a caller in your own home, surely! As kind as His Lordship is to Miss Delia."

Cook's amazement pricked Elizabeth's conscience.

"Why don't you go along upstairs and sit with your aunt and your guest now? That will make up for your earlier rudeness. I'll have one of the girls bring up fresh water and cakes, and you can have a nice chat and a nibble with them."

Now Elizabeth really felt foolish. Her task was to teach these girls how a proper household was run, and she'd just been scolded for avoiding her duties as mistress of the house. This was a fine example to set her maids-in-training.

She didn't want to go upstairs, though, to endure Lord Chandler's amused glances and amusing conversation when she hadn't joined them earlier. Still, Cook didn't need supervision to teach a child to make pastry, let alone three capable young women. She was in the way here.

"I can't bear to be cooped up any longer on such a fine day," she said as an excuse, before recalling the morning's earlier overcast skies. "I need a breath of fresh air after puzzling over scrawled bills until I'm cross-eyed." Searching for another reason to go out, she added, "Maybe I'll take the kittens into the garden for a while."

Cook gave her a measured look, then turned away from the table. At least she wasn't going to insist on Elizabeth's doing her duty in front of the girls. "Want a cake or two in a napkin?"

"Yes, please." Elizabeth felt like a little girl again as Cook bustled about getting a square of clean linen and placing half a dozen tarts and cakes on it. Little as she needed to eat sweets, the thought of sitting under a tree with the kittens and treats appealed to her. Maybe it would ease her mind to retreat to childhood pleasures, to a time before she had found herself alone to deal with worrisome responsibilities.

Taking the wrapped bundle, she headed for the scullery next to the kitchen. In a nook by that room's fireplace stood the large basket she'd lined with a soft old blanket for the kittens. The cat had moved them back to the dolly tub three times before finding it full of wet laundry and giving up on housing her babies in the preferred place. She was a devoted mother.

As she bent above the basket, Dolly rose and stretched each of her four legs in turn, mewing and sniffing toward the bundle of cakes.

"No, you don't need sweets any more than I do," Elizabeth told the cat. "I'm taking your kits outside where they can sniff the air and see there's more to the world than a basket, now that their eyes are open. Come along so you'll know they're safe."

Picking up the basket by its arched single handle, she headed down the passage and outside.

The morning mist had begun its retreat to the river

across the fields some time ago, and it looked as if the sun might break through. Even the lime tree's scant shade from pale new leaves might be too cool for the kittens. She'd sit on the bench against the stone wall with the basket at her feet. If anyone looked out the windows from the long drawing room upstairs, they wouldn't see her there.

Not that anyone would be looking for her. Lord Chandler had come to visit Aunt Delia. Though he spoke with her just as much as he did with her aunt, that was just common courtesy. He was unfailingly polite and almost proper during calls, quite unlike their first rude encounters. Or as proper as a rogue could be. Perhaps his gaze and smile didn't always behave.

Setting the basket on the ground, Elizabeth watched the powder-puff kittens with pointed tails squirm around and over each other in play.

When Lord Chandler looked at her in certain ways, she, too, often relived the time he seized her roughly and kissed her in her own office. Or remembered his ruthless arms when he snatched her off the road to Wells, forcing her against his muscular chest and thighs.

Even though the sun peered weakly past shifting cloud cover, Elizabeth felt warm. She needed to sit outdoors. Yet even out here, the house reverberated with Lord Chandler's presence.

Maybe eating a cake would distract her. Opening the tied napkin, she found two jam tarts under a handful of tea cakes. Cook knew she couldn't resist apricot jam tarts.

Leaning over the basket, she set her elbows on her knees and watched the kittens extend long necks as they lifted tiny questing heads toward this great new outside world. Munching on a tart while laughing over the round-eared babies filled her with contentment. She drifted on its welcome current.

Elizabeth looked around as steps approached the back entrance to the kitchen. Cook had probably decided she needed tea. A mug showed past the door frame first, but it wasn't a woman's hand carrying it. She stiffened, leaning back.

Lord Chandler stepped outside, turning toward her at once, as if he knew where she'd be seated. "Your aunt Delia dozed off, so I came to find you." He held out the mug as he reached the bench. "Cook asked me to bring you tea."

He would have to find her with a half-eaten tart in her hand. It felt as big as the kittens' basket as she stifled the urge to stuff it under the edge of her spread skirts.

"Cook climbed all the way up to the drawing room to ask you to bring me tea?" Elizabeth warmed under his engaging grin as she took the pottery cup from him. She didn't know if the touch of his fingers in the exchange or the heat of the cup startled her, but the tea sloshed over.

When he smiled down at her with that inviting tilt to one side of his tantalizing lips, she couldn't help but smile in return. It was impossible not to respond when his eyes signaled the start of that slow, lazy curve of his expressive mouth.

"Would I put your servants to extra work for no reason?" he asked, his strong chin raised. He stared down from under lazy lids. "Naturally I came down to the kitchen looking for someone. I couldn't help your aunt dream, since she's fallen asleep, and you were nowhere to be found."

Flushing, she knew that Cook had been right about her rudeness. "You have no engagements, nothing to do, so you're reduced to looking for company in kitchens?" she asked. Bantering with Chan was diverting, and she fell into it easily now. "Cook should have set you to cleaning pots or boots."

"Yours, I'll clean anytime," he said, gazing at her

crossed ankles in stockings and slippers with too much interest. "Though rubbing your feet would be a far greater pleasure."

Immediately she drew her feet back under her dress, uncomfortable when his teasing took a personal turn. This was no more than the usual flirtatious manner of people in society. She never had encouraged the false playfulness in other men's conversations.

Spreading the napkin of pastries open, she gestured to the bench on the other side of it. "Won't you sit down and share these?" she invited. "Cook always presses food on me as if I might starve between meals. I don't need to eat sweets, and you'll save her feelings if you have the rest."

Taking one of the tea cakes, he said with a twinkle, "Cook has the right idea. I never like women who are too slender. You can bruise yourself on their bones, and depriving themselves of good food makes them peevish."

Elizabeth felt his gaze meander over her generous curves. She'd never thought much about her figure. If anything she considered herself too plump. His expression during these overly familiar and too frequent appraisals seemed pleased enough with what he saw. Not that she cared about his opinion of her.

She threw the remainder of the tart a few feet away, where house sparrows hopped and pecked.

By now she didn't feel the need to fill every moment in his company with conversation. She leaned over the kittens again, enjoying their playful starts and stops as they learned to use wobbly legs.

"Your aunt seems stronger each time I see her." He put a long finger down among the kittens, scratching at the blanket. A golden fluff ball put its head to the side before gathering itself for a mighty leap at it. "Perhaps she'll soon feel able to go out. Let's take her riding out into the countryside on a balmy day."

His ongoing attentions to Aunt Delia pleased her, even if she knew she should discourage him from coming so often. Her aunt enjoyed his calls so much it seemed cruel to deprive her, though. Aunt Delia would revel not only in the ride, but in endlessly recounting Lord Chandler's efforts to entertain her. Depriving her of the double satisfaction was unthinkable.

"How considerate of you," she said, looking into dark eyes that felt too close on the shared bench. Drawing room chairs would have been safer after all. "A short drive some sunny day might not tire her too much."

"The length of the drive is up to you. Just give the word when you think she's had enough, and I'll turn back at once."

Wanting both to scoot closer and move away, she protested, "Your curricle would be too crowded with three of us on the seat."

"Your aunt takes up less room than a small child," he said, leaning over her to take another tea cake in long, sure fingers. "She can sit between us, and you can put your arm along the back of the seat to make certain she's secure."

Holding her breath even after he leaned back, she closed her eyes. The image of the three of them on the leather-covered seat in a curricle came clearly to her mind. She pictured her hand curved around her aunt's shoulders, brushed by his arm with each movement as he drove. She clasped her hand as it tingled with phantom sensations.

"We'll see how soon Aunt Delia's ready for an outing." She opened her eyes with reluctance. "For now, she loves for you to bring her the day's gossip. She may be finding her way back to the present, hearing your accounts of who's visiting the Pump Room and who stopped you on the street for chats."

"She's a sociable soul who seems to know everyone in the city and most of London." He took still another tea cake, and his arm brushed her midsection this time as he reached past her. His big hands made the generous, mounded cakes look minuscule.

"Yes, she's always enjoyed Bath's opportunities to get together with friends from various places." Elizabeth felt as if her voice had risen an octave from his touch. "She's far more outgoing than I, which I sometimes forget. I'd be happy to go out only for an occasional book discussion group and musical evening, but Aunt Delia used to attend every entertainment given publicly and privately in Bath."

"*Grandmère* was very much like your aunt," he said, looking at her with understanding. "As she became vague, she began begging off from invitations, too. Didn't want others to realize she slipped up at times. She had too much pride to let go of her dignity. It was sad to see her turning more inward, when being with her family and friends might have helped her hold on to her memories more clearly."

The idea that exposure to company might help hadn't occurred to Elizabeth. "So you think I should encourage Aunt Delia to go out more, even if she runs the risk of embarrassing herself by not recalling who people are, or forgetting what day it is?"

"Worse things than embarrassment can happen to us," he said, leaning on his hands, which were flat on the bench. "What will it matter? Anyone who really knows and cares about her will smooth over any rough edges when she makes little slips, and those who aren't perceptive enough to do that probably aren't worth knowing."

Trailing a long weed through the basket for the kittens to investigate and attack, she thought about it. Public embarrassment didn't seem as horrible to him as it did to her.

Maybe stimulation for Aunt Delia was worth the risk. Her aunt had never seemed to mind what others said about her, though she'd helped Elizabeth hide the connection with Lucinda. Come to think of it, that seemed odd, not her usual open way at all.

"Elizabeth, I want to ask you something, and I don't want you running inside for the oven rake. Promise?" Now he was grinning, his dark eyes glinting sparks like burning coal.

"If you think I'll want to hit you, I'm not sure I want to hear it." She couldn't imagine what he would want to know.

"It's really about Miss Lindsey as much as about you."

She nodded, concentrating on the golden kitten as it tried to climb up the blanket, and he continued. "When Miss Lindsey talks about Lucinda, she doesn't mean you, does she?"

Elizabeth sat back on the bench. Surely he knew that after meeting the true Lucinda. "Aunt Delia was my father's much older sister. For some reason she never married. She lived with my father and took care of his estate until he married late in life, I'm told. When my parents married, Lucinda and my aunt became very close."

There, she'd said the name aloud. It wasn't so difficult when she thought of the woman as past history. "Aunt Delia grew to adore Lucinda like a daughter, and after her brother—my father—died, she stayed with us."

That was enough family history to tell Lord Chandler, more than she'd told anyone else. She bent over the basket again, tickling fat tummies as kittens tumbled around her hands.

His large fingers appeared beside hers, and the golden kitten abandoned her at once to leap at his hand. "But Miss Lindsey chose to live with you after you left school?"

Her heart twisting in her chest, Elizabeth didn't look up. She didn't have to answer his questions. She could get up and go in the house right now. Though he'd been kind to Aunt Delia, she didn't owe him personal information about a family situation she had kept entirely private.

Without knowing why, except that it was easier to talk while bending over a basket of kittens together like this, she said, "Aunt Delia wanted to stay with Lucinda. She adored her, and she enjoyed the duke's friends. But I couldn't set up house by myself after finishing school, and none of the other relatives were speaking to Lucinda by then."

Early afternoon stillness gathered close, and street noises seemed far away, leaving the two of them in a private circle that inspired confidences. She almost felt relieved to talk about the time before her world had changed forever, leaving childhood, security, and trust far behind. "Aunt Delia has never left me, not even for a day."

His tone was as gentle as his fingers among the warm, furry bodies. "Then your aunt must love you very deeply, too, if she chose to do what was best for you rather than to follow her inclinations."

"Yes." The one word was all she could safely say around the pressure closing her throat. Recognizing Aunt Delia's love should make her feel happy, not choked with tears that burned at her throat and eyes. Her aunt loved her without doubt; why did she feel empty and lonely at his observation about her aunt's affection?

"It's obvious that you love her just as much," he continued.

"She's all the family I have." Leaning her elbows on her knees, she gripped her arms and gulped down emotions.

Dolly leaped easily into the basket, licking at her babies as if washing off human finger marks. Chan clasped both his big hands loosely between his knees as he leaned forward beside her.

"Not quite the only family," he said, still more quietly than before. "You have a mother."

The clamor from the street broke loose in her ears again, shattering the pleasant interlude they'd shared. Elizabeth didn't move, concentrating on keeping her voice steady as she answered. "I don't recognize her, as you surely realize by now. She sent me away years ago, and I accepted the separation she forced on me."

Chan looked at her; she felt his gaze. "Miss Lindsey doesn't seen to have accepted the separation as easily as you have."

Rising, she walked away from him toward a lime tree. She didn't want to discuss her aunt—and especially not Lucinda—with him further. Placing a hand against the rough ribbed bark, she rubbed the heel of her palm against it harder and harder. The heat building up in her hand, the drag of her skin against the rugged trunk, focused her attention away from inner pain.

She sensed him behind her, though she hadn't heard his steps. A breeze stirred, and she caught the slight scent of his crisp fragrance and starched linen. She wondered what scent he wore. Perhaps a special blend, made only for him.

His breath touched the nape of her neck, stirring unfamiliar longings as he spoke. "If she loved your mother and thinks she talks with Lucinda again in her periods of disorientation, she must miss her. We could take her to visit Lady Enfield."

"No!" The unexpected proposition was horrific. Sick and reeling, Elizabeth clung to the tree with both hands for a moment.

Then she whirled away from Lord Chandler, back toward the house. "Seeing that woman could imprison my aunt permanently in the past. I won't expose her to that danger."

He didn't follow, just spoke more gently still. "Is the

danger you fear really to your aunt? Be honest with yourself."

If he'd scolded or pushed for action, she could have screamed at him as she wanted to do. Instead, he asked his quiet question in that kind voice, as if she were as fragile as Aunt Delia. She wanted to pound on his broad chest and claw at the planes of his chiseled features. She wanted him to take his cool superiority back to London and leave her alone.

She didn't want to think about the answers to his questions. "You don't know what you're saying." She nearly panted for air. "I can't answer you honestly or otherwise. This decision was made long ago and it wasn't mine. I accepted the choice others made for me, and I don't intend to change matters now."

"You went beyond acceptance," he said with maddening logic. "While a door may have been closed between you and your mother while you went away for the usual schooling, you turned the key in the lock."

"What's the difference of a lock, when the door was shut by someone else?" Elizabeth gripped handfuls of skirt to hide her hands' trembling. "The door will stay locked now."

"You don't have to pass through if you unlock the door."

From the sound of his voice, he was coming closer. She tensed, pushing him away with her will and determination.

"If you don't want to see Lady Enfield, you don't have to. I can take your aunt to visit your mother."

The thin spring air boiled up around her, turning red as sunrise to her eyes. Elizabeth dug her nails into her palms to offset the flood of pain drowning her lungs. Gasping for breath, she turned around, holding up both hands to ward him off.

"You can't take her," she said. "I won't let you take her away from me. Aunt Delia took care of me when no one else would, and now it's my turn to take care of her. She's not your grandmother, she's *my aunt! Mine!* I'll see that she has everything she needs, and I don't need you barging in and telling me what to do."

Lord Chandler stood looking at her, and in his dark gaze she read pity. "You don't see what she needs."

"I won't have you coming here, thinking you know what's right for my aunt when you've barely known her a fortnight." Her fury grew, shaking her body and voice as he stared at her with reproach. "You don't know me. You don't know what it's like to be closed out of your mother's life at her lover's whim."

When he started to speak, she gestured him away with a violent sweeping motion. "Go away. I hate your insufferable assurance. Just go now, and don't call again. Not to see me, not to visit my aunt. From this moment, my door is closed and locked against you, too."

Chapter Eight

"Of course we'll be delighted to come." Aunt Delia didn't even glance at Elizabeth as she accepted Lady Rowe's invitation for an evening of conversation and cards.

Anxious, Elizabeth asked, "Are you certain Dr. Johnston would approve of your breathing the damp night air? You've hardly been out of the house for two weeks."

"It wasn't my idea to live like a hermit." Aunt Delia gave her an injured look before turning back to her young friend.

"My niece can be an old hen, clucking around me like I'm on my last legs, and shaky ones at that. Of course I feel well enough to enjoy one of your special evenings, Evie. I'll be bundled up all the way there and back, if I know my girl."

Elizabeth poured ratafia for Lady Rowe and passed cakes to Aunt Delia. Her aunt's appetite this afternoon certainly supported her claim to have returned to full health. During the last few days she had seemed like herself again, calling Elizabeth by the right name. Still, she wouldn't want her aunt to go out too soon and suffer a setback.

"You can't fault Elizabeth for wanting to protect you." Lady Rowe smiled reassurance at her. "I hope you come, for routs aren't nearly as lively without you, Miss Delia. I was pleased when Chan said you needed an outing and might accept a personal invitation to my little gathering."

Chan. Lady Rowe knew him well enough to call Lord Chandler by the name his close friends used.

Naturally they would be friends, since both of them belonged to the wider social circles of London. The ton was a small and exclusive group. Little wonder the two would be drawn together, for Lady Rowe was as beautiful as he was handsome. No doubt she flirted with the same practiced ease, too.

Feeling disgruntled at the thought of them together in a ballroom or even a more private salon, Elizabeth passed the plate of wine biscuits.

"I never turn down your invitations, any more than does anyone else in Bath." Aunt Delia was all smiles and making perfect sense. "I only wish you lived here permanently. This town wouldn't seem so stodgy if you were around all the time."

One of the most popular part-time Bath residents, Lady Rowe claimed to rest up in Bath now and then from the rigors of the London season. Surely she couldn't entertain any more there than she did here. Her elderly husband didn't go up to the city often, so Lady Rowe was often here with him.

How like Lord High-and-Mighty Chandler to arrange for his beautiful London friend to tempt Aunt Delia back out into society. He couldn't know if her aunt was ready to face crowds of people or not, because she'd had him turned away at the door every day this past week. She had instructed Cook to keep the back door locked against a rear assault on the house, too.

"You won't have to fret over getting your aunt to my musical evening the quickest and most comfortable way." Lady Rowe sent Elizabeth a reassuring look over her glass. "Lord Chandler has promised to hire a closed carriage to bring you both with him, and he assured me he'll order extra hot bricks and rugs to keep your aunt cozy."

As if she wouldn't hire chairs to carry the two of them to Lady Rowe's house. Elizabeth set her mouth in what would have to pass for a smile. He'd done it again, nosing into her business. If Aunt Delia didn't look so pleased at the invitation, she would send their regrets for the evening at the last minute.

The knocker sounded from the entrance hall downstairs. Perhaps Lord Nosy Chandler had sent another pretty young hostess to enforce his prescription of social engagements for her aunt, despite her concerns.

The sound of Sally's giggles ascended to the drawing room, and Lady Rowe's eyebrows rose faintly as she looked between Elizabeth and her aunt.

"That's just one of the workhouse girls Elizabeth's trying to polish into a servant," Aunt Delia explained. "My niece has taken this notion to train maids and then find them places in service. That's why her hair is halfway down on one side today. It's Nell's turn to act as lady's maid, and though she's willing enough, she'll never make a dresser."

"I hope to help young women who would otherwise be unable to support themselves with decent work." Refusing to put a hand up to check the coiffure that felt more insecure by the minute, Elizabeth smiled over a half-eaten tart at Lady Rowe. "Nell is a great hand with laundry, and Suze is becoming a first-rate pastry cook. These tarts are as good as those Cook makes. Won't you have one? You might hear of someone here or in London who could use additional staff."

Shaking her head at the proffered plate of cakes, Lady Rowe said, "How commendable of you. I didn't realize you were interested in social reform, let alone doing more than joining organizations to promote it. I'll ask around among my friends to see if—"

The door into the drawing room opened. Sally nearly backed into the chamber, looking over her shoulder. A visitor followed her in.

Lord Chandler.

Elizabeth slid the remaining piece of tart into her napkin, holding it loosely in one hand. She didn't want him to catch her eating every time he saw her.

As he strode confidently into the room, she seethed at his sneaking in when she was distracted with a visitor. He'd been lucky that Sally answered the door, as wheedling his way past the girl probably wasn't too difficult.

Going to Aunt Delia, the intruder leaned down to kiss her lightly on the cheek. "I don't need to ask how you're feeling today, for you're glowing. May I hope that's the effect of the port I brought by for you? The ladies in my family swear by it as a restorative."

"It's lovely port, dear, sweet enough without a cloying taste. Just as I like it best. I'm happy you finally stopped in when I'm *awake* so I could thank you in person for bringing it." Aunt Delia sent Elizabeth another reproachful look before turning to beam at Lord Chandler again. "You'll know Lady Rowe, of course."

"Indeed. We meet often in London." Turning, he took their other caller's hand but dropped a kiss on her forehead. "Evie! Don't you look charming in Cossack green. You're always first with the new colors, and they all become you."

Evie indeed! Elizabeth had known Lady Rowe for years and didn't use her pet name. A man shouldn't know about fashionable colors, anyway. She tugged her skirt hem to cover the faint scorch mark Nell had left while pressing it.

Looking up, she found Lord Chandler lounging before her with a lopsided grin. He drawled, "Miss Merriman. I'm glad to find you at home at last. You've had an excessively busy week, for I've been denied each time I asked if you were home."

No doubt he was gloating because he'd found a way into her drawing room against her best efforts to keep him out. Elizabeth gestured abruptly to a chair near her aunt in a grudging invitation for him to sit down.

Horrified, she watched the remainder of her tart fly out of the napkin she held in that hand. As the pastry hit his immaculate pantaloons, the sticky jam clung for a moment. Then the tart slid down his thigh, over his perfectly polished boot, and onto the carpet, crust side up.

"Oh, no!" she said with a squeak.

"May I?" Calmly he took the linen square from her nerveless hand and wiped the worst of the jam from his clothing. Dipping a corner of the cloth into the hot-water pot, he rubbed briefly at the remaining stain on his light-colored pantaloons.

"I'm so sorry," she said, mortified. "I can't think how I came to be so clumsy."

"Then you aren't trying to run me off by throwing food at me?" he murmured. Scooping up the bit of tart lying on the floor, he crossed to Sally and handed her the napkin and the pot. "You'd best bring up more hot water for the ladies' tea, and perhaps Cook might find a few more tarts for Miss Lizbeth to . . . enjoy."

His naughty glance at her set Elizabeth's face burning. What would Lady Rowe make of him using her pet name so freely? She shouldn't feel a little curl of satisfaction at his putting her on the same level of esteem with his friend Evie. Resisting it, she focused on his interference. The irritating man had ordered her servant around as if he lived here.

Looking up at him in near worship, Sally giggled and dipped a saucy curtsy. "Yes, milord," she said. "I'll bring up another cup, too, unless you'd rather have the decanter?" Turning to Elizabeth she added, "Did I get that bit right, miss? I'm to offer gentlemen the decanter?"

Nodding, Elizabeth waved her out. She'd rather offer this darkly handsome lord the door, but she couldn't be rude to him in front of Lady Rowe. That would most certainly kindle gossip in the small society of Bath.

Inhaling sharply, she wondered if he had arranged both calls with Lady Rowe. He must have known that coming with her here would likely get him back in the house with the least fuss.

Instead of taking the distant chair she'd indicated, he now settled on a less comfortable one beside her.

"You'd better watch that girl," Aunt Delia said, frowning as the door closed behind Sally. "She isn't suitable for any household with gentlemen under a hundred in it."

Feeling defensive in front of Lady Rowe, who might recommend her girls for jobs, Elizabeth said, "Sally just needs a good talking-to now and then. She'll learn to keep a proper distance."

Lord Chandler and Lady Rowe exchanged a look of amusement and understanding. Lips tight, Elizabeth wondered how well they knew each other in London.

Turning a shoulder on the other ladies, Chan spoke to Elizabeth in a low tone. "You must deliver very effective lectures on the subject of keeping men at a distance—and outside your door. I hope you won't banish me again."

Looking past him, Elizabeth felt uncomfortable that Lady Rowe, who after all was their first guest, might feel excluded. At once Lady Rowe moved closer to Aunt Delia, almost turning her back. "I must ask you before

I forget. Do you know anyone local who might be trusted to gild woodwork for me?"

Now Elizabeth was positive Lord Chandler had asked for Lady Rowe's help to worm his way back into her house. She vacillated between feeling irritated and flattered.

With Lady Rowe and her aunt occupied in a discussion of decorating, she might as well pick a bone with Lord Chandler. "You put her up to inviting Aunt Delia to her rout." Keeping her voice down didn't keep accusation out of its tone. "Did you also plan her visit here at a time I wouldn't be on hand to remind the girls to refuse you entry?"

"Then you admit you've been at home to everyone except me this past week?" he asked with a grin.

"You know that's true," she said in irritation. "I told you not to come back. I meant it. I don't have to allow just anyone inside my doors."

"I asked to see your aunt, not you." His slanted brows drew together. "Do you decide whom she sees, too?"

Warmth spread over her face as she clenched the chair's arms. "My aunt needs rest and quiet."

Aunt Delia laughed aloud at something Lady Rowe had said, her cheeks pink and her eyes lively.

"So I see," he said, smiling.

Feeling defensive, Elizabeth frowned. "Her mental fragility doesn't always show to outsiders in brief visits."

Chan leaned on his chair arm, looking grave. "I don't want you to feel uncomfortable if I stop in, but I like Miss Delia. I want to call on her and escort her to a few gatherings. She might benefit from mixing with her old friends. I know you want to protect her. But look at her with Evie. Can you truly believe she's best kept isolated from people she obviously enjoys?"

"We're attending Lady Rowe's rout, thanks to you." He was right about Aunt Delia's pleasure. Elizabeth felt guilty and confused at her aunt's animation as the two women talked. She wanted only what was best for Aunt Delia, but it was possible she might be a little over-protective.

"And you'll allow me to take you both to Evie's house?"

Nodding briefly, she didn't look at him. How difficult to discover she might be wrong in front of the last person she wanted to know it. She could feel his gaze on her face like the touch of the sun.

"You'll tell your maids to let me see your aunt?"

"I'm not an ogre," she said sharply, causing Lady Rowe to look around. More quietly she continued, "Come if you like, though I don't understand why you insist upon spending so much time with a lady you hardly know."

Light molded the hard contours of his face as he frowned toward the window where the other two now sat with their heads together over a book. "Partly I come because your aunt reminds me of my grandmother, whom I loved very much and miss. You'll like my other reason less."

Shifting on the seat, he leaned toward her. "I know you don't like to talk about her, but your mother is concerned about your aunt and you."

She started to rise, and he put a hand on her arm. Behind them, Lady Rowe pointed out the front window toward the Sydney Hotel, and both the woman and Delia seemed engrossed in that view.

"Don't begin that nonsense again if you want to keep visiting my aunt." She spoke fast and low. "I'm not taking Aunt Delia to see that woman, and neither are you."

"I won't take her anywhere you don't agree to," he assured her, looking affronted. "What kind of man do you think I am?"

"One bent on getting his way at any cost. The way

you maneuvered your way in here today is a perfect
example."

When he stayed silent, she turned to stare at him. He
sat looking at Aunt Delia but seemed focused on his
thoughts. She didn't understand the turmoil he stirred in
her. Surely the sensible thing would be to end all contact
with him, since she wanted no connection with Lady
Enfield.

And yet his visits brightened Aunt Delia's days.
Though he had flouted her orders to stay away, she
couldn't feel angry with that. She wasn't entirely unhappy to see him again.

With no reason to welcome his company, she enjoyed
the challenge of talking with him. After thinking it over,
she usually appreciated his way of making her recognize
her less worthy motives. He wasn't the most comforting
person she'd spent time with, yet she had said things to
him, felt things because of him, that she'd never experienced with anyone else. He was as exhausting and as
exhilarating as a long trek over steep, uneven ground.

"One more thing I must mention," he said. "I won't
come here without honesty between us. You need to
know I've visited Lady Enfield often since I went there
with you. That's part of a debt to my friend I can't repay,
and I'll go on helping him."

"I understand loyalty to a friend," she said. "But your
business with Lady Enfield has nothing to do with me."

"Perhaps not, but I don't want to mislead you even
by omission." He grimaced. "Lady Enfield asked me to
tell her how you are, how Miss Delia is. She won't see
me if I don't agree to that. Then I can't help my friend."

Anger jolted Elizabeth, but it wasn't the body-shaking
attack she'd felt during their last talk about that woman.
He questioned the quality of her concern for Aunt Delia,
thought her selfish and overprotective. She would show
him that she could be as logical as he.

"Your arrangements with Lady Enfield are your business. I don't want to talk about them. Just promise you won't mention her to my aunt. I don't want Aunt Delia to know Lucinda is anywhere near Bath or that you see her."

"Keeping secrets creates trouble," he said. "But that's your decision to make, not mine. You have my word on it."

Staring into his grave eyes, she wondered at herself for believing him. Her confidence in him came dangerously close to trust, and he was, after all, a man.

Letting her gaze slide down his long, muscular body on its way across to her aunt, she sighed. Oh, yes, Lord Chandler was every inch a man.

Later that afternoon, Chan bowed as Lady Enfield entered her drawing room, struck anew by the close resemblance between Elizabeth and his hostess. "Thank you for receiving me."

Even when she smiled, the sadness never quite left her eyes. "You know you're my lifeline to Elizabeth and Delia. You're welcome here whenever you care to come."

Though she was too polite to ask at once for the family news that seemed the only light in her days, he gave it to her. "Then I'm doubly welcome today, for I can give you good news about them both. Miss Delia is so much herself again that Elizabeth's agreed to let me escort them to a rout soon."

The tension in her posture relaxed. "That is excellent news! I've been so concerned since Delia wandered away and couldn't find her way home again. This failing of her mind, even temporarily, has to worry Elizabeth even more than me, for of course she would feel dreadfully responsible."

"You know your daughter's nature well."

"We were together until she turned twelve." Lady Enfield gazed beyond him, thoughtful. "Perhaps because

141

she had little company other than her aunt and me, she was such an adult little thing as a toddler. She copied everything we did or said. She learned to read much younger than I did, and anything she undertook, she did well."

Pride added a lilt to her voice and lit her features. Chan wondered how Elizabeth could have spent twelve years basking in her mother's attention and then come to doubt her love.

"But listen to me ramble on instead of making you comfortable." She gestured toward a sofa and chairs grouped before the cold fireplace. "May I pour you a glass of wine?"

Moving toward the door into the garden, he asked, "Would you mind a breath of air as we talk? I sat with Miss Delia and Elizabeth for an hour and then in a saddle for another. A stroll would suit me, if it wouldn't be too much exertion for you."

"Not at all." Pulling the dark shawl draped from her elbows over her shoulders, Lady Enfield joined him, leading the way to the glass-paned double doors. "I should have thought of a stroll myself. Will was an active man, too, hated sitting about except in the evening. We had some of our best conversations on long rambles and rides. I felt closer to him when we talked than any other time. He actually wanted to tell me things about himself, and he listened to what I said."

Had this woman's husband neither listened nor told this sympathetic woman his personal doings and doubts? What a waste of a good listener and a sharp mind.

As they stepped through the door onto the stone flags outside, she looked up at him, uncertainty widening her golden eyes. "Do you mind if I speak so intimately of Will to you?"

He'd rather not know about the old duke's love life, but whatever helped Ash, he would do. "Please, say what you like."

"One of the worst things about my irregular situation is having no one to remember him with." She gripped the shawl's ends tightly, wrapping them close across her chest. "I've now been widowed as both a wife and a lover. When a husband dies, no matter how businesslike the marriage arrangement, a lady has the support and understanding of her friends." Her tone tightened against tears. "But when a man is your best friend outside of matrimony and against society's rules, you lose him without anyone feeling you have a right to grieve."

Head down, she added quickly, "I made my own choices, of course. I have no right to complain."

Putting a hand under her elbow to steady her as they strolled toward the colorful border in the back cottage garden, Chan felt her tension. "Certainly you can complain—to me at least. You need someone with whom to let down your courage. I knew the old duke as Ash's father, which put him too much on a par with my own father to think about him as you do. But when you talk about him, it shows me who he was in reality—not the frowning man I often saw."

Nodding briefly, she touched the leaves unfurling on an elm tree branch as they passed under it. "I know the expression you mean. He often arrived at our house near London wearing it, and it gave me such pleasure to see it ease as we strolled the grounds." She looked up at him quickly and then away, reminding Chan of Elizabeth's sliding, sidelong glances. "He always held my arm like this, as if he were afraid I'd stumble without his support. It's good to feel a big hand touch my elbow again."

Gently Chan increased the pressure of his fingers, hoping to communicate a sympathy for her loss he didn't know how to put into words. The sun's shadows, lengthening across the shrubbery enclosing the garden, reached for them as they walked between flower beds full of spring color, vibrant behind her simple black gown.

Whisking a handkerchief out of her sleeve, she

touched her eyes briefly. "I don't want to take advantage of your good nature by going on too long about Will. Let's talk about Elizabeth instead. I'm glad to hear she'll be going out among people again. She's too young to be cooped up nursing her aunt. Do you know if she has many friends?"

"Probably, as bright and beautiful as she is. We haven't met Elizabeth at assemblies since I've been in Bath, though Ash and I have been included in the usual routs given by local hostesses."

"No doubt." She nodded once. "Both of you are highly eligible bachelors and attractive guests as well. An unmarried duke and viscount don't show up in Bath every day, or even every season."

Bending to pull a weed, she straightened again. "If you see Elizabeth in society, will you pay special attention to her? I wonder if she dances as gracefully now as she did at six on the lawn while our old gardener whistled. What a darling she was."

"She's a darling now," he assured her, laughing at the mental picture. He sobered at the straight look she gave him.

"Then you feel you're coming to know her well?"

The question, asked with that measuring gaze, made him consider his answer carefully. "As well as any male probably knows her."

Lady Enfield frowned. "You call at the house almost every day now. Do you base that opinion on seeing her with other young men who call?"

Rubbing his jaw, he shook his head. "Only ladies have called in Sydney Place while I've been with them."

Clasping her elbows, she insisted, "If you haven't seen her among young men, can you judge how she feels about them?"

With reluctance, he admitted, "I know what she says to me. She doesn't seem to have a high opinion of any males."

"Oh, no." Lady Enfield put a hand to her lips. "Delia hinted in letters a few years back that Elizabeth seemed distant with young men, but I didn't realize it was actual antipathy. She adored her father; I'm not certain I understand why she wouldn't enjoy the company of gentlemen."

"Elizabeth hasn't brought her father into our conversations, but she's made remarks that show she doesn't trust men in general." Her caution toward him was as irritating as a boot that rubbed wrong, and he meant to change it.

Sighing, Lady Enfield said, "Perhaps Lord Enfield disappointed her too many times, promising to be home for her birthdays or to send trifles he forgot. I tried to explain that he loved her very much but was busy with the prince."

If Lord Enfield had been part of the prince's worldly retinue, Chan could believe he had no place in his life for a wife and daughter. Few of the Carlton House set included wives in their exclusive gatherings, perhaps because of the prince's marriage with Mrs. Fitzherbert.

Lady Enfield laughed. "When Elizabeth was eight, she wrote a letter to the Prince of Wales telling him she needed her father more than he did. She couldn't understand why I wouldn't post it for her."

Picturing Elizabeth acting with purpose even as a child was easy. He grinned. "She's still inclined to deal with problems head-on."

His hostess frowned into the distance. "Yes, she was determined even as a small child. If only she had been younger when Will and I found each other. At an earlier age, she could have lived with us. Will and I would have worried less about the effect of our arrangement on her outlook and opportunities." Her voice snagged in her throat. "Then she might have seen that some men can be counted on in any circumstances."

Each time he talked with this woman, he felt more

compassion for her interrelated losses of lover, daughter, and friend. How alone she seemed in her shadowed house with only servants. It didn't seem right that her deep and true love for the old duke had ended like this, without familial comfort and acceptance. Society, too, condemned her for loving the duke enough to share daily life openly with him, instead of carrying on the commonplace passionate couplings of bodies in secret.

This wasn't a subject he knew how to discuss with her. Any support he wanted to offer could be tainted with insult. She was every inch a lady in his estimation, but to assure her he thought so implied that others did not.

Besides, she was Elizabeth's mother. Being with her always made him feel slightly off balance. It was difficult to keep his regard for one admirable woman from coloring his view of the other.

Worst of all, his ultimate goal was to separate her from the legacy the man she sincerely mourned had left her. The more he heard about their shared days, the less he wanted her deprived of it.

Changing the subject seemed the safest road to take at the moment. "I told Elizabeth today that I've been visiting with you and telling you about her and Miss Delia."

The sweet scent of wallflower wafted past his nose on a breeze as slight as her sigh.

"Was that absolutely necessary, telling her?" Lady Enfield sounded both wistful and worried. "Was she angry with you for doing so?"

"Not as angry as when I suggested Miss Delia would benefit from visiting you." He grimaced, recalling Elizabeth's explosion. She certainly displayed more temper than her mother, though passion and ire had something in common. "And yes, I did have to tell her. I don't like to wear a mask with anyone. It's easier to be open about what I'm doing, even if that doesn't suit everybody's ideas."

"No. Of course, you're right to be honest with Elizabeth. Perhaps then she can come to trust you." She shook her head. "What a pity if she dwindled into old age alone, believing no man could be more dependable than her father."

Much as he hated to wound her, he said, "It's Lord Ashcott she seems angry about."

"If only she knew Will as I did, but we acted so different in public than in private. If only she'd seen . . ." Her expression softened as she turned her face up to the pale sky. "It was obvious she blamed Will for her being sent away to finishing school, and then me for not leaving him to live with her later. But neither of us thought our improper household was a good influence or background for a girl growing quickly toward her own marriage. And by the time she finished her schooling three years later, I couldn't bear to leave Will. He'd been seriously ill, and I was afraid of losing him."

She stopped, looking at yet through him as her expression changed from concern to vitality. "He's the one man who ever encouraged me to feel truly alive and capable of doing anything I tried."

Chan couldn't remove his gaze from the quiet joy in her face. For the first time, the tasteful little house where he himself had installed demireps for discreet liaisons seemed like a tawdry hideaway.

Lady Enfield remembered her duke as a beloved friend. Chan envied this lady the voyage of self-discovery she'd made with her lover, each of them learning through mutual emotion and devotion.

Chan wanted that kind of loving.

Taking Lucinda's arm again, he guided her along the garden's paths. He wondered if his parents' scant years together had been a joy. Could marriage be a joint journey of discovery instead of a duty to continue one's family line and title? He had assumed the business of being married bunged a hole in the pleasure boat. Neither the duke nor Lady Enfield had found joy in marriages of convenience. Could he look forward only to a civil mating, with true contentment coming from some clandestine arrangement? The thought depressed him.

"I wish I could send Delia some of these." Lady Enfield stooped to cradle a bright polyanthus bloom. "She always loved early spring flowers. If only I could go to her or she could come here. It breaks my heart to realize I may never see her again." Her voice broke, and she bent lower over the bright flower. "Even worse, I may not be allowed to see her while she's fully aware of who I am or able to converse normally. I need to tell her I love her and appreciate her care for my daughter when I wasn't there to give it. She has done so much more than be a husband's sister."

Chan wondered if he had tried hard enough to persuade Elizabeth to allow a visit between the older women. It didn't sit well with him, seeing all three unhappy.

"I understand your feelings, even if I haven't yet changed Elizabeth's mind about a visit." He looked off into memory. "After my grandmother had slipped mainly into a world of unreality, an acquaintance visited her for the first time in years. The friend expressed regret more for her personal loss of the strong woman she had known than for *Grandmère*'s vague but contented state. She kept saying she wished she had come sooner, so she could have taken leave of her friend before the final curtain of confusion separated them as surely as death."

Lady Enfield made a sound of swallowed tears, touching his arm. "Yes, that's my fear. Having Delia follow Will behind the curtain, whether to death or loss of awareness, before I can talk with her again.

"So many losses." Stopping, she gazed up at him, speaking with urgency. "Take care how you love, Lord

Chandler. It isn't easy to know the best way to live with your emotions. Love should be boundless enough to cover everyone you care about without limitation, but it doesn't always work that way. Not when loving someone hurts another person you care about." Letting go of his sleeve, she seemed to fade a little, like the afternoon's sloping sunlight. "The two people I loved most just couldn't fit into each other's lives."

If only answers for people's hearts came easily to him. "It would have been difficult to leave the duke if he was ill. Did you explain that to Elizabeth?"

"Once I sent her off to school, she wouldn't see me when I visited her. Afterward, when she moved into Sydney Place with Delia, she refused to read my letters." Lady Enfield walked faster and he kept pace. "I enclosed letters for her in notes to Delia, but Elizabeth threw them on the fire when she realized they were from me. She'll never forgive me for sending her away. For loving Will so much I chose to live with him instead of her."

Lady Enfield clasped and unclasped her hands. "It was a mistake to let myself love Will so blindly. I was wrong to put him and my selfish need to be with him before Elizabeth. I thought I could have both him and my daughter in my life, but Elizabeth couldn't allow it. It never occurred to me that close as we'd been, Delia and Elizabeth and I, we wouldn't always love each other and want to be together."

Thinking about the price she had paid for loving, he asked, "If you could choose again, would you agree to live with the duke?"

"Aye, there's the rub," she said in a whisper that reminded Chan of Ash's father. "The choice would be just as difficult again. Either way, I'm bereft. I'm grieving the loss of the best companion a woman ever knew, and I'm agonizing over the daughter and friend it cost me to have his love. Neither is a pain I want to live with. If I'd given him up to be with Elizabeth after she finished

149

her schooling, the separation would have been as heart-breaking as his death. We belonged together, Will and I, as if we were two halves of a whole."

She flung out one hand. "But knowing such devotion wasn't without anguish. During every year of the past twelve, I've believed I would find the right thing to do or say to help her understand and forgive me." Her voice broke on a small sob. "I must have made the wrong choices. If I'd never given myself the joy of living with Will every day, maybe now I would have the pleasure of being with Elizabeth and Delia. Maybe she would be married like most young women her age, with children for us both to love."

Tears seeped from the corners of her eyes and slipped toward her jaw unchecked. "Oh, what damage have I done to her?"

He had to offer hope where he saw such wretchedness. "Perhaps your choices did her good as well as injury."

"I wish I could believe that." Stopping again, she stared into the dark shrubbery behind vibrant blooms.

"Elizabeth may have felt abandoned, but she has made choices to exclude you, too." He needed to find something in the chasm between mother and daughter to lessen this lady's pain. "Maybe you wish now you'd done things differently, but who ever had perfect parents? Children put themselves into the mixture of what they become, too. Besides, you must have given her a good start, for Elizabeth grew strong, independent, and confident enough to help other young women be self-reliant."

"You're being kinder to me than I deserve." Lady Enfield leaned across the flower bed to pull a dried weed stalk from the shadowed depths of the shrubbery. She stood winding its dead length about a fingertip. "I once believed that if Elizabeth saw me again, she couldn't reject the love I feel so strongly for her. I was utterly convinced that she would be reminded of how we loved each other and feel it stir to life again." A small sob escaped her. "I was mistaken."

Tugging at the dry weed's length between her hands, she blinked rapidly, and her voice rasped out of her throat. "My daughter's heart and mind are closed against me. All she wants now is for me to stay out of her life. That's the only meaningful thing I can give her. No matter what the gift costs me."

The dried stalk snapped and Lady Enfield held a separate strand in each hand without seeming to notice.

Staring at the browned, broken stems, once whole and strong with green life, Chan realized that some things couldn't be put back as they were.

Surely love couldn't be one of them?

Chapter Nine

Two mornings later, Chan gazed into the murky depths of his cup as he leaned against the cushioned leather back of a deep chair. "This tastes like it's left over from last week and heated again."

Ash grunted, his gaze intent on the printed sheets he held.

"Hazard's is sliding downhill on ice, if this is the brew they serve patrons these days. Too much success tends to spoil any business, even a circulating library that's been around long enough to serve our fathers."

Still getting no response from his friend, Chan finished off the bitter coffee and set his cup on its plate on the side table. For a reading room at ten o'clock in the morning, Hazard's sounded more like a London coffeehouse. Talk and laughter rose from every corner.

Idly, he leafed through the London *Times* and Spanish newspapers he'd already read while Ash scrutinized Irish gazettes. Still few reports on Wellington's activities in Portugal. That must mean significant plans were taking

shape. Pray God Old Hooky's plans didn't depend on
the Spanish fleet, with half its ships driven ashore by a
terrible storm in the Bay of Cádiz. Best check on the
ships he'd backed, see if those investments had been
dashed against a foreign shore.

"Yes!" Ash pronounced the one word with satisfaction before dropping his newspaper on the table between
them. He stretched as if he'd just awakened and looked
around. "Where's the man with the pot? I need another
cup before writing my letter."

"What's so important you'll write a letter yourself instead of waiting for Sims to do it?"

"Can't wait that long; we won't be back in London
for weeks at the rate you're working on Lucinda. I'm
almost tempted to do it myself"—he paused and caught
Chan's annoyed stare—"but I won't."

Ash held up his cup toward the servant across the
room. "Quigley's back at his Belfast estates. Must be
light in the pockets if he's in Ireland during the Season.
I have to get an offer to him on that two-year-old black
he raced at Wimbledon before somebody else figures out
he needs money."

Chan frowned. He wouldn't tell another man how to
manage his business affairs, but trafficking in racehorses
was always risky. Was Ash aware that death duties had
likely depleted the inheritance he had received? Chan
hoped his friend would consult his man of business before investing.

"Want coffee?" Ash asked as his cup was filled.

"No, thanks." Chan rose from his chair and stood at
the window behind their seats, looking down into Cheap
Street. Carriages and carts crowded the narrow lane, and
people on foot dodged vehicles and each other.

He was impatient to get on with his day's visits to
Elizabeth and Miss Delia, then on to Lady Enfield. Despite Ash's joke, his friend's interests had kept Chan on
the road almost daily since they had arrived in Bath. He

wasn't the one fishing and keeping tabs on racehorse owners.

"Good-looking black, that one." Ash rubbed the thigh of his lame, outstretched leg. "Might have some Fresian blood in the line, but more Arabian. I can race him a couple of years and then make back my investment in stud fees, even if not on bets."

Chan said, "If he wins tolerably."

Ash laughed and flexed his maimed foot. "My horses win often enough to pay a damned expensive Irish trainer."

Paying out instead of making deposits wasn't Chan's idea of good investing either. He leaned over to look up the street from the upstairs window.

"What's so fascinating out there at this time of day?"

Chan hardly heard the question. The particular grace of a woman turning onto Cheap Street off of High Street reminded him of Elizabeth. He grinned. Despite her confident carriage, the lady's blue figured muslin gown hung unevenly at the hem. Only one female would come out in public wearing a gown with a flounce tacked up so inexpertly he could see its dip from here.

Turning away from the window, he said, "I see someone I know. Finish your coffee and I'll join you again shortly."

Ash set down his cup. "Go ahead and stop him. I'll be right behind you."

Heading for the passage, Chan said, "It's no one you'd want to see. Have another cup, why don't you?"

"You trying to hint me away? Must be a petticoat you're chasing." Grinning, Ash picked up the Irish paper again. "In that case I'll take my time. Wouldn't want to outshine you when you're so afraid of the competition."

Relieved, Chan hurried into the passage and took the steep stairs two at a time. As he pushed open the entrance door to Hazard's Circulating Library, Elizabeth reached it. She stepped back toward the street without looking up past the brim of her straw bonnet.

"Don't drink the coffee here if you value your stomach's health," he said, surprised at the lift to his mood.

Wide-eyed, she looked up; then her beautiful face relaxed into an answering smile. "Lord Chandler! If you come to the best-stocked lending library in Bath only for coffee, you deserve what you get."

"If you use my title like a new acquaintance, I'll force a cup of the worst brew in Bath on you." No woman should glow with such glorious inner light in the morning, even with her hair poorly dressed and her hem uneven.

"I won't spare time for coffee, especially when you offer it as a threat. Aunt Delia finished the last volume of her novel last evening and feels at loose ends if she doesn't have another ready to devour at once." She flourished two volumes between gloved hands. "I know that fretful state of mind all too well, so I promised to come exchange it for her first thing today."

"That's kind of you. Let's see what we can find that she might enjoy. Then I'll walk you home." He'd send up a message to Ash before they left, for he wouldn't pass up an opportunity to have Elizabeth to himself all the way to Sydney Place.

Her uneven skirts swayed with fetching rhythm as she crossed toward the shop's counter. A clerk approached and held out a hand. "Good morning, Miss Merriman. Let me take these books for you and check them in while you browse."

Handing over the books with thanks and a smile, Elizabeth waited while the clerk led them into the library. Chan took her elbow as they headed for the glassed bookcases of circulating fiction, feeling her warmth like a sun-soaked peach against his palm.

The clerk opened the door of a bookcase for her as if he knew exactly what she would want. Chan disliked the fellow's proprietary air, acting as if he knew all about her, even which books she'd prefer.

Elizabeth thanked the clerk again and turned to the bookcase.

Moving close enough to show the lady was with him, Chan held the glass door so it and his body formed an alcove for her as she scanned the shelves.

"Do you have a particular work in mind for your aunt?"

"Not really. Aunt Delia and I both like gothics and Minerva Press volumes, and we read them between new books by authors like Maria Edgeworth and Mrs. Opie."

He knew enough to recognize that the works ranged from pure entertainment through stories with morals, even new ideas about women's place in society. "Can't say I've read much fiction. Mostly I read journals and newspapers."

"Then I won't expect advice from you on a book to please Aunt Delia." She smiled and made a shooing motion with her hands. "Don't wait on me. I lose track of time when I'm looking at books."

"If I get bored, I'll wander over for a look at biographies." He didn't expect to be tempted away. "Take all the time you want."

Accepting him at his word, she turned to the bookshelves and promptly appeared to forget he existed. So much for his reputation as irresistible to ladies. Grinning, he remembered the first time he'd seen her, staring in at a display of books on Milsom Street, totally absorbed.

Sobering, he wished he had been kinder to her that day. How impossible it seemed now that he had mistaken her character for a moment.

While she inspected the spines of books, he studied her. Between the back collar of her spencer and her bonnet's edge, her slender nape peeked. The small expanse of skin looked vulnerable, soft, and inviting. Idly, he wondered how she would react if he pressed his lips lightly against its enticing warmth.

Shifting position slightly to hide an instant reaction to the thought, he grimaced. From past experience, he knew Elizabeth would probably bash him with a book if he gave in to that temptation, particularly in a public place.

Though she stood in one spot, face hidden by her straw bonnet's poke brim, he knew which shelf and books she examined. Her browsing became a ballet. She leaned gracefully to one side as she checked along a shelf, then eased to the other. She bent slightly at the knees as she scanned lower shelves, rose on her toes to check titles above.

He'd never realized the back view of a woman totally engrossed in books could scorch him, body and lungs.

As she ran a gloved finger along the volumes, he felt as if its naked tip drew liquid heat across his chest. The lissome forefinger paused, traced its way up the book's spine to the title. He held his breath, his chest kindling with hot embers. Her yellow-gloved hand eased out the volume with teasing indolence, then shoved it home decisively.

The inferno in his chest blazed downward to increase the discomfort of his buckskin pantaloons. He nearly groaned aloud as her seductive hand caressed the next leather binding, then the next.

By the time she lifted a volume into both caressing hands, he longed to seize her shoulders and drag her back against the hard need she stirred without conscious effort. As she opened the book between graceful fingers and stroked down its spread spine, he ached to press her round, firm bottom against himself, rub his urgent desire across the mounds and valley of her beautifully curved backside, show her how intensely she could want him, too.

"This should be satisfying," she murmured.

"Most," he agreed with raw irony, taking the first volume of the work from her as she reached for the other two. Taking all three volumes, he held them strategically as a shield and closed the bookcase. He had to think of something besides Elizabeth's lush figure.

Walking with care, he followed her to the central counters, where she produced a subscription form from her embroidered reticule. He was glad her chip bonnet's brim obscured her face entirely, as it also hid his torment from her. Leaning his hipbones close to the counter beside her, he conjured the memory of a dip in the cold sea at Brighton, hoping to walk out of the library in a decent state.

"Chan!"

Ash's voice from the stairs cooled him off faster than an icy dip. He'd rather the duke and Elizabeth didn't meet here after the animosity between them at the Bear Inn. At least he stood between her and Ash's approach. Maybe he could warn his friend away without the two of them coming face-to-face.

As Ash swung his awkward leg across the polished wood floor in his direction, Chan heard a quick intake of breath from Elizabeth. A quick glance showed she still faced the clerk, shielded by her bonnet's poke brim. She must have recognized the voice.

Facing Ash, Chan screened her from his friend's view. Maybe he could still head this off without a need for the two to speak. He took a step toward Ash.

"If you've finished womanizing, let's get back to the Bear." Distracted by his own plans, Ash had apparently not noticed Elizabeth. "I need ink and decent paper to write Quigley, not the foolscap they offered me here."

Chan set his hands on his hips to close off more of the view behind him. "I'm about to stretch my legs in a walk. You go on to the inn and write your letter. I'll join you for lunch later."

Stepping around his elbow, Elizabeth faced Ash.

The duke looked startled; then wrath filled his features.

Looking stiff as a statue encased in ice, Elizabeth sounded just as cold. "No need to change your plans with your friend, Lord Chandler. I've been seeing myself home since I was sixteen, and I can do so today. Good day to you, gentlemen."

With a brief nod in Ash's general direction, she turned with a flourish of her uneven flounce and headed for the exit.

"Her again." Ash's eyes blazed and his mouth sneered as he watched Elizabeth march away. "Damn, Chan, isn't it a little early in the day to frolic with a strumpet?"

Chan quelled the urge to strike his best friend. Only a few feet away, Elizabeth couldn't have missed Ash's demeaning comment.

Hazard's clerk had no doubt heard it. The man looked after her with big eyes, then glanced at Chan with curiosity before busying himself.

Elizabeth came in here often to borrow books for herself and her aunt. The entire staff probably knew her. Chan wouldn't permit anything to threaten her reputation. He had to force Ash to retract his ugly words at once.

Fixing the duke with a cold look of clear significance, he said, "You've made a mistake. You don't know the lady who just left, very properly ignoring that crass remark. And you don't know me if you think I'll overlook an insult to another friend."

Outrage followed incredulity as Ash began an oath and bit it off. Chan held his friend's hot glare without blinking.

Finally the man made a dismissive gesture and looked away. "No, I didn't recognize her—if *she* was a lady." Expression and tone stiff, he headed toward the door. "I'm going back to the Bear Inn. Come with me, unless you'd rather follow your *friend*."

*   *   *

Chan caught up with Ash before he reached the door, hardly a feat with his friend's stiff-legged gait. Reaching ahead, he swung the door open.

Ash wrenched it from his grasp and stalked through, letting it swing loose behind him.

Closing the door on the way out, Chan stood looking toward High Street, hoping for a glimpse of Elizabeth. She must have already rounded the corner.

His inclination was to follow her. The sound of Ash's swallowed gasp, followed by a quiet curse, stopped him. The stubborn fool had limped off too fast and paid for it as his foot twisted.

Duty sent him after Ash, who had already hobbled on. Swinging his fists at his sides, Chan strode beside his steaming friend in the opposite direction from where he wanted to go.

With every step, he betrayed Elizabeth, yet following her would be a greater disloyalty. His physical response to her in Hazard's was pure lust. A man couldn't throw away years of brotherhood because a woman swamped his senses with every glance from golden eyes.

Though even a narrow view of her nape had been enough to steam his clams today.

"You still here?" Ash didn't look around.

Chan's irritation swelled. "Obviously." Elizabeth had just begun to respond to him with the ease of a comfortable acquaintance, after fighting him off at every encounter as if he were a French marauder.

Yet his irritation might have been excessive; he couldn't claim to be setting aside the love of his life. She was simply a beautiful woman whose company he enjoyed, whose presence fired him with an uncommon craving. Wasn't she?

"You can go to blazes, for all I care." Ash's jaw worked, probably from the effort of moving so fast. His shoulders were stiff and hunched. "I don't need you around. Go after the chit; go back to London. It's all the same to me."

Hurrying still faster, Ash slipped, and Chan caught his arm before he went down. He propped his friend upright.

Still not steady, Ash fought off Chan's grip. "I can take care of myself. I don't need you grabbing at me like a nanny."

Holding up both hands, Chan said with contained patience, "You damn near fell on your face and you know it. Stop acting like an ass."

Ash raised his fists for a fight. "Stop acting like a mooncalf over a whore's spawn and I won't have to."

For an instant, hot anger tightened Chan's muscles. He could easily flatten Ash with one blow. The moment grew taut, while people eddied around and past them, a few staring with open curiosity.

Gritting his teeth, Chan breathed deeply, deliberately. He wouldn't be drawn into a street fight at their ages.

Fisticuffs had erupted often between them as boys, for Ash had needed to prove his mettle and disprove any limitation assumed from the lame leg. Though he could have bested Ash easily with his superior reach and strength, Chan had always fought to a draw, letting Ash's exhaustion stop their affrays. He'd felt he owed Ash a chance to beat against something, since he couldn't lash out at Fate's unfairness. Later he'd learned to walk away without a word. Ash's temper always cooled with time.

Still, though he wouldn't come to blows in a public street, this was an issue Chan didn't want to walk away from. Ash wouldn't insult Elizabeth without hearing from him.

That realization surprised him. What feelings had begun to stir in him? Protectiveness?

Quietly he said, "I've never picked your friends, and you won't choose mine."

"Friends!" Ash flung the term away with a shove of one hand. "We've never quibbled over friends. This is about a woman. Women aren't for friendship; they're for pleasure or breeding. You can't marry the chit—not with her mother's reputation—and if you want her for pleasure, you don't have to call me out like a schoolboy in front of everybody in Hazard's."

The injustice of Ash's grievance balled his fists. "Bath is where Elizabeth and her aunt live, Ash. That clerk at Hazard's desk knows her by name. You didn't spare her reputation or her feelings, in front of a man who's probably known her for several years. That wasn't the act of a gentleman, and you know it."

Flushing, Ash grimaced. He surely saw Chan was right, even if he couldn't admit a mistake easily.

"I didn't even notice her until she stepped out from behind you, looking down her nose at me like a bishop," Ash said. "You know I don't consider her a lady, whatever you choose to think.

"That's the woman who tried to brain me with a poker, if you've forgotten it," Ash continued. As Chan frowned, he made a swipe in illustration. "We've been too close to start lying to each other now. If you expect me to put on a show of bowing and scraping around her, you can forget it. I've never shown you two faces, and I won't do it now."

Ash was right about that. He was honest to the point of lacking tact, always had been. Still, he shouldn't have said what he did, especially not in public.

Too, Elizabeth could have shown him a little less frost. Ash was touchy about slights. But he should not have gone so far in retaliation.

Annoyed with both of them, Chan started off again. Setting a slower pace, he headed toward the Bear Inn. "I'm not asking you to act dishonestly. Just behave with common courtesy if you happen to meet. Is that asking too much?"

For once Ash didn't answer immediately. Head down, he seemed to give the request serious thought.

Uneasiness churned Chan's guts, bitter as the morning's coffee. What would he do if Ash refused to behave with civility toward Elizabeth? Ash had been his friend as long as he could remember. If he'd had a brother, they couldn't have been closer. A man didn't end a lifelong friendship over a woman—not unless a shooting offense occurred.

Hands on his lapels, Ash stopped to rest his bad leg, staring up at the soaring front of the abbey. Angels on its stone facade climbed as endlessly up and down ladders as this dilemma scaled Chan's mind. Thoughts that went nowhere frustrated him.

Finally Ash looked at him, straight and accusing. "This isn't like you, Chan. You've always known the difference between women you bedded and those you might wed. This woman has knocked you off center. She and her harlot mother have their hooks deep into you for their own purposes, probably scenting more money."

Shaking his head, Ash looked troubled. "You're my *friend*. I can't watch you waste your life over a fancy piece like my father did. To let you stroll over the same precipice to perdition is more than I can take."

Standing in the crowd surging around the Pump Room entrance and the abbey churchyard, Chan had never felt more alone. The clutches of love could be cruel, even between friends.

Ash's face was sincere as he gazed at Chan with concern. "You've never acted like this over one of your flirts or mistresses. This one's different. Dangerous. She could lure you away from family and friends like her mother tempted Father. I don't want to lose you like I did him."

"You don't have to."

Looking away, Ash shook his head.

Chan couldn't fault a friend for caring what befell

him, even if Ash was wrong in his fears. More than a quarter-century of trust, brief quarrels, and extended loyalty bound them together in shared experiences. Neither had faced a sorrow or joy alone in that time. To cut Ash out of his life would be harder than losing a limb to the surgeon's knife without a deadening drop of drink.

It just couldn't happen.

Chan cuffed Ash lightly on the shoulder. "You're taking this too seriously. I've never lost my head over a female. Why would you expect it now? I genuinely like Elizabeth and her family, that's all. You have to admit I can do a better job of straightening out your estate mess if I'm on good terms with everyone involved."

"The terms don't have to be that good." Ash's dark look had lightened a bit. "I asked you to deal with Lucinda, not her daughter."

"Lady Enfield won't see me unless I talk to her about Elizabeth. I told you that. Only by feeding her daily news about the doings in Sydney Place do I get the opportunity to discuss the legacy." Maybe that wasn't the whole truth, but it was true as far as it went. No need to encourage Ash's unwarranted worries.

Ash didn't look convinced. "You could make up enough rubbish about what she does to satisfy Father's bed warmer. You don't have to show up at her door as often as the post."

Shaking his head, Chan said, "I don't like lying any more than you do. Telling tales to Lady Enfield would upset me as much as it would for you to talk politely with Elizabeth for an hour."

"Then I suppose we'll go separate ways for the first time in our lives. You paying court to mother and daughter, and I avoiding them." Holding out a hand, Ash said, "That's the best I can offer—to stay out of the chit's way."

Chan clasped the proffered hand briefly. "It's good enough. Make yourself scarce if I speak to Elizabeth when you're around. I'll make the excuses for you so it isn't offensive."

"Don't make any excuses on my account," said Ash, limping off toward the inn.

Chan followed. Though he should feel relieved to have matters better understood between them, a bleak landscape loomed ahead. This was the first serious rift in their long years of friendship, and it didn't sit easily in his mind.

Yet he couldn't stay away from the lively house in Sydney Place with its melee of young kittens and apprentice maids, a dotty old lady much like his beloved *Grandmère,* and a bristly beauty badly dressed by an abigail-in-training. Her fascinating golden eyes were glowing flames that enticed him like a moth, no matter how many times he flew away into the night.

He'd just have to keep those fires from flaring into a conflagration that destroyed the lifetime bond between himself and his friend.

Chapter Ten

Leaving Ash in the yard at the Bear Inn, Chan strolled
on. He hadn't been tempted by the offer of a pint, too
restless to sit in idle talk, too perturbed by their clash to
attempt a show of their usual camaraderie.

Two boys wove through the crowd on the street, slap-
ping at each other and laughing. Watching them, Chan
longed for a simpler time when he and Ash had been on
those easy terms.

Worst of all, a sense of injustice gnawed at Chan.
Elizabeth deserved better from him than a protest that
he couldn't fall under her spell. When he was with her,
he often felt bewitched, but not because she deliberately
worked any magic. The thrall she had conjured had
grown despite her attempts to shun intimacy.

Removing his beaver hat, Chan whacked it against a
thigh to scatter dust and frustration.

Though she admitted him regularly to the house on
Sydney Place now, or had before Ash's latest insults,
Elizabeth didn't allow him past a surface acquaintance

with her. Her emotional shield repelled approach better than any armor in a muniment room.

What would it take to win her confidence?

Finding himself outside the Guildhall, he gazed along the soaring columns and pediments fronting the plain Bath stone building. It housed representatives of local labor but also the most exquisite banqueting facilities in Bath. Like Elizabeth, its classical exterior hid an industry and inner beauty of which few would guess. He glimpsed her depths, wanted to unlock and explore them. No matter how he worked at learning who she was behind the lovely facade, the real Elizabeth eluded him.

Frowning at the tall structure, he wondered why he cared if she chose to hide inner secrets. It wasn't as if he could allow himself to seduce her, a young woman of good birth. She wouldn't give herself easily, with her horror of being known as a kept woman's daughter.

Despite Ash's fears she might trap him in marriage, Chan had no plans to wed for another ten years. Even if he wanted to be leg-shackled, he wouldn't risk his longest friendship in choosing a wife. The animosity between Ash and her was proof against Elizabeth becoming more than a valued acquaintance.

Ash was a blockhead, and he himself was another.

Chan's itch to breach her armor, no matter how much she fascinated him, made no sense. Plenty of females were open to him in every way with little effort on his part.

As if to prove the point, a pretty maid bumped her market basket against him. "Beg pardon, sir, indeed I do." She smiled back at him over a shoulder, a clear invitation in her glance as she passed under an arch in the screening wing on the side of the Guildhall.

A market basket. The servant had come to buy farmers' wares in the Guildhall marketplace.

Elizabeth had come to town to exchange her aunt's

books. Doing other errands while she was out, such as picking up perishables for dinner, would be the usual practice. While he stood here in useless fretting, she might be strolling among the stalls behind the Guildhall buying green peas or marrows.

After Ash's insulting comment in the circulating library, Chan owed her an apology on his friend's behalf. If he were lucky, he'd catch her here and not have to create a chance to talk with her away from her aunt.

Hurrying between the wrought-iron gates that opened back from the arch, he entered an area crowded with stalls and people. Despite the throng, he needed to find Elizabeth at once, before she finished her errands and returned home.

Looking at people instead of at farm and glasshouse produce, he twisted through the crowd. Earthy smells of soil, chicken dung, and onions wafted past him as people went about business in a pinwheel of movement.

Like the fresh scent of mixed herbs against a midden, one feminine form appeared, moving with grace through chaos. Then Elizabeth disappeared from his view behind a burly farmer in an embroidered smock.

Chan pushed forward with a new sense of urgency.

Elizabeth wandered through the marketplace, hoping to call her bruised feelings and tumultuous thoughts to heel. She couldn't take her distress home, not with Aunt Delia there. Even when her aunt mistook her for Lucinda, the older woman sensed her frame of mind far too well and, like a loving pet, reflected it.

The marketplace was ideal for recovery, as she could move at random, speak little, and not look as lost as she felt. Stall vendors called information and insults across rows in a dissonance that echoed her inner state. The blur of colors, shapes, and smells was a familiar part of her life and therefore comforting.

After the shock of the past hour, she needed normalcy.

Nothing the duke had said or done since arriving in Bath was right or normal. Each contact with the vile man left her feeling like a stranger to herself. How could he persist in seeing her as a reflection of Lucinda—something she was not and could never be?

Despite every effort to live a blameless and useful life, she was still being judged by her mother's reputation. It wasn't fair, but she had always heard talk about bad blood. People still believed the sins of the father were transmitted to the child.

Ahead of her, a litter of puppies wrestled in the dirt before baskets of produce, awaiting homes. Bloodlines counted in breeding hunting dogs and horses—but most of all, blood seemed to count in humans.

The duke saw her as a mirror image of her mother in more than appearance—because of their blood. And she doubted that even Lord Chandler could make his friend keep that opinion to himself.

Dissociating herself from Lucinda long ago had been the right thing to do, despite Chan's sympathy toward the woman. Holding herself back from the viscount was safer, too, and had been the right decision. When push came to shove, he had stood with his friend instead of standing up for her.

This dull ache in her throat and burning chasm in her chest were the duke's doing, and Lucinda's legacy to her.

A touch on her elbow made her leap away like a besieged cat, her heart pounding.

"I'm glad to find you." It was Lord Chandler.

Clenching her fists, she stared at his square-jawed, handsome face. With her feelings and reputation shredded publicly by his friend just minutes ago, in his presence, he should know he was hardly a welcome sight. "How did you find me? And why?"

"A hunch." His slanted dark brows bunched. "Why? Because I'm sorry. I wanted to explain."

Choking back distress, she swung wordlessly away to pretend absorption in the produce at the nearest vendor's stall. Speech wouldn't make it past the thick pain in her throat. He hadn't followed quickly enough. If he had appeared faster, she might have forgiven him; she couldn't talk now.

As she seized carrots and threw them down again, she knew he stood close behind her. His presence intruded itself even when she didn't look at him, whether he spoke or not.

Feeling a tug on the parcel under her arm, she realized he had taken Aunt Delia's books. He held them out of reach when she tried to take them back. Annoyance joined her pain.

His smile offered an apology. "If I hold on to these, you'll have to give me a chance to explain."

Turning back to the stall, she ignored the vegetable vendor's gap-toothed grin. "Talk doesn't mend broken plates. You've made the effort; go back to your friend with a clear conscience."

"You're a valued friend, too," he protested. "I have more than one."

"No doubt you have many." She brushed her gloves together to rid them of dirt from the carrots. The smirch left behind by the duke's hateful words would take longer to remove.

"Maybe as many friends as carrots in that basket." He reached past her, picking up a gnarled tuber and letting it drop again. "And most of them just about as indistinguishable."

Glancing around, he lifted a pineapple from the next stall. He balanced the brown oval on his fingertips. "One friend may be better company at one time, one at another. Both can be special enough to rate a place at my table."

The crone behind the vegetable baskets cackled, nodding at him, while the fruit seller took back his pineapple with a wink at Elizabeth. Lord Chandler seemed set on adding to her public embarrassment.

Replacing the carrots she had selected, she hurried to a stall across the way. Maybe now he'd get the message she didn't need his company or his ruinous friendship.

Within seconds, the prickle of his presence again spread along her shoulders and back.

"Best not pitch those eggs around like you did the carrots," he advised, removing a brown egg from her fingers. He held it up before her eyes so she couldn't ignore him. "Eggs must be handled with care if you don't want to lose them. Like two special friendships I want to keep."

Looking away, she fought to avoid sounding as wounded as she felt. "You're in no danger of losing the friend you value most. Just accept that eggs and carrots don't mix, and leave eggs alone."

Carrots? She should have presented herself as the tough root vegetable, not as an egg. A fragile image was the last impression she wanted to convey.

Yet the egg seller applauded. "Comb his head proper, miss! Then kiss and cry friends before that carrot lady grabs him away from you."

Flushing at the assumption that she cared whether another woman wanted this plaguesome devil, Elizabeth gathered her tattered dignity. "You'll have to excuse me," she said with an effort at cool civility. "I came to the market to find something that might tempt my aunt's appetite. This discussion isn't welcome or appropriate here."

Hurrying away, she found herself fingering carrots again when the brown egg came back into view. Chan reached for a root and held both comestibles easily in one big hand. "You're wrong, you know. These can be

171

delicious together. Hasn't your cook ever served you a carrot puff?"

Elizabeth set her teeth together, searching for the smallest and most tender of the vegetables.

"Granted," he continued, "the carrot is tough at first and has to simmer for a while."

Her lips trembled with the effort to hold back reproach. She was too deeply injured to smile at his silliness. The idea of boiling the duke had definite appeal, though.

"The cooked vegetable has to be riced before it mixes well with the egg." He waggled the carrot at her with an entreating look. "Even though the egg has taken quite a beating by that stage, which I very much regret, the resulting dish can be quite delightful."

Picking up a gnarled carrot, Elizabeth handed it to him. "Yet some ingredients are spoiled. Your duke is more twisted in character than in body. He won't mix in the dish you suggest. Not ever. All you'll get for trying to force this particular combination is indigestion that no amount of emulsion will cure."

The confident smile curving his lips didn't match the lines creasing his forehead. "Eggs are a particular favorite of mine. I don't mean to give them up."

Moving around him to a fruit vendor's wares, she chose not to answer. Metaphors made the conversation too confusing. She didn't want to mince words over insults that still cut to the quick.

Instead, she spoke to the vendor arranging a pineapple among pears in an inviting display. "My aunt might fancy one of these if they're fully ripened. When did you cut these?"

"Took them ripe and fresh from the glasshouse before dawn, miss, long before you left your warm bed." He looked over her shoulder, grinning. "Just three and tuppence, sir. The lady might forgive you for a sweet gift like this."

"I don't want a gift," she insisted. "I'm buying for my aunt."

Chan stood close again, his presence filling in every space between their bodies, wrapping around her like the warm hug of a feather bed. If she allowed it, he would suffocate her.

Mentally, she built a brick wall between them while she hefted, prodded, and sniffed at different spiny fruit, but Chan's gaze bored right through her barrier. His assault against her defenses was relentless, so she couldn't let down her guard. She didn't need his kind of friendship. This devil with dark brows saw too much, assumed too easily, and threatened her peace of mind with every treacherous word and smile.

As she rolled a diamond-skinned pineapple between her hands to check its ripeness, a thread of her glove at the thumb snagged on a sharp spine. Trying to free it, she broke the thread and the seam split. She bit back a word she wouldn't say in public, wondering what else would go wrong on this horrible day.

At once Chan took the fruit and set it aside, cradling her hand, turning it gently as he examined it. "Have you hurt yourself? Let me see."

The ragged, mixed emotions of the last hour heightened her senses, making his touch unbearable. "It's just my glove." Clenching her teeth, she tugged against his hold. "It's nothing."

Her unbidden reaction to his clasp was far from nothing. As he eased a thumb along the seam's growing slit, a sensation like warm candle wax oozed through. His fingers probed, his search seeping along her skin as if she'd sliced into the golden inner fruit of the pineapple, releasing its sweet juices to trickle over her palm and collect in a tantalizing pool.

Fighting off her body's betrayal, she hated him for inspiring it.

His slanting brows nearly met as he bent closer. His

breath warmed her skin, enervating and intolerable, as he prodded at the glove's split, widening it further as he searched her hand for injury.

Resisting his belated show of concern, she said, "Let go. I'm not bleeding."

Grimacing, he did as she asked and stepped back. "I don't like to see you hurt." With a quick glance around, he continued. "It's just the seam that's split. Let's go have your glove repaired now before you lose the entire thumb cover."

"Don't be silly." She handed the barbed pineapple to the vendor and quickly chose a brace of pears to go with it. "Mending a seam is no job at all, and my girls need experience with thin leather as well as fabric."

As Elizabeth searched her reticule for the right coin, feeling all thumbs between her agitation and the split seam, Chan handed over payment and motioned toward a handled basket near the vendor. "Put the pineapple in that, if you will, and add a dozen more pears."

But for Elizabeth, the gift didn't set aside the insult she had suffered. With stiff lips and growing resentment, she said, "I don't want you buying this fruit for me. I thought I'd made that quite clear."

Taking the basket and turning to select carrots, he shook his head. "But this isn't for you. I'm taking Miss Delia a few delicacies."

Paying without dickering, he arranged his rows of carrots to one side of the fruit, lining the basket with a cushion of green tops. Basket over his arm and books under his elbow, he crossed to the egg vendor.

Nearly running to keep up with his long steps, Elizabeth struggled against mounting irritation. She didn't want *anything* from him, for herself or her aunt, after his friend's slurs. "My aunt gets anything she can dream up to eat. I provide for her every need."

"Of course you do," he agreed, layering eggs carefully onto the nest he had formed with carrot tops. Tucking her books in beside the pineapple and pears, Lord Chandler slipped the loaded basket over one arm and took her elbow. "It never hurts to have more than you need, in gifts and friends. A person doesn't always know what they want to dream about. Come along. This basket is too heavy for you to carry. I'll walk with you and give it to Miss Delia myself."

Feeling annoyed and beset, she protested. "That's what you meant to do by finally coming after me, isn't it? You mean to beguile me with your nonsense all the way home, then pamper Aunt Delia so I will forget your hateful friend's insults. It won't work."

Pulling her to a stop, he set down the basket in the middle of the marketplace crowd and took her by the shoulders. Staring earnestly into her eyes, he said, "I wish I could have stopped Ash from saying that, Elizabeth. I don't want you offended in any way, by anyone. The slur was said, and I can't cancel it out any more than I can send rain back into the clouds. I have his word he won't say anything like that near you again, if that's any comfort."

Hardly able to bear the intensity of his sincere gaze, Elizabeth raised her chin but looked away. "How can I be comfortable when Mr. Williams and a dozen other people at Hazard's overheard what he said about me?"

"Look at me, Elizabeth." His fingers tightened and, blinking back moisture, she complied. "What good would a hot denial have done? Did you really want me to argue your virtue with Ash at that busy counter? We could have been there still, yelling at each other until every person within a block collected to hear it. I could have challenged him to a duel for insulting you and had the whole of Bath buzzing your name. Did you really want that much notice given to Ash's rude, brainless, cruel comment?"

The rough anger in his tone brought her the first relief she'd felt since rushing out of Hazard's. She peeked up at him past the chip bonnet's brim. "Did you say that to him, call him rude and cruel?"

"That," he said, frowning, "and worse." He let go of her and picked up the basket, his expression stormy and bleak. "We came as close to parting ways as I ever want to come with Ash."

Taking his proffered arm, she moved toward the arches leading to the street. Elizabeth looked up at his set jaw and mouth, and noticed fine lines pinching the outer corners of his eyes as he stared ahead. He had actually quarreled with his best friend over the insult to her, risked breaking a bond that he valued like a family tie.

The fury and pain inside her since the scene in the lending library burned down to embers. His defense acted as a salve to her sore spirits.

"I made Ash say immediately that he had mistaken you for someone else." He sounded embarrassed. "It was the best I could think of at once to spare your reputation."

New emotions washed over the embers of her anguish, nearly extinguishing it. She could return to Hazard's after all. She felt fiercely pleased that Chan hadn't allowed even so close a crony to malign her unchallenged.

"You can mend fences between you, can't you?" She felt as tentative about asking as she sounded. Little as she knew about lifelong friendships, she knew less about settling disagreements that arose in them.

Shrugging, he grimaced. "Maybe. I hope things go more smoothly for everyone now."

Relieved as he was to have made it this far in apologizing to Elizabeth for Ash's witless insult, more had to be said. Maybe the hardest part.

"Elizabeth, I need to ask something of you."

"I can't imagine what it might be."

176

They had almost reached Laura Place. "Let's turn here and head for Bathwick Park," he suggested. "The walk to your house from there won't be much longer, if you aren't tired."

"I often walk home by way of the park." Her rounded, golden eyes glinted curiosity at him. "Besides, you're the one carrying the burden."

"I hardly notice it." Sometimes he did feel laden these days, juggling Ash's, Elizabeth's, and Lady Enfield's differing needs. But he was a man of honor and would drop none of them.

They walked down the street, passing the many town houses rented out to Bath's visitors on long leases. "I asked for Ash's word on two things. He will be civil to you if you meet again, and he'll avoid you if he finds that difficult."

Her quick upward look pleased him. "Thank you."

But next came the hard part. "Can you try to overlook his outburst today and be civil to him if you come together again?"

This time her look was incredulous. "I'm polite to everyone. Are you implying I provoked the duke's insults?"

He shook his head and said earnestly, "Nothing excuses what Ash said, in public, about you. I'm not trying to defend him, just asking you to try to understand a couple of things about him."

Her face was now hidden by her bonnet's wide brim. "I don't like what I already understand about the duke."

"Little wonder." Though Ash and Elizabeth might never be close friends, he hoped they could come to tolerate each other. "The two of you got off on the wrong foot over this cursed legacy. But it's not the money involved that makes him determined to bring it back into the estate."

Her swift sidelong look was ironic. "Sixty thousand

pounds sounds like a considerable fortune to me."

"It is, but Ash can manage without it. He'd even be better off for learning better management of his assets." Getting rid of a string of racehorses would help for a start, but he wouldn't mention that to Elizabeth. "What Ash resented about the arrangement between his father and your mother was the attention it took away from him. He was angry that his father chose to spend time with a woman other than his mother, and not with him. To have a significant sum of money left to that woman he already resented just rubbed salt in the wound."

Head turned away, Elizabeth gave a bitter laugh. "I didn't care for that aspect any more than he did."

"Then perhaps you can see his viewpoint to a small extent."

"I'm not the woman he thought I was. I'm not Lucinda." She flashed him a molten look. "Perhaps you could make him see that obvious point."

"I try." If only Ash were less stubborn. "Another thing few people understand about Ash is that he's overly sensitive about his lameness."

Her tone was sharp. "I would never jeer at him about it, if that's what you fear."

"I don't think you would." How did one explain another person's outlook in a few sentences, without tattling like a gossip? "Maybe it's more accurate to say Ash takes offense easily because of being lame. It seems like he's battled everyone since . . ." Lord Chandler paused. "I'd understand if he wanted to fight me. He wouldn't limp if he hadn't taken time to shove me to safety during a cave-in when we were boys."

As she gazed up, her eyes seemed to search deep inside him, sensing more than he'd revealed. "You blame yourself for that."

Her focus on his reaction instead of his liability surprised him. The few women who had learned about his role in Ash's laming had clucked and shrieked over the tragedy, but Elizabeth was like *Grandmère*. While she felt things deeply, she recognized his feelings and acquitted him of blame, even though he couldn't absolve himself.

He tried to explain. "Having your life saved by a friend creates an obligation to do anything possible for him. Especially when he paid such a price."

Looking thoughtful, she said, "It could feel that way."

"The point I want to make isn't about that." His feelings made him uncomfortable and weren't relevant to the point he needed to make. "Ash's split-second choice as a boy changed him forever, and not just in his physical abilities. I almost lost his friendship then.

"His mother huddled over him while he struggled to recover, as if no one existed but the two of them. She wanted to keep him in bed, even when the doctor brought in crutches. She tried to turn him into a puling infant."

Anger at the duchess twisted his gut still. "From the moment I carried him home on my back, she detested me. Didn't want me near him again. The duke was the one who saw we needed each other's support and brought him to see me."

At mention of Ash's father, Elizabeth's posture straightened. Chan hurried to finish. "We needed to talk out what had happened in that cave. It had happened to us together, and nobody else knew the horror of it. But though we talked, Ash was never quite the same. It was as if he were set on proving himself as much a man as his father—even lamed. He came out of bed with his fists up, and he's been hot at hand ever since."

"Merciful heavens," said Elizabeth, eyes wide. "And I swung a poker at him. It's a wonder I survived."

"Ash can hardly hold loss of temper against you. He has too loose a grip on his own. But part of his problem is the constant pain, even if he won't talk about it. Often he's not angry at the people he attacks, so much as he's enraged at the pain he's always in. What I'm getting at is, it takes next to nothing to set him off."

"And I set him off at Hazard's?" She didn't look convinced. "The truth is, he doesn't like me because of . . . who I am."

"Because you're Lucinda's daughter. He *is* prejudiced by that connection, and I'm not certain he'll see reason anytime soon. You don't have much incentive to think well of him, but he resented your coldness toward him when you appeared from behind me at Hazard's."

Stopping at the edge of the park, Elizabeth set her hands on her hips and glared at him. "My coldness? He resented— Well! That man insulted me in my own house and upset my aunt. He did his best to seduce one of my maids. Before I said a word at Hazard's, he had announced to the room that you were womanizing. Since I was the only female near you, it seemed natural to take offense at that, even before he called me a . . . used a vulgar term."

"Your reaction is entirely natural." Setting down the basket, Chan clasped her widespread elbows. "I don't mean you shouldn't have been upset. But Ash assured me he didn't notice you as he came down the steps, and very likely he didn't. Steps are the devil on his twisted leg, so he has to pay attention where he lands his foot."

As she stared with doubt stamping her lovely features, he tried again. "If Ash said he didn't see you before he spoke to me, he didn't. Besides, half the time I don't recognize women myself under those blasted concealing hats you wear." He threw up his hands. "Footpads might keep their necks out of nooses longer if they used poke bonnets instead of mufflers to hide their faces."

Tension ebbed out of Elizabeth's expression as she gazed at him. Her curved lids half closed and a gurgle sounded in her throat. Hands going over her mouth, she giggled. "F-footpads in poke bonnets?"

The laughter she tried to smother set him grinning.

Then they were both laughing, shared looks sending them into renewed gales like schoolchildren. Relief lightened the weight of this horrible day. "If you don't get the full mental picture," he said in a gasp, "I can put on your chip bonnet to show you what I mean."

Clinging to his arm, she laughed harder. "Maybe you should do that in private to save your reputation."

As she pulled a handkerchief out of her tapestry reticule and dabbed at her eyes, he picked up the basket. They strolled into the park as Chan appreciated how quickly the day had brightened.

"To answer your initial question, I can be polite to your friend." Elizabeth tucked her hand into the crook of his arm and he savored the feel of its light pressure. "I'll make a point of it if we have to meet. Then if he's horrid to me again, I'll remind myself that he's probably in pain."

"I've made a mess of trying to explain." Chan smiled at her. He couldn't recall hearing her laugh this much before today, and already he craved more of the musical sound. "Don't make allowances for Ash if he's vile again. Just leave and let me deal with him."

"I don't need you to defend me," she protested. "And don't stand between me and your friend as you attempted to do at Hazard's."

The desire to protect her warred with his duty to Ash. Feeling split in two, he struggled to support Elizabeth without disloyalty to Ash. "Just don't believe you deserve his scorn and maybe you won't be as hurt by it. Sometimes when you understand people better, it's easier to overlook their mistakes. He's a much better man than he's shown you he is. So far you've seen only his worst side."

She sighed as gently as the current stirring leaves on nearby oaks. "That's hardly my fault, but I'll try to show better manners than he, at least. Whatever my personal opinion of the duke, he's important to you, and I don't want to stir problems between you."

He hadn't expected that level of acceptance from her when Ash couldn't give it. "You really care that he and I get past this? Even though he hurt you."

"I care about your feelings, not his." She was honest enough to admit the distinction, and he appreciated it. "I don't know what it's like to have a friend near your age, someone who has known you so long you have nothing to hide between you, important or not. I haven't been that close with anyone but Aunt Delia. It must feel good to have a friend you can tell anything you feel or think."

Chan rubbed the back of his neck. "It isn't quite like that with Ash. We tell each other what we think, and that can end up in arguments. Not that our wrangles ever mattered before." He shook his head. "As for feelings, I don't discuss them much with Ash or anyone else."

They emerged from Bathwick Park in mutual silence and set out across the rougher ground toward her house. Elizabeth seemed less upset than when he'd first found her at the market, and that was a relief.

"Aunt Delia will be delighted with her gifts." Her sidelong glance and smile buoyed his spirits. "Though friends have brought her fruit, no one ever gave her eggs and carrots before."

"I wouldn't want to become predictable." If only he could give something to Elizabeth she valued, too, after her generosity regarding Ash. Perhaps he could. "Tell me, does your aunt enjoy cheese and cider?"

"Both of us do, but you really mustn't show up at my door with food on every visit, or the neighbors will think I've lost all my money on exchange."

Her teasing gaze let him feel he'd brought something into her life besides trouble. "Tell me if you find yourself penniless. I'm a friend you can turn to in need."

Quickly, she said, "My father provided for me adequately, though I thank you for the offer."

Did Elizabeth really believe investments could meet every need? The thought of her losing her aunt, as he had *Grandmère,* then living alone for the rest of her life, saddened him. "Money was just an illustration. I'll be honored if you ask my help in any situation that might come up."

Pink-faced, she frowned and looked away. A strand of silence spun between them. Breaking it, she spoke. "Why did you ask about cheese and cider a moment ago?"

Maybe her reluctance to accept anything from him could be dodged. "The best cheeses and cider I've ever tasted come from an estate near Winsley, not five miles distant." Now he'd dangle the best bait. Leaning close he confided, "It takes extra dairy maids to make good cheese in the quantity they produce."

Her beautiful face glowed as she took his meaning. "And you think I might be able to place some of my girls there?"

He nodded.

"Oh, Chan! How considerate of you to think of that." She skipped once, to his delight. "Do you know the estate's owners well enough to talk them into taking on one of my girls? Are they the sort of people my girls would be safe with?"

"I wouldn't suggest a place for your girls that wasn't safe. You'd take the poker and shovel to me." He grinned at her obvious eagerness. "You may already know them. Have you met Lord Stretford and his pretty young wife?"

They neared the lime tree in her back garden.

"I may have heard Lady Rowe speak of them. They must be London acquaintances of hers and not frequent visitors to Bath. The town is hardly full of fashionable visitors anymore. Do you think Lady Stretford might need maids in London as well as in the country? Perhaps she would be willing to recommend my girls to others, if they give satisfaction."

Her enthusiastic expression shifted toward doubt. "Your offer of an introduction is wonderful, but what if my girls aren't well enough trained? They've had no experience in a dairy. I try to prepare them for all household jobs, but what if I'm teaching them the wrong things?"

"No one could teach them everything." A fierce desire to shield her from all worries filled him. "The attitude about working that you teach them matters more than specific skills."

Standing back, he let her walk ahead of him on the narrow path through the small kitchen garden. "You may not be impressed enough with Lady Stretford to send any of your girls to her. You'll evaluate job situations, too, you know, and not just wait for potential employers to sit in judgment on your training. It's an important part of helping your maids reach self-sufficiency, putting them with the right people in their first workplaces."

Stopping with her hand on the back door latch, Elizabeth looked at him with concern that was almost comical. "I hadn't realized the extent of the responsibility when I thought about training and placing maids. I need to watch for the lecherous husbands, sons, and footmen in households instead of just warning the girls to beware. At least you've warned me in time to think about it."

So she still saw men as villains. "Don't believe that only men threaten your girls' well-being. A self-centered mistress who doesn't care about her staff won't make their lives any easier, either."

"I wasn't fair, was I?" She opened the door. "You're right, of course. Women can create misery for other females, too."

As he followed her inside the dim lower passage between kitchen and scullery, she removed her chip bonnet and tucked up falling strands of hair before a small glass.

184

He longed to run his fingers into the loose arrangement, feel its silky texture. He ached to pull Elizabeth close against him, absorb her warmth as he stroked the full breasts thrust together by her uplifted arms.

What a shock it would be for Cook if she popped out of her domain.

Besides, it was hardly a proper urge for one friend to feel about another. Sighing, he admitted he didn't think too clearly at times. Especially where Elizabeth was concerned.

Chapter Eleven

"Don't leap down from the curricle by yourself; you'll look too eager." Chan's grin teased Elizabeth as she watched him step down the opposite side, hand the reins to a boy, and circle the carriage.

The past two days had dragged by in an endless wait for this visit to the Stretford estate. She had perched on the edge of the seat during the drive toward Winsley. Her eagerness to learn whether this might be a suitable place for her girls to work was matched only by her apprehension to know whether the mistress would consider hiring girls she had trained.

Chan had refused to tell her more about the lady of the house, saying she must learn to size up households and employers for herself.

Now he offered his hand and she turned to him readily, accepting his support as she stepped carefully onto the narrow metal step and then to the ground. Adjusting her shawl over her elbows, she tried to feel dignified and discerning, instead of nervous as a schoolgirl facing the headmistress.

"Chan!"

A feminine cry of joy scattered the serenity outside the imposing gabled manor as a lady flew out the massive doors and threw herself into Chan's ready arms. "You could have let me know you were coming, you wretched man."

He laughed as he swung their hostess off her feet in a hug that showed froths of lace on her petticoats. A little shocked, Elizabeth thought she glimpsed lace-edged pantalets.

"Do I need an invitation to visit you?" he asked.

"No, never."

Elizabeth stood apart on the wide stone stoop, watching the boisterous greeting. Such an extravagant display of warmth made her feel stiff and awkward. She wasn't accustomed to open displays of affection between men and women. She wondered if they were even proper. Was this a suitable mistress for one of her girls? Such easy manners might indicate too much familiarity among staff.

Chan didn't seem to think his welcome was too demonstrative, but then Lady Stretford was a beauty. Her perfect teeth flashed in the sun as she smiled at both her guests. Behind her the door still swung from her energetic appearance. Long curls bounced at her graceful neck, emerging from the profusion of hair piled elegantly at the back of her head.

Elizabeth pushed an errant strand from her precarious hair arrangement of the day under her bonnet. If only this had been Sally's day to help her dress and arrange her hair. This whirlwind of womanly perfection left Elizabeth feeling gawky and untidy. Being fashionable or beautiful hadn't mattered to her before, but the thought

187

of Chan comparing her with this lovely lady was dismaying.

Chan and the perfect portrait of womanhood both turned her way at the same moment, smiles matched in upward tilts to one side. Their eyes glinted with the iridescence of coal, elongated under sooty lashes that gave them duplicate looks of devilment.

"Elizabeth, this pretty butterfly is my cousin Ann, Lady Stretford. Ann, this beautiful lady is Miss Elizabeth Merriman."

His cousin. Relieved, Elizabeth dipped a curtsy.

Holding out her hands, Lady Stretford said, "I'm glad Chan brought you to visit. You're Evie's friend, too, for she mentioned you in a recent note." Her smile widened. "Come inside and catch your breath from that long drive. We'll have tea or lemonade or cider, whichever appeals to you most, while we talk."

"Thank you. Cider will do nicely." How stiff and formal her voice sounded, compared to the gay tinkle of this lovely lady's tone. Though this was meant to be a meeting on business more than a social call, she couldn't help noticing contrasts.

Chan's cousin wore light, delicate colors and embroidered, beribboned trims that suited her slight form. He obviously adored her. Perhaps he preferred dainty ladies with bubbling personalities to her serious ways.

Chan touched Elizabeth's elbow and they followed his cousin into the cool shadows of the long stone manor house with its eaves concentrated at one end. Elizabeth knew pure envy of another woman—not for the manor but for her manner.

Playfulness was foreign to Elizabeth's experience with men. Yet Lady Stretford chattered over a curved shoulder to Chan as she entered the house with a natural assurance Elizabeth longed to possess. How would it feel to hold his attention with this lighthearted informality?

Lady Stretford spoke in passing to the butler standing to one side of the entrance hall. "Masters, we'll have cider in the small drawing room."

The man bowed and took Chan's hat. "At once, Lady Stretford."

"How remiss of me!" Lady Stretford stopped halfway across the tiled entrance hall and turned to Elizabeth. "May I take you up to a chamber to freshen up and put off your bonnet? We can look in on the nursery."

Chan shook his head, pulling her closer. "If you take her off, I won't see either of you again for hours. I know how you are about your children, and you'll have Elizabeth playing doll house with your oldest instead of drinking cider with me."

Elizabeth was surprised. "You have a child old enough to enjoy a doll house?"

Lady Stretford laughed. "You are delightful. My daughter is eight and my son two years younger." She said to Chan, "Elizabeth can't play with the doll house until it's mended, for the children nearly destroyed it playing fire company. One corner burned off entirely before Nanny caught them and pulled it out of the nursery fire."

"Little brats." Chan's tone sounded affectionate. "They're as dangerous together as you and I ever were."

Hastily Elizabeth assured her hostess that she wouldn't take off her bonnet. Wearing it might help her stay focused on jobs for her maids, instead of being distracted by Chan's family. Though if his cousin was a doting mother, she might look after her maidservants, too.

Despite her effort to focus on her purpose, she had noticed his attitude about the children. Interesting that Chan sounded comfortable with their pranks. Someday he might make a far different father from hers.

Across the tiled entrance hall they paraded, then up dark, polished mahogany stairs lined with portraits of showy people and beasts. Lady Stretford led them on, laughing and talking in the same breath with Chan, neither of them waiting for the other to finish sentences. This was intimacy, knowing each other so well they didn't need to hear the completed thoughts. Elizabeth envied his cousin this level of closeness with Chan.

As they reached the top of the stairs, he touched her back. She knew he was aware of her despite the foreign conversation. They followed his cousin down the wide passage on the upper floor. Pretty benches and console tables stood like a color guard on either side of the carpet.

"Lady Jersey declares she won't forgive you for throwing her invitation to dinner in her face at the last minute to rush out of London with Ash. You unbalanced her table. Even Mrs. Percival told me you could languish in the country for eternity if you dared shun her birthday ball for the prime minister, after missing her last gala for the Persian ambassador."

Laughing, Chan interrupted. "Envoy extraordinaire and minister plenipotentiary, if you please. The ambassador doesn't want the formalities ignored when it comes to his honors."

"That's just with you." His cousin made a face at him. "You threaten his great popularity with the ladies. He lets me be as familiar as I like."

"I'm better suited to the ladies of Bath," he protested. "Let the ambassador have London's finest."

Elizabeth enjoyed the look he sent her way. She didn't know the London personalities they discussed as familiars. Kind as Chan had been to her and Aunt Delia, his world of foreign ambassadors and prime ministers was far above her quiet life in Bath. Soon he would return to it, and she really should prepare Aunt Delia to depend on him less. The thought lowered her spirits.

"Everywhere I go, people ask me if you're ill." Lady Stretford shook her finger at Chan and motioned her guests to seats. "You can't hide in Bath for the rest of the Season."

Elizabeth sank onto a sofa with a sinuous winged back and dragon's feet.

Chan sat by her, leaning an elbow on its raised, padded end. He stretched a long arm along the fanned wooden wing behind her, offering a wicked smile. "Tell anyone who asks that I never felt better. Something about Bath must agree with me."

Her delicate dark eyebrows winging upward like Chan's, Lady Stretford said in a knowing voice, "So I see."

Elizabeth felt a little ill at ease, sitting on a fierce dragon sofa with this devilishly handsome man. White and gold throughout the room brightened the Nile green upholstery. Light colors were at odds with the small-paned windows and heavy stone outside, though the dragon seemed at home.

"Never mind London's fripperies." Chan disposed of the topic with a suitable gesture. "Elizabeth's here for a purpose. She's training girls as maids. You'll want to speak up for at least one before they're all promised."

Elizabeth flushed at his blunt introduction of the subject. She hadn't meant him to foist her girls on his kinfolk. "My girls aren't ready for placement quite yet. They still have a great deal to learn."

Lady Stretford stared a moment, looking between Elizabeth and Chan. "Then this visit isn't what I thought, Chan. You never visit me with ladies on your arm. When you arrived with the most beautiful creature I've seen in your vicinity, I expected more than talk about maids."

Elizabeth stiffened at the assumption without understanding it. Then a whisper of satisfaction arched along her spine and shoulders. This elegant lady had assumed Chan brought her on a family visit—though of course that impression was quite wrong.

"Don't embarrass Elizabeth. She isn't used to the sly

insinuations of society." He spoke to his cousin but turned a tantalizing grin on Elizabeth. His fingers found her shoulder blade and traced its edge.

Looking at Lady Stretford as if he weren't making it impossible for Elizabeth to breathe, he continued. "I'm doing you a favor. You should appreciate the chance to get maids who have been trained by a lady to a lady's household standards. You're too accustomed to writing London agents when you need staff. It's time you used your flighty head to assure your husband's comfort at home."

Hunching a haughty shoulder at him, his cousin made a face. "My husband's comfort will never depend on maids, if he knows what's good for him." She turned to Elizabeth. "I'm curious about why you train maids. You don't appear to be in dire financial straits that force you into trade, and you aren't dressed for the part of an agency manager either. Those businesses don't train the people they send out anyway, from the complaints I hear. Tell me how you came to do such a thing."

Genuine interest showed in her expression, so Elizabeth answered honestly. "I haven't thought of what I'm doing as a staffing agency. I'm giving girls practical experience for positions in better households so they can make their own ways in life. I want them to have an alternative to depending on a man for a living."

"Why would any female want an alternative to marriage?" Lady Stretford clapped her hands, looking delighted and amazed. "You're an original!"

Chan grinned and ran a thumb along her back.

In her experience, people who were called "originals" were eccentric at best. Elizabeth felt old, cranky, and defensive under the label. "Your encounters with gentlemen must have given you a happy view of them. Many women without your good fortune are treated like any other piece of property when the knot is tied."

"You make marriage sound as deadly as parson's

noose, as men say." His cousin scrunched up her face at Chan.

"Another term is 'leg-shackled,' " he offered. "Hasn't Stretford complained of that feeling yet?"

Wishing Chan had never dumped her into this subject, Elizabeth tried to soften the impression she had left. "Many couples must be content in marriage, but girls from the workhouse rarely have the best prospects for husbands. I'm just offering them a way to look after themselves."

"How differently you think from most ladies." Giving her a searching look, Lady Stretford smiled. "I wonder why. But that goes beyond what I can politely ask you yet, though I long for the day I know you well enough to demand the whole story. Chan, I defy you to change her mind about gentlemen. She's far too lovely to remain on the shelf forever."

One corner of his mouth dipped in a mocking smile as he met Elizabeth's glance and held it. "Some efforts can't be hurried, and this one doesn't need you muddling in it."

Embarrassed by their banter, Elizabeth thought it must be typical of London's sophisticated circles. She felt as green as her girls the first time she had shown them finger bowls.

Chan's wicked smile teased her as she tried to look away. She slid her gaze away from his mouth. The languor of his lean body so close beside her provided no safer focus. No wonder men's lower garments were called *inexpressibles*. Chan's fitted pantaloons left her with a dry mouth and an empty mind.

Lady Stretford provided her with an escape. "Tell me how you train maids. I can't imagine telling Greer how to set up a refreshment tray." As she spoke, their hostess waved forward a black-garbed parlor maid who had entered with a footman bearing a tray behind her.

The footman set the tray on a pedestal table and carried both over to a place before Lady Stretford. He left the room quietly as she poured amber liquid into cut-crystal glasses that glinted rainbow effects in the light. Like a silent shadow, the maid took two filled glasses and handed them to Elizabeth and Chan.

Next she offered a plate of biscuits as Elizabeth used the service to illustrate her answer. "You glanced quickly over this tray before pouring out cider. You knew what you expected to find there, and had anything been missing, you would have asked your staff to fetch it. Training maids is little more than that. I believe that people learn best by doing, with guidance on how to do a task properly."

"As easy as that." Nodding dismissal to the maid, Lady Stretford slid a mischievous appraisal over Elizabeth's costume and hair. "Or perhaps not always easy. I suspect you're hardly a demanding ogre with these girls."

Elizabeth tucked the escaped strand of hair back into the confines of her chip straw bonnet and twitched her skirt over the faint scorch mark near the hem. It had faded enough so she had forgotten about it.

Raising a hand and his voice, Chan said, "Wait a moment, Greer. Do you have apricot tarts in the kitchen?"

Lady Stretford turned to the maid. "Bring an assortment of whatever sweets Cook has on hand along with a ripe cheddar. Chan, you've always preferred less sweet biscuits with cider, though you rejected even these plain cakes, I noticed. Why do you want tarts?"

"The occasional tart is a pleasure I don't deny myself." He frowned at his cousin as she giggled. "Mind your manners. Elizabeth prefers apricot tarts over any other sweet. I'm helping you entertain your guest."

Eyebrows raised, Lady Stretford smiled at Elizabeth. "This is more promising. He's bothered to learn your tastes. I've known him since he rode ponies, and though

I could tell you every food he likes least, he couldn't name one favorite food of mine."

Elizabeth spoke the first words that entered her head. "He only recalls my taste for apricot tarts because I smeared his pantaloons with one." Realizing how this might sound, she felt heat stain her throat on its way to her hairline.

"Promising indeed!" murmured Lady Stretford, eyes dancing.

Chan wagged a finger at his cousin. "You're even naughtier now than when we cousins played together at family gatherings. Save your teasing for the scandalous group you run with in London. Elizabeth isn't accustomed to your wicked banter."

Elizabeth gulped down the whole of her cool cider, grateful that Greer's entry with two additional plates ended this topic.

"Pass me Elizabeth's glass." When Chan complied, Lady Stretford filled it from the pitcher without taking it from him.

Elizabeth's fingertips grazed his on the crystal as she accepted the cool drink. Her fingers slid between his larger ones on the heavy-based glass. He didn't let go for a long moment, and their fingers lay entwined against the beautiful cut-crystal pattern. She was out of her depth, beyond her experience, feeling more lost every second. Worst of all, she wasn't certain she wanted to find her way back into the withdrawn woman she had been before Chan entered her life.

This kind of teasing talk must take place between ladies and gentlemen in society all the time, and by avoiding men, she hadn't learned to be at ease with it. She was unsophisticated enough to feel uncomfortable when it probably meant nothing.

"How do you choose the girls you help?" Lady Stretford's question came as a welcome distraction when

Chan finally released her glass. "Do you get recommendations of worthy girls from the vicar?"

"All women deserve a chance at a decent life. The workhouse is full of girls with no one to take an interest in them." Remembering those she couldn't house, Elizabeth sighed. "I would bring them all home with me if I could feed them."

Lady Stretford's teasing expression turned serious as she leaned forward. "You've been to the workhouse in Bath? I know those places exist, but I've never thought of entering one. Are the children not cared for properly?"

"The parish orphans' souls get more attention than their stomachs or futures, unfortunately. As a girl, I watched them march into morning services and felt for their motherless states." That much of their plight she had understood, for her mother, too, had abandoned her.

"The orphans learn only the dreary hardship of rough work," she continued. "Few could fit into better households. A few lucky boys may be apprenticed to a trade, but most children of either sex are sent off with the first master willing to put them to hard labor—as much as eighteen-hour days in mills and manufactories. Far too many unprotected girls end up maimed, molested, or dead."

"But I thought the situation had improved." Lady Stretford looked stricken by her description. "The bluecoat schools give orphans a better life, surely, and I've contributed to a number of societies that help needy children."

Chan set aside the plate of cheddar to answer. "Elizabeth isn't satisfied with writing out bank drafts. You should see the three girls in her care. They're healthy and eager, as well fed and dressed as any servant in your houses. When she places them, they'll know how to conduct themselves in a gentleman's house, and no lady will hesitate to have them appear before their friends. You'll be fortunate to have one of them, for Evie is telling everyone in Bath and London about Elizabeth's efforts."

Though a little embarrassed by his praise, Elizabeth basked in it.

Setting down her glass, Lady Stretford leaned forward, looking eager. "You won't let Evie have all three of them! Does one of your girls have a good hand for laundry?"

Chan grinned, twitching Elizabeth's skirt to uncover the scorch mark. "I wouldn't trust them with your best lace or linen yet. But the advantage of getting on her list now is that Elizabeth won't let them go into service until they're proficient. No London agency can promise you that. Even if they ruin every flounce and sheet in her house, she'll see that they take turns with every task to be done in a household until they get it right."

His hand rested lightly on her back, scorching through the spencer and thin muslin to her tingling skin.

Surprised, Elizabeth listened as he described the work her girls learned, even told anecdotes about their more humorous errors. She had no idea he knew such intimate details of life inside Number 6 Sydney Place.

Aunt Delia chattered, of course, which was how he knew. All those morning calls when Elizabeth had left Chan entertaining her aunt, he hadn't talked only about the weather or society, hadn't just listened to her aunt reminisce. He had asked about her efforts with the girls, taken her work seriously.

New warmth spread through Elizabeth, a sustaining glow of strength and pride in herself, lit by his sincere recognition and respect for her enterprise.

"Will you send one of your girls to me when she's ready for a place?" Lady Stretford begged. "I'll take whichever is available."

Elizabeth was grateful to Chan for stirring interest in her project, for without good places for her girls to work, her efforts to better their lives would be for naught. "If

I believe one of them would suit your household, I'll ask you to meet her. May I ask you a question now?"

Lady Stretford nodded and she continued. "What can you tell me about Greer, the maid who served us refreshments?"

Looking puzzled, Lady Stretford said, "Greer? She's the oldest daughter of our herdsman. Besides drawing room service, she helps out with fine sewing and waits on guests who come without their dressers. She made most of her sisters' clothing as they grew up. Why do you ask?"

Chan grinned at his cousin. "You're being interviewed to see if you'll do as an employer. You don't think Elizabeth will hand over her girls without knowing they'll get proper treatment, do you?"

Though she wouldn't have said it so bluntly, that had been Elizabeth's purpose. "I'll have to let them go in time, or I won't be able to train others."

Lady Stretford laughed. "If I'd realized I should try to appear responsible, I might have acted more staid with you."

"You can't be serious more than a few minutes at a time," Chan said, grinning, "and that doesn't make you any the less reliable. I'll vouch for your character, for you always took your share of the blame when we were caught in our escapades."

"No need for character references." Elizabeth smiled at Lady Stretford, liking her more every moment. "You know who your servants are. You're aware of their special talents and allow them to use them. I want that for my girls. To be seen as people."

"Then perhaps I can meet them when they're ready to be placed." Lady Stretford's smile for her was as warm as any she had given her cousin. "Of course, I'd do anything for my cousin, but this work is important. If Evie and I whisper the news to a few chosen people

with the warning that homes will be vetted before placement of your maids, you'll have far more requests than
you can fill in a lifetime." She threw her hands wide.
"Just think! Soon ladies will compete for a Bath-trained
maid like they vie for Madame Catalani to appear at
musical evenings."

"At least a maid will do them more good than an
overpaid warbler," said Elizabeth, pleased to her toes.

"A philistine!" cried Lady Stretford, jumping up to
hug her. "All three of the woman's chins and stomachs
tremble when she sings. You're as outrageous and out-
spoken as I am. Chan must have known we were kindred
spirits. What a joy to have you in the family!"

That dangerous assumption had to be corrected at
once. "But Lord Chandler and I are the merest—"

"Acquaintances," said Lady Stretford. "But Chan has
never brought any other lady to call on me—"

"And isn't likely to bring Elizabeth again if you go
on embarrassing her." Chan's scold didn't sound stern.

Arguing further would be rude, so Elizabeth didn't.
She and Chan had achieved a surprising friendship, considering his first impression of her. Friendship was more
than she had ever expected to know with a gentleman.

Rising, Chan said, "We don't want to be away from
Bath too long. Elizabeth's aunt frets if she's away for
several hours. May I take Miss Lindsey one of your
special cheeses?"

Laughing, Lady Stretford headed for the door. "I'd
best send two, for you'll visit often enough to eat more
than your share. I'll have a jug of cider put in your
curricle as well."

"You do know how to keep a man happy, though
Miss Lindsey will savor your cheddar. *Grandmère* al-
ways liked a good Winsley cheese when she came to
Bath." He approached her at the door.

He touched her shoulder with affection, and Lady
Stretford leaned her cheek against his hand briefly. "You

miss her still, don't you? That's to be expected, when she was more mother than grandmother to you."

Chan didn't reply, just exchanged a glance of close communication with his cousin.

Seeing this family affection between the cousins unsettled Elizabeth. Their touches and teasing showed feelings she hungered to know and to share. Her experience of female households left her with a yearning for this easy expression of male affection she hadn't realized she had missed.

The longing for closeness and warmth stayed with her as they took their leave and turned back toward Bath. The afternoon air was soft with spring's hope, balmy with the best of the day's sunlight. The rhythm of the horses' hooves keeping step lulled her with an enchanted sense of connection to Chan as they swayed in unison with the curricle's movement.

What a considerate man he was, supporting her effort to train and place her girls by taking her to meet his cousin. Even begging treats to tempt Aunt Delia's uncertain appetite. How fortunate she was to have such an ally, giving her a sense she was no longer alone.

When they reached the bustle of the city, she was sorry to have the ride through the awakening countryside end. Though they hadn't conversed, she had felt entirely at ease beside Chan, felt no need to entertain him or be entertained by conversation. She had never known how comfortable she could be, just riding at the side of a person, totally attuned without a word said.

At the stables behind the Sydney Hotel, he stepped down from the curricle, handed the reins to a groom, and rounded the curricle to her side. This time she didn't feel eager to come down from her high perch. She felt languorous and contented, like a cat lazing on a sunny sill after a good meal.

Chan reached up to lift her down from the carriage,

and Elizabeth couldn't look away from the strength and grace of his big hands. Holding her breath with guilty pleasure as he touched her, she wondered for the first time if her body felt supple and slim to a man's hands.

As he lifted her, she balanced herself with her hands on his shoulders. Where their bodies touched each other, the sensation reminded her of warmed currant jelly pouring over a trifle. How strange and wonderful to feel this delicious pleasure in simple touches.

He held her suspended between sky and earth for a brief, swooping flight that left her heart soaring. How marvelous the moment, for no reason at all. Her toes touched the graveled drive, curled within her half boots. These reactions were so unfamiliar they could be happening to someone else, yet the intensity of the experience seared itself deep within her.

As if her vision belonged to another observer, Elizabeth watched Chan claim her gloved right fingers. He tucked them securely around the curve of his biceps, which flexed against the blue Bath coating of his close-fitting riding jacket. Her fingers clung without instruction from her to do so.

Those were her knees, little control as she had over them, losing strength as he smiled. He pressed her hand closely against the slant of his side, captured it between the two flexing muscles of his upper arm and body.

Her traitorous, tranced body fell into the rhythm of walking beside him across the cobbled yard of the stable, through the grounds of the hotel, and out to Sydney Place. The mutual motion of simple shared steps beguiled her far more than the occasional dance she'd endured for the sake of polite participation in society. This was a revelation, the sweet torture of moving outside of time with a man without knowing or caring where the journey ended.

Then they were at the steps of Number 6, and she had

201

reached the familiarity of home, though even the stone of the row houses glowed with a more glorious golden light today. Sighing with contentment too rare to examine closely, she opened the door and led him inside.

Chapter Twelve

Though Sydney Gardens was only half-dressed in blooms to receive company, the grounds had several visitors for this early in the spring. Elizabeth felt more interest in Chan's hand under her elbow than in flowers or other guests at the breakfast that brought them here.

In the week since their visit to his cousin near Winsley, she had become increasingly aware of him in a new way. By now she could hardly string words together to make sense around him. She couldn't wait to see him and couldn't think what to say when she did. Maybe she was losing her mind.

Thank goodness Chan never lacked the ability to talk with anyone, for he and Aunt Delia had chatted together easily while she pushed food around her plate earlier. Now guests wandered the gardens while an orchestra played, and she felt tongue-tied and foolishly happy.

In rhythm with her pulse, her bonnet ribbons fluttered on a rising current of air.

"That's a strong gust." She pulled a tossed ribbon out

of her eyes. "Do you think we should take Aunt Delia home?"

Pale sunlight gilded his strong chin as he lifted his face, testing the breeze. He shook his head. "The day's warm. She's sheltered by shrubbery at the seat where we left her."

"We probably couldn't tempt her away from her friends anyway."

They exchanged an amused look, and she hugged the pleasure of sharing concern and affection for her aunt with him. After years of isolating herself from closeness with anyone but Aunt Delia, this harmony was both a revelation and an exhilaration.

What a joy Chan was, both to herself and to her aunt. Each day felt richer, brighter, with him as part of it.

"You skipped like a girl just then." Chan's dark gaze glinted over her as his mobile mouth curved upward. "What's made you this happy? Breakfast outdoors? Music? I want to arrange for you to have it every day."

Feeling carefree, Elizabeth laughed. "Everything and nothing. Sunshine, good company, and knowing Aunt Delia is happy with her friends. I know I owe a great deal of her good spirits to your influence, so you have nothing more to arrange."

Packed gravel pressed unevenly against the thin soles of her half boots as the two of them ambled along the main oblong walk through the gardens. He slipped his hand past her elbow to press her forearm gently, then cradled her arm against his side. "You made the choices about your aunt, whatever we discussed. I can't take the credit. I hope you'll always be happy in my company."

Of course he meant during the time he remained in Bath. She hugged his comment to herself anyway. A note in his voice caressed her ears and hidden places deep within her body and spirit. She wished for more with Chan without needing to define what it might be.

"You've done far too much for Aunt Delia and me

already." She almost ran her words together in her rush to divert herself and him from the unknown territory. This moment was enough for now, and she wanted to keep its perfection forever. "I can't thank you enough for introducing me to your cousin, for example. Did you know Lady Stretford wrote me after we visited her? She asked me to send the girls to her estate to learn cheese making in her dairy."

Her eagerness over the opportunity he had made possible bubbled out of her. "Think of all the estates surrounding Bath that produce their own cheeses. My girls can be assured of good positions if they know how to make Winsley cheddar."

"That's grand news. Sounds like my cousin wants to ensure she gets at least one of your maids." He nodded to a passing couple. "I'll drive the girls out when you're ready to send them."

"Thank you, Chan." She had known he would make that offer, saving her the worry of finding safe transport for the girls. "I want them to have this invaluable experience, of course, but they will have to decide whether one of them goes there to work or not. I'm doing this training so they will have choices. I don't mean to force them into situations they don't want."

"That's wise. People are more likely to work hard and be content in a job they choose." He grinned. "Somehow I can't imagine Sally making cheese for the rest of her days."

Nodding, she sighed. "No, and I'm afraid she won't be in service long, no matter where she's placed. Sally's far too fond of flirting to avoid marriage—or worse—for long."

"Why should she avoid getting married?" His tone was light but his brow creased. "The skills you're teaching Sally would prepare her to make some lucky farmer an excellent wife."

For the first time, she felt defensive about her attitude

toward marriage. "Becoming a farmer's wife, or any other man's for that matter, would make her an unpaid servant with no more say over herself or her children than a cow or sheep has."

"I call that a harsh judgment." The ends of Chan's slanted eyebrows rose toward his curved hat brim. "Most men are decent enough. She might be doted on; her husband might dance to her tune."

"Women are more likely to be beaten, abandoned, or ignored." The arguments came automatically, from habit. The trembling anger this subject usually swept through her limbs was oddly absent today. "I'm not training my girls so they can waste their lives as slaves or strumpets."

Uncertain about her long-held views despite her contentions, she challenged him. "You defend marriage to me, and yet you haven't wed."

Laughter was his answer as he glanced away at planned vistas down leafy walks at the sides of the main path. "It's too fine a day to argue about that or anything else. You're giving your girls the tools to build a future, and they'll use them well to construct what they need."

Of course he was right. She knew she must send her girls out into the world to make their way or to make ducks and drakes of their opportunities. She didn't look forward to exposing them to risks servant girls faced, but today wasn't the time to dwell on it.

"What's that sticking up above the shrubbery and trees?" He pointed ahead and to the right, where a tall contraption with a seat swinging at the top loomed into the sky. "It looks like a Merlin swing."

"So it is." Pride in her city welled up. She loved living in Bath. "You'll find most of the amusements here you find in London, despite Brighton's growing popularity. You have to earn your ride to overlook the park from the swing's highest point, though, for it's located in the middle of the labyrinth."

"Do you think I can't conquer it?" He guided her onto a side path, out of the way of strollers coming along behind them. "Even without the key to the maze, I could find my way in and out again. Let's go."

Chuckling, she looked up at him, taken with the curve of his hair onto his temples under the curly brim of his beaver hat. His eyes laughed with her, and she realized how often mirth seasoned their exchanges these days. Laughter had come back to her along with Chan, one of the best gifts he had brought her.

"I wouldn't dare question your abilities in any area," she said. "It must take more than a maze or a dangerous ride above the trees to strike fear into your heart." She shivered, smiling. "You won't get me on it, though."

"You're afraid of Merlin's swing?" His tone teased but he also sounded disbelieving. "You've never gone up in it?"

"No." She hugged herself. "I don't like heights, and that rickety contraption looks hazardous to me."

"I'd take you up with me, if the operator had a hope of winching up my considerable weight and yours at the same time."

"The seat's too small for us both, thank heaven, as broad as your shoulders are." She could feel herself flush as her gaze traversed his big, masculine body.

"You could sit on my lap, and I'd hold you so tight you wouldn't have room for fear." His arms encircled the air in a demonstration.

Elizabeth wanted to step inside that boundary. "That should start a scandal I'd never live down."

How horrified the Peplow sisters would be, who were even now walking past arm in arm, if she followed her impulsive inclination to hug him right in front of them.

"I'm not too cowardly to do daring things," she said, wanting his good opinion. "I've been as far as the second chamber of the Wookey Hole, for instance, and many of my schoolmates wouldn't enter the caverns at all."

"You've actually been inside the Wookey Hole?" His gaze and tone showed surprise as he took her arm again to walk along the side path. "Surely a dank, dark cave is more fearsome than a ride above the trees in the open air. I've heard the caverns talked about, of course."

"Then you've never explored it," she said, satisfied her courage was established.

Chan looked uneasy. "No, though I've heard the rock formations inside are impressive."

Glad to have experienced something he hadn't, she teased him with a description. "It's another world of sculpted stone walls like swirls of streaked frosting. Buildups from dripping mineral water look like misshapen organ pipes. You really must see it while you're so close. It's little more than a mile beyond Wells."

Looking away, he said, "I won't have time for seeing sights while I'm here, as busy as I am so far." He hunched his shoulders as if chilled. "A wet, cold cave doesn't seem like a place to take a lady. I'd rather spend time with you when I'm free than take in the most spectacular attractions."

Elizabeth sensed his aversion to the famous cavern even as she appreciated the compliment. He seemed to find time to do many things. "I suppose it's your friend's business that keeps you so busy."

"Yes," he agreed. "I've seen Lady Enfield nearly every day since you led me to her, but I can't claim to be closer to settling the legacy issue."

The talk about Lucinda and Ashcott made Elizabeth tense. "It seems important to you to help him, so I wish you success."

Stopping, he faced her. "Enough to help me?"

An inner door closed, and she regretted the retreat within herself. "I really don't see any way I could possibly help you."

"But you can." He took her hand, toying with her fingers. "Lady Enfield wants two things. If I can help bring either about, she's more likely to negotiate with me on the inheritance." He folded down all but her index finger. "One is an opportunity to talk with you, to ask your pardon for sending you away twelve years ago."

Looking into his dark eyes, she read his need and his reluctance to ask her to do this. Much as Chan had done for her and Aunt Delia, she wished she could give him what he asked. With reluctance, she said, "I don't want or need her apology. I don't want to see her any more than I ever did."

"Your mother really needs to see you, though." Cradling her gloved hand, he looked at it rather than at her. "Is it reasonable, refusing her even a chance to confess to you that she was wrong?" He shook his head. "Never mind. If you can't give her that much, maybe you'll consider her other plea."

"I'm not a priest, to grant her absolution." Elizabeth felt implied criticism, whether he intended it or not. She tried again to explain her feelings. "I can't be the daughter she seems to want at this late date, so seeing me would only hurt her."

Keeping a loose hold on her hand, he stood staring over her head. Finally he extended her first two fingers. "With your emotions still set against your mother, you may deny her second wish, too, even though I believe it's what your aunt wants."

"Which is?"

"Allow your mother and aunt to visit together."

Though she had half expected this reply, it unsettled her. Wanting to escape the entire subject, Elizabeth pulled her hand away and hurried off down a branching path beyond Chan. A small pagoda stood at the end in a secluded spot among shrubs.

As his footfalls followed, she flung words over her shoulder. "Please don't ask that of me, for I can't bring myself to do it. I can't have Aunt Delia upset by that woman."

"How can you be certain seeing Lady Enfield would distress her? Miss Delia seems anxious enough to talk to Lucinda when her mind is clouded." His voice sounded closer. "Think about it. Maybe that's the only time she's free to show what she really wants, given your stubborn attitude."

His reasonable tone crawled up her back like a hateful insect, and she shrugged it away. "I can't talk about this any more. Please don't make me. I've told you how I feel, and I can't help my feelings."

Reaching the small pagoda, she hurried into its shelter, hurt by his show of sympathy for the woman who had rejected her as a girl. She didn't want to cry in front of him. No matter how much he misunderstood her feelings, she didn't want to look like a typical female watering pot.

Big hands cupped her shoulders. She felt the heat of his body down the length of her back and legs even without touching him. Her desire to lean back against him, to feel his strong arms fold around her body, confused her. It made no sense, wanting to hide from him and at the same time longing for him to hold her.

The pagoda's small space swarmed with emotions buzzing from too many directions. She wanted to turn into his arms and cry out the despondence of that abandoned girl all those years ago. She wanted to drum his broad chest hard with both fists, damning him for caring about Lucinda, the woman who loved a mere man more than her child. She wanted him to understand her feelings, not protect Lucinda's. She felt betrayed.

Holding herself together by clasping her elbows, she hurried to the other side of the small enclosure.

"Maybe I seem stubborn to you, and maybe I am," she said. "I don't know anymore." She shook her head without clearing it. "I just can't trust her again, not with

Aunt Delia or myself. It was too easy for her to leave us before. She might do it again. Aunt Delia couldn't make that adjustment at her age."

"Listen to me," Chan begged, as quiet and reasonable as if he knew best. "To do the right thing here, you don't have to approve of what your mother did or forgive her for sending you away. She doesn't ask for your approval, and she doesn't believe she deserves your forgiveness." He paused. "But if you need to carry anger around for the rest of your days, that's a burden nobody can pry out of your grasp."

Stiffening, she gritted her teeth. He made it sound like her fault. As if she had chosen to be hurt and indignant, as if she wanted to feel agitated every time she was reminded of the woman's existence. Lucinda had created this nightmare for them all, not Elizabeth.

He approached her again, and Chan's big hands caressed the tight muscles of Elizabeth's shoulders. Pleasurable sensations washed up her nape and down her spine. She withstood their enticement.

Whispering next to her ear, he coaxed her. "Let go of the past. It's hurting you even worse than your mother. It's made you blind to your aunt's needs. Limiting your aunt's contact with family is cruel.

"No, don't pull away. I won't let you. Admit that your aunt Delia sees you as Lucinda in her mental confusions because she longs to see her niece again. Those two women were close friends before you were born. They shared anticipation of your birth and handed you back and forth between them before you could walk. They loved each other even before they loved you."

The vivid pictures he evoked were unfair. She had seen the close attachment between the two women who made up her world as a child.

A sob escaped Elizabeth's strained throat when she finally took a breath. She pulled free, putting her hands over her ears. His persuasive words and searing hands could make anything seem right. She couldn't think when his reasoning went against every emotion she harbored.

Stumbling to a shaped support under the pagoda's upturned eve, she leaned her forehead against it. Her bonnet bumped to the back of her head. Holding her breath often stopped hiccups; maybe it would work with tears.

A creak of the plank flooring warned her he was close. "I'm sorry; I don't want you hurt. Not by me or anyone else. Not ever." He sighed. "If I didn't care deeply about all three of you—Lady Enfield, Miss Delia, and you—I'd leave you to bumble this out alone. It's a family matter, and I'd stay out of it. But I take friendship as seriously as family connections, and I want to be a good friend to you."

"I'm not certain I can bear up under your k-kindness." She felt more torment than the sarcasm she put into her tone revealed.

He blew out a long breath. "No, it's not kind, but as I tell Ash, sometimes you do a friend a favor when you rub their noses in the dirt they blind themselves with."

Fists clinched against her distress, Elizabeth swung toward him. She wanted to push Chan away when he confused her like this. "Ash. That's who you're really concerned about. You aren't badgering me out of concern for what's best for Aunt Delia or me; you just want to make Lucinda happy so that you can get the disputed legacy back for your friend."

Chan shook his head, his lips tight. "If you'll use your head instead of your emotions, you'll know that isn't true."

Striking out at him left her feeling even more solitary. "Aunt Delia is the only close family I have left. You're asking me to give her up just because Lucinda's lost her precious duke and feels lonely—to give her back to Lucinda. Why can't my mother learn what it feels like to be cast aside, with no one to care if she wakes in the night feverish or afraid? It's her turn to be miserable."

Sobs broke loose in wrenching storms that shook Elizabeth to her toes. She gulped in an effort to contain the painful gusts of weeping and choked on the effort as they burst out despite her.

Then strong arms came around her, pressing her into the hard yet yielding wall of Chan's chest. Clinging to his lapels, she gave way to the flood gushing its way out, sweeping away all concern for time and place. Through the despair, she felt only the aching, empty places within herself and the comfort of the viscount holding her.

In time she came back to herself, and heard his consoling murmurs. She felt his hands caressing her back, steadying her, bringing her close against his body. She felt the hard angles and dormant power of his frame; it drew around her like a living shield, and she drew strength from it.

As her sobs slowed, she said with a gasp, "I don't even know why I'm crying with you."

"Hush," he crooned. "You don't have to know why. Something needs to get out, so let it come. I'm here." He pushed her loose bonnet the rest of the way off and cradled her head closer against his waistcoat.

Sniffling between sobs, she fingered the frill that had fanned stiffly out from his shirt placket. Now it hung limp and wet as laundry on the line. She couldn't have done it and his cravat more damage if she had dumped a pitcher of water over him.

The thought made her smile a little, when she had thought she'd never stop crying. Pulling back without leaving the protected enclosure of his arms, she searched in her dangling reticule for a handkerchief. Coming up with a scrap of linen graced with a broad border of needle lace, she shook it out. "Have you ever seen anything as useless as a lady's handkerchief? How could anyone be expected to do more than whisk away crumbs with this ridiculous thing?"

Fumbling at his inner coat pocket, Chan produced a manly square of white linen. He didn't let go of her, and returned both arms around her as soon as she had his handkerchief.

Using it with more energy than elegance, she drew in a deep breath and wondered at how much lighter she felt. "Bless you," she murmured. "You always seem to have just what I need."

"I want that to be true." His voice was low, and when she looked up, his intense gaze burned with tender concern.

"I've ruined your frill." She mangled it further, trying to press out the dampness. With an effort to speak lightly, she might keep herself from crying again. "What will people think, when you always look bandbox perfect, to see you with your linen wet?"

His devilish smile broke over his face like dawn over the horizon. "Never mind; I'll say I leaned too close to a fountain if anyone is nosy enough to ask. The important thing is, how are you?"

A finger under her chin, he tilted her face up.

Elizabeth turned her head, not wanting him to see her puffy red lids.

His hand firm but gentle, he laid a palm along her cheek and urged her face toward his.

She wouldn't look up. "I'd rather you didn't see me in this state. It's bad enough you watched me flood like a monsoon."

His warm mouth pressed against her lids, each in turn. Eyes closed, she drifted onto a warm sea, suspended above all cares. As his hands had made magic in every previous contact, his lips mesmerized in these drugging, intimate touches. Where his mouth claimed her face, she yearned for his heat and tenderness. How wonderful to come alive to him with this new awareness of her skin

214

and soul. She turned her head slightly to invite the rich favor of his lips for all of her face.

Deep inside, her body awoke to the warmth of his mouth, making her draw back even as she pressed forward. This consuming blaze could too easily burn out of control. Leaning her forehead on his sodden frill, she hid from the immense pleasure he offered. She didn't want it to end—but couldn't let it continue.

When he tipped up her chin again, she caught his hand and pressed her mouth against his fingers, drinking in its masculine scent and shape. Holding his palm against her cheek, she said, "That was lovely, and if you don't stop right now I'll have to run away."

"You leave me no choice then." He kissed her hair lightly and let her go. "I'm in no condition to chase after you at the moment."

He made a swift adjustment to his pantaloons as she moved away. She pretended not to notice, pleased and a little fearful that their unexpected sensuality had affected him as much as it had her.

"I didn't intend to create such a scene, let alone leak all over you." Her hands didn't know what to do, so they made senseless gestures.

"You've probably never let yourself go like that, and it was long overdue." His back turned, Chan leaned a hand against a pierced support of the pagoda. "I should have realized this subject is still too intense for you to talk about easily, especially away from your own home. I shouldn't have pushed you."

"No, I shouldn't be so emotional." She wiped her eyes and straightened like a soldier called to attention. "I'm not a fragile female to be protected from every disturbing thought."

"I'd rather protect than harass you. And expressing your feelings isn't a weakness for which to apologize." He grinned at her over his shoulder. "You can wilt my shirt anytime you need a good cry."

"Why is it called a 'good' cry when it hurts?" She sighed, feeling her raw throat protest. She still didn't understand what had gotten into her, to set off such a display of waterworks. "I don't want you to think of me as a silly female who cries over nothing. . . ."

His lips twitched in a smile as he propped a shoulder against the decorative support. "You're the strongest woman I know, if the most stubborn. 'Weak' and 'silly' don't apply to you. After all, you've been as far as the second chamber of the Wookey Hole. No one can dispute your courage."

Waving away the youthful triumph, she said, "It was a school outing. Part of a nature walk. Nothing to call brave."

Frowning, he said, "Seems odd, taking schoolgirls into a cave. What wonders of nature did you discover?"

Remembering those wondrous caverns should end her sniffling. "At twelve and younger, we were more interested in the legend of the witch than the bones of animals and natural formations." She shook her head, remembering how foolish she had been at that young age. "All of us took something to leave in the stream over the witch's stairs leading down to the second chamber. Whatever you place in the water is reputedly turned into stone, like the witch."

He shifted his weight and rubbed his neck. "The water turned her into stone?"

"No, a wronged lover did. The witch killed his sweetheart when he was a young man. Later he became a priest, and when she began harming others, he was sent to deal with her. He blessed a handful of the cave's water and threw it over her as she ran away. She turned into stone, and she and her demons still stand near the entrance as a warning to all not to interfere in matters of the heart."

"Bloodthirsty enough story to appeal to youngsters." His voice sounded odd, strained. "What did you leave

216

to be transmogrified by the Witch of Wookey's spell?"

"A little porcelain cat." She didn't care to remember, and her voice came out strained. "It was a gift from my mother for my sixth birthday. She told me to handle it carefully as I played with it so I wouldn't break it. I had a senseless fancy to have it turned to stone in the cave's water so it could never shatter."

Swallowing, she continued, hurrying to get it all out. "This was soon after I was sent off to school. I believed she would come for me at the end of that year. I didn't go back for the cat when the others returned the following year. I knew by then that I wasn't at school for the usual finishing girls receive. I knew then that I wasn't going home."

A long moment stretched between them, and he sighed. Finally he said, "And after that, you didn't care if the cat splintered into a million pieces."

She nodded. Chan understood, and his comprehension of her feelings eased her pain.

"People don't realize how much children can suffer— or be scarred." His lips tightened. "And not just outwardly, like Ash."

"What do you mean?"

Frowning, Chan crossed his arms over his chest. "I'd have to force myself to go into the Wookey Hole, even today. I don't like underground caverns."

"Oh, dear." Focusing on her own personal emotions made her forget those of others. "I should have remembered about Ash's accident. I should never have teased you to take in the sight as a pleasure trip."

Waving away her apology, he said, "It's an absurd weakness. If I'd faced up to it long ago, I wouldn't think twice about going into caves by now."

"No, I don't blame you for staying away from places that remind you of such a horrible event. Anyone would feel the same."

"Not Ash." He shook his head, his expression a somber study. "I couldn't even bring myself to talk about being trapped in there, but Ash wanted to go see the rock slide before he was off crutches. He couldn't get me to go with him, but he finally convinced his father he needed to return to that cave-in. The duke took him while he still had to be carried."

She shuddered. "I wouldn't want to ever again go near the place where I was so tragically injured."

"That was my reaction, and I felt like a coward." He shrugged, not meeting her gaze. "It's the same thing as getting back on a horse after a fall, after all. Ash doesn't let much hold him back—never did."

"I think you've been excessively brave about that disastrous day." Hurrying to him, she laid her hands on his crossed sleeves. "You've stood by Ash all these years, and he's the most potent reminder of that horror you could have."

He looked off, above her head, and she tried again to lighten his bleak expression. "Going back into that cave might have been an act of curiosity or even bravado on his part. Whatever it was, it required only a few minutes of effort, one time. You've stood by Ash for years, probably seeing him daily. Do you expect me to believe you don't wince inwardly every time you watch him limp?"

Now his gaze fixed on her, intense and surprised. "That's true. I've never said it to anyone, though."

"Give me credit for understanding human emotions, as much as I've displayed them today." She squeezed him forearm, feeling the taut beam of hard muscle though the superfine sleeve. "You'd have done still better if you had talked it out. You might have shrugged off some of the load of guilt you carry around over his lameness."

Straightening, he took her by the shoulders and stared into her eyes. "I'm no saint carrying his lame brother on his back, even metaphorically. Don't make me out to be

218

something I'm not." He shook his head. "Besides, Ash doesn't need my help or pity."

Elizabeth pulled free. "You don't need pity, either. But both of you were marked by that experience. We're all marked by the events of our lives, with the early ones perhaps cutting deeper than others do. Some leave scars."

Turning away, she went on to the difficult part of the comparison that had burst upon her with shining clarity as they talked. "What I'm trying to explain is that being abandoned by Lucinda left a scar on my deepest inner being. You urge me to see her, to forgive her enough to let her see Aunt Delia."

Facing him quickly, she felt petticoats and muslin swirl against her ankles. "Perhaps I should be as brave as you are and face the reminder of pain. But I'm not. It hurts too much even to think about that woman on rare occasions. Giving her another chance to injure me is more than I can force myself to do."

Chan stood staring at her, his mouth a straight line and his brow furrowed.

"Don't you see?" She spread her hands wide. "I don't want to be reminded of her, not by talking of her, seeing her, thinking of her. She pushed me out of her life and I prefer to stay out. Perhaps I could live with the constant reminder of what she did to me, as you live with the reminder Ash is to you. But I won't choose pain."

"I understand what you're saying." He propped a hand on a lean hip as he shifted his weight. "I was thinking about your comparison. What happened to Ash and me was an act of God, of nature, not human choice. So if Ash and I blamed anyone, it would have to be the Holy Father." His grin was rueful. "You were sent away to school, when you didn't want to leave your mother. You have someone you believe deliberately chose to hurt you. You have someone to blame."

His way of putting it left her feeling defensive again.

"You always make things sound as though I had a choice, instead of Lucinda forcing the situation on me."

"Do I?" He grimaced. "That's not what I mean to do. You were only a child. You didn't have the experience to deal with your feelings of outrage and loss as a twelve-year-old girl, away from your mother for the first time. You felt the way most girls would feel in your slippers."

His recognition that her emotions were justified salved the wound.

An arm across his chest, he propped his chin on the other fist. "You're older now. You've set up your own household. Instead of becoming a snappish woman frowning at the world, you try to give opportunities to girls who are truly alone. That's commendable."

His praise pleased her, and she stood straighter.

"But you aren't twelve years old anymore. You know more about temptations and making mistakes. You've seen that being grown-up is no guarantee of doing the right thing."

Flushing, Elizabeth saw at once where his thoughts were leading. "And I haven't changed my mind about what she did. It's unforgivable to abandon a child, just to live in sin with a man who can't marry you."

Sighing, he crossed the small space between them and clasped her upper arms. His expression was compassionate. "It was a terrible thing to live through. How could anyone ever leave you?"

Her breath stopped at her throat, snagged by an urge to shed more tears. Surely she had cried out every drop of moisture in her body. She swayed toward him, then caught herself as he spoke.

"But maybe you judge what you don't fully know about yet. Maybe you haven't been in love as deeply as she was with Ash's father. No, don't pull away, Elizabeth." His hands tightened, holding her in place. "I'm not saying what she did was right or pardonable. But

220

maybe if you had savored a scant measure of the devotion she felt for her Will, you could find it possible to bury the past and go on from here."

Elizabeth withdrew into herself again. For a moment she had thought he perceived the depth of the damage Lucinda had done her. "No, I certainly don't have knowledge of a passion so selfish it can take no one else into consideration. If that's what romantic love does to you, I don't want to love that way. I'd rather keep my good sense."

"You see in black and white, when your world could be a garden of miraculous hues." He let her go. "I wish you would get to know your mother now, from the perspective of the adult you've become. She isn't the ogre you've made her in your mind."

"She isn't a myth either like the Witch of Wookey." Elizabeth hugged the emptiness in her midsection. "I don't believe she's an ogre; I don't want to think of her at all. Can't we leave it at that?"

"If you choose to," he said, staring at her with a grave expression. "You advised me to face up to my fear of caves. Very well, I'm willing to try. Will you go with me to the Wookey Hole and help me face my demons of the past?"

The request took her off guard. She stood staring, openmouthed. A breeze stirred a long strand of escaped hair across her face. Reminded that she must look like she'd been dragged through a bush backward, she began tucking up loose locks.

Suspicion crawled through her mind. "Are you trying to shame me into changing my mind?"

He grinned. "You can retrieve your stone cat."

His gaze followed her hands, which were working to restore order to her tumbled hair, then fell to the tight front of her spencer. Her breasts tingled under his observation in almost the same way as when they had pressed against his hard chest. How could he make her

221

melt like a burning candle without laying a finger on her?

How could she think about wanton pleasures in the midst of discussing her mother's wayward choices?

That thought sobered her, and she let her hair go. Just like her mother, she could be distracted from common sense by a man's attention. Not that a few kisses in a hidden pagoda compared to Lucinda's loose past—living in public with a man not her husband.

An edge of uncertainty nibbled at the hard stance she had taken before. Maybe she should try to overcome the harsh feelings about her mother that abraded her mind and emotions. Reclaiming the cat figure was a small step, and she didn't have to keep it if it bothered her.

Offering her hand to Chan, she said, "If you want to overcome a reluctance to enter dark caverns, I'll come with you."

His eyebrows winged their way to their most devilish slant. "Done."

His firm clasp swallowed up her hand and swamped her with the desire to be in his arms again. Already she questioned the good sense of going off to a dark cave with the most irresistible of devils.

Chapter Thirteen

A stone cliff reared high above them, but that feature of the brushy landscape didn't make Chan sweat. It was the black mouth at the cliff's base, a silent, threatening snarl, that sent a rivulet of cold damp down his spine.

"We seem to have the place to ourselves this morning." As they neared the dark gap, Elizabeth talked on. "The entrance is through that little opening in the rocks. One might not notice it if people and creatures hadn't worn away the growth around it over the centuries, going and coming."

Elizabeth's hand on his arm kept Chan from letting a shudder ripple through him. He didn't want to show weakness before her. They had come for a purpose: Elizabeth needed to retrieve the cat figurine her mother had given her as a first step toward accepting the past and reaching beyond it.

Pointing upward, she said, "Early hunters drove animals over that cliff, then came down to dine here. Both humans and animals have lived in these caverns for centuries."

Chan prayed he wouldn't die here. Trying to appear controlled and cheerful, he headed for the dark maw of the Mendip Hills known as the Wookey Hole. "You said it opens up inside to a large space?"

"Enormous. Inside, you'll see smaller places like Hell's Ladder, leading down to the Witch's Parlor."

The names didn't reassure him about what he'd find down the gullet before them. Acting confident was halfway to reaching that state of mind, though, so he lit two torches from the glowing coals brought along for the purpose.

Steeling himself, he bent over and plunged into the murk inside the cave.

Cavern. Maybe if he called it a cavern instead of a cave, he could quell the screaming protests from deep within himself. Holding his torch aloft, he straightened carefully inside the Wookey Hole.

Elizabeth raised her own torch high beside him. Shifting views of rocks smoothed by eons of lapping waters flickered in and out of view. "See the striations of texture on these walls? That shows the river once flowed through here to shape this cavern."

Chan felt as if he were drowning in the river that no longer filled this space. The darkness beyond the small, changing circle of their flares danced toward and retreated from him in cruel intimidation. He wouldn't try to breathe deeply, just take shallow, quick wisps of air into his bursting lungs. He wasn't really smothering. That was only an illusion left over from the endless time he and Ash had lain in the dust-filled darkness of that other cave long ago.

"Aren't the muted colors and flowing patterns of the smoothed stone lovely?" Elizabeth stared about, her musical voice awed and magnified, echoing off the massive walls that arched over him. "I was too young to realize the full beauty of the place as a child. I'm glad you convinced me to come."

Chan hoped he could make it to the spot where people left items for the water to encrust, then get out again without disgracing himself. He grimaced. "I'm glad you're here, too."

Putting one foot forward, then another, took infinite will and determination on his part.

Following, Elizabeth continued to sound like a tour guide, though she might be talking to fill his silence. "This first chamber is quite high at the front. See?" She stretched up on her toes with her torch, and even at the highest reach of its thrashing light, he couldn't see the ceiling.

Plenty of air in here, plenty of space. No reason to feel this constriction in his chest.

"It smells dead." He had to make some comment to keep her from realizing his throat was as constricted as the rest of him. He tried mocking his fears, groundless as the imagination of a small boy who'd been told that child-eating monsters waited in here. "Probably that's the lime in the water, closed up in this restricted space."

Looking at him closely, Elizabeth said, "This chamber is twice the size of the next, as I recall. If you don't like tight spaces, you might want to stop here."

Not looking at her, he made himself hold up his torch, turning as if fascinated by sights his mind was too frozen to take in. She suspected his fear, but he couldn't bear to expose it fully before her. "No, this is fascinating, just as you promised. Besides, this doesn't look like the place you left your porcelain cat in the water. Let's go get it."

Elizabeth hesitated, a crease between her curved brows. "This way," she said, going ahead of him into pitch blackness. "The passage into the Witch's Parlor is in this direction. We'll soon come to it if we keep following this wall."

Their torches' light crept along the stone, slow as the flow of treacle in winter, as they made cautious progress around the chamber's side. At last the wavering light found the edge of an opening and fell a short distance into the black space beyond.

"This is the next chamber?" His echoing voice sounded hollow. Maybe that disguised the traces of his anxiety.

"It's the passage to the next chamber, the Witch's Parlor. This passage is quite narrow and low." She looked up at him. "As tall as you are, you'll probably have to bend over. Can you manage it?"

"Of course." Actually Chan didn't even want to think about that close a space. Tons of rock pressed down above them, and he felt every ounce.

Going on was all he would consider doing, though, despite the cold fist squeezing the air from his lungs. "Your stone cat will be in the Witch's Parlor?"

"Just beyond it, actually, in the water flowing down Hell's Ladder. I can't recall if I left it on the first step down or the second, but it shouldn't be difficult to find if it's still there."

She went forward into the darkness of the passage. "It has to be close to the edge, as my reach then was shorter than now."

Willing himself forward, Chan gripped his torch tighter. If he dropped it and found himself in darkness, he'd very likely burst his heart. He forced a step toward the passage and felt his boots fasten to the rock floor.

His heart tried to break his ribs, pounding its desire to be out of this black hole. Staring into the narrow shaft of his deepest nightmares, he tried without success to order his other foot to move.

Ahead of him, Elizabeth walked slowly in a puddle of her torch's wavering light. He couldn't let her go on alone. But his strongest effort of will couldn't stir his feet after her.

Panic swelled in his constricted chest, an echo from the past. His mind replayed the first sound of soil sifting slightly, making the boys he and Ash had been stop to listen. A few pebbles had broken loose in the darkness around them, tensing their muscles. Then boulders cracked like cannon fire and the hail of rocks began ahead of them.

Chan had turned tail and run, not looking back to see how close the rockfall might be. He raced neck and neck with Ash as more stones hurtled to the floor around them. Billowing dust rushed past, blinding them as they groped for the opening to the outer chamber.

"Here!" Ash had called, and Chan had run toward the sound, hardly able to see his friend through the thick air that clogged his nose and mouth, clouding his vision. As he caught up with Ash, his friend shoved him through the arch first and, in doing so, went down under the heavier stones piling through it after them.

Gasping for air, Chan clawed at his high collar. Around him was total darkness. Had their torches been extinguished? He felt deaf from the explosion of falling rock, blind without light, alone when he called to Ash and got no answer.

Shaking off stones that had knocked him to the ground, Chan put out his hands, searching frantically. Nothing but hard rock met his groping fingers.

"Ash, Ash, can't you hear me? Answer me! Please, God, make him answer!"

A soft hand touched his face and light wavered uncertainly before his eyes. He was still in the Wookey Hole, and an angel with Elizabeth's face stared up at him wide-eyed and troubled.

"I'm here, Chan. Don't worry. It's all over. I'm here with you this time."

He looked down into Elizabeth's concerned face, saw the gleam of reflected torchlight in her dark golden eyes, and shuddered back into the present.

Good God, he'd had the old nightmare while awake. Gritting his teeth against the shame, he groaned. "I'm sorry. This place must have brought it all back somehow, the darkness, the falling rock, the panic to escape." He wiped his hand down his face and realized it shook. Quickly he shoved it behind him.

Elizabeth took his arm firmly, laid it around her shoulders, and turned him around. "Come on, Chan. This was a stupid idea, not worth doing for either of us. We're getting out of here right now."

"No," he protested, feeling like the biggest coward in the kingdom or beyond. "We came here for a purpose, and it's important we follow through."

"You'll go alone if you do." She didn't pause as she made for the pale glimmer of light ahead. "Punishing yourself like this is senseless, especially to recover a meaningless trinket that may not even be here anymore."

"But your mother gave it to you." The objection sounded feeble to his ears. "You need it to . . ."

As he stopped, she gave him a yank that made him stumble forward.

"That was then; now is now." Her voice was shrill and bounced against unyielding stone. "The past, yours and mine, can both stay buried in their separate caves and do us both a great deal more good there."

They had nearly reached the opening into light and air. The rush of relief, the lightening of pressure in his chest and lungs, shamed him further.

"Bringing out that little cat figure wouldn't make me the innocent girl again who trusted her mother to come back for her." She sounded out of breath from hurrying. "No more than forcing yourself into this cavern will cure Ash's limp or your guilt at what happened to you both."

As they pushed out of the Wookey Hole's clutches, Chan put up his face and gulped in great drafts of air. He felt as if he were taking in a first painful breath after having the wind knocked out of him. Humiliated as he felt over his cowardice before Elizabeth, he was grateful she had insisted on getting out of the cavern. He had tasted death again in there, and its bitter terror was no easier to swallow than his first sample had been with Ash.

Throwing her flaming torch into the maw of the Wookey Hole, Elizabeth took his and sent it tumbling after. Wiping her hands down the sides of the plain brown dress she'd worn for their rough exploration, she looked straight into his eyes and soul. "Facing the past may sound very fine and good, but it isn't always so simple. Sometimes the past is best left in the past, if you're to live in the present with any comfort."

Feeling defeated, Chan followed as she turned abruptly and marched off with a straight back toward the carriage he'd secured a short distance away. She was wrong; he knew she was wrong. If only he hadn't been too hen-hearted to make it to Hell's Ladder. Now he'd never bring about a reconciliation between this mother and daughter. Elizabeth would continue to be as haunted as he.

"This one is yours." Chan bowed extravagantly to Miss Delia as he offered her the silver paper–wrapped trifle.

Pressing the other narrow package into them, he cradled Elizabeth's hands between his for a moment. "I hope you'll enjoy this small token of our evening together."

She smiled into his eyes as if he hadn't failed her in the cavern last week. "A gift! How generous of you. Aunt Delia, let's see what this pretty paper holds for us."

Joining her aunt on the sofa in their drawing room, she watched as her aunt unfolded her gift's thin wrapping with eager hands. Her aunt's purple half-dress gown set off the lighter lavender of her own, Elizabeth noticed with satisfaction. Their dresses might be a little grand for a musical evening, but each liked to look her best whenever Chan escorted them.

Taking out a furled fan with a stippled vellum leaf and carved, pierced ivory sticks, Aunt Delia laughed and turned a delighted face toward him. "It's been years since a gentleman brought me an elegant gift like this. Come kiss my cheek, dear."

Leaning over her, Chan kissed both pinkened cheeks and finished with a light touch to her lips.

Flirting with the lovely trifle, she peeked at him over the engraved central vignette of Venus and Cupid. Her eyes sparkled in the light of the evening fire, and Elizabeth could easily imagine her at twenty. "You rogue, you only brought it so you could take advantage of a lady."

While he laughed and agreed, Elizabeth felt the paper around the object she held. She wanted to prolong this moment before learning what he wanted her to have from him.

Chan turned to her and gave his heart-tilting grin. "If you open it, you'll know what it is faster."

"I'd rather savor the anticipation."

"I know precisely what you mean." His gaze drifted from her eyes over her mouth, lingering before caressing her throat. He took his time laving her shoulders with his full attention, before exploring the depths of her décolletage. She had never worn so low a neckline without a tucker of lace, but this evening she basked in his appreciation all the way to her toes.

From touch, she was certain she had a fan from him, too. Without looking down at it, she loosened the wrappings and freed the delicate thing. Lifting it above her neckline, she unfurled it stick by stick, holding his gaze when he looked up, his eyes widening. With the fan in full display, she held it over her heart, then lowered it with maddening deliberation.

His dark eyes kindled beneath half-closed lids as he

watched, his lips parting and curving into a smile.

"Lud, I didn't teach you that," said Aunt Delia, fanning herself vigorously with her new treasure. "Not that you appear to need instruction."

Turning her gift to see what he had chosen for her, Elizabeth caught her breath. Lovely as Aunt Delia's fan was, her own bone brise creation was a fairy's work of carving and piercing along the length of each stick. Its delicate construction suggested lace. A bride couldn't want a more beautiful object to occupy her hands during her marriage celebration.

It was too rare, too exquisite, too costly for one friend to give another. Raising her gaze in wonder to his, she shook her head, wordless.

"Don't even think about refusing it." His voice sank lower, isolating them from her aunt and the world. "You're the only woman I know who could do it justice or who would appreciate its beautiful simplicity."

"Of course she'll keep it," Aunt Delia insisted, breaking the spell he had created between them with a shared look and a few murmured words. "Fans are unexceptionable gifts to present a lady."

Unable to speak the myriad feelings he inspired, Elizabeth closed the fan halfway, touched it to her lips, and smiled only for him.

Aunt Delia did most of the talking as they put on their wraps and went out to the closed carriage Chan had hired. Even with her aunt between them for safety, Elizabeth felt the connection thrumming between herself and Chan, alive and growing stronger with every beat of her heart.

His gift and his gaze made her graceful, beautiful, desirable above all women. She luxuriated in her first full experience of knowing her power as a woman to draw a man to her. Best of all, the man who had been enticed was not just any man, but Chan.

In the carriage, he took the opposite seat to them, his

back to the horses. Almost directly across from her in the darkness, he talked with Aunt Delia easily while slipping his feet on either side of hers. She nearly gasped aloud when he pressed her entire leg from the knee down between his. With the faintest, mesmerizing movement, he rubbed the inside of her knee with his, caressing slightly upward to her inner thigh. She bit a fingertip of her glove to stifle sounds of pleasure.

By the time they reached Lady Rowe's house in Queen Square, Elizabeth was giddy and breathless, unfit for company. Chan sprang out of the carriage before the footman could let down the step, doing that service himself. Reaching in a hand, he steadied Aunt Delia as she appeared in the doorway, lifting her down to the carpet rolled out for guests.

Elizabeth gathered her cloak and courage close as she leaned toward the carriage door. Not only was she flushed, she felt feverish. Her bones had melted like candles set too close to the fire. If she made it to a gilded chair, she might manage to remain presentable for the evening's entertainment, but how was she to stand, let alone walk that far?

"If you don't come out, I'm coming in after you." Chan's murmur was a delicious threat that made her want to wait inside for him to carry it out. With regret, she scooted across the squabs and put her gloved hand into his. Pulling her gently into the doorway, he took her waist and lifted her slowly out of the carriage. She felt like a feather floating on hot currents above a fire.

When her slippers touched ground, she hardly felt it. Bystanders made comments she didn't comprehend as he tucked her hand over one arm, her aunt's over the other. They walked up the carpeted aisle between the usual gathering of onlookers outside major social events. Rushlights in scrolled ironwork frames over the steps made the scene as clear as any on a stage. Proud to be arriving with this darkly handsome gentleman, Elizabeth saw only him.

To avoid the press of guests waiting to go inside, Chan had suggested they arrive a little late. As they passed through the open door, she heard the strains of the chamber orchestra tuning their instruments from above. Vivaldi was to be played as part of tonight's program, and she especially enjoyed his compositions.

This would be an evening to treasure in her memory forever; the music, Chan's lovely gift, his blissful torment in the carriage. Perhaps on the way home— But no, best not to think about that until she was safely alone in Sydney Place.

Maids and footmen stood ready to take their wraps in the antechamber, and Chan was as attentive to Aunt Delia as he was to her. The brief sweep of his fingers along her shoulder as he removed her cloak evoked both madness and ecstasy. His fiery gaze as she looked back at him assured her his touch was no accident but a promise.

Her mouth still held the answering curve of a smile when she heard Aunt Delia cry out.

Whirling around to locate her aunt, the first face she saw across the room was the young Duke of Ashcott's. Chan's friend stood leaning against a column at the end of the grand entrance hall, his expression avid and satisfied.

The impression was fleeting but definite. She had no time to think about it, for Aunt Delia hurried away from her, her arms extended, sobbing. Conversations dragged to a halt as people turned to watch.

Elizabeth ran after her aunt, berating herself for taking her attention off her, but the profile of a lady across the chamber stopped her in the center of the marble tiled floor. In the cluster of people around their hostess, standing near the stairs, the lady dressed in dull black lace turned her head toward her aunt's repeated cry.

Aunt Delia reached the lady in black, throwing herself

into her arms. The lady's face radiated a light more golden than the brightest reflection off Bath stone.

"Lucinda! Lucinda, my dearest dear." Aunt Delia was babbling words among her sobs. "I thought I'd never see you again in this world after Ashcott—and I can hardly bear this joy."

Unreality settled over Elizabeth as the murmur of the company's voices raised to an excited rumble more often heard on the streets. Faces turned between her and her aunt, fingers and fans pointed. She felt naked in the midst of this nightmare, exposed.

Turning her reeling head, she looked for Chan. He would help her get Aunt Delia and herself out of this place, away from the rabid interest of the crowd.

When she found him by his dark head above the crowd, he was frowning toward Ashcott. The duke stood pointing toward her aunt and Lucinda, talking fast. The sweeping gesture ended on her.

Stunned and disbelieving, Elizabeth looked for Chan again and found him pushing through the milling mob in her direction. Their eyes met and clung. His showed the dullness of some terrible regret.

Clasping her elbows, she felt the coldness of the last few moments turn into shivers that racked her whole body. She gritted her teeth to keep them from chattering, then held her breath to stop the tears that obscured her vision of Chan pushing through the crowd toward her. This had all been a trick.

His main effort lately had been to push her together with Lucinda. He'd even attempted to retrieve the object from the Wookey Hole he thought might bring back memories of her childish love for her mother, despite the horrible ordeal he'd suffered in a similar space. He was obviously determined to give Lucinda one of the two things she craved in order to secure her legacy for Ashcott.

And since Chan hadn't been able to deliver the daughter, he and his dear friend had arranged to bring Lucinda together with Aunt Delia.

Betrayal. This was betrayal of the worst kind.

Chapter Fourteen

"The devil you say!" an elderly male in the throng near Elizabeth bellowed to another. "Ashcott's notorious Lucinda is the Lady Enfield? The old duke's golden kitten?"

"Guess we'll have to call her the golden cat now and this one the kitten." His companion laughed and motioned to Elizabeth. "Lud knows the chit's her spitting image. Must be her daughter. I wouldn't complain about finding either in my bed."

A matron frowned at them but drew her skirts aside as she tried to back away from Elizabeth into the crowd.

Still clasping her elbows, Elizabeth felt the cold of the other guests' scorn frost her skin. Glittering stabs from curious, calculating eyes assaulted her as the shrill sound of commentary rose. She gritted her teeth to keep them from chattering, held her breath to stop the tears that obscured her vision.

Her thoughts beat wildly as she stood trapped and alone in the cage of the crowd's eager gabble. Suddenly she knew the meaning of Ash's smug look of satisfaction.

Chan wouldn't do this to me.

Betrayed she might be, but not by Chan. Even before she had seen him turn his shoulder on Ash with an angry scowl and push through the crowd toward her, she realized she knew the sole agent of her downfall.

Through shifting curtains of people, she met Chan's gaze as he pushed people aside to reach her. The urgent message in his black eyes managed to bolster her courage. From the moment Chan turned his back on the duke and looked for her, she felt supported by his concern.

Arriving beside her, he took her hands into his reassuring hold. "I wouldn't have had this happen for the world. How do you prefer to handle it? We'll go or stay as you choose."

Grateful for being given a choice rather than a command, she couldn't think at once what to do.

Nearby, a woman's voice came. "Now I understand Lord Chandler sniffing around the scorched skirts of Bath's little saint Merriman."

Another female tittered, equally derisive. "Lord Chandler won't be disappointed after all. The apple doesn't fall far from the tree. Like mother, like daughter."

His expression dark as a thundercloud, Chan wheeled about, lightning flashing in his eyes. Nearby, all babble fell to whispers.

Elizabeth knew now what she must do. She wouldn't allow her aunt or herself to provide further fodder for these gossiping old cows. Her reputation and social standing might be ruined, but she would not provide public entertainment in her downfall.

Neither would she allow Chan to be derided by this mob. This concerned her family, her own smeared reputation. This was her problem. He had only tried to help people—she realized that now—and he didn't deserve to be mocked and ridiculed.

Distance from him was the only course open to her. The realization caused a sudden pain within her, but she couldn't deal with that in front of these social buzzards.

When he bent to her again, she was ready. "I want to get Aunt Delia away from here at once." Though her voice trembled, she kept it low. "She'll want to talk with Lucinda. Go order Lady Enfield's carriage for us while I get them out of here with as little fuss as possible."

Looking around angrily, he said, "I don't want to leave you alone with these slavering fools. I can send a servant for the carriage."

Her heart breaking at his insistence on doing the gentlemanly thing, she begged, "Please, make it easier for me by doing as I ask."

"I don't understand." He shook his head, frowning. When she couldn't explain, just made a mute gesture for him to go, his lips tightened. "Then I'll meet you at Sydney Place."

"Not tonight." She could barely force the words out. "I can't take much more, Chan. Please hurry."

A stifled curse escaped him as he glanced around at the crowd. He bared his teeth in a silent snarl, and those closest fell back.

Before he could speak again, she set off across the tile floor. The crowd parted before her as if she carried the plague.

Shaken and somewhat disoriented, Elizabeth pushed her way through a miasma of titters and dark looks toward Aunt Delia and Lucinda. From all sides, scandalized voices pecked at her like hens.

"Pushing herself in among decent folk with a mother like that."

"To think our sons might have courted her!"

"She never fooled me, holding up her nose at local fellows. Had her cap set for a viscount, no less."

"Only one use he would have for her kind."

"Bad blood will tell."

By the time she reached Aunt Delia, Elizabeth felt she had staggered through the scourging of a double-row military beating. Laying a hand on her aunt's shoulder, she said quietly, "Reunions among family members should take place privately. Let's go home."

Lucinda's expression as their gazes met assured Elizabeth that she had no part in firing off this public bombshell. Her face was pale and her features passed from shock to distress. "My dear, I had no idea—"

"I know." Elizabeth cut off the comment, wanting no discussion here where avid ears waited to catch and report every exchange. "We'll talk in the carriage on the way to Sydney Place. I've sent Chan to fetch your carriage."

"Yes." Lucinda turned to Lady Rowe, who had appeared, and their hostess stepped into their tight threesome. "Can we wait in a more private place?"

Lady Rowe didn't waste words or time. "Will the porter's nook do? I'll post a maid to keep everyone away and knock when the carriage is at the door."

Gratefully, Elizabeth nodded. With an arm around Aunt Delia, she turned her to find the small closet. Lucinda followed closely as they recrossed the cold marble floor of the reception room.

The march of the small cavalcade back the way they had come seemed endless. Elizabeth felt the eyes of onlookers like the buffet of branches whipped by a storm. Prattling voices beat against her eardrums.

"Fancy her living amongst us under an assumed name all these years."

"Brass-faced as a monkey and up to nasty tricks."

Aunt Delia kept stopping to look back at Lucinda, smiling when she found the woman close behind.

Before they had reached the safety of Lady Rowe's proposed haven, Elizabeth was horrified to see an acquaintance step out before them. "Why, Delia Lindsey, I would never have believed you would embrace a kept woman publicly if I hadn't seen it with my own eyes."

Her hand fluttering over her heart, Aunt Delia looked confused. "What's going on, dear?" she asked Elizabeth. "I don't understand."

A haughty man stepped forward and raised his monocle to an eye. "Lady Enfield and your family, is it? Do you mean to return to society after"—he paused to leer—"years outside it?"

From behind Elizabeth, a hand urged her on. Lucinda's voice sliced through the sudden silence following the rude question. "Only where I'm welcome, sir, and can feel at ease among friends."

Grim as she felt, Elizabeth applauded her mother's dignity and wit. Finding herself forced into this unwanted reunion, at least she had the advantage of a worthy ally.

Lady Rowe rousted the porter from his small side chamber and sent him off to watch for the carriage. Meanwhile, Elizabeth settled Aunt Delia in the man's comfortable chair.

Straightening, she looked Lucinda straight in the golden eyes that were so much a reflection of her own. The full impact of their resemblance shook her. She hadn't realized how closely she favored her mother, for she hadn't even glanced at Lucinda on that one forced meeting. In the crowd outside, she had been too distressed to notice. No wonder Aunt Delia called her Lucinda when her aunt's wits wandered.

This realization was another in the series of the evening's shocks, and by now she was too numbed to feel it as pleasant or not. "If you'll visit with my aunt," she said in a neutral tone to her mother, "I have a few questions for Lady Rowe."

With a nod, her mother switched places with her in the small, narrow space. "The same questions in my mind, I vow."

As Lady Rowe closed the door behind them, Elizabeth

asked, "How did you come to invite . . . to ask all three of us here this evening? Forgive me for questioning a hostess's prerogative to have any guests she wants, but the circumstances are unusual."

"Indeed." Lady Rowe spoke softly as she glanced behind Elizabeth at her aunt and her mother. "I must say I felt a moment's hesitation when he said Lady Enfield was ready to attend quiet evening entertainments like this musicale. But the duke assured me that all would be well. He said nothing would transpire that was unwarranted." She gave them all a look of regret. "It seems that I was mistaken in his meaning."

Lady Rowe put a hand on Elizabeth's rigid arm. "I'm so sorry this happened. I wouldn't have had you taken unaware and embarrassed like this for the world. From what the duke said, I didn't realize your mother's presence here would come as a shock to you. Can you forgive me?"

Nodding, Elizabeth hardly knew what she replied. "You only tried to do a kindness, as you always do."

Lady Rowe frowned. "This turned out to be a disaster, not a kindness to anyone. I didn't expect people to remember such an old scandal, as your mother was never active in society even while married to Lord Enfield. I doubted anyone would associate the title with . . . with—"

Elizabeth was in no mood to mince words. "With the sixth Duke of Ashcott's mistress. This wasn't your doing."

She didn't blame this lady who had befriended her aunt and herself. The blame for this unmasking lay squarely upon Ashcott's shoulders. He hadn't given her a civilized look or word since he arrived in town, and she had no doubt now that he had plotted her downfall.

His plan was perfect. Not only had this unveiling of her heritage struck her out of every social register forever, Ash had likely counted on an ugly public scene to besmirch Lucinda, Delia, and herself all at once. At least Elizabeth had stuck one spoke in his wheel by quickly escaping into a private place and refusing to provoke a row.

She shivered. The fury chilling her veins was not about the duke's vendetta against her mother. Lucinda had made her bed and could expect to lie in it for a lifetime. The woman had probably expected this to be a gathering of Lady Rowe's more raffish friends, for her even to appear this evening.

Elizabeth didn't mind her own disgrace by association as much as the damage done to those close to her. Delia was a social creature, and if acquaintances spurned her, it would cut deep. As for her girls, finding them places in decent houses would be impossible when everyone knew a jezebel's daughter had trained them.

A knock at the door signified that the carriage had arrived. The maid outside handed in cloaks to Lady Rowe when she answered it. The three fleeing guests threw on their outer garments and took hasty leave of their hostess.

Lady Rowe squeezed Elizabeth's numb hand. "I'll come by to see how you all are soon."

"You're a good friend." Tears tickled her eyes at this lady's kindness. Whether she ever came to call again or not, Lady Rowe had shielded them from prying eyes and eased them out of her house as comfortably as possible.

As they left the porter's room and hurried to the carriage, Elizabeth looked about for Chan. The ugly clamor of the guests again rose. Although it was time for the music to begin, no one had climbed the stairs to the rooms where the chamber orchestra waited. Instead they crowded the entrance hall, spilling through the double door from the reception rooms.

Before she stepped out to the entrance hall, Elizabeth finally glimpsed Chan across the room. He had Ash by the arm. Both men seemed to be talking at once, their faces grim.

Like hurled rocks, raised voices and harsh laughter bounced off her back as Elizabeth shepherded her aunt, clinging to Lucinda, out the main entrance.

"At least they have the decency to leave at once."

"I've never been so taken in by anyone in my life."

"To think I've actually had them in my house!"

A shield of resolution hardened around Elizabeth. Ash would pay for this. He had stirred a hornet's nest, and people she loved would not be the only ones stung.

As the closed carriage stopped before Number 6 Sydney Place, Elizabeth spoke for the first time since leaving the musicale. Leaning forward, she murmured urgently to Lucinda, "Will you go in with my aunt and see her settled for the night?"

"Gladly. But aren't you—"

"I expect she won't quiet down quickly, and she may want you to stay with her until she falls asleep. That could take some time." Elizabeth didn't want to explain her sudden willingness to see the two together. Delia's joy at seeing her mother again had made Elizabeth feel petty. "Ring for one of the maids to bring a posset and help her undress. Cook knows what to prepare."

Lucinda nodded. In the restless light from the flambeau at their door, she looked troubled. "You're going elsewhere?"

"Yes."

"And you don't want to discuss it."

"No."

Lucinda sighed. "You feel I gave up my rights long ago to advise you, let alone question you, so there's nothing more to be said. The carriage is yours to use, of course. I'll remain here with Delia until you return."

"Thank you."

Amazing how little emotion she felt about turning

243

over her aunt to Lucinda now that it had been forced upon her. She had far worse to deal with at present.

"Use the extra chamber and sleep here tonight if you prefer," she told Lucinda. "You can use my night things."

Elizabeth waited while Lucinda descended: then she helped ease her aunt down the step to her and the waiting footman. As the two women entered the house, she itched with impatience for the footman's return so the carriage could move on.

He put up the step and asked, "Where to, miss?"

"The Bear Inn," she replied. "Drive to the stables in the mews. I'll enter through the back."

After he communicated her orders to the coachman, the carriage dipped and swayed as the footman mounted the back of the vehicle. Elizabeth shifted to the forward-facing seat. As the horses leaned into the harness, the coach set off with a slight jerk.

Rolling through darkness punctuated by the flambeaux at most doorways, the coach turned at the end of the street for the return trip across the Avon River. Elizabeth felt as wooden as the vehicle's bench seat under its squabs. Only her brain felt alive—with feverish plans to deal with the duke.

Nothing she could do or say to him would compensate for the heartless cruelty of tonight's snare. His abuse of his personal power in society would injure Aunt Delia and Elizabeth's girls. That damage was done, but Ash would not go unpunished.

Her weapons were few, but she would make use of what she had. The duke wanted the return of his wealth, every groat his father had bequeathed to Elizabeth's mother. He couldn't bear for the old duke's paramour to receive any of it.

Well, if Elizabeth could help it, he would never see a shilling of the bequest. Surely she could influence Lucinda. Few people had to be begged to keep an inheritance.

Lucinda wanted her place in the family back. She wanted to be with her daughter and sister-in-law. Elizabeth would set her doors wide open, on the condition Lucinda held fast to her lover's legacy.

Association with her mother could cost her nothing more than she had lost tonight. Her reputation and peace of mind were gone, thanks to Ashcott. It made no difference now who knew she was the daughter of the old duke's mistress, the infamous Lucinda with the sleepy golden cat's eyes.

The young duke's activities hadn't interested her as long as he left her in peace. But she had nothing to lose, and she would make certain the seventh Duke of Ashcott gained nothing.

Minutes later, Elizabeth climbed down from the carriage behind the Bear Inn and spoke to the footman. "Go to the Sydney Hotel and stable the horses. Your mistress will send for you when she's ready to travel, probably tomorrow."

Bowing, the man turned away to put up the step.

She would have to find a hackney to get home again, but an inn was a likely place for the purpose. Hurrying across the dim expanse of the cobbled yard, she pulled up the hood to her cloak, clutching it close under her chin. Without impassioned purpose propelling her through the night, she would be afraid in this place no lady should go alone, yet having lost everything she valued most, she found fear had deserted her.

Cold rage swelled in her as she glanced at the windows above the ground floor. From here, she couldn't tell which were the duke's rooms. She would find and wound the enemy who had struck out at her, ending her efforts to train girls from the workhouse, making an outcast of her aunt.

Wrenching open the back entrance to the inn, she pulled the hood of her cloak lower over her face. Clamor and fumes from the taproom sent her feet and heart racing for the back stairs.

She dashed up them without looking over the rail to see if she had been observed. Anyone seeing her dark cloak would assume a strumpet was headed upstairs on the business of the night. She no longer cared if she was seen or what anyone thought of her. Her anger filled her with reckless resolve.

At the top of the stairs, she turned toward the duke's suite of rooms. The last time she had traversed this passage, Chan had followed close behind her, half carrying Sally.

Chan would never forgive her for what she was about to do; he valued his friend too much. He had hurried to her side at Lady Rowe's, but he would eventually forgive Ashcott. He always had made excuses for the duke before, and Elizabeth had no illusions that Chan would change now.

Not that it mattered. Chan was lost to her. Tonight had proved that her name and Chan's could be linked only in sordid jests. The thought pained her. She couldn't bear for the precious time they had shared to be cheapened.

But she needed to be strong. With the legacy lost, he and Ashcott would return to London. Chan's respect for his family name made any lasting contact between him and Elizabeth impossible.

She leaned against the wall. Chan, gone forever. No more warmth, support, closeness, laughter.

Her heart squeezed in her chest with such force that she bent nearly double. Anguish stole her breath. A realization came upon her: the impossibility of continuing a mere friendship wouldn't make her gasp in pain like this. The loss of a friend, no matter how dear, wouldn't feel like the end of all meaningful companionship and joy. To lose Chan was to extinguish light from the rest of her days.

Friend or companion, Chan was too vital a part of her life to lose. Yet Ashcott had made knowing Elizabeth a blot on anyone's good name. No decent man, let alone a member of the aristocracy, could know her for any but one purpose. Ashcott had truly stolen all from her.

No one should have the power to take everything from another person.

Pressure built within her head and chest until she panted with the need to relieve it. She felt dizzy from alternate waves of despair and anger as she approached the duke's door.

When she laid a hand on the knob, it rattled from the tremors racking her whole body. Gritting her teeth, she twisted the door's handle. It turned without opening.

She shook it, hard. The damned duke had to be in there, hiding in cowardice from retribution. She wouldn't be denied the satisfaction of telling him precisely how he would pay for his treachery. Now. Tonight.

As rage rampaged through her veins, Elizabeth beat on the door with both fists. "Come out, you revolting weasel. Face me and be done with it, for you won't escape if I have to camp across your door all night!"

Fury mounted as he failed to respond. Losing all reason, Elizabeth beat at the panel wildly, bruising her hands in the need to break through the boards and confront her tormentor. Tears of frustration streamed down her cheeks, enraging her more as the mark of weakness.

Then she was seized from behind, a hand slipping over her mouth. She fought hard despite the hampering folds of her cloak, kicking back at her captor's legs and biting at his fingers.

Arms banded her like steel against a hard chest, and a cheek pressed against her hot, wet face. "Quiet, love. You're safe. It's me."

Even before she recognized his voice, the taste and scent of Chan's hand reached her senses. Heart pounding, she went slack in his arms and nodded.

At once he freed her, steering her away from Ash's door and across the passage to his. Feeling bereft of his arms, she reminded herself that the greatest kindness she could do him now was never to let him near her again. She choked back a sob.

At the sound of boots and voices on the stairs, he yanked her hood down to her nose. Making quick work of the lock, he urged her through his room's door, glancing down the passage before following her.

"I don't think anyone saw you," he said, dropping the iron key into his hat on a side table as he hurried to her. "The public room is teeming with loud drinkers tonight. Maybe no one heard you over the boisterous crowd down there."

Hugging her cloak tight, she said, "It hardly matters now."

"It matters to me." He rubbed her arms through the fabric, and she longed to lay her cheek against his white waistcoat. "I followed you to Sydney Place as quickly as I could, but your mother said you only dropped them there. Why in the name of all saints did you come here by yourself?"

The less she told him, the better. "Was that your friend coming up the stairs?"

He bent to look at her but she avoided his gaze. "You didn't come here after Ash. You can't want to see him again after tonight!"

Raiding his inner coat pocket for his handkerchief, she scrubbed at her face. She didn't want to sound as determined and grim as she felt. "I have a crow to pick with him."

"An overgrown buzzard would be more appropriate." The jut to his chin showed his dark mood. He lit a candle from the night lantern waiting on the side table, then rounded the room, touching wicks. "You'd have to wait on him until dawn, for he left Evie's house in a raging furor after I finished with him."

Teeth set together, she said, "So did I."

"With far more reason." His eyes glinted hard as granite when he turned, holding the candle. The light from below cast strange shadows up his face, and she shivered at the dark force he emitted.

Her lips felt numb as she spoke. "Where did he go?"

"Probably off drinking with someone who thought better of his conniving tonight than I did." His black scowl fell on her and transformed into tragedy. "I'm sorry; beyond words I'm sorry."

Setting the candle into a holder with such haste it leaned to one side, he came to her, his palms up and his expression bleak. "Elizabeth, I didn't know about Ash's plans. Believe me, it wouldn't have happened if I'd caught a whiff of it."

His hands on her arms were hot, even through the cloak. She hadn't realized how cold she was. Shivering, she looked up at him, putting conviction into her gaze and tone. "I know you didn't."

As he swept her into his arms, he blew out a long breath that stirred her hair. "You're a wonder. Any other female would be pounding on my head instead of Ash's door. Like a sensible woman, you know me well enough to trust me."

"I don't feel sensible." She pushed away, needing to escape this warm place she most wanted to be and felt no right to occupy. "I feel like Ash ran over me with an iron harrow, and I'm bleeding from every s-slash of its spikes."

"You're cold!" He hurried to the fireplace, where fuel lay ready, touching it to life with a spill lit from a wall sconce. "Your teeth are chattering and you're shivering."

Hugging herself, Elizabeth tried to hold still. Her voice trembled as she said, "I don't feel chilled; I just can't stop shaking. I'm so disgusted it's just as well you stopped me from seeing Ashcott tonight. I'll make more sense if I face him tomorrow."

"I've had one round with Ash, and he hasn't heard the last of it." Brows lowering over eyes that flashed black lightning, Chan smashed a fist into his palm. "I've never been this angry with him. I didn't know I could be this furious." He paced within the rectangle of the room, dragging his fingers through his hair. "I pulled him out of Evie's house after you left. Literally. He refused to come with me, said he had a victory to celebrate, that he'd saved my life again."

Shock and humiliation weakened Elizabeth to the point that she leaned against a chair, clutching at its back for support. Ashcott had done what he did tonight to save Chan. This time his efforts were not against a rock slide in a cave, but against *her*.

His mean comments and ugly actions all made sense now. He wanted to keep Chan from getting involved with a woman whose connections could only embarrass him, a woman whose mother was exiled from society.

As if he hadn't noticed her insight, Chan still paced. "I forced him out into the street to tell him what I thought of his nasty tricks. He went too far this time, beyond what I could overlook or excuse. He insisted he'd done me a favor, that I'd realize one day what a friend he had been. Then he took a swing at me. I knocked him on his ass for the first time since he took to crutches."

Elizabeth's breath caught in her throat. Though she didn't expect Chan to approve of what Ashcott had done, she hadn't expected this. "You hit him?"

The blaze of righteous fury dimmed in Chan as he stared at his fists. "I hit him hard. He's had it coming for a long time."

Though she felt the young duke deserved far worse, she could hardly believe what had happened between the two friends. "But he's no match for you. It can't have been a fair fight."

Chan's shoulders slumped. "You're right." Opening his hands, palms up, he said in a dead voice, "I shouldn't have done that. It *wasn't* a fair fight. But I couldn't let him get away with hurting you like that."

Anguish tore from his throat. "I punched him out. Still, I love him like a brother."

Anger at Ashcott welling up again, Elizabeth wished she could take away the torment Chan felt. "I might have hit him myself if I'd found him in his rooms. What he did tonight was despicable."

Chan slammed a fist into his palm. "I've overlooked too much. Maybe if I'd had it out with him earlier, he wouldn't have gone this far." Hands clenched, he squeezed them against his temples. "It's my fault, too, what happened."

"Stop protecting Ashcott from his own behavior." She wouldn't allow Chan to make this his own fault. "He's ruined too many innocent people tonight for me to feel sympathy for him. Aunt Delia will be crushed when former friends avoid her, and who will want my maids in their houses now?" She shook her head. "You had nothing to do with that."

She might as well not have spoken. He stood looking at his big fists as if they were cudgels. "What was I thinking? I'm a head taller and a stone heavier than Ash. He couldn't move fast enough to dodge a hit from me. Bashing him was brutality, and it didn't change a thing he did or said."

Chan's dismal expression as he berated himself broke her heart. "I'm no better than the lowest lout in the meanest hedge tavern."

If only she could relieve his anguish. Little as she expected it, Elizabeth discovered his pain searing through her. The reason for his misery didn't matter anymore, only that he suffered, and she wept within herself for him.

What was this sharp inner experience of his grief, this desire to ease it, this longing to lessen his suffering? It felt different from her concern for Aunt Delia, for she knew he could bear it by himself if he must. She didn't have to share his pain, but she wanted to help him get past it.

Nothing she had felt for Chan seemed ordinary. She had realized without admitting it for several weeks that friendship seemed a pallid word for the joy she knew when he came to the house each day. Though she didn't know when she had stopped pretending he came only to visit Aunt Delia, she knew now that his visits meant everything to her.

Though begun with fear and fury toward him, her feelings had inched through suspicion to trust, and drifted to delight in his company. From a threat to her comfortable life, he had become its greatest champion.

Even when he nudged her toward changes she didn't want to make, he had her best interests at heart. She saw that now, in the blink of an eye. He could have settled his business with her mother long ago if he hadn't wanted to make things better for all of them—mother, daughter, and aunt. He cared for her peace of mind and had tried to contribute to it every way he could.

Looking up at his strong-boned face, she saw the upward slant of Chan's black brows gathered into a tight knot of disgust at himself. From his lowered lids, a sweep of black lashes smudged his eyes with regret. Remembering his mouth against her closed lids in Sydney Garden's pagoda, she wanted with every ounce of desire within her to touch his lids with comforting lips, to know the feel of his face between her hands.

More, she wanted to hold him against herself, to feel their hearts and breathing match pace, to ease his distress with long strokes of her hands over his back and shoulders, to show him he wasn't alone.

Elizabeth wanted more than to comfort Chan. She wanted to support, encourage, and share with him. She wanted to experience everything possible for two people to partake of between them. Her head to one side, she stared up at his dear face with a growing certainty of what to call this burgeoning feeling for Chan.

This was love.

Chapter Fifteen

Caught up in the wonder of knowing she loved Chan, Elizabeth didn't hesitate to express it. Going into his arms, she urged his face down. As she touched his mouth with hers, he groaned and clasped her, hard, his hands sliding under her cloak. She wasn't shaking now.

Chan had hit his best friend because of injustice to her. Yet his actions had hurt him far worse.

Comfort was her intent as she pressed her mouth to his, for she felt the anguish within him at what he had done. She wanted to relieve him of its burden. "Let me share the hurt," she whispered against his mouth. "I care."

Wanting him to feel the tenderness welling from her full heart for his distress, she caressed his lips with hers. Stretching against his tall, hard frame, she wanted to ease the bitter twist of his sculpted mouth. Tonight had changed so much.

Needing comfort herself, she absorbed every sensation of his questing mouth. His big hands slipped along her spine in hungry strokes; then his hard arms crossed to pull her against his length.

"Yes, hold me," she murmured. "We'll hold each other."

As her mouth molded against his with increasing urgency, her body sought to fit with every hard angle of his torso and legs. Surely if she pressed close enough, she could soak up the desolation dragging at his eyes and mouth, send her loving comfort deep within him.

Yet sharpening desire for more than comfort drew her into a swirling vortex of sensation. Like sunshine breaking through clouds, emotions brightened and flooded her with increasing warmth and awareness.

Closer, closer! sang her pulse as it hummed in her ears. Any space between them was too much as she gave him every measure of her being and, yes, her heart.

The need to meld wholly with Chan in one joyous if poignant moment would warm her for a lifetime. She could have nothing more than tonight in his arms, but she couldn't ask for more. Tonight she would give him all of her being, take all of his own into herself. Tonight must be enough to sustain her for all time.

This was all she would have of love, and she would have it to the last full measure.

Tears gathered behind her lids as she kissed him with fervent yearning to do so forever. Knowing even tomorrow with him to be impossible was all the more reason to love him with all her heart tonight. A joyous forever wasn't given to everyone, but memories of shared tenderness must surely salve the empty ache of existing alone.

Tonight she would love him, take all the tenderness and joy he offered her, and give him all of hers. Forever without him didn't have to start before the dawn.

Enraptured by the scent of her hair, Chan felt her reach for the clasp of her cloak with one hand and fumble with it. Then the heavy dark fabric parted and pulled away over her rounded pale shoulders.

His senses reeled as she smiled with trembling lips, damp lashes lying against her cheeks like shadowed ferns. Fierce need to protect her against every harm sped his pulse. Tucking her against him, he gathered her close, wanting her to feel his heart pounding near hers, pounding with need.

"You're too precious to let out of my arms or my sight," he murmured against her temple, feeling her blood pound under his lips.

Hungry to taste every inch of her lush body, he found the delicate shell of her ear and touched it with his tongue. She went still in his arms for a moment, then curled her face into his shoulder to expose it more fully for his exploration.

As he nibbled gently and whispered love words at the same time, she hunched a shoulder against his cheek and shuddered down the length of her exquisite body. He burned to possess the curves writhing gently against him, had to entice more of the sweet innocence of her responses to his mouth and hands.

"You're my bud on the brink of blooming," he whispered, "and I want you to unfurl for me, only for me."

"Yes, Chan," she murmured, eager, shy, and breathy. "I'm yours, just yours."

As she fumbled at ties hidden in the placket at the back of her gown, her breasts pushed forward against his expanding chest. Unable to resist the invitation, he nuzzled the bounty of her beautiful cleavage, the skin soft and radiant as any rose.

Her skin tasted as good as it smelled, warm and faintly floral with a hint of vanilla. He tasted her with his tongue and then with his whole mouth, delving over the mounds of her breasts and then into the deep valley between them.

Eager to have their ripe fullness in his hands and

mouth, he reached for the ribbons binding her into her pesky garments. Together they sorted out the ties and tugged in the right places to release her from gown and shift.

Teeth set against his growing need, he drew the sleeves of dress and undergarments farther down her lovely arms, bringing half her breasts into view above her stays. He held his breath at the rosy peaks pushing out of confinement, held aloft in mute petition for his gaze and touch.

Elizabeth didn't hide from him like the virgin he knew her to be. She stood proud and erect, with shoulders slightly back, offering herself to him fully.

Shrugging out of his coat and waistcoat, he tugged at yards of cravat, feasting on the vision of Elizabeth in her stays and thin linen petticoat tied at the waist. As he unwound the confining neck cloth, he felt his throat thicken with desire and words of praise for her loveliness. "If I could paint like a master, I couldn't brush half your beauty onto canvas."

With her skin burnished by candlelight, her eyes gleamed a brighter gold for him than ever before. "If you find me beautiful, that is enough."

He had to feel the soft skin burgeoning above her rigid stays, to press both textures against his chest. The contrast of restraint and abandon overwhelmed him. She was his. He would stoke this fire of her longing into an inferno of passion, and together they would burn with all the glory of heaven and the fury of hell.

Wrenching his linen shirt over his head, he dropped it without caring where it fell. He laid his arms around her bare shoulders, careful of their porcelain fragility. Within his loose hold he cradled her while staring with wonder at the beauty of body and soul she offered.

Elizabeth's spirit shone from her golden eyes, reflecting the flickering flames of the candles around them. They consoled and consumed him at the same time. Her skin was gilded with the same glow of soft light, luminous and warm.

"I'm afraid to touch you but can't keep my hands off." Bending, he tasted the column of her throat and traced a languorous journey across her shoulders and collarbone to the softness below. Sinking onto one knee, he pulled her to him as he raised his face, laving the darker nub of her nipple with his tongue and mouth, covering the tip to savor it gently at first, then with growing passion, as he felt her response.

Her head fell back as if pulled by the weight of her glorious hair, and he wanted his hands in it. He wanted the long mass of it spread around her face below him while he worshiped her with his gaze, his mouth, his hands, his whole body.

Leaning to the side, he quickly spread her dark cloak over the carpet. Taking her shoulders, he urged her to her knees, too, bracing her against his raised leg.

"I want to love you tonight, Elizabeth," he said, looking from her to the cloak. "I want to fan your bright hair over that darkness and see you become a part of me in the way you've never been part of any other man. I need to hold you and touch you until we're both mad with wanting each other, and then I want to hear you say you want me."

As she nodded, eyes radiant and lips curved into a smile, he lowered her tenderly onto the black of her cloak. As he plunged his hands into her hair to remove every pin he could find, she explored his bare chest with her hands and gaze. She touched him with curiosity and wonder in her fingertips at first, then spread her palms and fingers flat against him as if drawing the heat and heart out of him and into herself.

Chan yearned to give her more than he'd ever found within himself to offer any woman, to take her deeper into the spiral of unity than he'd ever been. "I'm going to love you tonight until I feel you love me back."

Her huge golden eyes swam with moisture as the curved lids grew heavy with passion. "Yes," she said on a long sound.

Time spun out between them into a place that had never existed before. Chan stepped into its seclusion and took possession of it and her.

When their hands and mouths had explored every wonder of this private place they had created between them, he dipped into the heated spring of readiness between her legs. He wouldn't let her feel a twinge from their first joining. Holding himself sternly in check, he focused only on giving her long, slow strokes with a finger until she met his rhythm eagerly. Easing in another digit, he felt the warm honey of her need flow over his hand and gritted his teeth against the desire to plunge himself after its depths.

Hands fluttering over him as she writhed beneath him, Elizabeth found his nipples, rubbing and fingering them into taut need. Groaning aloud, he leaned into her hands while inserting another finger to avenge the luscious torment of her touch. His thumb found the delicate spot of greater pleasure, and, moist as she was, it bloomed at once.

Holding on to his shoulders, she braced her hips against his hand for a long, shuddering moment, her eyes widening with incredulous delight. He laughed with the joy of her discovery, his gift to her, and bent to kiss the soft mouth that parted to him in renewed passion.

Her whole body matched his in heat and need. Her mouth begged him to plunder her as her hips arched and bucked. Her hands danced over his shoulders, singed his sides, and clung to his rump, drawing him toward her in a wordless plea.

"I want more," she said in a gasp, "more. Now. Please. Love me completely, my darling Chan, love me."

Her flushed, pleading face, her swollen lips and breasts, her long limbs reaching for his body were overwhelming, more than he could resist. Doffing his pantaloons, he covered her with his body. He cradled her in his forearms, holding himself away from her on his elbows for the double joy of watching her response.

Easing himself into position as she welcomed him between eager legs, he nudged gently at the hot center of her desire. He would go slowly, advance only a centimeter at a time to avoid giving her discomfort in this first joining.

Elizabeth, his darling, impetuous Elizabeth, had her own ideas. With unconscious wantonness, she pressed herself over him in small, sensuous side-to-side hip movements. He gasped as she took him into her, and both from a far distance and within himself heard echoing gasps from her. The great pools of her eyes widened as she pushed again, gradually taking almost his entire length into her innermost place. Balanced above her, he hung on the endless moment with the same awe and discovery he saw in her expression.

This was his delight, his place of belonging, his woman. For the first time in his life, he truly knew what it meant to make love. Every exchange of their bodies tonight was a culmination of emotion, he recognized with awe and wonder. He loved Elizabeth with his body, his soul, and his life.

In full acceptance of that knowledge, he pulled out far enough to make the long stroke of total claiming memorable. Sliding slowly into the oneness they made together, he said, "You are mine now, forever, my love."

On a long breath, she said, "Yes" with lingering sibilance.

He felt the word sink into his soul like a pledge, a vow between them. Gazes and bodies linked in total harmony, he loved her with every movement of passionate coupling he could devise, and received in return the full gift of her eager response.

Together they clung and reached and rose beyond

themselves to a new height of giving and taking, vision and touch and sound amplified beyond bearing. Just when he knew he couldn't hold back longer or reach higher to give her the heavens, she cried aloud, arching her back and lovely throat, pushing herself against him and holding on to him as if she could never let go. He felt the undulations deep within her that gave him the freedom to join her in surrender to mutual ecstasy. Clasping her close, he carried her over the threshold of joy and joining, into the fulfillment they created for each other.

Lying spent with his darling in his arms, he breathed as though he had run a long, hard race. He had. And he had won the prize of his life.

A few moments later he rolled to his side, taking her with him. He wasn't ready to let go of her, not certain he could ever let her out of his arms again. Half-dazed with the glory of their mutual discovery, he touched light kisses to the damp hair clinging to her temples.

"I doubted many times I'd ever hold you like this," he murmured against her hair. "I thank you, I thank every power in the universe that brought you into my life and arms."

Moving away just enough to smile at him, Elizabeth kissed Chan with lips that trembled despite her efforts to control them. "And I thank you for showing me this magical togetherness."

This time the meeting of their mouths was tender with repletion. Through unshed tears, she savored him, sought to feel him with all of her skin in an effort to commit him to memory.

Every moment of the night's magic blended both joy and sorrow within her. Even as she exulted in their joining, she endured the anguish of their parting. She must savor and remember every instant against the rest of her nights in a solitary bed. Tonight was all she could have of loving.

Stretching out the enchantment, she melded against him, her eyes tightly closed to feel him more fully. Almost, she could feel the separateness of them disappear as she lay within his arms and they breathed in unison.

Then a fist battered the door.

Before she could think, the door exploded open.

Ashcott limped in, shoving the door closed behind him as he glanced around the room.

In the same instant Ash stepped inside, Chan swung himself in front of her. He pulled the cloak over her nerveless body and grabbed his shirt.

"Get out of here," he ordered as he pulled the garment over his head.

"You're through, aren't you?" Ash said.

Elizabeth cowered behind Chan, stunned.

"Nothing I haven't seen before or done myself," she heard Ash say in a careless tone. "We need to talk. Send your little tart on her way with a handful of coins."

Chan sounded urgent and desperate as he reached for his pantaloons. "I'll come to your rooms in a few minutes. Go on now."

"Let me have a peek at her first. She might do for a nightcap later."

Elizabeth swathed herself in the folds of the cloak Chan had freed and thrust back toward her. This nightmare grew more grotesque by the moment.

"What's this then?" The sound of Ash's movements stopped and she heard the rustle of silk. "Lavender! Fine feathers for a tavern wench, I think."

With a swift backward look to see that she was decently covered in her cloak, Chan rose to his full height, buttoning his flaps. "Ash, I've had all of you I can stomach for tonight. Put that down and get yourself out of my room or I'll carry you to yours and drop you out the window."

Elizabeth struggled against slight soreness and an unreal feeling to stand, glad she still wore stays and petticoat under the cloak. Wrapping it tighter around her, she stood erect and defiant beside Chan. She would face down this villain.

Sneering, Ashcott looked her straight in the eyes. When she didn't blink at his scorn, he finally looked away.

Ignoring her, he spoke to Chan. "At least you've come to your senses and realized what to do with the—"

"Don't say another word, or I'll have to knock you down again." Chan's voice sounded angry and harsh. "I can't even stand the sight of you right now. Go pack and call for your carriage. I want you out of this inn tonight."

Ash snarled, baring his teeth and curling a cut lip. "This is the most feeble-witted thing you've ever done, Chan. A woman like her doesn't come between two men who have been nearly brothers all their lives. You'll be tired of her in a week."

Chan took a step toward him, his arm raised and his elbow back. Then he stopped and dropped his fist. "You're wrong. Wrong like you've been about her from the start. Go back to London. Decide if you can treat my countess with the respect she deserves. If you can't, I won't have you in our house."

No! Elizabeth breathed deeply without getting enough air. Chan didn't mean it. She wouldn't let him mean it. He was just protecting her, the way a gentleman would.

Beseeching now, Ash shook his head, his hands outstretched. "Chan, you can't marry her. You owe your family and your name better than that. You can't taint an ancient and honorable bloodline over a woman you tumbled on the floor of an inn."

"Don't belittle the lady I'm marrying if you want us to know you in the future." Reaching for her, Chan put an arm around her shoulders and pulled her forward, against his side. "Elizabeth is everything any man could want for himself or his family. And if I hear a word of gossip about tonight, I'll know its source and act accordingly."

Ash stood with his hands still out, his expression desperate. As his hands folded and fell to his sides, he looked stricken, almost ill. "Chan, reconsider—"

"You reconsider." Chan's grip on her shoulder was painful. "I've told you how things stand with me. You have to make your own choice. I've made mine."

Unable to watch the agony of acceptance kill the last light of hope in Ash's face, Elizabeth looked down at her bare toes, clenched on the carpet.

The door slammed.

Wincing, she looked up, wishing only to deny the horrors of the last few minutes. One glance at Chan's beloved face showed her the same expression of desolated misery Ash had worn. This final break had hit him harder than the earlier unforgivable punches he had thrown. He looked as though he'd just been told of a brother's death.

One certainty froze into rock-hard shape within her: she loved Chan far too much to marry him.

Chapter Sixteen

Fumbling at the lock in the uncertain light from the flambeau outside her door, Elizabeth floundered between feelings of loss and frustration. Flickering shadows scattered her thoughts and her field of vision. The night's upheavals had left her too exhausted for further arguments with Chan about a union that would bring shame on his family name.

Wishing that weren't true, she said, "Thank you for seeing me home."

"I wouldn't let my betrothed travel alone in a hackney in the middle of the night." Chan's voice behind her sounded more stubborn than loving, after the wrangling between them all the way from his rooms at the Bear Inn. "We'll talk again later today."

With the door slightly open, she put one last effort into making him understand. "Please don't come back here, Chan. Knowing me has cost you too much already. I can't endure having you caught up further in the scandal that will flood Bath over the next hours. If you care for my peace of mind, stay away."

The warmth of his big hand settled onto her shoulder. She resisted as he urged her to turn. "Please, I'm so tired. Just let me go without further useless debate. I can't deal with anything more, and I know what has to happen."

His groan ripped at her shredded heart. "I'm sorry. Of course you need to rest. I'll come back later."

Now it was her turn to groan. Chan simply wouldn't hear her refusal to marry him.

His voice behind her was like dark chocolate, bitter and sweet. "Give me a kiss to dream on."

Despite her resolution to send him away without another soul-scalding touch, she couldn't resist that plea. He tilted her chin up. They kissed gently, sweetly, with promise that couldn't be fulfilled. Her longing to claim all the night's pledges foreshadowed the agony of getting through all the days and nights ahead. Without him.

When chill air touched her mouth again, she stumbled inside her house. Leaning her cheek against the closed door, she felt her bonnet twist and plunge downward like her heart. The ribbons cutting into her throat choked her less than the torrent of loss pinning her against the wooden panels.

With her ear and hands against the door, she could feel as much as hear his footsteps depart. The sounds of harness and carriage retreated into the night as tears slipped from her lids and down her cheeks. He was gone, and the forever of loneliness had begun.

The throttling strands loosened from her throat and the weight of her bonnet was gone. Smaller hands touched her shoulders and turned her, taking her into a warm clasp.

"There, my Lillybet, there. Cry if you must, but don't cry alone. I'm here, my little Lillybet." The familiarity of the old pet name, the remembered lilac scent of comfort, took her back to a younger self who knew the power of Mother to make bad things retreat.

Exhausted and overwrought, alone too soon after the release and exhilaration of joining with Chan in body and spirit, Elizabeth accepted solace. She clung to the strange yet familiar source of support and let the tears flow unimpeded.

Later she would be strong. Now she needed to grieve. Sobbing painfully, Elizabeth lamented all the losses of her life: the adored father who rarely came home, the mother who chose a lover over her, the beloved aunt slipping away into senility, the lover whom she must forsake for his own good.

Love's legacy in the past had been only anguish. It could be no different for her now.

What seemed eons later, painful hiccups began to interrupt her stormy gusts of tears, and she fought to regain emotional control. Her throat burned raw and her eyelids felt too saturated to open.

Accepting comfort from a mother Elizabeth didn't want wasn't fair. She pushed away from the haven of encircling arms.

Without protest, Lucinda unfastened Elizabeth's cloak, slid its weight off her sagging shoulders, and laid it over one arm. Urging Elizabeth toward the stairs, she said quietly, "Up to bed with you. Rest is what you need most."

Relieved that she didn't have to make even these small decisions, Elizabeth went like an obedient child under her mother's hand to the stairs. Tomorrow she would make matters clear with Lucinda, when she could think.

Tonight conscious effort was necessary to effect even ordinary movement. Spent and empty, she pulled herself up from one step to the next, gripping the smooth curve of the dark banister.

Following the pool of light from the night lantern Lucinda held up, she made it down the passage to her bed-chamber. Inside, Lucinda set down the lantern and lit a candle from it, then touched wicks at the dressing table and bedside.

Without conversation or fuss, she helped Elizabeth with the fasteners of her gown and petticoat like a lady's abigail. Handing her the soft linen nightdress she took from its embroidered case, Lucinda turned her within the limp puddles of her clothing to unhook her stays.

Elizabeth stepped out of the circle of her garments and stripped off her stockings. She slid the bed gown down her arms and over her head. In the white night-dress so little different from those of her childhood, she crept to the high bed with its downturned covers. Once up the two steps, she sank into the soft depths of her feather bed. Its enfolding warmth was especially wel-come tonight.

Lucinda arranged pillows behind her as she settled, then pulled covers over her and tucked them around her shoulders. Though these gifts of attention were offered without extra pats and entreating looks, Elizabeth felt troubled about accepting them. She wished Lucinda would go away.

Like a servant, Lucinda gathered up the garments left on the floor.

Elizabeth didn't want more of these services that laid unwanted claims upon her. "No, please, leave them. You've done too much already."

As Lucinda smoothed out the crushed, damp petticoat, Elizabeth realized what it might reveal about her eve-ning. She hadn't untied the garment from her waist; Chan had simply pushed it out of the way.

Sitting up in bed, she met Lucinda's gaze as her mother stood with the telltale petticoat taut between her hands. Stains like watered red wine marked the white linen clearly, evidence of the passion she had shared with Chan.

No words came out when she opened her mouth. Shoving her feet over the side of the bed, she landed with a thump like that of her heart.

Taking the petticoat, Elizabeth fanned it carefully over the back of a chair to dry. This garment would be tucked away, not sent down as usual with her personal laundry. Her girls didn't need to see evidence of this once-in-a-lifetime night. She wished Lucinda hadn't seen it, for she didn't want to share this with anyone.

Lucinda had taken up her crushed lavender gown and hung it for airing. Not a word had been exchanged.

Elizabeth didn't have to explain herself to this woman who had abdicated the role of mother. She didn't feel guilty about the adult choice she'd made, to have what she could with Chan before letting him go out of her life forever.

Lucinda stooped to gather up her stockings. "You must love him very much. I'm glad. He's a good man."

Colder than the night air warranted, Elizabeth climbed back into bed. Piling up pillows against the headboard, she pulled the covers to her chin as she leaned back, shivering with regret. If not for her mother's choices in loving, she might have had a future with Chan. "He's far too good to suffer for knowing us."

Lucinda stood erect in her black evening dress and touched a locket on a golden chain. Fingering it, she said, "If he loves you in the best way, nothing would be too much for him to suffer with you."

The complex pain twisting through Elizabeth produced simple words. "I love him too much to hurt him."

Clasping her hands, Lucinda bowed her head, her mouth against her fingers. She stood that way a moment as if praying, then looked up, blinking rapidly. "Then you've learned a sad thing about loving; it can do serious damage to people you don't want to hurt."

Elizabeth sat dumbfounded, not ready to answer. If she agreed, would that excuse her mother for years of

269

harm done to her child through loving her duke? She wasn't ready to absolve her.

"I won't let my feelings damage him. Not if I bleed inside for the rest of my life." Out of old hurt, she added, "Not everyone chooses to be selfish."

Lucinda walked away to the window across the room as if she could see out its closed draperies. "You believe you can protect him from hurt by renouncing him." Her womanly shape in the dark gown merged with the night's shadows as she clasped lace-clad elbows. "The choices love gives us aren't that simple, my darling. Once expressed, love isn't an object you alone hold and can hide away in a cupboard. It's more like a stream. It flows between you and your beloved, and the waters wash against all those closest around you."

"I can dam it inside myself." Fighting off exhaustion, Elizabeth refused to allow this woman her easy excuses. "Love doesn't have to drown anyone but myself in sorrow. I won't let those I care about pay for my unrestrained emotions as you did."

Across the room, Lucinda's shoulders sloped forward and shook in silence. Elizabeth fought against feeling sorry for the tears the woman's self-indulgent choices had brought her.

"There is no way to dam love. It always spills over." Lucinda raised her bowed head and spoke. "Much as you want to believe it exists only between you and the holder of your heart, its overflow can't be contained within two lives. Love warms those who rejoice in it, but scalds those who feel it to be a threat."

The implication of being in the wrong offended Elizabeth. "Any child would have felt abandoned, not just me." She couldn't let the moment pass without venting a small part of her grievances. "You closed me out. How was I supposed to be 'warmed by love' when you decided to live openly with your duke instead of me? I had no choice!" She thought of the love her mother must have known, then felt even angrier.

How dared her mother lecture her? The purity of her feelings for Chan couldn't be compared with Lucinda's unholy alliance, an indiscretion that had branded so many people and ruined them. Her mother had chosen to ruin them all, too. Had she simply allowed herself a discreet affair, society might have overlooked it, but since they had lived in sin for all to see . . . "You left me alone to go off with your duke and now your disrepute forces me apart from the man I love. Can't you see the damage you've done?"

Lucinda turned slowly, her white hands contrasting with the darkness of her sleeves. From the shadows across the room, her eyes glittered with tormented life in a wan, deadened face. "If you look only for the harm, that's all you will see. I love you, Elizabeth. I loved you then and I love you now. You're a part of my heart as surely as my body, and to hurt you was to hurt myself." She stretched a pale hand into the dark space between them. "I have paid for my misdeed every day of the past twelve years. From the first visit to your school when you refused to see me, I mourned my mistake. I had thought to protect you."

Elizabeth looked away, unable to watch the grief-twisted features any longer.

"I wish I could say more than that I'm sorry. I know it isn't enough, but I'm grievously sorry."

The woman's voice broke, and she was quiet for a moment. "Maybe it doesn't have to be all loss between us if you learn from my errors. Life is more than loving one person, and I never loved you less, though I loved Will. I thought I could hold on to you both, and I believed it wasn't good for you to live in an irregular household, as close to womanhood as you were. I expected to spend time with you at your school and in this house. I didn't realize you couldn't let me love both of you."

Her hands to her temples, Elizabeth shook her aching head. "You make it sound like it was my fault, but I was only a child. I couldn't help how I felt. I can't help how I feel now. I don't want to heap misery on you— I don't want to hurt anyone. I just want to make things right for Chan."

Lucinda's sigh drifted across the chasm between them. "You're wiser than I, perhaps. If I can help you, I will. Even if I can help only by staying away, as I've done for so long."

"You can do one thing for me, something I want very much." Help from Lucinda was the last thing she wanted to ask, but the need to strike back was still greater. With resolution, she wrapped the covers tighter and made her request.

"Promise me you'll keep the duke's legacy. Don't relinquish any of it to his son."

Staring at her, Lucinda said, "You want me to keep it? With your attachment to Chan, I thought—"

"I know what I'm asking." The seventh Duke of Ashcott had taken away everything she valued, and Elizabeth would deprive him right back. "Your lover's son set up our meeting tonight at Lady Rowe's. He's the one who spread censure and scandal around the room. He's the one who made it impossible for Aunt Delia to go among her friends again with comfort. As much as you love her, I'd expect you to want to repay him as much as I do."

Shaking her head, Lucinda crossed to the fireplace and stared into the grate.

Elizabeth hugged herself under the covers, still cold to the core. "Why would you object to keeping what the duke wanted you to have? Isn't that what you intended to do all along?"

Facing her, Lucinda put a hand to her brow. "Will

wanted me to have that money in the event of his death because I went to him with nothing of my own. I set up the funds your father left in a trust for you. And Will and I knew that, after all we had done, you would be unlikely to want to share your home with me."

Coming to her, Lucinda leaned her hands on the bed. She gazed earnestly at Elizabeth as her lilac scent filled the air between them. "I've made so many choices already—so many important choices that you consider wrong. This one will be even greater. I love you, Elizabeth, and I want to show you that. The choice to keep Will's legacy will have repercussions far beyond his young son—you know that. But I think it's a decision that *you* need to make."

Urgency set her features and filled her tone. "You alone can make this choice, Elizabeth. Will's legacy is yours to deal with. I give it all to you."

Heavy of head and heart, Elizabeth sat silently at the breakfast table the next morning. Though the meal should have been luncheon this close to midday, the household had slept late after the fractured evening the night before. Elizabeth had ordered breakfast instead. She felt little appetite for any meal.

"I'm afraid I never got the upper hand with her," Aunt Delia said to Lucinda. "We spoiled her far too much when she was small. However, she could run this household as well as I by the time she was fourteen, and I've hardly turned a hand since."

Breaking a roll into smaller pieces, she watched Lucinda serve Aunt Delia another spoonful of stewed apples. Her aunt ate them greedily as she talked.

"Her embroidery never improved much beyond what it was, though none of the slippers she made me ever fell apart." Considering, Aunt Delia added, "Not that I'm hard on my belongings."

At least Elizabeth didn't have to worry about making

conversation with the houseguest she didn't want to entertain. Aunt Delia seemed determined to describe every incident of the past twelve years to Lucinda. In detail.

Left with her own thoughts, Elizabeth brooded. Had her mother meant what she said last night, dumping the decision about the old duke's legacy in her lap? Surely not.

She had seemed serious. Perhaps the woman had wanted her conscience soothed. Elizabeth had asked Lucinda to keep the legacy, so by turning the choice over to her daughter, perhaps her mother expected the bequest to stay as the old duke left it. And now it was Elizabeth's concern.

Still, sending the young duke off without hope of recovering a large chunk of his father's estate was within her power now. She could now have her revenge.

Elizabeth looked at Lucinda, who was bending toward Aunt Delia as if hanging on every girlhood story. Lucinda wanted her to think about the consequences of her decision.

If she gave back the inheritance, she would have to support Lucinda. While the prospect of having her mother around wasn't as impossible as it once seemed, it wouldn't be entirely comfortable.

Yet more important, what would Chan feel toward her if she ended Ash's effort to recover the legacy? Helping his friend had been Chan's main goal during his time in Bath. Would he hate her for hurting the man who had saved his life? Much as he disliked what Ash had done, she had seen clearly that he still loved his friend like a brother.

Chan had said recovering the money was more an emotional need for Ash than a financial one. He'd said it represented lost affection and time between himself and his father.

Which was exactly what losing her mother to the old duke had meant to her. Odd that she and Ash had both felt the same loss of a parent from that long love affair.

What if she gave back the money and pleased Chan? How would Aunt Delia take her niece's decision to deprive her mother of Ashcott's wealth?

No decision she could make had entirely positive outcomes. Had Lucinda felt this same confusion about her own choice years before? How could anyone know what was best when so many lives could be changed by each decision? If Lucinda indeed had saddled her with this choice, Elizabeth would refuse to make it.

Sally came into the dining room with a fresh pot of hot water, followed by Suze with a rack of toast and Nell with a covered serving dish. All three must have insisted on waiting at table today, probably to see their mistress's mother. At least her girls had turned out well, even if she was the only one who would employ them.

As Nell uncovered the main dish with only a slight clang of its lid and presented it to Lucinda, the distant sound of the door knocker reached them. Elizabeth clenched her hands in her lap.

Sally set the pot before her mistress. "I'll take care of that, Miss Lizbeth, and I won't forget the message."

The girl flounced out of the room with far too much sway to her hips. For once Elizabeth didn't care that she left the door slightly ajar.

Chan had probably returned for the second time this morning. Because she was still in her dressing gown, she hadn't received him the first time.

Dressed, she couldn't bear seeing him again only to send him away. She hoped he would read her note and return to London. That would end the torment of knowing he was still in Bath.

Down the passage she heard the door open and Chan's deep voice ask a question. Sally's lighter tones answered, then sounded again with more urgency. A short silence followed.

Feeling her gaze, Elizabeth met Lucinda's considering

stare. She reached for her teacup, then changed her mind and seized her napkin instead. She didn't feel steady enough to hold a cup of hot liquid above her lap, not with Chan reading the message she had penned to him earlier.

After several efforts to find words that would convince him to go back to London and forget her, she had finally settled for a bald statement of facts.

We can't be together without hurting too many people, you most of all. I can't marry you without blackening your family's good name and breaking up your longest friendship. I could never bear it if I divided two men who are all but brothers. Seeing you again would cost me too much heartache, so if you care for me, go away without another torturous parting. Let last night be our final, beautiful memory of each other.

Pressing the napkin against her lips as she felt the sacrifice anew, Elizabeth waited for the sound of the door closing behind Chan one last time.

Instead she heard boots stomping down the passage despite its carpet.

The door swung open with such force it banged the wall. Lucinda jumped and Aunt Delia cried out.

Chan stood glowering, shaking her best hot-pressed notepaper in his clenched fist. "If you think I'll slink away with my tail tucked like that of a hound beaten from your door, you can forget it." He didn't seem to notice anyone else in the room. His fury rose in volume. "I'm not afraid of scandalmongering."

As he headed around the table toward Elizabeth, she sprang off her chair, knocking it over backward. "Why couldn't you just go away quietly as I asked? You're breaking my heart."

"Your heart is made of marble if you can send me

away over this!" He shook the tearstained note at her again and kept coming.

"Don't touch me again, please." Clutching the napkin, she backed away from him as he rounded the table where she had sat. She wasn't certain what either of them might do if he caught her. "I must let you go, and you'll just make it more difficult if you touch me again."

"You'll get used to it." Kicking the fallen chair out of the way, he shadowed her down the side of the dining table. "Stop dodging me; you didn't run from me last night."

He nearly caught her, and Elizabeth twisted away, hiding behind Lucinda and Aunt Delia.

"Last night can never happen again, never. I was selfish, but I wanted you just once, and it shouldn't have happened, but I'm not sorry it did, though it can't happen anymore."

"Listen to yourself." Black eyes flashing with diabolical fire, he came on, relentless as temptation. "You're making no more sense than this silly drivel you scribbled."

Incensed, she edged along the table. "Drivel! I poured out my heart to you."

Flinging her note down, he ground it into the carpet with his boot heel. "That's the product of deranged thinking, not your heart." Now he was behind Lucinda and still coming after her like a great black panther. "One minute in my arms and you'll know you don't mean a word of it."

"No, Chan. You have to forget me." Even in dread of being caught, she had to convince him of his best interests. "Find yourself a proper countess."

Since the absorbed ladies at the table offered no protection, Elizabeth dashed past them and sprinted for the door. Maybe she could reach the sanctuary of her office and lock its door against him.

Almost at the exit, she ran into the wall of his chest.

Seizing her arms, he lifted her onto her toes. "Damn it, I won't have this. I'm not a maid you can order to go or stay; I'm a man. Don't think you can tell me what to do or how to love you."

Pulling her hard against his chest, he branded his mouth against hers. Nothing about this embrace was tender. He plundered and claimed, possessed and dared defiance. He stole her reason along with her breath, and Elizabeth clung to him with her mouth and body to stay on her feet. They fought to the finish of the most draining, enlivening kiss they had ever shared.

Then she stood free of him, released before she was ready to breathe on her own again. He glowered with nearly as much rage as before.

"You want to fling that away?"

Arms holding herself together, Elizabeth panted as if she'd run uphill to the Royal Crescent. "I don't want to lose you but I must. Too many people would be hurt if I thought only of myself. You would be damaged most; don't you see that?"

"Do you think I'm a coward? Afraid to face the censure of people who can't let others' mistakes die a natural death?"

Big as he was, Chan seemed to loom even larger in the confines of the room. "Just because I couldn't plunge into the depths of the Wookey Hole doesn't mean I'm a weakling you have to protect. I can face down anything, censure or the darkest hellhole in the earth."

"I never called you cowardly. If you want to give up your place in your rightful world, that's one thing, but what about your children?" Caught up in the duel with Chan, she gestured toward Lucinda. "Do you want your daughters ostracized from decent society because of the sins of their licentious grandmother?"

As soon as the words were out, Elizabeth wanted to snatch them back.

Lucinda put a hand to her mouth.

Chan's face showed her she had gone too far.

"You've ridden that particular horse to a lather, and it's time you put it out to pasture." Grim-faced, he took her arm and dragged her around the table across from Lucinda. "That's your mother sitting over there by your aunt, who loves her. You love and respect your aunt, and she thinks well of your mother. Yet you're so rock-headed stubborn you won't allow yourself to see any view of Lady Enfield you didn't chisel out of stone for yourself."

Making a sound of disgust, he walked away. "Your view is set as solid in your mind as Coady stone, your own secret building mixture no one else shares: I have to go away for my own good. Your mother has to stay away because you can't allow her human mistakes."

"I didn't mean—"

"You need to break some of the molds in your mind." Striding away, he stopped outside in the passage, framed by the doorway, raking her with a hungry, angry glare. "*Nothing* is set in stone. Not even your wrongheaded opinions. I'll prove that to you."

Then he was gone, his swift steps resounding down the passage. The entrance door slammed hard.

Dazed, Elizabeth righted her chair and took her seat at the table again. She didn't want to look at anyone. Putting a hand to the pot under its cozy, she murmured, "I need a cup of tea in the worst way. May I pour for anyone else?"

Lucinda met her cautious glance with a faintly sad smile, watching her with curiosity. Against the far wall, Suze stared with her mouth hanging open, and Nell hugged the chafing dish of coddled eggs. Sally beamed, her hands clasped over her heart.

"Isn't it lovely," said Aunt Delia as she spooned up apples, "having a gentleman around at breakfast time? So much livelier than a house of women alone."

Chapter Seventeen

Over tea that afternoon, Elizabeth reached for another apricot tart at the same time as her mother. Offering the plate, she said, "I'd forgotten you like these, too. Have all you want; Cook bakes them almost every day."

"Your first solid food was the filling from one of my tarts." Smiling, Lucinda gazed beyond her into the past. "When the weather permitted, we had tea on a rug on the lawn, you, Delia, and I. We were reading when you helped yourself to my tart. You'd licked it clean and begun gumming the crust when I noticed what you were doing."

"Apricot glazed her cheeks and even her hair." Aunt Delia laughed. "I called her greedy, but you said she was clever, knowing what she wanted and helping herself to it."

"She was always a clever child, right from the start." Lucinda's tone and expression reflected pride.

Memory stirred similar moments from the past for Elizabeth. Not just of having tea together, the three of them, but of the loving praise that reassured her she was special.

Uncertainty brushed across her. Was she as unfair in her attitude toward Lucinda as Chan had charged? She didn't like to think so. It wasn't neglect as a child that made her distrust Lucinda; it was the abrupt end of her love, when her mother chose to go live with her duke.

Chan had been right about other things, though, like her aunt's need for contact with Lucinda. She couldn't remember when Aunt Delia had looked so lively. Despite the ugliness at Lady Rowe's last evening, her aunt wasn't at all vague today. She had eaten well and had hardly stopped talking with her sister-in-law.

"Do you remember when she was four and insisted on having a book, too, while we read?" Aunt Delia set down her cup, laughing. "She recited the most improbable stories, 'reading' to us with the book upside down."

This was good for her aunt, having Lucinda stay here a few days as distraction. After their interrupted breakfast, Elizabeth had urged her mother to send her carriage for clothing.

Her motives for the invitation hadn't been entirely praiseworthy. Part of her wanted to thumb her nose at Ashcott and every other cruel member of society in Bath. The young duke had forced the door open on their family secrets, but she was happy to deal with the consequences in her own way. It was somewhat invigorating to flout conventions.

However the outcome of Ash's handiwork was already evident. A morning post had brought regrets from several local hostesses. Since Elizabeth didn't believe a dozen upcoming social events had been canceled overnight, the message of ostracism was plain.

At least Lady Rowe had sent flowers with a note that she would visit soon. A true friend stood by them.

No other supporter had called or left cards so far today. Society had sentenced them to isolation. With her mother here, though, Aunt Delia hadn't noticed.

The thought led to another: maybe Aunt Delia wouldn't miss her circle of friends in Bath if she moved out to the countryside with Lucinda. For years the two had been best friends to each other, far removed from other society. Aunt Delia might be content in that situation again.

Setting down her cup, Elizabeth touched the linen napkin to her mouth. Seeing a contented future for Aunt Delia brought a small sense of relief from her personal wretchedness. If only a way could be found across other chasms, far deeper than Cheddar Gorge, dividing her from Chan. She sighed.

Her mother extended the plate of sweets in her direction, her golden eyes alive with sympathy.

The usual balm for anxiety hadn't helped today. Elizabeth shook her head. "No, thank you."

"Even apricot tarts won't help a sore heart." Lucinda set the plate near Aunt Delia, who took a seedcake. "I wish I could tell you the ache lessens in time, but it never did while I held out against Will's entreaties."

"Those years nearly killed you." Aunt Delia took another nibble of cake. "I never saw anyone go into such a decline."

Lucinda looked uncomfortable.

Suspicion crawled across Elizabeth's mind, and she searched her memory. "I remember you were sad for several years before I went away to finishing school. But that was after Father died."

Aunt Delia dusted crumbs off the front of her gown into her napkin. "A girl might think her mother was grieving her father's death. I knew differently. How could a young wife grieve for a husband she'd hardly seen either before or during marriage?"

"Hush, Delia." Lucinda spoke quietly, not looking above her folded hands. "Elizabeth adored her father and she doesn't need to hear any of this."

"Perhaps she does." Aunt Delia sipped tea and set the cup down again. "You protected her far too much from the real circumstances in Enfield Hall. Maybe if she'd seen my brother's clay feet clearly, she could have found more forgiveness in her heart for you."

Lucinda shook her head. "I don't deserve forgiveness."

"Don't be as silly as Elizabeth. If forgiveness had to be earned, heaven would be empty."

Despite her heavy heart, Elizabeth smiled at her aunt. Maybe she had expected Lucinda to win redemption for her error in judgment. Yet she could think of nothing her mother could do to change those lonely years without her. Past mistakes couldn't be mended—another reason to avoid making one over Chan.

Had Lucinda known when she fell in love with her duke how much misery would result? Elizabeth knew very little about her mother's affair. "When did you meet the sixth Duke of Ashcott? I don't recall that you were ever away from home for more than an afternoon or evening."

Aunt Delia shook her head. "Young folk always think the world began with their births. Your mama knew him long before you were born. Before she married your father."

Lucinda nodded. "One of the duke's estates was near Rochester, where the Merrimans own land. Do you recall living with my brother after your father died and we had to leave his estate?"

Elizabeth nodded, rediscovering that memory. Aunt Delia had come with them instead of living with the new heir at Enfield Hall, explaining that she felt closer to her sister-in-law than to any blood relative.

Having them both with her for those three years had helped Elizabeth. Losing a parent and her home at the same time had unsettled her whole world.

"While he was in the country, Will was never too

proud to join in local festivities. He called on my family, of course, though the duchess wasn't much for mingling with country folk."

The wistfulness in her mother's expression struck a familiar cord within Elizabeth. "At my first assembly, I was terrified. Will saw me hiding in a corner and he very kindly asked me to stand up with him. I didn't sit out a single dance after that, for he brought over every young man in the hall. I came to admire him more than any man I've known."

This wasn't the image of illicit lust and seduction Elizabeth had harbored over the years. It reminded her of coming to know Chan and learning his great capacity for compassion and helpfulness.

"But he was married by the time you came out?" For the first time, Elizabeth felt interest instead of aversion for the relationship that had taken her mother away.

"Yes, he was several years older than I. Will was married very young." Lucinda looked at Aunt Delia, who confirmed the impression with a nod. "As a duke, he married suitably, a lady of fortune and high birth."

The sort of lady Chan must choose as a bride. Elizabeth's heart shriveled like a dried apple.

"A woman seven years older than he." Aunt Delia chose another seedcake. "Young people married to oblige their families in those days. None of this modern rubbish about falling in love."

Lucinda grimaced. "The tragedy of it was discovering the power of mutual love after marriage vows bound you to someone else."

This was a view of her parents' union Elizabeth hadn't considered. If last night she had been forced to submit to a man she hardly knew in a cold marriage bed, how different the experience would have been. She shuddered.

Perhaps she had judged her mother too harshly. At least she could understand the dilemma Lucinda had faced, even if she couldn't imagine sending away her own child.

Drawn to a man she could never marry, wed to a man she didn't know, longing for warmth and tenderness in her life, a young widow had fought love's urgent call for three years.

If Chan came to her three years from now and begged her to be his mistress, would she be strong enough to send him away? Even if he had married, could she deny herself and him after endless yearning? She had no doubt love would only send deeper roots twining into her being, as it had her mother's.

Even so, she must deny love. Expressions of passion could bring children into the world who would suffer far more than she had, safely at school under her mother's family name with a doting aunt nearby.

Children.

Dread flowed through her veins like poison. She laid a hand on her flat abdomen. Looking up in horror, she met her mother's understanding gaze. What if she and Chan had already created a new life?

Marrying her to give their child a father would do worse than besmirch his family name. It would bind them together in disrepute instead of devotion. But not to wed would brand a child a bastard.

Already she might have set events moving that would make another child's life miserable. She had made love with Chan without counting all possible costs. Taking a step that ruined another's existence could indeed happen without the least intention. And she was learning that firsthand.

Brushing at his sleeve impatiently, Chan took the stairs two at a time.

From the doorway below, Sally called, "You'll find her in the drawing room taking tea with her mum and aunt."

Elation empowered him. He could face Elizabeth with confidence and persuasiveness. She wouldn't doubt now that he could face down any adversary that threatened to wedge them apart.

Wrenching the door open, he burst into the drawing room. The three ladies around the table turned startled faces his way, but he focused on the only one who mattered. He didn't care who heard what he had to say.

Striding to the tea table, he plopped his prize among the violet-painted china on the tray. "Now try to deny me."

Three chairs scraped back in unison.

"Merciful heavens, Lord Chandler, what is that?"

"My dear boy, have you brought a stone to tea?" Aunt Delia sounded delighted. "I can never guess what you'll do next."

Elizabeth reached a tentative hand toward the odd-shaped trophy, then picked it up. "It can't be."

Turning it over, she peered at the bumpy surface, like light-colored rough stone, from all sides. The general shape reminded her of a cat. Looking up with an expression of horrified concern, she gasped. "You didn't!"

Jumping up, she flung his victor's spoils onto her chair seat and began wiping at his coat and hair with her napkin. "Look at what you've done to yourself." Her languorous, golden eyes glistened like the wet rocks of the Wookey Hole, and her lush lips trembled as much as he had in the guts of the earth. "You could have been killed, going there alone."

Sounding puzzled, Miss Delia said, "He looks as if he's rummaged through a box room or cellar, from the cobwebs and dirt he's wearing. Was he truly in danger?"

"Danger is the least of it," Elizabeth declared, dropping the napkin to take his face between her hands. "It's a wonder you didn't go mad, alone in that horrible dark place."

Catching her at the waist, he said, "You've already

driven me mad. The terrors of the Wookey Hole were nothing compared to spending the rest of my life without you. I've proved myself; I can best any demon, past or present. Now will you marry me?"

Her eyes widened and tears spilled out. Collapsing onto the chair again she sobbed, bent over. "Please, Chan, don't tempt me to b-blacken your family's honor and separate you from everyone you've known. We can't build love on a damaged foundation. We'll bring everyone nothing but unhappiness."

Swiping Lady Enfield's napkin, he thrust it into Elizabeth's hands and knelt beside her. "What about us? Don't we deserve happiness, too?"

"How can we be happy when your friends and family"—she stopped to gulp—"will h-hate me for marrying you?"

"We don't need anyone else. I don't want anyone but you." What would convince her? "You don't have to worry about Ash. He headed back to London at first light this morning."

Elizabeth didn't have to know he'd damn near cried as he watched Ash's curricle pull away from the inn, worried that he'd lost his best friend forever. What mattered now was convincing her to marry him. "You heard me tell him he could either accept you or keep away. It's up to him. I mean that, Elizabeth. You're more vital to me than any friend or family member. I can handle anything with you beside me, but I don't want to face tomorrow without you."

Shaking her head, she pushed back several strands of fallen hair. "If only we could be together."

His heart twisted at the sight of her pink nose. "I hate seeing you cry. Please don't. Nothing has to keep us apart if we don't let it."

With her nose burrowed into the napkin, her voice came out muffled. "I love you too much to hurt you. If I didn't, I'd go straight to the nearest vicar and get the banns called at once. Then you'd be sorry for the rest of your life."

The glower she gave him made him laugh. "Let's go. You can't torment me any more than you're doing right now."

Her chin quivering, she said with exasperation, "How many times do I have to say it? I will *not* marry you and tarnish your family name."

"This isn't the way I expected an offer of marriage to go when I finally found the right woman for me." Plunging a hand under her bottom, he found his prize while she leaped out of the chair. He rose, brandishing the knobby clump at her.

"Do you see this encrusted thing, Elizabeth? Your china cat is locked under limestone deposits like your heart is by your stony will. You believe you can layer your heart away from your mother and from me, but you can't. You haven't. You need us, both of us."

Shaking her head, Elizabeth stood on the other side of the chair, defiant and exquisite despite her disarray. "Please don't keep asking. Saying no hurts horribly."

As close as he'd come to dying of a smothering apoplexy in that cursed cave, he wasn't giving up now. Holding out the crusted childhood gift from her mother, he opened his hand and let it drop onto the carpet. Elizabeth cried out as she lunged for it over the chair.

"It won't break, any more than your fixed notions." Deliberately he set his heel on the encrusted keepsake. "I can crush this right now. Grind it to powder under my boot."

"No, don't!" She leaned forward, her hands on the chair's arm.

"It's covered by twelve years of layered stone that never should have hidden it." He gestured toward Lucinda. "This little china cat represented your need to keep your mother's love intact, but you pushed her out of your life as surely as you left this bit of china in the

Wookey Hole. You didn't consider that the only way to keep love growing and alive is to act on it. Don't repeat that mistake by trying to enshrine the love between us instead of living it."

"Please," she said. "Please don't break that. I want to keep it." Her golden eyes full of entreaty, she held out her hands, palms up. "I want to keep you, too, but how can we be together without hurting anyone?"

Impatient, he shook his head. "I'm not asking you to be my mistress, if you think I'll settle for less than having you as my wife."

"No, we can't risk bringing children into the world on the wrong side of the blanket." A small sob escaped her. "It isn't right to have children who would suffer for our loving."

To Lucinda, she said, "I don't mean that as a further insult to you. Really, Mother."

Turning back to him, she continued. "I'll always love you, Chan, together or apart. I won't ever forget you. But the best thing to do for everyone is to put distance between us."

Rolling the lumpy object over the carpet under his foot, Chan shook his head. "Every time you love someone, you sprout new branches—limbs that grow through use and care. All these years, you could have been thickening branches by loving your mother. Instead you let your emotions petrify like this misshapen figure. Now you have another chance to keep love growing. Don't ruin what we have by hiding it away."

"But I've forgiven Mother, and I can never forget you." She pleaded with him, her tear-stained face still terribly beautiful. "You don't have to crush the figurine she gave me to prove your point. It will always remind me that you taught me to love and trust again."

Looking at Lucinda in hope, he saw her smile. Glad as he was to have Elizabeth reconciled with her mother, he couldn't stop now. Not if he was to win the most important battle of his life.

Positioning his heel over the stony cat again, he asked, "What about me? Can you risk yourself with me?"

"For heaven's sake," said Miss Delia. "Put the boy out of his misery and take him. His country estate would make a perfect home for Dolly and her kittens. And me, too, of course."

Putting his heart into his gaze, Chan looked into the depths of her eyes and soul. "What's it to be, Elizabeth? I can break through all the layers you've allowed to build up over the years between you and trust in one step. I'm telling you, nothing is set in stone."

Her mouth opened and her gaze dropped to his hovering boot. She glanced quickly at Lady Enfield and back to his face. He hardened the determination in his expression and heart.

Her cry tore at his will. "I would marry you if I could without hurting you!"

Their future was lost. Raising his foot, he stomped downward.

His shin took the impact of a hard edge and he toppled backward, cursing the sharp pain. Lying on the carpet, he hugged his screaming foreleg. Through the haze of hurt, he saw Elizabeth looking down at him in horror, still gripping the chair she had shoved against his leg.

Then she was on the floor beside him, cradling his head against the luscious swell of her breast. "Chan, darling, I'm sorry. Don't you understand? I love you too much to hurt you."

Turning his face into the welcome curves of her generous bosom, he said, "But not too much to lame me."

Tenderly she stroked his face.

"For heaven's sake, girl, marry the man," Delia said. *Bless the woman for her impatient order.* "I certainly would."

Looking up at her aunt, Elizabeth smiled. "You probably gave that same advice to my mother about living with her duke."

"Countless times," the older woman said. "I don't mind repeating myself when I'm right."

Shaking her head, Lucinda frowned. "Delia, Elizabeth has to make this decision for herself."

Holding him almost as close as he wanted to be held, Elizabeth placed a kiss on Chan's eyebrow. He turned his head to give her better aim at his mouth, but she talked instead.

"One of us has to hold fast to good sense," she said with finality. "Giving in to what I want most in the world would only drive us apart in the end. Pride in your family is important to you. You think you can get through life with only my company, but you need your family and friends."

When he tried to disagree, she laid a soft, lavender-scented hand over his mouth. "You've inflicted tortures on yourself in the Wookey Hole caverns to make me admit I need my family, whatever has divided us in the past."

The look she exchanged with Lady Enfield brought him a measure of satisfaction, even if it was cold comfort.

"How can you ask me to believe you value family little enough to taint your name with a disreputable marriage?" Her lips quivered. "I won't be the hammer that cracks your family honor and crushes the lifelong brotherhood between you and Ash."

Slipping an arm around Elizabeth, Chan resettled himself in her arms. He had one more arrow in his quiver. "I can be as hardheaded as you, love. I'm not leaving this house until you say you'll marry me. We can stay here for years, as far as I'm concerned. At least we'll be together."

He grinned up at her. "Though I hope it won't take

you as long to come to your senses about marriage as it did about your mother."

"You're impossible!"

Dropping him onto the carpet, she rose and flounced away. His view of her trim ankles in pink stockings blurred as his head bounced on the floor. As she exited Elizabeth slammed the door behind her, hard.

Miss Delia picked up her cup and nodded to Lady Enfield. "Just like your Will, he won't take no for an answer. Elizabeth might as well give in and wed him."

Lady Enfield's brow creased. "I don't know if she can. She still hasn't realized the difference between loving people and making choices for them."

Down in her office, Elizabeth paced and punched the cushion she had seized off the sofa. Chan had leaned on it once, so it could stand in for him.

If the sixth Duke of Ashcott had shown as much endearing persistence and frustrating persuasion as Chan, she didn't wonder that her mother had capitulated and gone to live with him. It had taken all of her will to hold out against Chan.

Still, she couldn't cave in and risk doing greater damage to more people than her mother had.

To think he had put himself through the agony of the Wookey Hole to prove his courage to her. Not that she needed the evidence, but he obviously had. She was glad he had conquered his fear but wished she had been with him to ease his way through that waking nightmare. Impossible as it was, she wanted to support him through every difficulty.

Stopping, she rubbed her chin on the cushion's corded edge. She loved Chan and he loved her. Each was determined to protect the other, one by marriage and the other by refusing it. In the tales she'd always loved to read, her favorites, love always found a way over every obstacle.

Surely if she pondered enough, she could find a route past the rock standing between them. Something that persuaded Ash to tolerate her, reconciled the two men, and put a decent face on her mother's reputation.

Pressing the cushion over her face, she cursed. It was beyond impossible.

No. It couldn't be. She couldn't give up all hope. Chan had made it all the way to Hell's Ladder in the Wookey Hole, despite paralyzing fears from his past, to break through her barriers to loving. Surely she could find an effort as heroic—and less foolhardy—to give them a chance to be together.

Pacing, she wrestled with hope and despair until dusk gathered in the corners of the room. Night wasn't far behind, and no answer had come to light her dark future.

A knock sounded at the door.

She didn't want the interruption. "Who is it?"

The door opened and Sally slipped inside. "Gorry! Can't see your hand before your face in here, miss. Should I light the candles, or will you come out for your dinner?"

"I don't want dinner, but I'll sit with Mother and Aunt Delia."

Sally grinned and turned to leave. "Lord Chandler will be ever so happy to see you, too."

"Wait!" Surely he hadn't meant his silly threat to stay until she agreed to wed him. He had to stay away from her. "Did you say Lord Chandler is dining here?"

"Yes, miss. He sent for his traps from the Bear Inn, and Miss Delia said to put him in the extra room. Your mum's going in with Miss Delia." Sally opened the door. "Don't fret over dinner. Cook put a nice joint in to roast this morning. Even a big man like yours won't leave the table hungering."

If only he could be her man. The entire household seemed in league to push them together, when she had to do the right thing and let him go. "Take my cover off the table before you call the others. I'm not joining them for dinner after all. Lord Chandler will keep the ladies well entertained."

Sally lit the candle on her worktable. "You'll need to eat, miss. Let me bring you a tray. Cook braised a nice bit of fish with lemon and dill, and I found asparagus at market."

Rubbing her aching head, Elizabeth waved Sally out. As the door shut, she resumed her pacing.

The worst thing Chan could do to himself was to settle into her house as a permanent guest. Even now the news would be leaching through the city like rain into dry soil. Lord Chandler's movements interested everyone in this society, and his move to her house would bloat the blather about all of them.

Once again, circumstances had been thrust on her by the choices of others. Chan hadn't meant to multiply her troubles by his impetuous move into her house; she was certain of that. He loved her and was bent on marrying her.

Hugging herself, she longed to find a way to make that happen. The ache in her throat spread despair throughout her soul and body.

Her life had been rich as clotted cream only a few weeks ago: girls to train, an aunt to look after, more social engagements than she wanted to attend. Now she had maids she wouldn't be able to place and a steady cancellation of invitations from Bath hostesses.

Hot on the heels of the scandalous revelations at Lady Rowe's party, an attractive nobleman moved into her house. No one would believe she wasn't his mistress, just as her mother had been the old duke's. Nothing could redeem a shred of her reputation now.

Taking up the cushion again, she threw it across the room. It bounced against the wall and fell to the floor like her dreams.

Much as she loved him, she was filled with exasperation at Chan. If only the viscount had followed his friend back to London, talk would have died down in a few weeks. Though social doors would have remained closed against her, she could have lived here in quiet solitude. She wouldn't have been happy without him, but she wouldn't have had decent people look away, scornful or embarrassed, if they met her on the street.

Crossing the room, Elizabeth kicked the cushion.

From everything she had read, this wasn't the way falling in love should feel. Where were the joys, the dizzy delights of loving and knowing she was loved? She felt cheated.

Outside forces had fenced her in for most of her life, dictating where and how she would live. Now she had been compelled into a corner where she couldn't even exist in peace with the man she loved.

Leaning over her worktable on both hands, she saw her life burning away like the candle in front of her. Resentment grew as she stared into the wavering flame. She wanted more than the few brief days of light and warmth she'd enjoyed with Chan.

Giving up real love felt wrong. Maybe she could still work out a way for them to be together. Maybe it was time to act instead of react.

At least she couldn't make matters any worse.

If she did nothing, Chan would eventually believe her refusal to marry him and get on with his life. His estate would need his attention and his relatives' needs would draw him back to the demands of daily life.

If she didn't choose action now, she would continue to live in social isolation. No more maids would receive training from her—at least not with a chance for a decent, self-supporting life. She would grow old and bitter, and end up talking to herself and a horde of cats, her only companions over the years.

Pushing away from the table, Elizabeth hugged her elbows at the thought of the deadening days before her.

She would rather sail to Australia on a convict ship and start over with a new identity than live here without love. With nothing more to lose, any wild plan she could conceive was better than that.

Instead of agonizing over the effects of others' choices, she now had to make decisions of her own. Perhaps disaster would be the outcome, but her world had already tumbled down like Nell's worst efforts at arranging her hair. At least any further catastrophe would arise from her choice, not from circumstances pushed on her by others.

Besides, she might succeed. If she did, a future with Chan was her prize. The gain from the risk was glorious enough to outweigh possible failure.

Straightening like a soldier, Elizabeth turned her pacing into a determined march.

The candle on her desk had nearly guttered out an hour later as she sat down to write. Inspiration had finally come like a frightened dog. She was far from certain this desperate measure would work.

Sanding the sheet, she folded it, consulted Burke's Peerage, and inscribed an address on the outside. Over the folds, she dripped a black wax seal as the best color to convey the spirit of the message.

Elizabeth sorted out guineas from the cash box in a cabinet behind her worktable. Leaving the room quietly, she headed for the servants' stairs to send her girls on a special errand.

This missive required a special messenger to ride through the dark night. The cost of such delivery was high, but she was gambling in a high-stakes game.

If it worked, even the full sum of her mother's inheritance wasn't too much to pay.

Chapter Eighteen

Up and dressed early the next morning, Elizabeth hovered on the first floor to stay near the entrance. Like a bird watched by a cat, she couldn't alight.

From the dining room where breakfast would be laid out, she wandered into her office, where she couldn't focus on household accounts. Returning to the morning room at the front of the house, she stared down the street. This early in the day, the only activity centered on the Sydney Hotel.

A watched pot never boiled, she knew. She would sit on this elbow chair with her back to the front windows. A bit of mending would occupy her time better than fretting.

At least she didn't have to deal with Chan's whereabouts yet. If she were lucky he would sleep on into the morning, remaining in the best possible place for her purpose.

Early sunlight slanted in over her shoulder as she opened the needlework table beside the chair. Aunt Delia's cap lay just inside, needing a ribbon reattached. She could have it back in place before her aunt awoke.

What if nothing happened today? She might have misjudged circumstances or even made things worse. No, she mustn't endlessly play out the worst possible outcome in her head. Her choice had been made and she had to live with whatever happened.

The uncertainty of outcome in any choice was now clear to her in a personal way. Never again could she heap blame on her mother for the effects of choosing to live out her love with the duke. Being with the person who helped you become your best self was a necessity. Predicting every outcome of combining your life with another's was impossible.

Taking a needle from its embroidered cover, she searched for white silk among the ivory spindles in a lidded compartment. Measuring off a length of thread, she snipped it with the dainty stork scissors. Holding the needle's eye to the light, she jabbed at it once, twice, three times.

A thunderous knock on the entrance door sounded as if someone were beating on it with a cane. Dropping needle and thread, she jumped up, and Aunt Delia's cap fell from her lap.

Hurrying out of the morning room, she rushed to the door. With a hasty wrench at the knob, she hauled the door open, finger to her lips.

"Hush!" she said. "You'll wake the whole household."

The seventh Duke of Ashcott pushed past her, white as his loose, crumpled neck cloth. "Is he still alive?"

"I'll take you up to him at once."

Guilt gnawing her midsection, she closed the door and hurried past him to the stairs. Ashcott looked as if he hadn't slept in days. He needed a shave.

To come this early, he must have left London within minutes of receiving her late-night message. Anxiety had traveled with him throughout the dark hours, for deep lines etched the corners of his tired eyes and grim mouth.

Pulling air into her tight chest, she wished a kinder way to bring him here had been possible. Still, she hoped the outcome would justify the cruel means she had used.

Behind her, Ashcott labored up the stairs. She could hear pain in his breathing and slowed her ascent. At the top of the staircase, she went directly to the chamber Chan occupied and tapped on the door. There was no answer from within.

With a quick glance at Ashcott's haggard face, she turned the handle and stepped over the threshold. Limping badly, he hurried past her.

In the dim light from the draped windows, Chan lay facedown, spread corner to corner across the bed. He must have passed a restless night. Pillows were bunched against the headboard to one side, and tumbled covers tangled with his long, muscular legs.

His broad shoulders and back lay bare above the quilt. His cheek was flattened against the mattress, nearly off its edge. One long arm dangled toward the floor. He needed a larger bed if he were to sleep with a wife. Elizabeth held back a smile to avoid spoiling the somber expression she had put on for the duke's arrival.

Ashcott hobbled to the bed and reached for Chan's shoulder. His hand hovered above his friend and he cast a look of mute appeal at her. "Will I hurt him if I touch him? Should I let him sleep?"

Chan stirred, blinked, and stretched his legs. Elizabeth held her breath as the covers shifted to reveal the rise of his lean flank.

The duke's hushed questions must have awakened him, for Chan squinted up at Ash. Rolling onto his side, he frowned and rubbed his eyes. "What the devil are you doing here?"

Ashcott stood with his mouth open, staring as Chan sat up.

By now Chan had discovered her in the room as well. A slow grin suffused his sleepy face. "This would be a dream except for him."

"You're not dying." Ashcott pushed his hand through his hair, dislodging his curly-brimmed beaver hat. He didn't even notice as it bounced on the carpet behind him.

Sweeping his hand down his face, Chan said, "Dying?"

The duke's voice rose from disbelief to ire. "You aren't even injured."

Elizabeth bit her lip.

"You don't have to sound disappointed about it." Chan tousled his hair further as he rubbed his head. "What are you doing here? How did you know I moved from the inn to Elizabeth's house?"

"You're asking the wrong person for answers." Turning abruptly, Ash glared as he snatched up his hat. "I should have known better than to be taken in by a message from a light-skirt."

Chan shoved himself out of bed and came after his friend.

Elizabeth sucked in air, staring at Chan's magnificent bare body in full morning light. His laundry apparently wouldn't include nightshirts.

Catching the duke by the shoulder, Chan said between clenched teeth, "That's enough, Ash. I meant what I said. If you can't treat my countess with courtesy, don't come around us."

"Did you think I was here to mend fences?" Pulling a folded, crushed sheet of paper from inside his coat, he threw it on the bed.

"This letter says you're near death from an accident and want to make peace with me."

Chan picked up her letter and unfolded it, looking at her with his slanted eyebrows raised.

Elizabeth shrugged, swallowing her guilt at the deceit she'd used. "It isn't entirely untrue. You would never have broken off your friendship with Ash except for our accidental meeting. The effect of that break is killing something vital between you, and you both need to make peace."

"I should have known you hadn't come to your senses." Ashcott nearly snarled as he looked Chan up and down. "At least put on your drawers. I'm tired of finding you undressed with this woman."

Glancing down at himself, Chan looked startled. Grinning at Elizabeth, who returned his smile, he pulled a creamy woolen dressing gown off the bed's footboard and shrugged into it. "Then stay out of my private rooms."

Ashcott limped toward the door. "With pleasure."

Faster, Elizabeth reached the door first and closed it, clinging to the handle as she leaned back against the solid panels. This wasn't the way she had hoped things would go. She had to keep the duke here.

"Get out of my way."

The young nobleman's glare as his fist tightened on the ebony cane made her heart bump her ribs. This was the only chance she would get; she had to talk fast and with persuasion.

"You rode most of the night to reach Chan's bedside when you believed he was dying." She tried to steady her voice, when she wanted to shake reason into him. "Surely that shows you have enough feeling left for him to stay and talk out the trouble between you. Can't you make as much effort for a living friend as a dying one?"

A menacing look twisted Ashcott's face, and he took a step closer. "What's between Chan and myself is no business of yours."

"To an extent you're right, and in most things I won't

interfere between you." Straightening, she faced him with the dignity of knowing her purpose was worthwhile. "You and I have one thing in common that makes the misunderstanding between you my concern: both of us love him."

Flinging away from her, the duke sneered. "Yours is cream-pot love."

Chan growled. "Watch your tongue!"

Angered at the charge that she wanted only Chan's wealth, Elizabeth gripped her hands together and clung to her temper. "It's reasonable for him to think as he does, Chan. Plenty of other people must believe the same thing." Again she spoke to the duke. "You need to understand that I don't mean to marry your friend if doing so will bring him more grief than happiness."

Ash thumped the floor hard with his cane. "Then don't order your bridal clothes."

Temper flaring, she spoke with vehemence. "What kind of love turns its back on a man for following his heart? What kind of friend abandons another over a choice he doesn't like?"

Red-faced, Ashcott gripped his cane. "I care enough about Chan to want a wife for him who won't be a public embarrassment."

Advancing on the duke with his fists clenched, Chan stood over him. "I've never been embarrassed by Elizabeth or her family, which is more than I can say for you since we came to Bath."

Men were worse than animals. The last thing she wanted them to make of this meeting was another opportunity to fight.

"Stop this right now." Hurrying to stand between the two men as they faced each other like snarling dogs, their jaws jutting, Elizabeth held up a hand toward each of them. "Recriminations won't repair relations between you. I want you to sit down and cool off, first of all."

Figuring he would be more responsive to her, she

stared at Chan first. Grimacing, he gave in and went to prop himself against the edge of his bed.

Ashcott was harder, looking at the door for a long minute before glaring at her and then Chan.

Quietly she asked him, "What do you have to lose by listening, except a lifelong friend?"

Muttering something that sounded like "Damned interfering woman," he swung himself to the chair by the window and threw himself into it. Scraping its legs on the floor, he shoved himself around so he didn't face Chan.

Clinging to a bedpost for support, she searched for the right words to reach two stubborn hearts. "Think about why you've been friends so long."

"Not because Chan knew who had his best interests at heart."

"Not because Ash let a man know what was best for himself."

"You're blind as a mole if you think you know what's good for you where women are concerned," Ash said with a snarl.

"Fine words from a man who favors tavern wenches."

This would get them nowhere if the two men only took potshots at each other. Elizabeth felt hope slide away.

Taking a deep breath, she grabbed for their attention. "Chan, what's the best thing your long friendship with Ashcott has brought you?"

"Nothing springs to mind."

Ashcott shot him an angry look. "Your mind's too full of ruining yourself for anything else to be present."

Between cursing and tears, Elizabeth snatched the duke's cane and poked Chan in the naked chest with it.

Frowning, Chan rubbed the spot she'd struck.

Ashcott grabbed for his cane.

Holding it out of his reach, she glared at each of them in turn. "That's enough schoolboy nonsense from both of you!" She handed the duke's cane back. "Act like the adults you are and face up to losing the longest association of your lifetimes, aside maybe from your parents. Surely you can admit you've been closer than brothers in the past."

Shifting position so the bed creaked, Chan ducked his head. "You're right," he said in a gruff voice. "I owe Ash; he saved my life."

Tapping the floor between outstretched legs with his cane, the duke said, "Much good that did, considering you can't wait to throw it away."

Impatience made Elizabeth snap at Ashcott. "Chan's making an honest effort here. Try to say something positive, if you're going to speak at all." When he only threw her a sullen look, she redoubled her efforts on Chan. "What do you think you owe the friend who saved your life?"

Two voices answered her at once.

"Too much," said Chan.

"Nothing!" said the duke.

The two men glared at each other, then glanced away.

Walking away from them in order to force out the next question, Elizabeth joined her hands tightly under her chin. The next question could bring answers that didn't help, but she had to trust in his good sense. "Chan, if you owe the duke so much, why would you ignore his advice about a wife? How could you even consider marriage with a woman he can't accept?"

From the sound the bed made, she knew Chan had shoved to his feet. The duke stopped tapping his cane.

Chan stared into her eyes, rubbing his neck and frowning. She forced herself to look back with love and trust, hiding her fear of losing him.

Finally he spoke as if discovering the words as they emerged. "My choices have to suit me first, for I have to live with the consequences. I'll always be grateful to Ash for making it possible for me to live to have choices, but my life has to be my own or it isn't worth living."

Chan stared steadily at her, his slanting black brows bunched together.

Nodding with relief, Elizabeth turned to see Ash staring at his boots. Though he frowned, he appeared thoughtful.

Getting the duke to respond with reason to her would be far more difficult. For any hope of a future with Chan, she had to succeed. "Ashcott, what value do you place on Chan's life?"

"I don't know what you mean." The duke sounded sulky, reluctant to answer. "You can't put a price on a man's life."

"Of course you can," she said in a reasonable voice. "Men have been sent off to die in Spain for no more than a few pounds a year in military pay. Is a viscount's life worth more than that to you?"

Shifting on his seat, Ash said in an angry tone, "This is nonsensical."

"Not at all." Going to stand before him, Elizabeth spread her hands. She felt she risked the worst loss of her life. "The price you want Chan to pay for your friendship is to hand over his life choices to you. That would leave him with no life of his own."

Ashcott glared at her, his eyes hot and his lips tight.

As she clasped her hands against his fury, her great need rose in her throat and choked her voice. "I want to buy back that right for him, so he can make decisions for himself, yet still have you as a friend."

When both men tried to speak at once, she hurried on. "Let me finish, please. I have a proposition that will give you both something you value highly."

Swallowing, she put her hands over her mouth, realizing the enormity of what she must do. Her mother's choices had changed Elizabeth's young life forever, and

305

now her last hope required that she act in a way to alter others' paths forever.

Distraught but determined, she faced the duke. "My mother has relinquished her legacy from the sixth duke to me. Ashcott, I'm willing to return it to the estate."

"No!" Chan took a step toward her.

"What?" Ashcott looked stunned.

"I won't let you do this," Chan said to her.

"The whole sixty thousand pounds?" Ash's eyes widened.

"The sum doesn't matter," Chan informed Ash. "Lady Enfield is keeping it. You're not going to pay him for a right I already have."

"You're both demented," Ash said in wonder. "No woman gives up a fortune of sixty thousand pounds."

Surely she had said it simply enough for them to understand. "My mother gave me her inheritance, and I'm giving it to the duke. You're free of all obligation, Chan."

Chan shook his head. "You can't do this to your mother."

"It's done." She felt terrible enough, sacrificing her mother's last gift from her beloved. If only Chan would make it easier for her. "Mother said she wanted me to make this decision. I've made it."

Turning back to the duke, she continued. "Ashcott, you'll pledge in return for that legacy to give Chan your ongoing friendship and freedom to make his own choices. Chan, you'll accept that Ashcott doesn't have to like every person you do. The two of you can enjoy plenty of time together, whatever place I might have in Chan's life."

Struggling up from his chair, the duke balanced unsteadily as he stared at her. "You don't mean you'll hand over sixty thousand pounds like it was a brace of pigeons."

Chan waved his arms. "Of course she isn't handing it over. It isn't even hers."

Elizabeth returned the duke's incredulous look with a direct stare. "I do."

The duke stood searching her face with his gaze, and she didn't look away. She raised her chin a notch.

Finally he shook his head and wheeled toward Chan, dazed. "Maybe you know what you're doing after all. Damned if I thought any female in the world would give up a fortune without being forced into it. This is one hell of a woman, Chan."

Dropping his arms, Chan beamed. "That's what I've tried to tell you. My lady is no ordinary woman. I should have known you'd finally recognize that."

"I'm a reasonable man." Ashcott rubbed his chin. He grinned sheepishly. "Sometimes I just have to vent my temper before I see things clearly."

Sobering, he grimaced. "I didn't get past the first toll-gate out of Bath before I knew I'd been a sapskull. Nothing's worth losing the friendship of a man who's stood by me like a brother."

Chan held out his hand. "You might try listening once in a while, but your heart's in the right place."

Ash took the proferred hand and wrung it. "I never learned how to admit I was wrong, or I would have reminded you years ago that I was the one who insisted on going to that cave. Father warned me to keep out. You don't owe me anything for dragging you out of a bad situation I badgered you into in the first place. I didn't know you felt obligated."

Chan shook his head, waving aside the explanation. "It's not as if I hung around purely out of obligation. You're a tolerable drinking companion."

Ash tapped his boot with his cane. "You'll do when nobody else is around to take a bloody hand of cards."

They shared a long, wordless look.

Wondering how faint praise had accomplished it, Elizabeth felt confident the two men were friends again. She was less certain where she stood between them. Tentatively she asked, "Do we have an agreement, then?"

Two limping steps brought Ashcott before her. He reached for her hand. "You've shown more nobility than I have. Chan is right to be embarrassed at the way I've acted, compared to you. Can you forgive me for behaving like a prize ass?"

Bending in a bow suitable for a duchess, he dropped a salute on her hand.

Bemused, she murmured, "Of course I forgive you."

Straightening, he grinned. "You could have argued a bit about the ass part." Then he said with sincerity, "I wish you both great happiness. I hope you'll allow me to visit in your home once you're wed."

Fervently she assured him, "You'll always be welcome."

Chan joined them, laying a hand on Ash's shoulder and putting an arm around Elizabeth. "This makes me happy, seeing you two on good terms. Elizabeth wasn't willing to come between us, but that's no longer a problem. We can be married at once."

Hating to dim the mellow mood filling the room like the morning's golden light, Elizabeth pulled away from the warmth of Chan's hold. "That's half the problem solved. We have another hindrance to get past."

"Only in your stubborn mind." Fists on hips, he frowned. "I don't care what gossips and scandalmongers say, now or ever. We'll be married."

Shrugging, she looked at Ashcott. He could ease this problem, too, if she could persuade him to help.

"The duke pointed out the other obstacle early on, so you can't say it's just my opinion. My mother's liaison with the duke's father made her infamous. Now it's known I'm Lucinda's daughter, not just another of the numerous Merriman family."

"I'm to blame for that," Ashcott admitted.

Her purpose in restating their problems was in part to set them out before the duke. If he accepted that responsibility, he might also offer aid.

Earnestly she said to Chan, "I don't want to taint your family name. I know you would stand up for me or hide away with me, but I can't like to bring shame into your family. How could I bear for our children to be taunted or shunned?"

Chan clasped her hands with tender possessiveness, holding them against his heart. "I won't let you sacrifice my happiness. You've preached Ash a fine sermon about him wanting to make my choices for me. What are you doing when you won't let me choose my own wife? I dare anyone to snub you in my presence."

Elizabeth shook her head. "We must think through all the consequences of this choice, not just blindly follow our hearts. I've promised Ash my mother's legacy. She has nothing else to live on, Chan. I'll need to keep her and Aunt Delia with me. People won't forget the scandal, with her living in our house."

Gesturing at Ashcott, she hoped for the best. "How do you think Ash will feel, visiting you with Lucinda always present?"

"Your aunt and mother could live in the dower house," Chan said, "except that two widowed aunts are already installed there."

"Let me answer for myself," Ash said. "I'm not the brute I've looked like."

"He knows how to act in a lady's home." Chan grinned. "You just haven't seen him on his best behavior."

Ashcott stepped in front of Chan. "Elizabeth is acting as her mother's agent, so I don't have to deal with you anymore."

Holding up his hands, Chan stepped aside. "Don't expect her to give ground without a fight."

"You and your mother have made me feel ashamed

309

of myself." The duke shook his head. "When it comes right down to it, I can't go against my father's wishes."

"Good man," Chan said, clapping him on the back.

"If your mother would give up an inheritance so you can be happy, especially if she's left with no income, she's a better person than I've judged her," Ashcott said. "She'll keep the legacy my father meant her to have."

Grimacing, he continued. "Maybe I can't warm up to her entirely, but I promise to be civil. I'll dance with her at your wedding breakfast if you want. That should silence a few of the old biddies' wagging tongues."

"That's very big of you, Ash," said Elizabeth, her lips trembling into a smile. "Thank you."

"I doubt that your reputation would take much tarnish off Lady Enfield's." Chan grinned at his friend. "Might do more good if you make certain Prinny comes to our wedding. Elizabeth's father was the fifth Lord Enfield, a friend from the Prince of Wales's salad days. The prince might put in an appearance if you propose it to him."

"Indeed." Ash gave her a speculative look. "The prince showing up for your wedding breakfast would put a different face on things. You'll have to be married in London, of course. But you can count on all the society sheep to follow where royalty leads."

Laughing, he shook his head. "You might want to warn your mother to wear a dark veil for the marriage festivities. Our prince prefers ladies of uncertain age, especially when they're as beautiful as your mother is. She's likely to find herself not only noticed but propositioned by him."

Accepting a jest from a friend, Elizabeth smiled. "If he chooses to pursue my mother, he'll have to put up with Aunt Delia as well. I doubt she'll ever want to be separated from her Lucinda again."

Groaning, Chan shook his head. "Even the prince wouldn't intimidate your aunt. I can just imagine her offering him one of Dolly's kittens for Carlton House."

The three laughed together, and Elizabeth's heart rose with the welcome sound.

Ash looked around the room, grinning. "I hate to see a warm bed go to waste. I'm heading down the street to the Sydney Hotel to see if I can find one of my own. Thanks to straightening out all your problems, I haven't slept for two days."

"Much help you've been," Chan scoffed. He held out his big hand to his friend again. Ash took it and they stood for a moment, staring into each other's eyes and grinning like monkeys.

"Ungrateful blockhead," said Ash with affection.

"Cocky know-it-all," said Chan with friendly derision.

Turning away, the duke limped toward the door, waving a hand in the air. "Don't follow me down to the door. I can show myself out. I'm sure you can find something better to do up here."

Chan pulled her close against his side and they both watched the door close behind Ash.

Running his fingers along her rib cage to brush the side of her breast, Chan looked at her with tenderness. "Not a bad idea, going back to bed. It's still a couple of hours before we can hope for breakfast."

Elizabeth turned into his fierce embrace, her arms around him, her cheek nestled against his chest. Rubbing her face against the soft robe, she felt the fascinating contrast of hard muscle flexing underneath. She couldn't resist teasing him. "Now that we're going to be respectable, shouldn't we wait until after the ceremony to leap into bed together?"

Kissing the top of her head, Chan murmured, "You want ceremony?" He heaved a gusty sigh and sank onto one knee. Taking her hand between his, he looked into her eyes with a purposeful twinkle. "My dearest Miss Merriman, you must realize after the passion of my lovemaking two nights ago that I love you with my heart, soul, and body." He grinned wickedly and put his arms around her hips, his face burrowing toward the center of her growing desire. "Especially my body at the moment. Will you be my cherished and hard-won wife?"

Laughing, she tugged at his crisp black hair. "Stand up, Lord Chandler, and take your punishment like a man. With the greatest pleasure we can create between us in a lifetime, I accept your kind and flattering proposal, sir."

Coming quickly to his feet, he swung her off the carpet and into his arms. "That takes care of ceremony. Shall we get on with pleasure?"

As he headed for the tumbled bed, she slid her arms around his shoulders and murmured against his ear, "You didn't wait for my answer to your second question."

Stopping, he groaned. "I'll drop you like I did the china cat if you say no. Don't tell me you're going to make me wait until after our wedding ceremony to show you how much I love and want you."

Elizabeth nibbled his jutting chin and laughed. "I want to be your mistress for a little while before I combine that role with being your wife. My mother's best legacy to me is understanding that a man who is both friend and lover is the right life mate."

Laying her gently on the bed, Chan sank down beside her and traced her mouth with a tantalizing finger. "It should take us a lifetime to spend that legacy."

Raising her head, Elizabeth met Chan halfway. A kiss was a good beginning.

Fairest of Them All

Josette Browning

A true stoic and a gentleman, Daniel Canty has worked furiously to achieve the high esteem of the English nobility. Therefore, it is more his reputation than the promise of wealth that compels him to accept the ninth earl of Hawkenge's challenge to turn an orphan wild child into a lady. But the girl who's been raised by animals in the African interior is hardly an orphan—and his wildly beautiful charge is hardly a child. Truly, Talitha is a woman—and the most compelling Daniel has ever seen. But the mute firebrand also poses the greatest threat he has ever faced. In the girl's soft kiss is the jeopardy which Daniel has fought all his life to avoid: the danger of losing his heart.

___4513-3 $5.50 US/$6.50 CAN

ENRAPTURED
KATHERINE DEAUXVILLE

The twelfth duke of Westermere is simply out for a peaceful drive, until the Amazonian beauty tosses herself into his coach demanding he do something about the dreadful condition of his estate. This alone would not have flummoxed Sacheverel de Vries, but when the strange woman in the threadbare cloak babbles something about equal rights and social justice, rips open her dress, and claims he has attempted to ravish her, there is only one thing he can do. Skillfully maneuvered into a betrothal with the handsome aristocrat, Marigold Fenwick begins to regret her impulsive actions. And when Marigold decides to seduce the esteemed duke into an enlightened social consciousness, she hardly knows what she is getting into, for the aftermath will leave her thoroughly enraptured.

___4540-0 $5.99 US/$6.99 CAN

Dorchester Publishing Co., Inc.
P.O. Box 6640
Wayne, PA 19087-8640

Please add $1.75 for shipping and handling for the first book and $.50 for each book thereafter. NY, NYC, and PA residents, please add appropriate sales tax. No cash, stamps, or C.O.D.s. All orders shipped within 6 weeks via postal service book rate. Canadian orders require $2.00 extra postage and must be paid in U.S. dollars through a U.S. banking facility.

Name_____
Address_____
City_____State_____Zip_____
I have enclosed $_____ in payment for the checked book(s).
Payment <u>must</u> accompany all orders. ❏ Please send a free catalog.
        CHECK OUT OUR WEBSITE! www.dorchesterpub.com

THE IMPOSTOR
ELAINE FOX

Melisande St. Clair knows who she is and what she wants, and when Flynn Patrick steps out of the water and into her life, she knows that his is the face of which she's dreamt. But when she is forced to travel with the handsome stranger, he claims he is from another time and makes suggestions that are hardly proper for a nineteenth-century lady. Although she believes no one could mistake him for an English gentleman, the Duke of Merestun swears that Flynn is his long-lost son. Suddenly, Flynn seems a prince, and all Melisande's desires lie within reach. But what is the truth? All Melisande knows is that she senses no artifice in his touch—and as she fights to remain aloof to the passion that burns in his fiery kiss, she wonders which of them is truly . . . the impostor.

___4523-0 $5.50 US/$6.50 CAN

Dorchester Publishing Co., Inc.
P.O. Box 6640
Wayne, PA 19087-8640

Please add $1.75 for shipping and handling for the first book and $.50 for each book thereafter. NY, NYC, and PA residents, please add appropriate sales tax. No cash, stamps, or C.O.D.s. All orders shipped within 6 weeks via postal service book rate. Canadian orders require $2.00 extra postage and must be paid in U.S. dollars through a U.S. banking facility.

Name_____
Address_____
City_____State_____Zip_____
I have enclosed $_____ in payment for the checked book(s).
Payment <u>must</u> accompany all orders. ❑ Please send a free catalog.
    CHECK OUT OUR WEBSITE! www.dorchesterpub.com

Lady of the Night

Cordia Byers

Manacled to a stone wall is not the way Katharina Fergersen planned to spend her vacation. But a wrong turn in the right place and the haunted English castle she is touring is suddenly full of life—and so is the man who is bathing before her. As the frosty winter days melt into hot passionate nights, she realizes that there is more to Kane than just a well-filled pair of breeches. Katharina is determined not to let this man who has touched her soul escape her, even if it means giving up all to remain Sedgewick's lady of the night.

___4404-8 $5.99 US/$6.99 CAN

CINDY HARRIS

Sir Adrian Vale has earned his spurs at the battle of Crécy, as well as King Edward III's gratitude. But things have changed since that great victory. Branded a traitor, the knight is given a task he alone can achieve. Infiltrating Oldwall castle is child's play, but plumbing its secrets requires his most expert touch. While Philippa's duty requires that she wed Lord Oldcastle and bear his children, nothing can prepare her for Drogo's monstrous plan—or for the fascinating stranger who will carry it through. Adrian's soft caresses electrify Philippa's virgin flesh, while the answers he seeks fill her with dread. Who is this handsome warrior whose eyes hold such fiery longing? This man has come for not only the lord of the keep, but the castle's maiden bride.

___4650-4 $4.99 US/$5.99 CAN

Unveiled

Jenni Licata

When a disguised courtier delivers him a secret message from Queen Anne, Alexandre Rawlings has no idea that he will later find the man murdered. Standing over the victim is a mysterious woman in white, and one look at her lush figure tells the Earl of Carlton everything: She is innocent, but hardly for long. Determined to protect the naive beauty, Alex spirits her away in his carriage.

Rescued by the man known as the Devil Lord, she is captivated by his potent kiss. Victoria wonders if trusting Alex is wise, but though the handsome lord is shrouded in mystery, she is certain that when she unmasks his heart, a passion for the ages will be unveiled.

___4542-7 $4.99 US/$5.99 CAN

Dorchester Publishing Co., Inc.
P.O. Box 6640
Wayne, PA 19087-8640

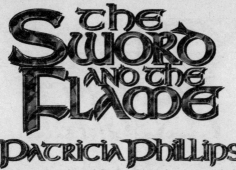

The Sword and the Flame

Patricia Phillips

The fire that rages in Adele St. Clare is unquenchable. The feisty redhead burns with anger when King John decrees she marry against her will. Then her bridal escort arrives—Rafe De Montford—and the handsome swordsman ignites something hotter. But Rafe has been ordered to deliver her unto a betrothed she cannot even respect—let alone love. But Rafe's smoldering glances capture her heart, and with one of his fiery kisses, Adele knows that from these sparks of desire will leap the flame of a love everlasting.

Lair of the Wolf

Also includes the seventh installment of *Lair of the Wolf*, a serialized romance set in medieval Wales. Be sure to look for future chapters of this exciting story featured in Leisure books and written by the industry's top authors.